"*The Audacity of Dop*ian road novel that's al[ready laugh-out-loud funny, fea]turing an anti-hero so potentially iconic you'll be surfing eBay for 'Riley Mansfield' tees before long. Imagine if *The Big Lebowski* had wandered into a Larry McMurtry novel and decided to write the common man's sequel to *Primary Colors*. *Audacity* is the rare combination of satire and sentiment, a look at our country during its most divisive decade, and a toe-tapping yarn spun with threads so pungent you might get a contact high just reading it. Dutton is without a doubt one of the South's freshest voices."

—Peter Farris, author of **Last Call for the Living**

"Not everyone can take a pot-smoking, song-writing, guitar-picking, down-to-earth Southern boy and turn him into a loveable and truly unforgettable folk anti-hero, but that's exactly what Monte Dutton has done in his equally vibrant stick-to-your-ribs novel, **The Audacity of Dope**. I dare anyone to read this book and not fall in love with the character of Riley Mansfield. Whether you share his political views or not, the sheer inescapable magnetism of this character is undeniable, as are Dutton's finely crafted skills as a writer and story teller. A truly worthwhile read with a heart of gold."

—Devon Pearse, author of **A Lighter Shade of Gray**

The Audacity of Dope

by

Monte Dutton

Neverland Publishing Company
Miami, Florida

Cover Design by Joe Font

Printed in the United States of America

ISBN-13: 978-0-9826971-15

www.neverlandpublishing.com

In memory of Jim Cypher,

the only man ever willing to be my agent.

CHAPTER ONE
WHOLESOME GOODNESS

Riley Mansfield sat quietly in a world of dull glistening. The stool was wooden, and the floor was brick tile, but everything else emitted the blurred reflections of pots and pans, sinks and spigots, steel cabinets, steel stoves, steel everything. It wasn't exactly charming, Riley thought, but charm wasn't likely to be a priority for the kitchen of the First Baptist Church, Killeen, Texas. Nor should it be.

He was hiding. His Aunt Sally didn't know he was here. She didn't know he was within eight hundred miles of here. Through the double doors, Riley could hear people talking about her, paying homage, offering up tributes and all kinds of other heartwarming shit.

Riley was the picture of relaxation. He wore khaki trousers, a black dress shirt and red-and-blue striped tie. His hair, which had extended to his collar, had been freshly shorn at the Great Clips in a nearby strip mall. He looked at himself, the likeness distorted in the reflective door of a stainless-steel refrigerator.

By God, I could almost still pass for a quarterback. A veteran quarterback, but still…

The emcee sounded like a coach. He had to be. He might be an administrator now, but like most male principals and superintendents in public high schools, he had once been a coach. Riley was sure of it. He imagined Darrell Royal.

"Now, Sally, next up we've got someone real special, young lady," said Coach Royal's voice. "I'm pretty sure you're not expecting this, but you've got a relative from way back in South Carolina, and I'm told he writes pretty fair songs."

Riley heard Sally Sue Ramseur Lollis gasp. She was a drama teacher and had once been an actress. People could hear Aunt Sally gasp on the rifle range at Fort Hood. Riley had written a song for

Sally's retirement party. When he had played it for his mother, he had fretted that perhaps Sally might cry. Sara Mansfield had lowered her chin, looked over the top of her reading glasses and said, "Riley, you know Sally Sue. She's gonna cry."

Sally cried as Riley grabbed his guitar, pushed open the double doors, walked behind tables littered with valuable Aunt Sally memorabilia, blew her a kiss and plugged in his guitar to a public-address system that, in Riley's professional estimation, might or might not work. He sang the song he had written on Tuesday, worked out on Wednesday, studied on the plane on Thursday and played over and over in a Fort Worth motel room on Friday. He had sung it over and over in the rental car driving down I-35. His fingers were trembling now, oddly.

He spoke a few words to test the sound, strumming the guitar to make sure the audio was going out into the "fellowship hall" with some rough semblance of balance. "It is apparent to me that all you folks in Texas know my aunt merely as Sally," he said, "but back in South Carolina, where her family's from, we still know her as Sally Sue."

I knew you, Sally Sue, back before I could walk
I knew you, Sally Sue, before I could talk
Your mother wrote me letters
Your boy shared my name
Your cousin was my father
Your heartache was my pain
I remember you in Panama
You told me of L.A.
You came to town for Christmas
And stayed past New Year's Day
I remember back when Texas
Was a trip of several days
When Frances was my tour guide
But Cas knew the way

CHORUS
Riley's sense of humor
Matched up with my own
I shared his love of baseball
I can't believe he's gone
I argued with his father
A most insistent man
But you raised Riley gentle
Molded in your hands
CHORUS
So now I'm back in Texas
This day belongs to you
I finally get to see just
Exactly what you do
I knew your sense of drama
Was advanced and well-conceived
But you don't have to tell me now
How well it's been received
CHORUS

Though his fingers continued to tremble as he strummed the guitar, Riley pulled it off the way he always did, looking relaxed even as inside he felt nervous. Sally Lollis, who had for thirty-two years been drama coach at the local high school, continued to weep throughout it, and when it was over, Riley stepped down, leaned his guitar against the stage and walked into the crowd to embrace his aunt.

"I tried to put some little phrases in there that would mean something to just you and me," he said, "and at the same time, I tried to make it where it would be entertaining even to people who didn't know all the little hidden meanings."

"Oh, Riley, this means so much to me. You performed magnificently."

"I reckon," he said. After Sally released him from her robust hug, he awkwardly walked over to a table nearby and watched as would-be Coach Royal introduced the next testimonial.

The remaining tributes were equally divided between fellow faculty members and former students. Coaches talked about how much Sally's late son, Riley John Lollis, had meant to them when he played baseball and football for them. A struggling actor told about how "Miss Lollis" had helped him earn a scholarship at the University of North Texas. Two other young college graduates talked about their friendship with the son and enduring love for the mother. Afterwards, cake, punch, cheese-and-sausage balls, chips and dip were enjoyed by all. Then Sally invited Riley to join a small group of friends for dinner at a nearby Italian restaurant favored by "officers from Fort Hood." Sally's father had been an officer at Fort Hood, which is why her part of the family had settled there after he retired.

At the restaurant, Sally explained to her friends that her nephew still lived in Henry, South Carolina, from where her family had moved when they settled in Texas. She told them he made a living as a musician and that his songs had been recorded by Jimmy Buffett, John Hiatt (actually it was John Prine) and others. She also told them that he had played football in college and that she had known him since he had lived at his grandparents' house, along with his parents, until he was two.

Sally wasn't precisely Riley's aunt but rather his second cousin. Her first cousin had been Riley's late father. Just like her mother, also deceased, she often called Riley by his father's name. Riley never corrected her. She'd been doing it his whole life. He was sure it was confusing to Sally's friends, though.

"Yeah, Buffett recorded a song of mine, and I guess that's the song some people know me by," Riley said. "It's just a feel-good song, I reckon, not much heavy lifting. It's funny how the simplest little songs you write are the ones that wind up being the most successful."

"Did you ever think about becoming a recording artist yourself?" asked the only other male member of the party, whom Riley remembered as being Riley John's baseball coach at some point. Riley was pretty sure he'd said he "played a little guitar," too.

"Well, I am, a little. I've recorded several albums, one that came out just a couple months ago. But I guess you'd say that I make a living off royalties from my songs, and I kind of just break even selling CDs and appearing in person," Riley said. "I think it's good to try to stay visible, and I don't think there's anything I enjoy more than singing my songs in front of audiences, but I haven't ever really had that burning desire to be a big star."

The coach nodded and said "I hear you," but the look on his face suggested that he found Riley's attitude similar to a third baseman who wanted to play but didn't care about winning.

To each his own, Riley thought, determined to remain convivial. He had Diet Coke with his ravioli and refrained from the use of profanity.

"I just kind of like to do my thing," Riley said. "Not that I'm good enough or anything like that, but I've been around famous people, and there's a trade-off. I believe I'd rather make a little less money and have a little more privacy."

It was impossible to explain it to people who had plenty of privacy and didn't appreciate it.

Sally invited Riley to stay over, and she may have even meant it, but he explained that he had a flight to catch the following morning and that he needed to be heading back up the interstate to Fort Worth.

Back on the road, Riley realized why his hands had been trembling. He couldn't remember it ever happening before. It was because he was sober and he didn't often play music in front of people sober. He'd known he should've smoked a little weed in the parking lot, but after all, it was a church and it would've been a really stupid way to fuck up a surprise party. Riley hadn't come all the way from South Carolina just to mess things up.

♫

The next morning Riley rose early, blazed a little and took special care to hide the rest of his weed in his overnight bag. Then he ate voraciously at the motel's free breakfast and headed for the Dallas-Fort Worth airport and an American Airlines flight home.

As it turned out, it wasn't that easy. The flight from DFW had a big, flashing "canceled" blinking on the video boards when he walked in with his laptop in a backpack, carrying a guitar and the overnight bag. Riley checked his cell and found a text message with essentially the same information. After fifteen minutes in line, he found himself rerouted through New York's LaGuardia Airport, which, in turn, meant that he would be getting home five hours late. It wasn't a big deal. He had a gig on Monday night at a small bar in Columbia, so, as long as he got home sometime on Sunday, everything would be cool, though slightly more complicated. He checked the bag with the airline and proceeded through the security check points with the backpack and guitar.

For two hours, Riley consumed a blueberry muffin and cup of coffee, reading first the *New York Times* and then a couple of Annie Proulx short stories from a collection he'd bought secondhand in Dover, Delaware a month earlier and never removed from his backpack.

For a time, Riley watched the people bustling through the airport. He thought it amusing to separate the commuters by parts of the country. Some people could be from anywhere. Others were obviously either from abroad or obviously still connected there. Some wore their regions in their hair, their footwear and maybe even the looks on their faces. Women were particularly interesting, he thought. Many Northeasterners, Riley reasoned, tried with some diligence not to be particularly attractive. He thought there might be a song in it but couldn't come up with a hook.

Riley got mildly annoyed when the gate agent hassled him about his travel guitar.

"You may have to check that," she said.

"Ma'am, whatever you say, but the very reason people use undersized guitars like this one is so they can carry them on planes. They're really pretty easy to fit in the overhead bins."

The woman frowned, disappointed at Riley's lack of submissiveness.

"Well, check with the flight attendant," she said, waving him reluctantly past.

Riley looked around, reckoning that the plane was only going to be half full. It was hassle for the purpose of hassle. "Another glamorous day of air travel," he mumbled, drawing a nod from the businessman filing in behind him.

"Woman must be a Yankee who don't like Southerners," he muttered to no one, because the businessman might himself be a Yankee.

CHAPTER TWO
SHIT HAPPENS

Riley Mansfield considered the words of the old Simon and Garfunkel tune "Homeward Bound." He wondered whether that was originally Simon and Garfunkel, or whether it was by Tompall and the Glaser Brothers. Simon, he thought, but wasn't sure.

In any event, home was where Riley Mansfield was finally headed. *Jesus*, he thought, *it's a prop plane. Whoever heard of flying in a prop plane all the way from New York City to South Carolina?* Damn cash-strapped airlines, cutting corners at every turn. The plane was called a Dash 8, and Riley had flown on more than his share, though usually in short junkets from Philly to Allentown, or LaGuardia to Elmira.

With both his Baby Taylor and the backpack safely "stowed" (as the flight attendants insisted on saying) in the overhead compartment, Riley settled in for the long flight to Greenville-Spartanburg, in his native South Carolina. Riley still remembered when it was fashionable to call Greenville-Spartanburg Airport "the Jetport," as if it didn't cater to aircraft that were technologically obsolete. "Jetport" gradually came to sound as stupid to the natives as it did to the cynical outsiders flying in, so the term had gone out of fashion.

Greenville was where Riley had gone to college. It was where he had played quarterback, though not with overwhelming success ("I had my moments," he was fond of saying), for the Piedmont Bobcats. It was where his country-folk music was still well known. He'd been a gypsy for so long that he no longer considered himself fit for any other life. Home was where he washed clothes, paid bills and cut grass. He lived in Hampton Inns, Motel 6's and Microtels. Home he yearned for in theory. In practice, home was not without its complications. Home, in fact, was forty-five minutes away from both Greenville and the airport. But both were in range. Greenville was his home metropolitan area. His agent would call it his home market.

Monday night was going to be good, though, he thought. Riley was scheduled to appear at a bar north of Columbia. He couldn't remember the name, even though he'd appeared there before. He'd check out his MySpace page when he got home, probably shortly after he loaded some dirty clothes in the washer. There would be a decent crowd, even on a Monday night. Friends, or maybe merely fans, would be there. He'd just be on stage, guitar plugged into an amp, but that wouldn't be as desolate as some coffeehouse in Blowing Rock or honky-tonk in Little Rock. This would be intimate. This would be cool. Riley was tired. His long legs felt cramped. Sometimes that restless feeling in the legs—the legs worn down by years of athletic contests and repaired by a succession of surgeries—was the only warning in his psyche that he had become fatigued. *Thank God for small favors. Thank God for exit rows.* He leaned back, stretching those legs as far under the seat in front as space would allow, closed his eyes and took a deep breath.

"Excuse, please." It was a foreign voice. Riley looked up. A man with olive skin stood above him. Apparently the aisle seat was his. Riley yawned and slid next to the window. No more words were exchanged. No "Thank you." The man just sat down, nervously. *Oh, well, it's the language barrier.* The man's eyes were expressionless, cold even, but Riley thought little of it. *These are desperate times*, he mused. A man who looks like this one could be Indian, American or otherwise; or Mexican; but in the wake of terrorism and the war in Iraq, the first thought was Arab and the second was terrorist. He couldn't help but be suspicious. He scolded himself. *A terrorist who looks like me could blow up anything he wanted.*

Riley wanted to make some attempt at conversation but couldn't figure out a way to break the ice. The man likely wouldn't understand his humor or would take any comment the wrong way.

Riley sighed and said nothing, but now he couldn't sleep. He pulled the book mark from Annie Proulx and began reading.

The flight attendant arrived. She was a young black woman, her enthusiasm not yet quenched by flight after flight, day after day. She explained the obligations of sitting in an exit row. Riley didn't even try to act like he was paying attention. He could've recited the spiel for her.

"Are you willing to assist the captain in the event of an emergency?" she asked.

"Yes," Riley said on cue. The other man merely nodded.

"I'm so sorry," she said. "You have to say it verbally."

"Yes," the man said, a bit impatient. "Yes. Whatever."

Riley gave the woman a look that said "Wonder what this guy's problem is?" Just a momentary opening of the eyes wide and the slightest shake of the head. It was enough to make her chuckle.

"What's your name, ma'am?"

"Shawna."

"It's a pretty name: Shawna. Don't you worry about a thing. I ain't on as many of these buckets as you are, but I've been on more than my share, and in the 'unlikely event of an emergency,' I will promptly obey your every command."

Riley's gregariousness seemed to make the nervous man...more nervous.

"Why, thank you..."

"I'm Riley."

"Thank you, Riley," she said, turning away.

"And, oh, Shawna?"

"Yes."

"I won't even think about tampering with any of the lavatory smoke detectors, either, because I know it's prohibited by law."

"That's so considerate of you," she said with an agreeable touch of sarcasm. "I would like to wish you a pleasant flight, Riley. By the way, the seat across the aisle appears to be unoccupied. Would you care to move over? It might be a bit more roomy."

The Audacity of Dope

"Why, yes, Shawna, I appreciate the consideration." As he moved over, he thought about asking Shawna if she'd like to come to the show, which was kind of ridiculous since it was more than twenty-four hours and a hundred miles from Greenville. It even occurred to him, ever so lightly, to ask her if she would marry him, or if she was married, or if she'd like to fuck, or if she'd like to get high. But, oh, hell, she would undoubtedly be turning right around and flying somewhere else. He'd never actually been with a black woman, unless a lap dance in Indianapolis counted. That'd go over well at home, though, in retrospect, probably not any worse than a kid with an honors degree and acceptance to law school deciding he wanted to play guitar and write songs for a living. Home was accustomed to weirdness.

The plane took off. Riley studied the Gotham skyline, squinted to see if he could find Yankee Stadium and the Meadowlands in the distance but settled for Shea Stadium, which was in its last year of operation. Riley soon became drowsy. Vaguely, he had lyrics in mind. He gave up on the book. The words were darting across his mind without having any effect. He wanted to write a song about the president, one that made fun of the fact that the president had been a college cheerleader. The name he had in mind was "Go! Fight! Win!" He sat there happily floating in the nether land between the conscious and unconscious, lyrics and rhyme flitting about with a lessened awareness that he was riding on a plane and that the trip would soon be over. For over an hour, he slept. The plane began its descent toward Greenville-Spartanburg Airport. Riley awakened and glanced out and looked for golf courses, a favorite hobby. He never failed to marvel at how many suburban homeowners owned pools. And how many occupants apparently played golf.

The man who had once been sitting alongside him had inexplicably gotten up. Riley felt like informing him that the fasten-seatbelts sign was on, but he wasn't completely sure it wasn't a dream. If Shawna noticed, she wasn't saying anything.

Riley looked up the aisle and saw her strapped into the little fold-down seat, apparently preoccupied with writing details into a logbook of some sort. Riley's mind was hazy, and it was hard to differentiate between the real and dream worlds. The plane was definitely close to landing. The man opened the overhead bin. *Wait a minute.* There wasn't anything in that bin but Riley's guitar, the Baby Taylor he could carry on a plane. The man hadn't had anything with him when he came down the aisle. The realization brought Riley wide awake. He started to get up, but unfortunately he failed to allow for the fact that a seat belt held him in place. Bouncing back when he sprang against the strap, he realized that he probably should think this through. *No need to panic. Stop obsessing over the color of the man's skin.* He closed his eyes again. The man wasn't necessarily an Arab or a Muslim, and if he were, the odds were overwhelming that he wasn't some fanatical nutcase. Radical Muslims were to their faith no different than what the Ku Klux Klan, or the Oklahoma City bombers (*Sounds like a roller-derby team*) were to Christianity. There were, however, no more than five or ten minutes until landing.

The man returned to his seat, closing the overhead bin, and to Riley's eye, seemed a bit stiff. Riley looked at him directly. The man avoided his gaze. *Goddamn it, he sure looks suspicious.*

Riley unbuckled his seat belt and got up himself. He reopened the overhead bin. Nothing there but his guitar. He reached for it. Everything seemed okay. *Shit. What's wrong with me?* Riley started to sit back down. He stopped, though. Just for safety's sake, he unzipped the side of the cloth gig bag. Something was glowing inside. A red light, dancing ever so slightly around the meshed polyester. It came from beneath the strings, down inside the guitar. Riley was positive this wasn't normal.

Oh, fuck, Riley thought, but he said not a word. He looked at the man. This time their stares met. Neither said anything. The man's eyes were full of uncertainty, not hate, but a certain resentment showed up, too. Perhaps the resentment was for the infidel, the American with long brown hair and a denim shirt. Perhaps the uncertainty was that of a man ready to meet his maker, ready to become a righteous martyr for his cause. This man's eyes seemed to be saying that nothing could be done to prevent a random act of violence.

Or, then again, Riley could be embarrassingly deluded. His mind raced. *Is it possible that this isn't a bomb? Well, fuck, what else would it be?* It certainly was remarkably compact. *Shit!* The laidback strummer of guitars had to disappear. Riley had to go back in time and become a man of action again. He had to make quick decisions, audible at the line. If this was all some horrible misconception, he was going to wish he hadn't been a quarterback.

Without a word, he yanked the guitar, bag and all, out of the overhead bin, wheeled around, pulled the emergency latch and kicked the door. It made the slightest bounce because it opened to the inside. Wind whistled through the cabin, but the altitude was low and there wasn't much problem with depressurization on a prop plane. An alarm went off. Lights switched on in the floor and blinked. Other passengers shrieked. One burly man leaped to his feet and, staggering, tried to shove him. Curiously, the could-be Arab remained in his seat, almost serene. He didn't appear to be worried. Shawna, on the other hand, did appear to be worried. She was alongside him now, trying to get him to stop, trying to close the exit door.

The burly man had him by one arm, struggling to tear the guitar from his grasp. Shawna had him by the other, stunned by the fact that this man who had been so pleasant just two and a half hours earlier had now yanked open the emergency exit while the plane was still in the air.

Riley had no choice. He let go of the guitar with the right hand, caught it and yanked it back with the left and, in so doing, shed Shawna's grip. She bounced off a seat and landed on the floor. Riley then punched the other, presumably innocent man, nailing him in the nose. He called Riley "a prick" as he fell, blood starting to squirt. Riley retrieved the guitar case, pulled the emergency door inside, threw the guitar case out the opening and watched it fall. *Goodbye, little Baby Taylor.*

"What the fuck are you doing?" It was Shawna. He barely knew her but doubted her words came from a training manual. The terrifying possibility that he might have overreacted occurred to him. *No, no*, he thought, it was a rational decision, a conclusion any man would've reached. *Wonder if she'll say "fuck" again?*

Just above the tree tops, the case exploded. Riley and Shawna saw it, because the plane was banking toward the runway and they were looking backward and peering out the space where once an emergency exit had been. He had the edge of the overhead bin in one hand and Shawna's waist in the other. He continued to hold her as the plane descended. The plane's wheels touched down. The landing was smooth, all things considered.

Riley grabbed Shawna and placed his hands on each side of her face, as gently as adrenaline would allow.

"It was a bomb, Shawna," he yelled above the swirling wind. "A bomb."

"No shit," she said, smiling. Riley felt mildly aroused. Shawna got cool in a hurry.

"He put it in my guitar," Riley said. "When I opened it, the bag, I saw a red light flickering. I looked inside it. I was barely awake, but I got up and saw what was happening."

The flight attendant headed back to the front of the plane. In the cockpit, undoubtedly, there would be some interest in what had occurred.

The man still sat there, strapped into his seat. Now he appeared to be praying, lips moving, and it must have been frustrating in that atmosphere to determine the direction of Mecca. Riley wondered why he wasn't screaming that God would bring destruction to the infidels even if this particular messenger had failed. He didn't. Somehow he'd managed to get a bomb on the plane, but he didn't appear to have any means to kill himself or others with anything less subtle than a bomb. *No backup plan*, thought Riley. *No hatred in his eyes, just weird resignation.* Gradually the peaceful expression gave way to a look of frustration. Riley, on the other hand, had a look that translated roughly to: "Thank you, Jesus, thank you, Lord."

With extraordinary swiftness, it was over, though it seemed to take an inordinately long time to taxi to the terminal. The plane stopped several times before resuming. When it finally came to a decisive stop, it was nowhere near the terminal. Squad cars converged. Armed men climbed on board to arrest and remove the thwarted bomber. They handled him harshly, though he offered no resistance, this abject failure in the cause of religious martyrdom. Riley's transition from nutcase to hero was immediate. Word had drifted ahead of them somehow, probably from the pilot's cockpit. Shawna's composure had been impressive, apart from the f-bomb. Few women—or God forbid, male—flight attendants could've let the cockpit know what happened with such clarity. Riley thought about that morning, how he'd almost worn a Todd Snider tee shirt and shorts instead of a button-up shirt and jeans. If he had, he'd be getting off a plane, with TV cameras arriving and sirens wailing, with these words across his chest:

TREE HUGGIN'
POT SMOKIN'
PORN WATCHIN'
LAZY-ASS HIPPIE

The pilot and co-pilot shook his hand. At the top of the steps, out on the tarmac, Riley thought that the scene made it look like he was a real star, someone people knew. SUVs were arriving, television call letters emblazoned on the sides. How could they possibly have gotten there so quickly? It was as if the Stones had arrived on US Airways Express in a prop plane. Shawna was back. He hugged her.

"I really loved the fuck out of that guitar," he said. Some choice for the last words he would likely ever say to her.

Interrogation, from a progressively higher ranking assortment of law-enforcement officials, lasted into the night. They sheltered him from the press and told him to keep a low profile and not go anywhere. Every time they told him that, Riley lied and said he would. He told them he didn't know yet where he would be staying, but he gave them a number and said he could be reached via cell phone. When his mother called, Riley gave her his love and said he didn't have time to talk.

"Watch the news," he told her. "I'll be home sometime tonight, but I'll be tired, so I'll be over in the morning to tell everybody all about it."

Everything went fine until the Federal Bureau of Investigation came calling. Agents Henry Poston and Ike Spurgeon introduced themselves. Poston reminded Riley of Willem Dafoe in Mississippi Burning. Spurgeon was mildly reminiscent of Sidney Poitier's character—Tibbs, "They call me *Mister* Tibbs," was it Virgil Tibbs?—circa In the Heat of the Night. Movie characters were Riley's only reference point. The only FBI agents he'd ever experienced were in the movies. No, come to think of it, he had talked to an FBI agent on the phone once, but that was when a college classmate had interviewed for a job and the agent was doing a background check.

The possibility that he could be a suspect had totally eluded Riley. The bomb had been concealed in a guitar he owned. On the other hand, he obviously hadn't wanted to blow up the plane, or else he wouldn't have risked his ass getting rid of it.

Poston asked, "Why did you place an explosive device in your guitar, Mr. Mansfield?"

"You're kidding, right?"

"Not at all. You don't mind me calling you Riley, do you, Mr. Mansfield?"

"No," he replied. "All my friends call me Riley."

"You're a musician," said Agent Spurgeon. "Are you struggling with your career? Did you need some stunt to give it a boost?"

"You think this was all an elaborate publicity stunt?"

"No," said Poston. "Agent Spurgeon merely asked a question."

"I'm assuming you arrested the Muslim-looking fucker who stashed that little bomb in my bag."

"Well, Riley, it turns out that he was about as unlikely a suspect as you are," said Poston. "He's actually not Muslim. He's from South Florida. Cuban descent. He runs a hardware store."

"I mean, you do have him in custody?"

"Of course, Mr. Mansfield. With whom do you think you're dealing?"

A chill ran down Riley's spine. This was about as scary as the incident itself. The reality of what had happened hit him. His guitar. Bomb inside it. Everything blown all to hell in a grove of peach trees.

"Did you interview the flight attendant? Shawna?"

"We have a statement. We haven't talked to her yet. The sheriff's deputies have debriefed her," said Spurgeon, who pulled a notebook from his open briefcase. "Miss…Williams."

"All I know is her first name's Shawna," Riley said.

"That's right. Shawna Williams."

Riley collected his thoughts. "She had to see everything," he said. "It's her job to pay attention, right? She was facing back, because she was strapped into one of those fold-down seats at the back of the pilot's cabin. She had to see the man get up, open the overhead bin and jam that thing through my guitar strings. I mean, it wasn't much larger than a baseball, and I didn't really see what it was. I wouldn't know it was there except there was a red light flickering from inside the guitar. But Shawna had to see him get up, tamper with my guitar bag. I was asleep and just kind of came to. After a minute, I realized there wasn't anything but my guitar in the bin he was fiddling around with. She had to see him get up, sit back down, and then me get up to see what the hell was going on. Besides, when I told Shawna what he did, he didn't say a word. He didn't protest or anything."

"How could he do it, Riley?"

"Do what?"

"Get the bomb through the guitar strings."

"It's easy. I always loosen them before I get on a plane."

The rest of the interview was somewhat perfunctory. Riley guessed he had passed some sort of test. The agents left, and Shawna apparently corroborated what he said. At 9:45 p.m., they returned to tell him he was free to go. He took their business cards and told them he would be back in touch if he thought of something that might be useful to the investigation.

The cops gave Riley a ride back to GSP, where he picked up his car. He decided he needed a drink, so he headed toward Greenville instead of home.

Timmy's Bar had a redneck name but was really sort of a hybrid between a honky-tonk and a coffeehouse, a tad funky to be relegated fully to honky-tonk status. It was also a private club, which meant that under South Carolina law, it was open to its members on Sunday. Membership was hardly exclusive, though. Scarcely anyone was there at ten thirty, when Riley walked through the door.

Harvey Kitchens stood behind the bar. "Shit," he said. "If it ain't the big hero."

Riley rolled his eyes. "What can I say? A man's gotta do what a man's gotta do. Pour me a shot."

"Jack?"

"Fine." Riley knocked it back. "Now give me a Budweiser, we'll talk a little and I'll be on my way. I'm looking for no trouble, barkeep."

"So what the fuck?" Harvey asked. Riley told his story.

"You don't got a cigarette, do you?"

Harvey flipped open a pack of Marlboro Lights. Riley lit up.

"I thought you only smoked after you got high," Harvey said.

"It changes a little," Riley said, "after I've foiled an international terrorist plot."

"Ah," said Harvey.

"Sometimes, in rare instances, I smoke before I get high," Riley said.

"So, when you want to play here?" Harvey asked.

"When's the next open night?"

Harvey pulled a clipboard from under the counter, leafed through a couple pages and said, "Tuesday. Be damned. We got nothing scheduled Tuesday."

"Tuesday it is," Riley said. "Now I'd better be headed home.

"Ain't got the shakes no more."

CHAPTER THREE
S.N.A.F.U.

At quarter past six, Riley awakened, staggered into the kitchen, tapped out vitamins from five different bottles, popped a fistful into his mouth and washed them down with a glass of water from a pitcher in the refrigerator. Without any notable body of evidence, Riley considered vitamins a counterbalancing force to ward off the potentially deleterious effects of his dysfunctions.

The vitamins induced, or at least seemed to induce, the call of nature, so, now almost fully awake, he strolled into the bathroom, grabbed his trusty bong from the cabinets under the sink, sat on the toilet and proceeded to offset the vitamins.

Even the home phone, which Riley didn't use nearly as much as the cell, was jammed with messages. *God.* His name was in the phone book. There was a message from a preacher whose church he hadn't attended in fifteen years. He was still a member, though, as Reverend Something-or-Other reminded him. The chairman of the county Republicans. The local paper. The local radio station. The county paper. The chairman of the county Democrats. Three former teammates from college. Seven from high school. A history professor. A Driver's Ed teacher. No telling how many musician chums. Predominantly friends, but a sampling of enemies. A beautiful girl he had once loved secretly in high school.

Riley grabbed a legal pad and took notes on the very small minority of the calls he planned to return. The first he tried was the girl from high school. No answer. Frustrated, he set the legal pad aside, picked up the guitar leaning against the living room couch and played a few songs. Then he erased all the messages—he hadn't even been through half of them, turned on the TV and smoked a cigarette.

He placed his laptop on a small, rollable, lightweight desk and hit the power switch. While he waited for everything to load, Riley

The Audacity of Dope

picked up *ESPN: The Magazine* and read Rick Reilly's column. He had no idea why it came to his house. He hated it, all except for the Reilly columns, and definitely hadn't ordered any subscription. It had merely started showing up in his mailbox every week. This was "The Body Issue," which perfectly illustrated why he hated the mag.

Even "Reills"—that was what they called him on TV—sucked in this one. It was mainly about a career encountering naked athletes in locker rooms. Elsewhere in the pages, an Olympic hurdler had a face that reminded Riley (not Reilly, at least as far as was known) of Sheryl Crow. Riley read the four paragraphs about her and shoved *ESPN: The Magazine* into Rubbermaid the Trash Can.

Absentmindedly, Riley switched on the TV and surfed between *Sportscenter*, *Imus in the Morning* and *Wake Up with Al*. Charles McCord, Don Imus's news director and sidekick, spent two thirds of his allotted time talking about the mysterious musician who had foiled an apparent terrorist attempt to blow up a small passenger plane.

In the mail were two royalty checks, so Riley filled out a deposit slip and attached it to the checks with a paper clip. Then he roughly deducted what he had just added from his checking account by paying bills. With each of the mail-in bills, he affixed a stamp and a sticker from the Disabled Veterans with his return address.

Oh, yeah. The laptop. Riley signed onto the Internet and spent ninety minutes mostly deleting emails. He replied briefly to perhaps one of every twenty, usually with a single nondescript sentence. He signed onto both MySpace and Facebook, leaving the same terse comment: "Please indulge my reluctance to be a hero at least as long as things remain crazy." He listed his status as "numb."

Riley turned off the laptop. He leaned back, almost flat, in the recliner and pulled the line out of the back of the phone. On the coffee table was a biography, half finished, of the writer Terry Southern. He started reading and grew sleepy. While he was thinking about waking himself up by playing a few songs on the guitar, he fell asleep. One of his last waking acts was to hit the on-off button on the remote, silencing the television.

The sound of wheels rolling down the gravel road to his house somehow awakened Riley, who obviously wasn't slumbering soundly. He fairly leaped up, squinted between the shades to see a van, one with some kind of satellite boom on its roof, carrying the call letters of WYFF-TV 4 rolling up. Riley thought the vehicles of television stations looked as if they were painted up to be race cars. Quickly, quietly, walking softly, Riley turned off all the lights and lowered himself silently back into the recliner. Then he just sat still as the doorbell rang over and over for five minutes.

I can't fucking deal with this.

Then he remembered. He had a gig. Just him and his guitar, for tips, CDs and tee shirt sales at a bar north of Columbia. He'd scheduled it to try out a couple new songs and gauge the response of the twenty-five or so who might presumably show up on a Monday night.

Cool.

The scene repeated itself—doorbell ringing, Riley hidden inside, quiet—with Spartanburg's WSPA-TV 7. It occurred to him that, logically, Asheville and Columbia would soon come calling and logically were lagging behind because the cities were farther away. Desiring to escape this self-enforced imprisonment in his own house, Riley shaved and showered, fancying himself in a race against time and television. The weather was clear, so Riley placed his gig bag, five CDs and a couple tee shirts of each size in the farm truck, left his two other vehicles in the garage, opened the barbed-wire gap at the foot of the hill behind the house and drove across the farm to his mother's house instead of using the highway.

Riley's mother was in her bedroom, reading, when he dropped by. She had her back turned, lost in thought.

"Mama?"

Sara Mansfield turned around, peering at her son over the top of her reading glasses.

"Well, how's Sally Sue?" she asked, exhibiting a touch of satire in her expression.

"I barely remember, at this point," he said.

"My God," she said. "You certainly are all over the television. I'm glad our number is unlisted. People have been looking for you over here all day."

"I wish mine was unlisted. I'm a prisoner in my own house."

His mother was unflappable, a virtue she inherited from her father, "Papa," who had died in 1995, while Riley was in college. Riley told her the story as quickly and delicately as possible.

"I don't want to be a hero," Riley concluded. "I don't want to be on TV. I don't want to be anybody but me before all this happened. I feel like just taking off and going on the run until all this blows over."

"It's pretty amazing what you did," she said. "People are gonna want to know all about it."

"Wasn't no heroism to it," Riley said. "It was just a matter of being afraid of being blown up and feeling like I had to do something about it. I just had to do something or not do something, and when I decided not doing something was likely to mean getting blown up...I did what I had to do."

"Well, thank God you did, Riley, thank God you did."

They looked at each other for a few seconds.

"Well..."

"What?"

"What about Sally Sue?"

"Well, when last I left her, before I got on a plane somebody wanted to blow up, she was very happy and emotional and touched by all the people who showed up to tell her how much they loved her and appreciated her," Riley said.

"What'd she think of the song?"

"Just like you said. She cried her eyes out, but they were tears of happiness."

"Well, that was awful sweet of you to go out there, Riley."

"It was damn near the last trip I ever made."

"I know it," his mother said.

"Mom, I gotta go. I got a gig in Columbia tonight, and I'm damn glad to have it because it'll get my mind off all this craziness."

"I wouldn't be surprised if you didn't get down there and find a pile of people waiting."

"Good," he said. "Maybe I'll say they got to buy a tee shirt or a CD if they want to interview me."

"I'd say you better have a few to sell, in that case," she said. "Give me a kiss before you leave."

"Love you, Mama."

"I love you, too," she said. "You be careful."

♫

The cell phone had been rendered useless. Every time Riley turned it on, it rang immediately. The message box was way full. Increasingly addled and frustrated, he headed down Interstate 26 for the Corner Pocket, a bar just off an Irmo exit, north side of Columbia, the state capital.

Somehow, on the road, Riley got a call through to Tom Logan, his agent.

"Where the hell have you been? Why haven't you returned my calls? Why haven't you returned anybody's calls?" Logan, undoubtedly seeing Riley's name on his cell phone before he answered, didn't even bother to say hello.

"Whoa, Tom, hang on. Good to fuckin' hear your voice, too," Riley replied. "It's impossible. Here that beep? Calls are coming in constantly. I can't function like this, man."

"Sure you can," said Logan. "This is an unbelievable opportunity, Riley. You're an overnight sensation. Everybody on earth wants you. Do you know what this could do for your career?"

"I'm more worried about what it could do to my life. Fuck this, man. I didn't sign up for this shit. People tailing me. Everybody wanting a piece of me. I thought the fuckin' FBI was going to arrest me for blowing up the plane instead of the piece of shit who tried to do it. Fuck. I just want to play music, Tom, you know that."

"You could be playing your music in any concert hall you want if you play this thing right," said Logan. "Carnegie Hall. Hollywood Bowl. Grand Ole Opry. Whatever you want. There's quite a market for heroes, my friend. What'd you tell the White House?"

"I ain't heard from the White House. I got a message. I'm not taking calls, man."

"You've got to take calls from the…the President of the United States."

"I know, I know, I know. But, see, Tom, I don't like the fucker. I'm against him. I think he's evil."

"Riley…"

"Hang on, man, let me finish. I'm gonna be civil. I'm just gonna politely decline. You know, 'preciate it, dude, but I just want to go back to being a guy who likes to play his guitar."

"You just can't do that!"

"Fuck I can't, man. Ain't this a free country?"

"You've got to respect the office…"

"I do, I do. I told you I'm gonna be polite. But it's not right to lend myself to be some…some photo op for everything I can't stand. I'm against this guy on everything. I'm against the war, pro-choice, soak the rich, legalize weed, you name it. If some guy wants to burn the flag, I'm for his right to do that, particularly as a protest against this fucked-up, true-believin' dumbass. I mean, it's not just that he's conservative. He's got that right, and the people who elected him, if they elected him, good for them. But it's more than that. It's natural that I hate the fucker. I'm liberal. But I don't understand why conservatives like him. He's turned everything they believe upside down. I'm not gonna stand up with this guy, matching shit-eatin' grins, right when he's trying to brainwash the country again. No fuckin' way."

"You through?" asked Logan.

"Yeah."

"Ever heard of the Dixie Chicks, Riley?"

"The Dixie Chicks are big, Tom. I'm just a guy who plays in bars, sells CDs out of his trunk and lives on song royalties. I'm not big, man. It's not like I'm blowing something big. I just want to do what I'm doing. All these people are calling you, too, right? Just tell 'em I'm not interested. Just tell people that want me on TV that I'm not interested in talking publicly about this. If they want me on their show, they've got to let me sing.

"And...besides. I'm not saying all this stuff to the world that I'm telling you publicly. I'm not gonna shove my views on other people. I'm just not gonna deny everything I believe. I'm not gonna be some campaign gimmick. That's all."

"All right, Riley, settle down. Just listen to me. You can't avoid this. By doing that, it's just going to get worse. You don't have to do anything but talk about the incident. You don't have to do anything but go to the White House, be polite, respectful of the office and shake hands with the president. Take advantage of this. Play it smart. Get some benefit out of it. What you did was admirable."

"What I did was self-preservation. What I did was avoid getting blown up. I'm no hero. I just did what I had to do. I don't want to be forced to act like I'm somebody I'm not."

"Riley, my advice is to make time, just for a few weeks, for your life being really, really hectic. This could give you everything you've always wanted. It could put your music in front of millions."

"You through?"

"I'm through," said Logan.

"Well, I can't...do that. It's not in me."

"Well," said Logan, "an agent's job is to advance the career of an artist. If the artist doesn't want his career advanced, effectively he defeats the purpose of having an agent. I have no choice except to tell you that I can't represent you under those circumstances. It's not in me."

"Fine," said Riley. "Thanks for everything."

He hung up and cut the cell phone off again. Then he thought for a few moments and realized that he really had no other choice. He had to do it.

So he threw the cell phone out the window.

♬

The first sign something was amiss was the absence of those ubiquitous TV vehicles. The second was the sound of music playing inside the Corner Pocket. Riley could tell it wasn't smooth enough to be coming from a jukebox. He left the other stuff in the truck, for the time being, and walked in with his guitar bag slung over his shoulder.

A guitarist, bassist and drummer Riley didn't recognize were onstage. He was an hour early. Maybe they booked a lead-in, but that seemed awfully unusual on a Monday night. No one with any sense would open with a band and headline with a singer.

Then again, this one did really suck.

Riley walked up to the bar. "I'm Riley Mansfield. I'm supposed to be playing here tonight."

The bartender was a kid, and the look on his face underscored the fact that something was amiss.

"Jo-Jo, cover for me a minute," he yelled to his partner, then met Riley's gaze. "Stay right here. I'll be right back."

The manager—George Something-or-Other—came out.

"We didn't expect you to make it," he said. "So we booked somebody else."

"Today?"

George looked over at the band, which sounded as if it arrived straight from the garage. "You were all over the TV. We didn't figure you could make it. I tried to call you. These guys been bugging us to death, and the lead singer's dad is the city manager's son, and you know how it is."

"If I couldn't make it, I would've called you," Riley said. "This sucks incredibly."

"I'm sorry. Maybe…"

"Forget it," said Riley, rage rising as he walked rapidly out the door. He knew better than to hang around and argue. He didn't lose his temper often, but when he did, he was prone to being wildly irrational. No good could come from doing anything but getting back in the truck and settling himself down on the way back to Henry.

Unbelievable shit storm. World of shit. Shit to the nth degree. Life as Riley knew it was coming to an end.

CHAPTER FOUR
IN THE ELEMENT

Tuesday was another day in Riley Mansfield's fortress of solitude: shades drawn, TV off, laptop on. He didn't even feel like he could play his goddamn guitar. He was glad he didn't have call waiting on the home phone. If he called someone, no one else could tell that his phone wasn't just off the hook. So he left it off the hook unless he wanted to call someone. Sometimes it rang in the couple seconds between plugging the line in and dialing the number.

The effect was smothering. His ten-year-old Toyota Corolla and two-year-old Tacoma truck were locked in the garage. The twenty-year-old Ford was out of sight. The hill where his house stood was shaped like the back of a two-humped camel, with the house perched on the first hump. He parked the farm truck in the dip between the hills. It could be seen when looking out the back windows of the house but not from the front yard.

Riley called the local newspaper and gave the editor an extended interview. He didn't want to be a recluse to the home folks. He also snuck down to the local radio station and taped an interview with the station manager. Riley ran his errands, taking a deposit to the bank, and a fistful of letters, mostly bills, to the post office. He picked up three tomatoes and a bunch of bananas at the curb market; a bottle of dishwashing liquid, a box of cereal and a half-gallon of milk at the Family Dollar; left five plastic trash bags at the dump; bought two pounds of homemade sausage at the meat market and a Diet Dr. Pepper and a pack of Marlboro Lights at a convenience store.

Either people in town were gawking and pointing at Riley as he passed, or he was slightly paranoid because he was mildly buzzed. He wasn't stoned or baked. He wasn't quite high. He was merely buzzed, and that was a manageable way to go about his affairs.

Besides, what was a man imprisoned in his own home supposed to do? Bake brownies?

♫

Timmy Barefoot liked to call the music he hosted "literate country," which played well for the liberal-arts majors, not to mention a few of the intelligent people in the area who didn't, or hadn't, gone to the University of the Piedmont. At Timmy's Bar, Riley was at home. It was the first place he had ever played, back when he'd learned enough chords to play a passable guitar and pick up familiar songs by ear. Riley would never be anything but a passable guitarist. He'd just started too late in life. He needed someone else to play the guitar breaks while he strummed along in rhythm. For Riley, the guitar was merely an instrument that helped him sing and write. Words, not music, were most important to him, and a guitar was the key that unlocked the words.

There would've been a good crowd, anyway, because he was local, familiar and playing tunes for the home folks when he got the chance. He always stopped off when he was home for a day or two. Two weeks' notice, and he could play there at any time. Riley was famous at Timmy's, as famous as he was obscure most everywhere else. Timmy's was more home than home.

Way more, actually.

Now, though, the crowd outside, waiting for the doors to open, was huge, unwieldy even. All the local TV stations were there, too, their SUVs embellished with the call letters and channel numbers—the NASCAR Sport/Utility Series!—parked up on the sidewalk because they could. They were past "details at eleven!" and on to "more on the foiled terrorist plot!" stage. Harvey Kitchens ventured outside to tell the mob that Riley just wanted to play his music for the fans and was trying to get his head straight—actually, at the time, he was trying to get his head jangled—and concentrate on his performance. If they'd hang around or come back, Harvey said, he'd try to get him to answer a few questions once the show was over. When would the show be over? Well, he didn't know, Harvey said. It'd probably be late.

Riley was smoking weed back in the dressing room with what passed for the band. This would've been likely to occur even had he not foiled a terrorist plot. Timmy, the club owner, was going to play lead guitar. Chad Dunham, an old classmate at Piedmont, had brought his set of drums. Harvey would play the bass and, occasionally, the fiddle.

"So, why didn't Abdullah, or whatever his name was, do something?" asked Chad. "How come he didn't just, you know, set off the bomb?"

"You're not gonna believe this, man," said Riley. "It's pretty wild. See, the FBI guys think the bomb, once it was activated, or whatever, was set to explode at a certain altitude. It went off automatically. The idea, according to what the FBI thought, was that it would blow up just as the plane was about to touch down."

"Wow. That sounds kind of high-tech," said Harvey.

"Well, you know, when you think about it, it's the same principle as a depth charge, only it's altitude above the ground instead of depth beneath the surface," opined Riley. "Apparently he activated it right before he shoved it into my guitar. It wasn't designed to blow up the plane. Apparently, the idea was that a small explosion would cause the plane to crash, throwing it off kilter just as it was about to touch down."

"So why'd the guy stick it in your guitar?"

"Well, you know how the guy hid it?"

"How?"

"They think he had the thing—I don't know, it wasn't a whole lot bigger than a coffee cup, or, no, it wasn't that shape, maybe it was more like a chocolate éclair, something like that, I don't know, maybe about the size of a baseball. But, anyway, get this, they think he had the thing rammed up his ass."

"No shit?"

"You can't make that shit up, man, I swear." Everyone laughed.

Timmy, who was rolling another joint, looked up. "But, why did he pick the guitar? And, when he fetched it out of his butt crack, did it not stink up the whole plane?"

"Well, I guess nobody knows for sure," said Riley, "but, best anybody can figure, he got up because, when it came right down to it, the little shit couldn't bear the thought of having it blow up inside him. They think he couldn't cope with the image of having himself blown up—and everything else, the plane, the passengers, me, everybody—from the inside out. And my Baby Taylor just happened to be…there."

"Did he tell them that?" asked Chad.

"I don't know, man. I ain't seen him since they drug him off. I don't know whether they got that from him or figured it out for themselves. I mean, they don't know that. Either it's the only thing they can figure, or that's what they got from him. Last time I seen him, he just looked like he was praying. Funny thing is, the FBI told me he wasn't even Muslim. Cuban, maybe, something like that."

Silence. Everyone digested the information.

"Well, like, how could he get a bomb through security, even if it was stuck up his butt crack?"

"Why come you always ask me all the tough questions? Fuck, I don't know."

Another short period of contemplation.

"Cuban, huh? Did anybody bother to tell the dude that Kennedy was already dead?" Harvey asked.

"And…Che Guevara, he's gone," said Riley, taking a hit. "Viva the revolution, I guess.

"Isn't this funny? We're laughing our ass off bullshitting about a guy who tried to blow up an airplane."

"So, how's it feel to be a hero, man?" asked Timmy.

"Feels pretty fucking numb," said Riley. "Or maybe it's the weed."

They all laughed. Timmy fired up another J.

The Audacity of Dope

♫

As always, it was Timmy Barefoot who walked up to the mic, Telecaster strapped on his shoulder.

"Ladies and gentlemen, welcome to another night of live music at Timmy's Bar," he said. "This particular night is pretty special, and not just because we got our very favorite singer-songwriter in the house. I'm sure everybody knows the story, and it's pretty cool, but what we're here for tonight is music. Let's give it up for the hometown boy, the ex-Bobcat, man, make welcome Mr. Riley Mansfield!"

Harvey yanked a little zip-zip out of his fiddle, and the makeshift band rolled briefly into what passed, barely, for the Piedmont fight song. A few frat boys next to the stage yelled. Riley walked out to thunderous applause, waving as he strapped on his electric-acoustic and plugged into the amps. The cheering wasn't going to subside, it seemed. Riley bowed. He had on the Todd Snider tee shirt, partially visible beneath a beige flannel shirt, unbuttoned.

"Thanks, everybody. It's good to be back home, back to Timmy's Bar. It's been a weird fuckin' day, man, and a strange and unusual week."

The applause rose again.

"Nothing makes a crowd roar like gratuitous profanity," Riley said. "Yeah, it's just another big night. Sorry I dropped an F-bomb there. It just kind of slipped, but, no, it's been a big week, y'know. 'Cause, like, I bought a new pair of sneakers!" He lifted up one foot. "They're New Balance, I think. Feel good. You know me, man. Whatever's on sale in ten and a half or eleven."

It was a weak attempt at humor that no one got.

"What about the plane?" someone yelled.

"Oh, the plane? It had propellers, man. Kind of a bumpy landing, but, you know, I reckon it could've been worse. Well, nah, I guess it couldn't. My guitar got blowed up."

Once the smattering of applause subsided again, Riley nodded, waved his arms downward and said, "Enough about tennis shoes and fuckin' airplanes. I wrote this song about a little adventure I had in Nashville, man. I'd been playing for tips just like I am here. Yeah, man. Hint, hint. I don't get the good gigs, man. I had been up onstage at Robert's Western World, down on Broadway, from, like, five to eight, and another band followed me. A better band, well, a band, not just me plunking on this little guitar I recently lost."

The applause rose again. One of the frat boys expressed the opinion that Riley kicked ass.

Agreeably, Riley said, "What, man? You ain't got no tests to study for? It's exam time, best I remember."

Smattering of applause. Ripple of laughter.

"To make a long story short, well after I got through, and got this gal, Flo or something—barmaids in Nashville are named Flo or Reba or Eileen, yeah, Ruby, that's good, not a Jessica in the bunch—anyway, I got Flo to store the guitar, and I just watched the band perform, and drank some beer and wrote little notes to myself on a cocktail napkin about, hey, I love that old song and I ought to learn how to play it, shit like that, but after a while, I met this girl, man, and, yeah, probably because I started drinking…and there wasn't nobody much there that I really knew…and, all by my lonesome, I was kind of, you know, uninhibited, and I had this little adventure that was cool but probably the good Lord was looking out for me or else I'd have got myself killed.

"I probably need to rethink the deal about living dangerously, but, then, how the fuck am I gonna come up some more tunes? I'd lose my niche. So, here goes. It's in 'G,' boys, little tune called 'Tattooed Gal.'"

I never liked tattoos and bright-red hair
But I love women
Somehow I came across a gal

The Audacity of Dope

Who had all of those things
She had a man with cold, mean eyes
He was bad to fight
He stomped away
She turned and asked me
If I had a light
I didn't love her
It wasn't right
But I tried to help her
Just for one night.
She said we've got to go or else
Bobby, he'll be back
Next thing I knew we left the bar
And wound up in the sack
When she was nude I found that she
Had many more tattoos
She taught me a new way
To observe the golden rule
I didn't love her
It wasn't right
But I tried to help her
Just for one night.
I put her on a Greyhound bus
Bound for New Orleans
I hope that Bobby followed her
And didn't follow me
It goes to show what happens when
Liquor leads the way
I asked Jesus for forgiveness
But He turned and looked away
I didn't love her
It wasn't right
But I tried to help her
Just for one night.

No, I didn't love her
Well, maybe for spite
But I tried to help her
Though…iit…wasn't…riiiiiggghhht!

Applause once again rocked the building. Beers arrived on the bandstand. Riley handed them out to Harvey, Chad and Timmy. He wrapped his hand around the remaining beer, hoisted it and took a slug.

"Okay, okay, thanks so much. I appreciate it," Riley said, bowing again. "We'll mix in a few of my songs here and there, and we'll do some old country standards, and a little rock-and-roll. Hell, I might get moved and weepy-eyed and play some out-and-out pop, Elton John or some shit, but that's only gonna happen if you start buying wine coolers for the band.

"On the other hand, if you start sending shots up, we'll have to play really easy rock-and-roll where a man has to hit notes drunk he wouldn't think about sober. In that case, we'll be doing one Steve Miller Band song after another—'cause they're like, really easy— just shortly before some, uh, mishap happens up here and I have got to get a Band-Aid."

The crowd laughed nervously because, collectively, it wasn't sure exactly what Riley meant. He didn't know, either.

About an hour in, Riley put a capo on his guitar, second fret, and performed a medley of Jerry Jeff Walker standards—"music y'all may not know already, but you need to"—then excused himself for, as they say, "a brief intermission."

He almost forgot to be a huckster. He returned to the microphone to say, "Uh, tip your bartenders. Buy some shit at the table at the back. Got CDs, man. They're right back there. Keep the faith, hang loose, be cool, all that other shit, and I'll be back directly."

Backstage, the looseness evaporated into what felt like an odd numbness. It was true that the word could readily be used to describe at least part of the sensation of smoking weed, but it didn't normally offset the exhilaration of a live performance. Inexplicably, given what he perceived as an emotional flat line, Riley felt tears welling up. His first reaction was embarrassment.

"I think I'm going to step outside. I think I need some fresh air, but, just in case it's too fresh, I think I'll take these," he said, retrieving a pack of cigarettes from a coffee table. "Be back in a few."

Riley peeked out the back door to a loading dock. Miraculously, there were only empty cars, with no one milling around them. He half-expected reporters and television cameras. No one, it seemed, had anticipated he might step outside, so he sat down on the concrete steps, where, indeed, he began to cry. Still, he felt no corresponding emotion, which perplexed him. Literally, Riley cried and didn't know why. He lit a Marlboro Light.

"Riley?"

He looked up. It was a girl from his hometown, one he'd known in high school. Melissa Franklin. She'd been a cheerleader. Pretty girl, sweet and unaffected. One he'd wanted to love but just never got around to it. Riley vaguely remembered that she had left a message on his home phone.

She noticed he was crying.

"I'm sorry," she said. "I guess this is a bad time."

"No, no, Melissa. It's great to see you. For the life of me, I don't know why my eyes are wet. Sit down. Been a while."

She stared into his bleary eyes.

"Guess, you see, I started smoking."

"Can I bum one?"

"Sure," he said, lightly tapping the pack on the back of his hand. She pulled it out, and he gave her a light.

"My mother came with me. She's back inside. I told her I'd be back in a few minutes. I think she'd probably like to see you after the concert."

"I gotta say, I'm surprised," Riley said. "I don't guess you'd be up here with your mom if you had a husband, kids."

"No," she said. "I guess I'm still just, uh, adrift. I'm teaching now. At the high school."

"What do you teach? Let me guess. Social studies."

"English."

"That's cool. Can't be smoking at school, though."

"I guess hiding it keeps me from smoking more. With Mama, it's all about appearances. She'd be worried somebody would see me if we were alone in the desert."

"That's a song right there," Riley said.

"I heard about you and your plane almost getting blown up, and how you're this big hero. Funny thing is, I had been thinking about catching up with you. I'd sort of been looking for a chance to come see you play."

"So how's your mama doing?" He didn't much want to talk about being a hero.

"She's good. She and my dad split when we were in high school."

"Yeah, yeah, I remember. You never did make a big deal out of it," Riley said. "It seemed like everybody else was more upset about it than you were. You ever see your dad?"

"I used to. I think he always held it against me that I took Mama's side...I actually haven't seen him in, like, five years. I think he called the year before last at Christmas."

"Well," said Riley, "I don't got a daddy neither."

He wasn't the only one eager to change the subject.

"I wouldn't have imagined," she said. "I mean, you were the big football hero, went off and played in college."

"Something about playing guitar and singing and being in a band."

She was leaning against the banister. Riley wished she had sat down beside him.

"But," he said, "I think I really started smoking—I mean, I really don't smoke that much—because I started getting high. I started getting high because I started playing in a band."

Melissa laughed.

"So, I guess I'm, like, spilling my guts and shit, huh?" *Why am I spilling my guts about this shit?* "It beats talking about international terrorism."

"Your secrets are safe with me," she said.

"A man's got to have friends he can depend on," Riley said.

The door behind them opened. It was Timmy. "Time to go, bro," he said. "Natives getting restless."

"I hope that's because they've all bought CDs and tee shirts, and if we play some more music, the guy at the table can put some more stuff out. Fat chance of that, huh?"

"C'mon, superstar," Timmy said.

"Ah'ight." Riley turned back to Melissa. "I'll give you a little head start so you can wash your hands and smack on that gum. You and your mama hang tight. Timmy knows what you look like, so I'll get him to usher you back to wherever the fuck it is I am. We'll work it out."

"Okay, bye," she said, and kissed him on the cheek.

"Don't just leave, now."

"I won't."

CHAPTER FIVE
A BIT MUCH

Riley met the media outside Timmy's at about 11:15. He buttoned his shirt, hiding the Snider tee shirt, sat on the steps in back, the same place where he had chatted with Melissa. Lights illuminated the darkness. Riley wore sunglasses, which, given the lights, didn't seem unusual in the slightest. He did not at all want his eyes showing up on television.

"Would you stand up, please, Mr. Mansfield, and come over here?" a pretty blonde from Channel 4 asked.

"If I stand up and talk into your microphone, my guess is I'd be favoring your station over all the others," Riley said as quietly as he could. "Why don't we just do it this way? I'll sit here, all of you can run your cameras and everybody will get the same thing."

"We want to go live," she said.

"Well, you can all go live, and then I won't be favoring one station or another, or TV over radio, or radio over newspapers."

"You'll be favoring radio and TV just by talking to everyone at the same time," yelled a reporter from The Greenville News. "They'll have it before we do. That's just the way it is."

"Well, there's nothing I can do about that," said Riley, "or let me put it this way: There's nothing I'm gonna do about that. Ask me questions. Try to behave, you know, like, pretend you're polite and civilized. Or I'll just blow it all off. I don't mean to be uncooperative. I just want to get this shit over with."

For perhaps two seconds, there was quiet. Riley took that to mean at least one of the stations was already "going live," which meant at least one had just televised America's newest hero saying a bad word.

"Sorry, folks out in TV land," said Riley, reeling a bit. "I did not know my remarks were, like, apparently, live. I didn't mean to offend all you law-abiding citizens good and true.

The Audacity of Dope

"Questions, anyone?"

"Describe the incident at the airport, please."

"Oh, c'mon, there's already been news at six, hasn't there? Don't we already know the basic facts?"

"What was it like when you confronted the alleged terrorist?"

"Um, there wasn't much of a confrontation. It was more like I confronted my guitar in the overhead compartment of the aircraft," Riley said. "How'd you like that? The aircraft...I never thought I could sound like a flight attendant. Eventually, come to think of it, I think I 'de-planed.'"

No heads were nodding. No one was laughing except Riley, who said, "But, seriously, folks. Buh-boom-chuh! That's, like, a drum roll. For a joke. Get it? Whatever."

Even through the weed-induced haze, Riley was getting this sinking feeling. *Wow, this isn't really going to come off well.*

"I was, like, suspicious, because I was sort of half-asleep, and the alleged terrorist was standing up, messing with something in the overhead bin—that's what they call 'em, in aircraft lingo, overhead bins—and even though I was sort of half asleep, half awake, it occurred to me that there was nothing in the overhead bin except my guitar.

"So, like, the alleged terrorist sat down, and I sort of jumped up, and when I looked in the bin, sure enough, there was only my guitar—my poor, soon to be, late, great guitar—and when I unzipped the gig bag, there was this red light, blinking or flickering, inside it. I got wide awake in a real big hurry when I realized that what was inside my guitar, my poor Baby Taylor, was, most likely, a bomb. I felt I had to make a really quick decision, which, I guess, if it had not been a bomb, would've made me look really stupid."

A cacophony of questions rose, which Riley quieted by raising his hands.

"I can't believe you guys. Nobody's gonna ask me a real important question, one like, 'Well, Riley, tell us, why do you play a Baby Taylor?' 'Well, thanks for asking that, Bob. I play a Baby Taylor because it's a compact model suitable for carrying on an airplane, and, yet, its sound is remarkably resonant, and in this age where we have to be ever vigilant to prevent terror from striking our airports and, for that matter, our homes and our gigantic skyscrapers, it comes in handy to pack a guitar that will speed the understandably tortuous path through security. In most instances, I understand, the small guitar doesn't actually get blown up, as mine did.

"But, once again, I digress, don't I?"

Riley expected laughter again. He got very little. Eyes rolling, mostly.

"In my mind, I was, uh, sufficiently sure of myself that I knew I had to do something fast. So I looked at the dude, and he was staring back, and I didn't take his look as being indicative of any goodwill on his part, so I decided I was right and that, quite possibly, I was about to blow up, along with the plane. Once that realization is in place, it's really not that hard to do something drastic.

"I was already sitting in an exit row, so, luckily, having sat in exit rows before and understanding the mechanics of such things, I grabbed my guitar, and pulled the lever, and all hell broke loose— Hell's okay, right? Guess so—and people tried to tackle me, and there was this one guy who I punched 'cause, like, understandably, he thought I was nuts, and I chucked my late, great guitar out the opening where the door had just recently been, and before they stuck me with a needle or shot me with a…poison dart or something, down below, the bomb went off in the tree tops, and I, like, suddenly became a big hero.

"All because I didn't want to blow up."

The cameras all started to move away, which Riley took to mean Leno and Letterman were about to come on, and the various TV personalities strode away, leaving Riley largely alone.

"And, hopefully, we all lived happily ever after."

A few more questions were hurled in the darkness by lingering scribes.

"What did you tell the president?"

"I don't know what you're talking about," Riley replied.

"I understand," said a short guy in a blue button-down, "that the president has invited you to the White House."

"Nope. Sorry. Don't know nothing about it."

"Well, would you like to go to the White House?"

"Dunno," said Riley. "Reckon he likes my music? I'm kinda doubting it, man."

They all had deadlines. They all had to run back to phones and stations and laptops. Amazingly, in seconds, there was only Riley in the dark. And Melissa, who had apparently been watching from nearby.

"You were good," she said. "Really."

Riley smiled. "I can be an eloquent fucker," he said, "but, honestly, you're just trying to make me feel good, right? I think I really screwed up."

"No, you didn't."

"I did. Look at how late it is. I don't think I was on live TV all that time. Maybe just a few minutes. Maybe just up to where I cussed. I think they were shooting a bunch of footage for others. The networks. CNN. Fox. That's what that was all about.

"I wonder if I was on, like, Fox, live? I'm so fucking stupid. Smoking that joint before I came out might not have been the best idea I ever had."

Melissa laughed, which Riley had noticed she did a lot.

"My mom's inside," she said. "Try to be good, okay?"

"Check."

♬

At two a.m., Riley, obviously too fucked up to drive home, found a room at a nearby Hampton Inn, sadly, sans Melissa, with whom, in his jangled state, he realized he had obviously fallen in love. The woman at the front desk asked him to sign one of the cardboard slips that hold the plastic room keys, but Riley found one of his CDs in his bag and signed that to her instead.

I'M NO HERO. JUST A MUSICIAN…

AND THEY AIN'T THE SAME.

RILEY MANSFIELD

WEE HOURS, 5/27/08

Safely lodged in Room 117, Riley's hands began shaking as he undressed. It was vexing. He didn't feel anxiety consciously. First the unexpected tears, now the trembling. Anxiety escaped the numbness that had enshrouded his psyche while he wisecracked with friends, smoked weed, guzzled beer and shots, performed, talked with Melissa and made a fool of himself with the media.

He tumbled off to sleep quickly but not soundly. Once he dreamed it was he, not the Baby Taylor, that had plummeted from the plane. Riley awoke before exploding in the tree tops.

Good sign.

♫

When Riley pulled into his mother's driveway, at about noon on Wednesday, he was pleasantly surprised not to see a dust cloud raised by satellite trucks and passersby. The scene could have been any day at the well-worn brick home.

That being the case, Riley tried to act normally. He walked into the kitchen and asked his grumpy older sister, "Where's Mom? I need to pick up my mail."

The former Louise Mansfield, twice married, twice divorced, sat at the kitchen table. Riley rarely saw her when she wasn't sitting there, smoking cigarettes and sipping Natural Lights. She worked, of course, but Riley never saw her there. He didn't even know the name of the company or where it was. Louise and he did not get along in long stretches, and it was his general view that no good could come from any but the most basic of conversations. For instance, in asking Louise where his mother was, he merely wanted her to say "in her bedroom" or possibly "gone to the store."

After a handful of forced pleasantries, Riley escaped his sister mainly unscathed—perhaps there were modest advantages to being a hero—and walked past the living room and down the hall to his mother's room.

Riley saw one of the nephews through a cracked door, playing a video game, and said hello, but all he got was a perfunctory "hey Uncle Riley, love you" because seventeen-year-old Davis was trying to get through a trap door or a secret closet or whatever he called those crafty maneuvers that enabled gaming enthusiasts to reach levels unattainable by mere skill.

"Love you, too, Davis."

His mother was ready when he entered her bedroom, where she was reading. She still knew the rhythm of his footsteps on the hardwood.

"I told everybody who stopped by here I didn't know where you were and didn't know when you were coming and if you were coming home," she said. "And I told them to get off my yard, and while they were at it, get off my property or else I was going to call the law."

"I love you, Mama. You always could read my mind."

"I saw the film of you outside that honky-tonk you were playing," she said. "That was your daddy coming out in you. Come hell or high water, you're not going to be inclined to do whatever it is the world demands of you."

"What's going on here?" Riley asked. "I mean, besides all the crap related to me deciding I'd just as soon not get blown up by a terrorist."

"Well," she said, "it's been a very difficult couple of days, even by the standards of this family."

Riley and his mother talked quietly. He left her some books to read. She returned some he had given her.

Back home, after placing a garbage bag full of mail and an armful of books on a couch already covered with clutter, Riley brooded the way a man broods when he believes himself right and no one else does. He sat in his recliner and tried to read a Wallace Stegner novel. His reading materials were as muddled as everything else. He was in the middle of four different books at the same time. His eyes ran across pages without perceiving so much as a sentence. Then he tried the Annie Proulx short stories again. He felt his shoulders, hell, his whole body, slump. His hands trembled. His neck stiffened.

Then Riley turned on the television and began flipping channels. First he tuned to MSNBC, where he heard biographical details of his life repeated over and over. Even on Fox News, Riley Mansfield was still being portrayed in a positive light. Riley knew in his bones this wouldn't last much longer. He felt a hopelessness all his own because he knew he couldn't handle all this any way other than the suicidal, me-against-the-world mode that was his nature.

Two words blinked on and off in the neon sign that was his brain.

Fuck me.

CHAPTER SIX
CLOSING IN

It was drizzling in Our Nation's Capital. The National Security Adviser, David Branham, spent a minute or so staring out into the dank morning fog from his office in the White House's West Wing. Branham welcomed the Deputy Director of Homeland Security, Banks McPherson, into his office.

"Morning, Banks," said Branham. "What you got?"

McPherson opened his briefcase and removed a dossier on Riley Mansfield. He placed it on Branham's desk.

"This is the guy who foiled the bombing attempt," said McPherson.

Branham looked at photos of Riley, one a posed shot and the rest concert photos.

"Jesus," he said. "A musician. What are the odds?"

"He's a pretty interesting fellow," said McPherson. "He played quarterback at the University of Piedmont. Academic All-American. Accepted to law school. Instead, he became a songwriter."

"Ever wrote anything good?"

"He's had a lot of songs, mostly by artists kind of below the radar. One of his songs, recorded by someone named Nanci Griffith, was nominated for a Grammy."

"I know that name," said Branham. "She's a Texan."

Branham was a Texan, too, his rise in government boosted by an affiliation with other Texans like Rick Perry and Phil Gramm.

"Banks, here's the deal," said Branham. "All right, this has happened. Nothing we can do about it. Now the mission is to make this work to our advantage. The President is sagging in the polls. The election is a little over five months away. We need this Riley Mansfield to go to bat for the President's reelection campaign. We need him on the stage, standing behind the president, at campaign rallies. He needs to be made a symbol of the President's strong stand against terrorism."

"So far, since the incident occurred, Mr. Mansfield has avoided most media contact," said McPherson. "Almost everything the TV networks have used is footage from a makeshift press conference outside a bar where he, Mansfield, had been playing. Radio is using clips from an interview he gave his local radio station, and newspapers are using quotes from a story in his local weekly newspaper."

Branham chuckled. "Good for him," he said. "South Carolina's a good Republican state. This boy ought to be willing to go to bat for the President. We'd make it worth his while."

"As best we can tell, sir, he's fairly apolitical in terms of, uh, any activism."

McPherson pulled a CD from a suit pocket.

"Some of his songs suggest, I think, sir, that he's somewhat liberal."

"Well, we'll make sure he doesn't play any of those songs at our rallies, Banks. We need to get him on our side, whether he wants to be or not."

"An offer he can't refuse, sir?"

"You said that," said the National Security Adviser. "I didn't say that."

The two exchanged mischievous looks.

"But I liked it," said Branham, signaling an end to the meeting.

As McPherson reached the door, Branham said, "Wait a minute, Banks."

Branham wrote a name and phone number on the bottom of a yellow legal pad. He placed a ruler above the note and sliced it cleanly.

"Make this call," he said, handing the note to McPherson. "Explain the situation, and tell him I told you to call him. He'll know what to do."

♪

Riley lounged in his recliner and heard the word "recluse" used in relation to him on MSNBC, CNN, Headline News and Fox News. Each used footage of Riley, looking quite impaired and notably wearing sunglasses, outside Timmy's Bar.

Jesus. It was just last night.

So far, no TV trucks since he got home. Maybe it was dying down. More likely, it was just the eye of the hurricane. The footage had them occupied for a while. If Riley could just get out of town, maybe he could elude all the people who wanted a piece of him.

He got up and started washing clothes. Once he got a load started, he rolled a joint and went out on the back patio. Feeling wary, he looked around the corner of the house, saw that the coast was clear and walked downhill to his semi-hidden truck. He smoked half of the joint and slid the remainder in the pocket of his tee shirt. After sitting on the tailgate for a few minutes—*Damn, why didn't I bring the guitar?*—he walked back up the hill, wobbling slightly as he went.

Back in the kitchen, Riley spun the timer dial on his George Foreman Grill and had a cigarette while he waited for the grill to warm. On television, Joe Scarborough was wondering aloud if this Riley Mansfield had something to hide. *Great.* Riley returned to the kitchen, smiling at the absurdity of it all, and cooked breakfast: sausage on the grill and a cheese omelet in the frying pan. He placed a couple slices of bread in the toaster.

The phone started ringing, and Riley waited to see if the caller would leave a message. Miraculously, no. He pondered the question of how comprehensive his moratorium on electronic communication should be. Should he just give up cell phones, or phones in general?

He decided to keep the land line once he realized that he still wanted Internet access. Didn't the wireless have something to do with the phone line? Riley thought so.

The toast popped out. Riley spread butter on the slices of bread hurriedly, making sure it would melt before the toast cooled. He ate from the recliner, sitting the plate atop the closed laptop on the rolling table. He listened as Pat Buchanan upbraided Scarborough for tainting Riley with speculation.

"Look, we don't know anything about this guy, but there's no evidence he's anything but an American hero," said Buchanan. "I don't know why he's apparently turning himself into some recluse, but I'm sure this fellow is under an unbelievable amount of scrutiny, and maybe he just wants to be left alone. I understand that."

I'm fucking being defended by Patrick J. Buchanan. This is really, really scary.

Riley picked up the guitar leaning on the front of the sofa and this time walked out the front door to sit on the steps there, strum the guitar and sing to his heart's content. At least if someone came to bother him, he'd see them coming. It occurred to him that the guitars had become his dogs. Since he traveled almost constantly—and since no one at his mother's house could possibly be depended on to feed his dog—he'd had to give Fenway, his Newfoundland, away.

The guitars, though, were worthy successors. They were each like different breeds. The Pawless, mellow and resonant, best in show. The Martin, slightly more expressive in the upper strings. His battle axe, the electrified Lazy River, a bit the worse for wear from so many bleary nights onstage. The red Telecaster he'd bought in a pawn shop. He didn't play it as much as he should because who wanted to plug in when the acoustic was right here in the living room?

Strumming away at the Pawless, he absentmindedly mourned the loss of the Baby Taylor and realized he would need to buy a new travel guitar—*How about a downsized Martin?*—before his next plane trip, which he reckoned wouldn't be for a few weeks, anyway. *Geez. Flying. Will it ever be the same?* His schedule was on his MySpace page and scribbled in the little appointment book American Express sent him every year.

The vibration of the strings soothed him. The guitar never got mad or disapproving. He communicated through it, and it was never judgmental over what passed through.

No heavy lifting this bright, clear day. It was warm, not hot. A cool breeze reflected just the slightest touch of spring still in the air. Hank Williams fit his melancholy perfectly. Riley felt like "a rolling stone, all alone and lost." His bucket had a hole in it. He could relate to the wooden Indian unable to communicate with the similarly wooden maiden. He wondered if he could get out of this world alive.

With his throat a bit charred, Riley sang mostly in the key of D. He tried to lift his spirits by moving from Hank Williams to Buck Owens, but Buck seemed absurdly chipper so Riley switched to Merle Haggard, who, like him, was "tired of this dirty old city," though not this one, mind you. His dirty old city was metaphoric. After bemoaning the futility of a mama who tried, it occurred to Riley that he'd like to settle down if only "they" would let him. Then he just belted out "Fightin' Side of Me" for old times' sake. He was pondering a switch to Lefty Frizzell and the blues that accompany smoking cigarettes and drinkin' coffee when he heard the sound of automobile tires rolling over the gravel on the quarter-mile road to his house.

It was a squad car. It was, in fact, the Sheriff in the flesh. The car was fairly crammed with three men in suits and a woman in a pantsuit. The woman owned a real estate office and, as best Riley remembered, was either the county Republican Party chair or used to be. He didn't recognize the men, save the Sheriff, but that was probably because Riley didn't often mingle with Republicans, local or otherwise. Riley pulled a stick of gum out of his pocket and began chewing it with mild diligence as the squad car came closer. Reflex action.

The Sheriff got out first.

"Hey, give me a second, will you?" Riley fairly yelled. He then went inside, closed the door behind him, washed his hands industriously and gargled. He considered changing tee shirts but thought it might look suspicious. Then he came back out.

"Mind if we come in, Riley?"

"Sheriff, I'd really rather you not," he replied. "You know, I travel all the time, and the house is just a place to flop when I come home. I'd really be right embarrassed to have y'all come in, and besides, the couch and the love seat are both covered up with magazines, guitar strings and God knows what else."

The more open air, the better.

"Tell you what," Riley offered. "I'll raise the garage door and we can just set a piece on the tailgate of my truck and a couple of chairs I got out there. Give me a sec."

It wasn't a comfortable summit meeting.

Sheriff Horace O'Shields introduced Riley to the other visitors, one of whom was a Baptist preacher, another the aforementioned real estate saleswoman, then there were the bank president and the car dealer. Riley nodded, but their names went straight through his brain without leaving a mark. They all acted remarkably as if he knew them.

The bank president took the lead. He was beefy and bespectacled. At first he praised Riley for his heroic act, tossed in a paragraph about how the whole town, the whole county was proud to have him as a native son, and Riley tried to act interested, nodding with what he hoped was a respectful façade.

"Mr. Mansfield—or should I call you Riley?—we have some really exciting news."

"Riley's fine." He wondered if it would've been okay to call the bank president by his first name but discarded the thought since he didn't remember it.

"We need you to get packed up and ready. The President of the United States wants you to come to Washington, where you are to be honored at the White House."

"The White House?"

"Yeah, you know, in Washington." It was the preacher talking. "The Executive Mansion."

"Yeah," said Riley. "Gotcha. Rose Garden. West Wing. Oval Office." *Swimming pools. Movie stars. Black gold. Texas tea.*

"President Harmon wants to publicly honor you for your service to the country," said the bank prez. "I understand that he wants to present you with the nation's highest civilian honor."

"What's that? An Oscar? An Emmy? A Grammy?"

Silence.

"Sorry," said Riley. "It was a joke. A bad one, obviously."

Then, of course, they laughed.

"I appreciate it," Riley said, "but right now, I'm kind of booked solid."

Sheriff O'Shields piped up. "Well, what difference..."

"No, Friday night I've got a gig," Riley said. "I've got to play a club in St. Augustine, Florida. St. Augustine Beach. Been scheduled for months. I'm sorry. Can't get out of it. I'm headed down there in the morning. Then I'm playing in Florida about every night next week."

"When the President of the United States issues an invitation, you do what it takes," said the car dealer. "This, these...concert appearances...surely, you can get out of 'em to be honored by the president."

"No, I really can't. I'm a man of my word where playing live music is concerned."

Obviously astonished, they all began to talk at once. The general consensus of the babble, as best Riley could gather, was that he should meet the president out of respect for the country and the office.

"Look," he said, waving both hands, "I'm not a hero. I just did something because it was there and I recognized it, and I had enough sense to know there really wasn't any option. Either get blown up or do something to prevent it from happening. That's not being a hero. That's just not giving up. That's just avoiding disaster because there's no other choice."

"Easier said than done," said the car dealer, versed in the art of persuasion. "How many people do you think have the guts to do something like that? Not many."

"Oh, I don't know. Given the choice of dying a horrible death and doing something to stop it..."

"That's easier said than done," said the preacher. Again. *Is there an echo?*

"Okay," said Riley, growing impatient. "How many people would want to resume their life—their life that they're happy with—when the whole world wants a piece of them? A lot. Most of them would succumb to all this pressure. It takes some guts not to do that."

The real estate lady was the most strident. "See here, Mr. Mansfield. The President of the United States wants to honor you. As an American, you owe it to your country to accept his praise."

"No," said Riley. "I owe to this country, this free country, my right not to have myself misrepresented and used as a tool of partisan politics. That's what people fought and died to give me the right to do."

"You don't like Republicans, do you, Mr. Mansfield?" said the woman, bristling.

"Not a bit. Some of them, though, I respect. Sam Harmon ain't one of 'em."

"He is the President of the United States."

"I respect the office, not the man who occupies it."

Now it was a shouting match between a belligerent middle-aged woman and an unshaven young man, standing in his front yard wearing a pocket tee shirt purchased at a truck stop and blue shorts from a Goodwill store. (He had been on a road trip when he discovered he had failed to pack anything to sleep in.) The banker and the car dealer stood on one side, expressionless and appalled. Sheriff O'Shields was on the other, frowning.

"This is a time of war. Men are fighting and dying to protect our freedom," said the real estate lady.

"If they are protecting my freedom, and I can be forced to prop up the image of a corrupt and inept tyrant, then truly, Mrs. Whatever-Your-Name-Is, those men have fought and died in vain.

"Goddamn you! Now get out of my fucking yard."

"There's no reason to get nasty," said the lady.

"Yes, there is," Riley replied. "Now get out of my yard."

All but the Sheriff beat a hasty retreat. He spoke quietly.

"I can't even describe how big a fucking mistake this is, Riley Mansfield," he said. "You are doing something you can't do, and you will pay for it."

"Well, Sheriff, I guess you're in a unique position to know," Riley hissed. "Take your best shot."

O'Shields and his delegation pulled away. Riley set on the steps again and lit a cigarette. His hands were trembling again, which they hadn't done when he was standing in the aisle of a passenger plane, winds swirling and warning lights flashing, hurling a door open and chucking a guitar out the emergency opening. But now they were doing it…most all the time.

To hell with the president. Lots of times he doesn't matter. But the Sheriff! There's a man who can fuck with your life.

Gripped suddenly by paranoia, Riley spent the next thirty minutes writing a song, his first protest ditty, in fact. It settled him. He sat the notepad at the top of the steps and hashed out the chords. Then he wondered just where in the world it was that he was going to play this song.

Sitting on his front porch, slightly buzzed, Riley played "The Fightin' Side of Me" again. It was a Haggard song that he disagreed with but, somehow, also liked, or else he wouldn't have known all the words to it, would he?

CHAPTER SEVEN
ROOTS OF HIS RAISIN'

At Christmas during Riley Mansfield's junior year of high school, his father had bestowed upon him a gift he would later regret. He gave Riley a Harmony guitar. The two shared a love of country music, cultivated throughout Riley's boyhood by exposure to late-night radio broadcasts of the Grand Ole Opry.

The guitar didn't come with lessons. Riley bought some music books and figured, correctly, that the little dots in the grids represented guides to where he should place his fingers, and that's how he learned enough chords to proceed. He spent a month in vain learning how to tune the guitar, finally discovering that there were electronic tuners that enabled one to get the spruce guitar's strings vibrating together properly.

By March, Riley was playing songs. In April, he learned he could figure out how to play simple songs without relying on sheet music. By May, he was writing his own simple songs, and by summer, he was spending most nights jamming with other musicians. Before football practice began in August, Riley and his friends had played several Wednesday-night gigs at the YMCA.

Word gets around in small towns, and the football coach wasn't overly pleased at his soon-to-be quarterback's new hobby.

But it all worked out handsomely.

Riley hooked up with his lead guitarist because they were working together in the cotton mill at the time. The drummer was a football teammate. A former teammate—actually he had been a star running back while Riley was playing junior varsity—played bass. Riley was the least proficient musician but by far the best singer, and already he was writing songs with an edge of cynical humor.

At seventeen, Riley had his own band, which he named Johnny's Boys because his father, Johnny Mansfield, had given him the guitar. It was a popular choice because his father was beloved by most of his friends, most of the people in town, everyone who played football at the high school and everyone who knew him, with the possible exception of his elder son.

Several times Johnny Mansfield dropped by "the clubhouse," which was on a farm near a rock quarry, way out in the middle of nowhere. If anyone came at all, it was undoubtedly Riley Mansfield's old man, who, more often than not, had already been drinking for several hours and was only too happy to arrive with a couple six-packs in tow. This only enhanced his popularity with Riley's band mates. Usually, though, Johnny had the modest sense to wobble off after hanging out for an hour or two, and the band could proceed with other business, nicely uninhibited from the brew.

Johnny wanted Riley to drink, play football and chase women, though he didn't often just come out and say it. Straight "A"s, which were usually etched across the boy's report card, impressed him not a whit. Years later, Riley realized he couldn't recall one incident in his entire life in which his father had said anything positive about his intelligence, his grades or the fact that he had been named editor of the school newspaper as a junior and was included in all that who's who shit.

It was almost Independence Day when the lead guitarist, Charles Terrell, decided they should learn some new songs, songs they could play at rowdy bars instead of the YMCA, which was supposed to be a wholesome place for teens to congregate, and where, obviously, no drinking was allowed. In point of fact, most of the kids who attended made sure to get drunk—or high—before they got there.

Mostly, Johnny's Boys was a country band, but they quickly learned some songs by the Eagles, Boston and the Steve Miller Band, mostly because they were easy and the kids needed something to dance, not clog, to. Many of their country songs were slow, chosen because sweethearts could "slow dance" to them.

The first song they heard was a song by the New Riders of the Purple Sage called "Panama Red." The second Charles suggested was John Prine's "Illegal Smile." The third was Kris Kristofferson's "The Pilgrim, Chapter Thirty-three: Hang On, Hopper," which began with the descriptive details surrounding a male personage who was wasted on the sidewalk wearing a jacket and jeans. None of the songs was likely to be heard on the radio anywhere besides NPR.

After listening to the songs on a homemade cassette Charles had brought along, Riley said, "Hmm. Do I detect a trend here?"

And Charles Terrell said, "I don't suppose none of y'all wants to get high?"

And Riley Mansfield's best friend, Donnie Skidmore, said, "In a word? Yeah." Had he been sitting behind his drums, there undoubtedly would've been a drum roll.

"You know how, right?"

"Shit, yeah, I do," said Philip Parker, the college boy.

"Well, I mean, I know how to smoke a cigarette," said Riley, who'd learned when he was fourteen because, on a vacation in Myrtle Beach, he had desperately wanted to pass for a couple years older. Lots of good-looking women smoked, particularly when they were at the beach being rebellious, and Riley had needed an excuse to strike up conversations.

Charles Terrell was already rolling a joint. "You'll be fine," he said to Riley. "Ain't nothing to it. Just a mite harsh."

It wasn't difficult at all for Riley to get high, though he was fairly sure a small chunk of his lungs was sticking to the wall by the time things started getting slightly slower and infinitely cooler.

As a football player, Riley had been a late bloomer. He never started until his senior year. When August arrived, his old attitude had changed. No longer was Riley meek and subservient, trying not to make mistakes. He had a new recklessness that translated well to the practice field. He became bold and a bit too adventurous for the coaches' taste, but he got results. Riley morphed into the kind of roguish leader that teams rally around. Whether by coincidence or not, Riley's partying ways received positive reinforcement.

Meanwhile, Melissa Franklin had been a cheerleader, a year younger than Riley. During her junior and senior years, she had dated a football player named Sammy Crenshaw. Crenshaw, though, had quit the team during the first week of practice back in 1992. His departure had, in fact, simplified Riley's rise to the position of starting quarterback.

From nowhere Riley became one of the more celebrated football players in the state. His good grades drew considerable attention. The Spartanburg TV station even ran a feature that showed him playing his guitar, singing a song he'd written. It was the only time in his life he ever came close to pleasing his old man.

Crenshaw, meanwhile, had become indignant at the team's success. In the words of his old man, following the general consensus in Henry, Crenshaw had "gone to the bad." Most days, Crenshaw could be found hanging out around some corner of the school building, smoking Marlboros and telling anyone who would listen that he could kick Riley Mansfield's ass and would've been the starting quarterback had the coaches not been such assholes. Riley gave him a wide berth.

Riley hadn't really wanted to play football in college, but a state-championship season and his dad's relentless lobbying sucked him toward the scholarship offers that flooded his way. He told Johnny he was too banged up and tired to go with the family to Clemson games, and his old man bought it because he saw it as giving Riley the opportunity to be recruited elsewhere.

After being a good boy all week, Riley had the house to himself most Saturdays, and after allowing the rest of the family a half hour or so on the road, Riley would pull his stash out of its hiding place, the breast pocket of a blazer that was already two sizes too small, and spend those Saturday mornings watching TV and reading the paper with a blissful buzz. Then, about noon, he'd shave, toke up one last time, take a shower and head off to be mildly entertained on the sidelines watching a small-college game.

Riley didn't get to play in the Shrine Bowl, the annual all-star game matching the top players from the two Carolinas—he had never been placed on the preliminary list before the season started—but he was named to the North team in the in-state all-star game. During the week leading up to the game, he and his roommate, a combination punter-tight end from Easley, shared a joint late each night in the dorm room where the team was lodged.

After being named most valuable player in the North-South Game—and tossing a touchdown to his buddy the tight end—Riley started getting scholarship offers from schools larger than the ones that had initially recruited him. All his visits occurred during basketball season, when he found his ass being kissed at Clemson, South Carolina, East Carolina and Piedmont. He hit it off best with the upperclassmen who showed him around at Piedmont. One Riley liked particularly well because he was instrumental in getting him laid. But it was another player who allowed in passing as how the only time anyone at Piedmont was ever drug-tested was during preseason practice, a week before the season, and if a player didn't smoke or snort anything until after practice started, there was no way he could test positive.

Riley hadn't ever seen anyone snort anything, but he signed with Piedmont three days later, anyway.

Once in college, Riley learned to drink things stronger than beer. He mainly played football in obscurity, quarterbacking a junior varsity team that only played five games. He learned fascinating things about fellow freshmen like whether or not they smoked marijuana and about co-eds like whether or not they were inclined to fuck.

He continued to make good grades because, goddamnit, he actually liked reading and shit. His academic strategy had evolved in high school, and after some attention dedicated to the bullshit advice they doled out in seminars, he went back to it. If he really liked a class, he tried for an "A." If he didn't give a shit, he tried for a "B." "B" was always the minimum target. Once in his freshman year, he miscalculated and made a "C," but twice he miscalculated and got "A"s by mistake, too. It was like his high school coach had said: Luck only exists in the short run. It all evens out in the end. That wasn't the way it had been phrased—"There's no such thing as luck"—but Riley had his own translation.

In large part because Riley seemed weirdly attracted to academics, the coaching staff didn't seem to know what to make of him. It didn't really bother Riley, who, deep down, wasn't all that interested in being there. Playing football to fulfill obligations was old hat. What'd made him good was learning how to have fun doing it. Fun sometimes comes across as selfish within the context of an athletic team.

Fortunately, Riley didn't give a fuck, and not giving a fuck had become functional. Riley learned to cultivate a balance. On the one hand, when he didn't care, he relaxed, and when he relaxed, he excelled. On the other hand, relaxing too much meant he didn't pay attention, and when he didn't pay attention, things wound up really bad.

This lesson Riley learned when he had an afternoon lab on the day of a junior varsity football game against a junior college less than an hour's drive away. The coaches had let him drive over after the lab ended. Driving the two-lane roads, he and a student trainer, who had also been in the lab, proceeded to share a joint. It seemed as if all the managers and trainers knew how to score weed. It occurred to Riley that it was a pretty thankless job, otherwise.

Riley threw three interceptions despite the fact that he attempted only seven (passes, not interceptions). There were three dozen people in the stands. Every game in high school had been watched by at least five thousand. Luckily, Johnny Mansfield hadn't been able to make it that day, but if he had, Riley probably would've played better.

I wasn't that bad. I mean, two of the three picks bounced off the receivers' hands. They're the ones who looked like they'd been smoking something.

In the season's seventh game, the starting quarterback, a senior, injured his knee. Riley found himself promoted to the varsity. For some ungodly reason, Riley returned punts against Appalachian State. For some ungodly reason, he almost broke one in the third quarter. And did break one in the fourth.

The next week, he played three series at quarterback. He started the tenth and eleventh games, both of which the Bobcats won, to finish the season 6-5. Riley kept the starting job in the spring, and he completed fifty-five percent of his passes for more than 3,000 yards as a sophomore. Piedmont won eight games, lost the Independence Bowl to Houston in the final minute, and Riley made second team all-conference.

Meanwhile, Riley began making a name for himself sitting on a bench in the student center and playing songs he had written in what were described as "coffeehouse showcases." The coaches likely weren't wild about this, even though Riley managed to schedule his gigs after the last film sessions and meetings had been completed. His 3.4 grade-point average had earned him immunity from mandatory study halls. He never told the coaches about his singing, and even though they had to know, they never asked. He was playing well enough—football, not guitar, though he was getting better—that they didn't care.

Then, however, a knee injury wiped out most of Riley's junior year, and by then he was living in an apartment off campus, and between twice-daily rehab sessions, he mainly blazed and watched Chicago Cubs games until baseball season was over; then he turned to reading Kerouac and Kesey and kept on blazing. He never started watching soap operas because he had standards.

The knee came back but some arthritis developed. The team had won but three, lost eight, with Riley not even on the sidelines most of the time. During spring practice of his junior year, the coaching staff grew desperate and ornery. Riley, the same free spirit he had always been, landed in the doghouse.

"Your shit don't play no more, Mansfield."

Mansfield? Since when did I stop being Riley? Motherfucker.

As a senior, Riley, who, mind you, had once returned a punt for a touchdown, turned into a designated passer, brought in on third-and-long to drop back and pull a completion out of his hat. He got no benefit from play-option fakes and faced down huge linemen and blitzing linebackers, all teeing off and most frothing at the mouth. Football basically became synonymous to Riley of getting his ass constantly kicked.

Thankfully, the whole coaching staff got fired when it was all over.

CHAPTER EIGHT
WHEELS TURNING

The public-relations firm of Sedgwick Sanford & Van Buren was one of many Washington firms that worshiped at the altar of Prince Machiavelli. One of its clients was the Republican National Committee.

Two enterprising junior partners, Garner Thomas and Sue Ellen Spenser, regularly plotted strategies designed to elevate their stock. They had gradually, in tandem and over time, learned the usefulness of amorality.

"I was scouring the blogs this morning," said Sue Ellen, leaning into Garner's open door, "and I came across something."

"Do come in," he replied, "and close the door."

She sat in front of his desk, beaming.

"Are you familiar with any scuttlebutt about that guy down south who prevented some raghead from blowing up a passenger plane?"

"Riley Mansfield. A third-rate musician. Lives in a small town in upstate South Carolina. We should be well on our way to making him a hero to the cause by now," said Garner.

"Uh, don't think so."

"What?"

"According to a blog I found this morning—it's on that lefty site, MoveOn.org—this character isn't going to consent to being honored by the President."

"Fuck them," said Thomas. "Fuck him. I don't care what kind of a hero Riley fuckin' Mansfield is. He can't turn down the President of the United States. Is he quoted?"

"No," Spenser replied, referring to her notes. "No one can reach him. He talked to some reporters and TV people after some show in a honky-tonk two nights ago, but since then, nothing. Anyway, Priscilla Hay apparently talked to his former agent, one Tom

Logan. According to her blog, Logan and Mansfield split because he, Mansfield, didn't want to exploit the, uh, potential stemming from the incident on the plane."

"What's he? Smoking crack?"

"According to the blog, this Mansfield character doesn't want to see what he did used to advance the President's political fortunes."

"Has this Mansfield character expressed this view himself?"

"No," Spenser said. "Or, if he has, I can't find it. Everything's secondhand."

Their eyes met. "We should...do something about this...This is what we do, Sue Ellen."

"Yes," she said. "But which way do we take this guy? Penthouse or outhouse?"

"Well," said Garner, "I'd say we should find out what the situation is. Talk to him or to someone who has talked to him. Either we put the screws to him to make him play ball with us, or we turn those screws the other way and destroy him. Simple as that.

"You book a flight to South Carolina. I'll check with black-ops boys down at the Committee and see what the holdup is on getting Mansfield together with the President. I'll do the legwork and figure out which way we're going to go. You find out where he is, keep tabs on him, feel him out and I'll let you know what we're going to do. Either way, this could be big."

"In other words," Spenser said, grinning, "we need to decide whether we're going to fuck him or I'm going to fuck him."

"I didn't say that," Thomas replied, smiling coyly. "You said that."

♫

Only a block away, in another brownstone, the writer of the aforementioned blog, Priscilla Hay, was meeting with George Grinnell, a senior partner in a firm, Clark Powell Morgenthau

LLC, that was affiliated with Democrats, who were gradually getting better at dirty politics and, in particular, attack ads.

"Priscilla, have you actually made an effort to contact Riley Mansfield himself?" Grinnell asked.

"Why, yes, of course," she said. "He isn't answering his phone. I mean, home or cell, either one. I talked to his sister. She said she doesn't know where he is. She said she saw him briefly yesterday and, as best she knows, he's at home. I got the impression they don't get along. I also got the impression she had been drinking."

"We've got to get him on our side, Priscilla."

"And your suggestion is?"

"What's your schedule?"

"I'm supposed to go to Colorado on Tuesday."

"Can you get out of it?"

"Won't be easy," she said. "There's this problem of that being my job and this not, officially, being it."

"I'll talk to Leon," he said. "I can't think of anyone more persuasive than you. I'll get it cleared, and I'll take care of the arrangements. Go home and pack. You're going to South Carolina to recruit a new spokesman for the Democratic Party. It doesn't sound like this worm is going to take much turning."

"What we need to do," said Hay, "is have Mr. Riley Mansfield appear with the presumptive Democratic nominee for president."

"It's ticklish when we don't know exactly who it is yet," said Grinnell. "On the other hand, it would be quite the rage if we could get to him first."

"I get the impression that not only does he not want to stoop to the level of the Republicans; he doesn't really want to talk to anybody."

"For right now, let's see if we can get him to talk to you," said Grinnell.

CHAPTER NINE
DEEPER SHIT

Riley awakened, feeling better than expected. All systems were "go," but the lights were flickering. He piddled around on the Internet a while, mainly erasing emails but replying to a few. Then he made breakfast and watched MSNBC. Again he found himself in a mood to write a song.

> *Woke up this morning feelin' kinda bad*
> *Must be the worst hangover I ever had*
> *I played my guitar till I broke a string*
> *My voice so shot I almost couldn't sing*
> *I'm absolutely sure I've got to piss*
> *Wondering where and how I've been remiss*
> *I've got a little pain beneath one eye*
> *It's turnin' red and blue, I don't know why*
> *First I'm gonna wake*
> *Then I'm gonna bake*
> *Get in a zone*
> *Of my very own*
> *Make a few calls*
> *Break a few laws*
> *Turn the stereo on*
> *Play a John Prine song*
> *I don't want to contemplate no bills*
> *Or operate my Sears cordless drill*
> *The hole in my screen porch that I can't hide*
> *Will have to wait until this buzz subsides*
> *I'm getting in the mood for scrambled eggs*
> *Once I regain control of my legs*
> *Grits and sausage might just hit the spot*
> *It satisfies me when I've gone to pot*
> *CHORUS*

I'll get around to what I've got to do
Once I can shake these triflin' blues
I wish that I could find my shoes
But for now I think I'll watch the news
A cyclone has wrecked Bangladesh
Yet somehow I still feel quite refreshed
I'm bored with the New York Stock Exchange
My money's all tied up in mary jane
CHORUS
Turn the stereo on
Play a Jeeerryyyy Jeff Walkerrrr sooooong

It occurred to Riley that a call to Melissa Franklin might be appropriate. He plugged in the phone line and dialed the cell number she'd given him at Timmy's Bar. She answered on the fourth ring.

"Hey, wanna get away?"

"Riley?"

"Yeah."

"So, what is this? A Southwest Airlines commercial?"

"Nah," he replied. "I kind of had a cosmic trip in mind. A gonzo trip. Want to come over to the house?"

"Are you baked?"

"Nah," he said, "Are you at school?"

"Just got out. School is out for the summer."

"Well, I'm waiting for you."

"Waiting to see me, or waiting to blaze?"

"You, baby, you." He laughed softly.

"Well…"

"Aw, c'mon. I'll sing you some songs. We'll get some of the world's problems solved. That's easy. My problems? Those are hard. I need someone to talk to. I need a friend. I'm all fucked up emotionally. The world is crashing in on me, and I'm a prisoner in my own house. I need some counseling. Aren't you a guidance counselor?"

"English teacher."

"Same difference. We can conjugate."

She laughed. "Okay. I'm assuming you live in that brick house across the field from your mama?"

"Nah, that's the lord of the manor. I'm in the shack with no running water and an outhouse in the back."

"Liar. I'll be over in a few minutes."

"Wow. I couldn't get a pizza that quick."

"Particularly not at ten in the morning," she said.

A half hour later, having kept an eye on the shades, he answered the door with a guitar strapped around his neck. As soon as she sat down, he sang an old John Denver song, "Poems, Prayers and Promises," the one that mentioned sitting around a campfire and passing a pipe around. She got the message. They got high.

"Don't worry," Riley said. "Nobody ever comes up here but politicians." Then he told her about the visit from the county's leading Republicans.

"You know, I wasn't really kidding when I said 'let's get away.' I think I gotta get out of here. I think I gotta go on the lam. I think the world's closing in on me."

"I think you're paranoid," she said.

"Could be," he said, "but I need someone to help me with things. I need someone to get on a cell phone and make some arrangements. I need to go play music on the fly. I need you to make some calls for me and line up some impromptu gigs at places where they know me and they'll let me stand up behind a mic and do a few sets. I don't got a manager anymore."

"Why's that?"

"He dropped me, man. He said he couldn't represent me anymore as long as I was unwilling to capitalize on all this attention. You can be my manager. We can do that on the fly, too. I need a friend. That's all it really takes, is someone I can trust. Someone who'll look out for me. Someone like you."

Melissa shook her head. "You're so fucked up," she said. "I got no training. I got a job here. I got a life. I got some security. I don't know anything about music."

"You know everything about helping me," Riley said. "I need guidance. You're a guidance counselor."

"English teacher." They both laughed. Riley lit a joint, took a hit and passed it to her.

"I really think I might be in trouble if I stay around here too long. I'm not trying to be a troublemaker. I want my life back. My life is on the road. It's where I'm comfortable. My life is about observing things and writing songs and playing them in smoky little bars and hoping there's somebody out there who'll play them and go to all those big-time places and record my songs and let me make a living off the royalties, while at the same time, performing at the level where I'm comfortable.

"I gotta run. Not because I don't want to face reality. Because there's no choice," Riley concluded.

"What about your family?"

"Oh, that's just as totally fucked up as everything else. I'll spare you the details. We can talk about it on the road. But I need you. School's out. It's summertime. If you don't like being my manager and constantly getting my stubborn ass out of various and sundry scrapes, I'll have you back in time for school to start up again, or you can stop anytime. I know you're not that happy with your life. You've got security. Well, fuck security. I'll pay you. You can make just as good a living. I got money in the bank. I got a laptop. You can open it up in the driver's seat of my truck—we'll take the truck so we can haul shit—and pay my bills going down the road. Hell, you can pay yourself going down the road. We'll sleep in motel rooms and on couches when some friends will take us in. You'll love it. I mean, you will. I know you will. You want some adventure. You want some meaning. You don't want to be stuck around here."

"I don't see how," Melissa said, but wheels were turning, and Riley could sense it. "I need time to think."

"Well, while you're thinking, be packing some clothes, too," he said.

Riley's digital camera was on the coffee table. He turned it on and showed her pictures of him playing at a place called the Birchmere in Alexandria, Virginia.

"It's kind of ironic, don't you think?" he asked. "The last place I played, I mean, in a gig, before everybody wanted me in Washington was…"

"Near Washington," she said.

"Exactly. From there I went to Texas, but that was for a family thing. I sang at a retirement party for my aunt." Riley didn't think the distinction between second cousin and aunt was worth making.

They both heard a noise outside. Riley peeked through the blinds.

"Fuck," he said, "it's a squad car."

"Asshole." Melissa thought he was kidding.

"No, I mean, seriously. Hold your voice down. Look in the cabinet in the kitchen. There's some air freshener. Quietly—don't make much noise and let whoever this bastard is know you're here. I'll go out the side door and open the garage and talk to him in the yard. Meanwhile, you spray shit everywhere. Keep calm. Everything'll be cool if we don't lose our shit, okay?"

Melissa was impressed by Riley's ability to be calm. She listened and nodded. He tiptoed out, started walking through the door to the garage, then stopped and ducked momentarily into a bathroom. Melissa heard him gargle and wash his hands at just about the time the doorbell rang. He tiptoed back through the supposed guest bedroom, which was mainly strewn with guitars and amplifiers. She heard the garage door open.

"Hey," Riley yelled, "over here."

Melissa, really getting nervous in Riley's absence, sprayed the room with melon-scented spray. Then she sat on the couch and fished out another cigarette. She hesitated lighting it, thinking, well, this defeats the purpose of the air freshener. *No, silly, it's not marijuana; it's tobacco.* And it would probably take away from the odor of the weed, not to mention the suspicious odor of the cantaloupes and honeydews. Then she almost started laughing, imagining Riley saying, "Nah, deputy, we was just settin' around enjoying some fresh cantaloupes. I love me a good slice of cantaloupe."

In the yard, Riley walked up to the officer.

"I'm Riley Mansfield, sir. What might be your name?"

"Deputy Barton Fleming."

It occurred to Riley that the man had a Southern name but a Yankee dialect. He had thought local law enforcement the final bulwark against carpetbaggers and scalawags. Generally, they were assholes, but they were our assholes.

"Well, what can I do for you? I apologize for being unshaven and nasty. The morning's off to a kinda slow start. Been up a while, but I just hadn't got the chance to get things going yet."

"If you don't mind, Mr. Mansfield, I'd like to take a look around your property."

"Sure, Deputy. I ain't here enough to get into any trouble."

"We got a report that there's some marijuana growing on your property."

"Well, first of all, sir, knock yourself out. There's nothing of the kind, but, as a citizen, I think anybody accused of anything ought to have the right to know who's making such accusations. It ain't right to have your reputation muddied up. I don't know of any enemies I got, but I can assure you, ain't nothing illegal growing in these two acres, or on the farm in general, for that matter. The only thing I'm worried about growing is these damn fire ant mounds."

The deputy stood, silently watching Riley rattle on with a certain weariness.

"Let's walk around," he said finally. *Humorless sort. No rapport. Didn't respond to folksy charm.*

"We might want to check out the whole property."

"You mean, the farm?"

"Yessir."

"Fine. If you got all day to find nothing, I've got all day to show you nothing."

They walked around to the back of the house.

"Deputy Fleming, is there any particular reason you feel compelled to carry that shotgun?"

"Just standard procedure, Mr. Mansfield. I've been told there was a possibility you were armed and dangerous."

"When, in fact, I'm barefoot and wearing gym shorts and a tee shirt."

"Nonetheless…"

"No problem, sir. I don't want no special treatment like I'm a big hero or nothin'."

"That's right," said the deputy, not so much as cracking a smile. "Same treatment for everybody."

Meanwhile, Melissa crept toward the window in the kitchen but kept far enough away that she couldn't easily be seen. Then something occurred to her. *What if Riley isn't being paranoid?* She went back and fetched the camera off the coffee table.

As Riley and Deputy Fleming walked around the back edge, the deputy peering under the wooden deck, Melissa was figuring out the none-too-difficult way to operate the camera. Unerringly, she set the dial to "auto."

"What's that down there?" Fleming asked.

"Well, it used to be a dog pen, but I had to give up my dogs because I'm not around enough to take care of 'em, and I can't trust my nieces and nephews to do it for me. It's been getting overgrown for, like, five or six years, maybe more."

God, I'm talking way too much. Cool it, will you?

"Let's take a look."

Melissa had discovered the zoom lens and was now looking through the viewfinder. Then she figured out how to switch the view to a small video screen on the back. She crouched down a bit, aiming the camera through the window over the kitchen sink.

Just as a precaution, and a little out of curiosity, she started snapping photos of Riley and the deputy standing at the edge of the overgrown dog pen.

"What's that down there?" asked Deputy Fleming.

"Uh, sir, I believe that's called poison ivy," said Riley. "Ain't never heard of nobody smoking it."

"Don't mess with me, son. Not that. What's that leafy shit over there?"

"It's a weed, I think, but I don't think it's marijuana. It's more like poke salit," said Riley, thinking this Fleming was really stupid. His Yankee ass probably didn't know what poke salit was unless he'd been a big Elvis fan. On the other hand, it wasn't actually poke salit.

"Tear me off a piece of it, Mr. Mansfield."

"Deputy, it's got purple berries on it."

"I said, tear off a piece of it and show it to me."

Riley leaned over and reached for the plant. Fleming grabbed the shotgun by the barrel, swung it like an axe at Riley's back and knocked him to his knees. The force was such that Riley's eyes went black for a second.

"Mother…fucker."

"What'd you call me, boy?" The deputy whacked him again, this time knocking Riley flat.

Melissa snapped one photo after another.

The beefy deputy reached down and tore half Riley's shirt off. Failing that, he took a handful of near-black hair and yanked.

"Get up, boy."

It didn't take as long as it would've.

Fleming calmly leaned the shotgun against the corner post of the rotting pen, put his beefy arms around Riley and pulled his automatic from the holster. He shoved it against Riley's nose.

"Don't move, boy."

Riley did nothing but breathe heavily and wince.

"When the President of the United States wants to see you, son, you go see him and you do whatever it is he wants. You understand me?"

"As well as I have…ever understood…anything…in my life."

When Fleming let him go, Riley dropped to his knees again.

The deputy grabbed the shotgun, holstered the automatic and said in parting, "Now let me give you a little piece of advice. You're a hero because we want you to be one. It'd be the easiest thing in the world to take the facts of your case, scramble 'em around a little, lay a few hints, and turn you into a stinking terrorist.

"You have a good day, Mr. Mansfield."

Melissa went back to the front of the house and watched the Ford cruiser idle slowly, back into the yard, turn around and cruise leisurely back out to the highway. After waiting until it turned left, away from town, she dashed into the backyard, where Riley had crawled over to a chinaberry tree and slowly gotten himself up off the ground.

"I thought he was gonna fuckin' kill you," she said.

"I almost wish he fucking did," said Riley. "Goddamn, I'm hurt."

"We gotta get you to the hospital. Where are the keys to your truck? You're too banged up to get in my Corolla."

"Relax. I've been hit hard enough on a football field to know there ain't nothing broke. He hit me on the back. I'm just really, really bruised…I'll get over it. Just walk with me slowly back to the house. The steps might be a problem. I got, uh, some, uh, ice packs in the freezer. I just need to sit down a while."

"You need to go to the fuckin' hospital!" Melissa absolutely screamed.

Riley started laughing and wincing at the laughter.

"Shit. I need to go to the fucking bong."

It stopped her in her tracks. She tried not to laugh and blew a very undignified clot of snot from her nose. It was painful to watch, mainly because Riley's back was slowly changing colors and everything was painful.

"It's cool, Melissa," he gasped. *How can getting whacked in the back fuck up your ribs?* "That asshole didn't kill me. He just knocked the shit out of me. I'm gonna be fine. When we get back up there, just help me place the ice on my back.

"I think there's some Aleve in my backpack. I think I want about four of them."

"Right."

"Do you now understand that I need to get the fuck out of here?"

"Yes."

"Will you go with me?"

"Yes."

"Why are you carrying my camera?"

"'Cause I took pictures of everything."

"No shit?" Riley asked.

"No shit."

"I'd hug you if it didn't hurt so goddamn much. What can I do for you in return? Would you like me to lick your pussy or something?"

Melissa frowned.

"You'd slap the shit out of me if I wasn't hurt, wouldn't you?"

She almost smiled.

"Go ahead. Laugh. It's funny. It's a joke. This isn't. You are the most amazing woman in the world. How could that be? How could I know you all your life and not realize how amazing you are?"

Riley, knowing the drill from all those training rooms of yore, kept ice on his back for the recommended twenty minutes, got fucked up—yes, he did have a small bong—and mainly remained silent. They hardly spoke for some time. Each took a couple swigs from a decorator bottle of Crown Royal that Riley had forgotten he had until Melissa found it behind several bottles of steak sauce in the cabinet.

"Melissa, hand me the phone."

Riley got the phone book and looked up a number. Melissa didn't ask whom he was calling. She just watched intently.

"Yes, ma'am," Riley said. "Could you please get Sheriff Shithead on the line? Tell him it's Riley Mansfield."

Riley heard the woman suppress a laugh and then call for Sheriff O'Shields. She didn't mention what Riley had called him.

"Well, hello, Mr. Mansfield," he said. "What can I do for you?"

"I got your message," Riley said.

"What message?"

"Deputy Fleming paid me a visit."

Silence.

"We ain't got no Deputy Fleming," said O'Shields.

Silence.

"Mr. Mansfield?"

"Well, never mind," Riley said. "Nice talking to you."

Riley hung up, looking bewildered. Melissa waited. Riley said nothing. He was thinking.

"Melissa, go home and get packed. What's today?"

"Thursday."

"Maybe we'll go to Washington to see the president. Maybe we'll go to Florida to buy some weed. Seriously, I got a gig in St. Augustine. I don't really need weed, particularly not from Florida...Long story."

"Okay. I'll go. Shit. How could I not?"

"Make whatever arrangements you need to make. Go up to the Circle K and get me a bag of ice and some Zip-lock bags. I'll pick you up in the morning at eight, and I'll make some arrangements. Let me think this thing through. Make sure you bring your cell phone with you. Don't tell anybody, except your mother, and tell her not to tell anybody else. I'm not leaving this house till I can do it without looking like I've had the shit beat out of me, but I'm a quick healer. I'd say we can strike out early in the morning."

"Why the cell phone?" asked Melissa. "Just out of curiosity."

"I haven't got one."

"How could you not have a cell phone?"

"I threw it out the window of my car the day before yesterday," he said. "It's a long story, and we'll have plenty of time on the road. I'll call and get the account canceled. Bring whatever bills and shit you've got. I'll pay them and go by the post office before we leave. I got to do some serious thinking here, but I'll figure things out."

As she opened the front door, heading out, Riley asked, "How's your mama gon' take this?"

"I'll manage," she said. "Worry about yourself."

CHAPTER TEN
NOT A BAD WAY TO BE ON THE LAM

Riley showed up at Melissa's house, as promised, at eight. He'd been up since five because getting out of bed wasn't particularly easy until he got limbered up, and it took about thirty minutes to get limbered up.

In the bed of the Toyota Tacoma, his "late-model truck," he had an ice chest, a suitcase, his camera and a shoulder bag containing a portable printer. Behind the seat atop the bench seats were two guitars in gig bags, a laptop in a backpack, a box of CDs and tee shirts and a pair of cowboy boots. Melissa brought two bags. Riley put them in the bed and locked its watertight cover. Neither was particularly talkative as Riley headed down the interstate. As he was headed down, not up, Melissa gathered they were going to Florida, not the District of Columbia. Riley opened a zip-up sleeve and inserted a Hayes Carll CD in the stereo. One song was about Jesus stealing a man's girlfriend (and if he ever found Jesus, he planned on kickin' his aaaassss), Riley started playing along with a harmonica for a while. The inhales and exhales caused Riley to produce the occasional lateral grunt. Melissa couldn't help but chuckle a bit. He finally gave up.

"It's a new sound," said Riley. "I thought maybe tooting on the harp might numb up the pain. I was wrong."

"Why so quiet?" Melissa asked.

"Well, I'm, uh, sore, worse than yesterday," he said. "I'm...sober. I thought about blazing but I also thought about...coughing. It's kind of okay unless I'm still for a while. I mean, it's okay, as long as I'm still, but then, when I move, it really hurts. Until I move a lot."

"Then it stops hurting again," Melissa said.

"Exactly. Or...doesn't hurt as much.

"It'll be all right. Just gonna take some time. The lower back absorbs a bruise well. It's best not to favor it. That just strains the muscles everywhere else."

"Pull your tee shirt up," said Melissa.

"It probably doesn't even show," said Riley.

"Did you look at it in the mirror?"

"If it shows, I don't really want to see it."

"Lift up your shirt."

Melissa reached over and pulled the shirttail out. "Lean up a little," she said.

Riley reluctantly complied.

"Damn, Riley, your back's black as coal. It's like it changed races."

Riley cringed. "Shit, Missy, don't make me laugh." He laughed. Almost cried. "Fuckin' racist."

"Okay, I'm sorry," she said, "It's dark blue. Kind of gray, too, around the edges."

"School colors," he said. "Go, Bobcats."

Interstate 26 bore right north of Columbia, heading eventually to Charleston but, for their purposes, to I-95, Savannah, Jacksonville and beyond. Melissa slept for hours. Riley listened to satellite radio, flipping between "Outlaw Country," "Willie's Place" and several stations that featured comedy. Down around Brunswick, one of his songs played on "Outlaw Country," but, afterwards, when the disk jockey, Dallas Wayne, mentioned the plane incident, Riley switched the channel. *Well, that's one more message I threw away with the cell phone*, he thought.

"Riley," Melissa said.

"Uh, huh."

"Do you know how long we're going to be in Florida?" He'd just driven by the Sunshine State's welcome sign.

"Uh, no. I think I need to keep moving and do things on the fly. I got good credit, about fifteen grand in the bank, I think, and we won't be going nowhere there ain't Laundromats and motels.

"I'm still making this up as I go along, but I'm thinkin' right now we'll stay the weekend along around St. Augustine, Daytona, down that way, then we'll double right back and head to Kentucky."

"What's in Kentucky?"

"Friends," he said. "Good friends. Maybe we'll crash there a couple nights. I kinda got things set up. I got on the phone, and online, last night. For some reason, there's an unusual amount of interest in having me play music at all these little haunts of mine. Did I tell you about getting blown off Monday night in Columbia?"

"No."

"Well, I had a gig canceled because they thought since I was such a big hero, I wouldn't show up. Now I'm snapping my fingers and they're probably getting rid of people just to schedule me. I bet that dude at the Corner Pocket is catching some serious shit right now."

"So…what's up tonight?"

"I'm just playing for tips at this little seafood shack just south of Flagler Beach. Tomorrow night'll be better. I'm opening for some friends, guys I've holed up with and written songs. I'll play an hour, and then I'll probably join them onstage for a while, maybe play again when they take a break. It'll be cool. It always is."

"A lot has changed," she said.

"I know it," he said. "That's why I need to turn back the clock a little."

"Back any better?"

"I popped three Aleves before I left the house," he said. "I left them in the kitchen, though. I'm glad you mentioned it. Look in the backpack behind my seat in the left-side, zip-up pocket."

She swung the backpack between the two bucket seats and pulled out the Tylenol bottle.

"There's all kinds of pills in here," she said.

"The Tylenols are the capsules. Just don't give me one of the blue ones."

"What are the blue ones?"

"Ambien. About six weeks ago, I hurt my foot and it was really painful. My doctor asked if I needed something to help me sleep. I said yeah, so he wrote a prescription and gave me a coupon for a free sample."

"Did it work?"

"Too well. It made me feel weird. That's the only way I can describe it. I never took but one, but I guess I've got an aversion to throwing things away. I think there are five still left. Maybe I'll take one if I really need to sleep, but I doubt it."

"Marijuana make you sleep?"

"Weed is an all-purpose medicine," he said. "You hungry?"

"I'm good."

"Wanna blaze?"

"I've never done it in a car."

"You should never do it in a car. Fortunately, this is a truck."

The Tacoma was exiting Jacksonville. "Traffic's thinning out," Riley said. "We just beat rush hour. I guess it goes without saying that you haven't ever rolled a joint going down the road?"

"Uh, no."

"There's a rest area coming up. You can watch to make sure nobody's coming. I can do it fast."

"Okay." She kind of left it hanging in the air.

"Be cool, Missy. It'll be all right. Trust me. In the opposite side from the Tylenols, there's a little black film canister with some weed in it. Under the little zipper on top, there's some papers."

Melissa fetched the film canister. "This isn't all you got?"

"'Course not. It's all I got in the backpack. It's road weed. There's a little empty Aleve bottle, kind of nasty. Where the weed was. We can put the roach in there."

"Gotcha," said Melissa.

Riley pulled off, scoped the lot for law enforcement and pulled down at the end of the lot, leaving five empty spaces between his truck and the last car. He began rolling a joint in his lap.

"Gotta use the bathroom?"

"I could," said Melissa.

"Well, go ahead. It's cool. I can keep an eye on the mirror."

"You sure?"

"I 'bout got it finished now. No prob. Relieve thyself."

She laughed a little. "Be right back."

When Melissa returned, Riley handed her the joint and said, "Don't let this explode into flames in your hand. I might as well use the bathroom, too."

After returning to I-95 and driving along for three miles or so, Riley said, "Okay, traffic's light. Give me the J."

Riley stuck it in his mouth and lit it, keeping one hand on the wheel. He inhaled deeply, hit the window switch on the door and cracked the window.

"Crack your window about an inch," he said, then exhaled a stream of sweet smoke and handed Melissa the joint. "We won't burn it all the way down. Wouldn't want to drop it or anything."

They each took three hits. Riley cut Melissa a few glances while driving and noticed she pulled voraciously on the weed.

"I'm good," Riley said. "Save the rest...unless you want it."

Melissa took one last hit.

"Just put it in the Aleve bottle and screw on the top," Riley said. "It'll go out. No oxygen, I reckon."

Riley lowered the windows. "Let her air out," he said. "I don't suppose you'd have some of those Listermint strips?"

Melissa laughed. "Never go anywhere without 'em."

"Bet you're hungry now, too, huh?"

"Yeah," said Melissa. "Really."

"We're almost to St. Augustine," he said. "Flagler's a little bit past. We'll stop at a barbecue joint on the exit."

Riley fumbled with his right hand through the center console. He untethered one air freshener, Little Trees, from the mirror and unwrapped a new one. Pine scent.

"It's strong," he said, "but it's not that different from the smell that preceded it."

"You're something," said Melissa. "I'm, like, so impressed."

"What?"

"For a guy with a buzz, you're so careful. Always thinking."

"It's a little more than a buzz. I'm probably more paranoid than careful. I can function high. Drive fine. Pay attention to the road. What I lose is the big picture. I'm absentminded. I'll drive perfectly fine, keep my mind on the road, check the mirrors, and then I'll realize I just drove twenty miles farther than I wanted to. Also, everything seems a little slow. Cruise control is a must."

"I know what you're saying."

"Know what I'm saying? I thought you said you never smoked dope in a car before?"

"I haven't," she said, "but I can relate."

♫

"Have some Brunswick stew," Riley said once they were seated. "It's good."

"So what are you going to do?" Melissa asked.

"I think I'm gonna have some, too. Then, maybe, some ribs."

"No, I mean, about visiting the president."

"Well, I went online and replied to some emails. I said I didn't want to take part in some ceremony but that I'd appear at some function if they'd let me do a song. A patriotic song. Something like 'This Land Is Your Land.'"

"Was there a reply?"

"Dunno. I'll check in the morning. Right now I just want to sit on a stool with my guitar and do what I do. I gotta get a hold on normality."

"Good luck."

"I just want to do what I gotta do to get my freedom, get my life, back. I just want to fade back into the background with the least amount of resistance."

"What's wrong with being famous?"

"A fucked-up back comes to mind."

It was only four in the afternoon, and the restaurant—it was actually a stretch to call it a barbecue joint, since it wasn't too dissimilar from a Shoney's except for the folksy sayings on the wall—was sparsely populated. Woody's, it was called.

Riley ordered a Diet Coke. "Have a beer if you want," he said to Melissa. "I just figured I'd wait until we got to the gig. We can drink for free there."

"Diet Coke," Melissa said to the brunette waitress, who looked about twenty-two.

"Get us both a cup of Brunswick stew, and we'll figure out what else we want by the time you get back with it."

Riley glanced at the waitress—"I'm Brenda, and I'll be taking care of y'all"—and paid particular, if fleeting, attention to her ass as she walked away. No focus. No prolonged leer.

"You know what's good? This chef's salad. It's got smoked turkey and smoked pork and ham. Boiled eggs," Riley suggested.

"Sounds good."

"Cucumbers. Cherry tomatoes."

Brenda arrived with the Diet Cokes and stew.

"I'll have a chef's salad," said Melissa.

"Me, too," said Riley. "The one with the smoked barbecue meat on it."

"Good choice. Will that be all?"

"Best I can tell right now," said Riley.

Riley ordered blue cheese dressing, Melissa Italian. Once Brenda had run along, Melissa looked Riley straight in the eyes. "Can I ask you a question?"

"Well, obviously."

"Why aren't you married?"

"The same could be asked of you."

"I asked first."

"I guess I'm too independent, too set in my ways. I think a lot of it's got to do with the family."

"How so?"

Riley winced. "Well, I've never known, never experienced, a marriage that worked. My mom and dad fought like cats and dogs. My brother has been divorced twice. Both my sisters have had at least two marriages. Annie's had three…and outlived one of them. I guess I'm kind of…scarred.

"You?"

"Oh," she said, "nothing ever seems to work. I fall in love with someone, and he merely likes me."

"I can't imagine that."

She smiled. "Guys fall in love with me, and I don't give a shit about them."

It was an awkward silence.

"Maybe…"

"What?"

"Maybe, like, you're the one," Riley said.

Melissa blushed.

"There's this middle ground," he said.

She had been looking at the table. Now she looked up, eyes widening.

"I can't find the middle ground," said Riley. "There are wild women, the ones you hook up with because they hang around, fucked up, after you play, and they take you home with 'em, but you can't respect 'em because of the way you got hooked up with 'em."

"Literally," said Melissa. They laughed.

"No, seriously. Then there are women who really like your songs, the ones who come to see 'artists' at coffeehouses, the ones who go see songwriters sit around tables and swap songs, the ones who tell you your music moved them."

"What's wrong with that?"

"Nothing, other than the fact that half of them are very detached, which may or may not mean they're lesbians, but they're kind of sending that, I dunno, formal message. But that's beside the point. With women, I seem to get fire and rain. Either it's just getting laid by someone who's gonna hook up with the next guy in line and fucked you because you were at the front of the line she ran into, or it's a really intelligent, wholesome, goodhearted, humorless woman who's just too tame for my tastes. The kind of woman who'd never put up with you getting high.

"What I need is a good girl with a twinkle in her eye."

Melissa's expression was tentative, at a crossroads; it wasn't clear whether she was going to smile or laugh.

"Your eyes twinkle," Riley said.

She smiled.

Riley and Melissa were seated in a booth next to the front window. The only other patrons—nicely dressed man, wife, two grade-school kids—sat around a table near the bathroom. Riley was vaguely aware they were sort of whispering to one another.

A little boy walked over.

"Mister?"

"Yes?"

"Are you the man who kept that bad guy from blowing up the airplane?"

Riley looked first at Melissa, then looked directly, through kindly, bloodshot eyes, at the boy with his tousled hair and round, clear face.

"No, son, I'm not that guy. I wish I was, so I could be your hero…but I'm not."

Disappointed, the boy turned and walked back to his family.

Melissa's one-word response wasn't overly harsh. She smiled slightly when she called Riley an asshole. It was a soft "asshole," though, whispered sympathetically, Riley thought.

When they got through, Riley reached behind the seat of the Tacoma and tried to slip something into his cargo shorts before Melissa, first listening for the sound of the passenger door electronically unlocking, opened the door.

"Damn," said Riley. "I better go back and take a leak."

"That's such a charming expression."

"Be right back."

In the bathroom, Riley ripped the cellophane off a CD and signed:

BEST WISHES,
RILEY MANSFIELD
5/29/08

He walked out and gave it to the kid who had approached the table.

"Let your daddy listen to it first and pick out some songs you'd really, really like," Riley said.

The parents thanked him and he returned to the truck.

"You're a good egg, Charlie Brown," said Melissa, who obviously had been watching from the truck.

♫

As they drove over the bridge into Flagler Beach, Riley said, "I gotta warn you, we're probably going to be staying at a little beachfront motel that's a tad shabby."

"That's okay," she said. "You should've seen the dumps in Myrtle Beach where my daddy used to take us."

He pulled into a motel that was a little the worse for wear. It had two parallel stretches of rooms, all on the bottom floor. The overriding color of the buildings was robin's egg blue. Blue-tinted white. Riley stopped under the overhang at the office and sat there for a moment.

"I know exactly what you're thinking," said Melissa.

"What?"

"Just get one room," she said. "Two will cost too much."

"That's all I needed to know," said Riley, turning to her. "Thanks. Be right back."

They were in room eight. One digit. Across the way were all the double digits.

"We've got, like, an hour," said Riley.

"I see," said Melissa. "Really."

"Want to blaze?"

"Sure. Why not?"

They blazed. Riley fetched a can of Lysol from his bag and sprayed it around the door. "Can't be too careful," he said.

"Want me to play you a song?"

"Yeah," she said. "One you wrote."

"I'm not sure I've written one that exactly applies," he said.

"How so?"

"All my love songs are either about heartbreak or sordid fucking or humorous failure. We need something lighthearted and romantic."

He played "Peaceful Easy Feeling," singing softly and thumb-strumming the guitar.

"Kiss me," she commanded gently. He did, trying to be tender. Melissa's response was…assertive.

"Would you hold it against me, would you think me a tramp, if I sucked your dick?"

"Not at all," he said with some degree of urgency.

Afterwards, Riley turned the air conditioner, which already whined, up to high. He played another song. They smoked.

"Wanna take a shower?" he asked.

"Let the games continue," Melissa replied.

♬

"What's the name of the place?" Melissa asked.

"Don't know."

"What do you mean, you don't know?"

"It's right up ahead on the left. I'm really not sure. The sign says 'High Tides,' but under it, it says 'Snack Jack's.' There's something that looks like an old motel, one that may or may not be open anymore. Maybe that was 'High Tides' and the seafood joint is 'Snack Jack's.' It wouldn't make much sense to call a motel 'Snack Jack's', but I really haven't ever been sure."

"How do you list it online? On your website?"

"I list it 'High Tides/Snack Jack's.'"

"Oh. Well, whatever it is—I assume that's it up there—there's a damn good crowd," she said.

"Seafood's good," Riley replied.

Riley carried his gig bag and the small cardboard box of CDs. He had rummaged through the large box and stacked in Melissa's arms two tee shirts of each size: medium, large, extra-large and extra-extra-large. A boom mic stand had already been set up. All Riley had to do was plug into the sound system. He sound-checked with a medley of old country tunes, pausing from time to time to tell the resident expert how to adjust the dials. Then he retired to a table on the deck to share a pitcher of Bud Light with Melissa. He had a half hour to spare before the time the barmaid who seemed to be in charge said he should take the stage, even though, technically, there wasn't one. Melissa held up her end of the bargain on the beer.

"So, how you feeling?" she asked, a bit on the exuberant side.

"I'm fuckin' good."

"Me, too," she said. "Do you think it helps to perform…"

"Stoned?"

"Yeah."

"It does. It sheds inhibitions, makes it easier to relax. There's a point of diminishing returns, but I'm not there. Think peace. Sometimes you can get a little loose-tongued, so I try to concentrate on being funny and cool and not political or, uh, strident."

"I don't often hear people use the word 'strident,'" said Melissa.

"I don't often make wild, crazy love before I perform," replied Riley. "Weed and sex and hot water from a shower make miracles with bruised backs."

♪

The tee shirts, color-coded by size, simply had the following message on the front:

The Audacity of Dope

RILEY MANSFIELD
No matter where you go,
There you are

As such, Riley opened with his song titled "There You Are," chosen, obviously, to sell tee shirts. Melissa's title as his "manager" included many evolving functions, one of which was selling merchandise. From the stage, he introduced her as his "girl Thursday," adding that the next night she would be his "girl Friday." Melissa thought his goofy joke matched his goofy looks in general. Once he plugged away a few introductory chords, though, he was right on.

I know a guy who's a first-rate prude
Puts a lotta effort into really bein' rude
Prob'ly try to catch me doin' somethin' crude
But he really don't mean no harm
Another guy I know don't like black folks
One won't drink nothin' but Diet Coke
One's been known to make up quotes
But he can write like a sonuvabitch
If you ain't an outlaw
You can't sing outlaw music
If you ain't got money
You can't buy no car
If you can't drive
You can't race in NASCAR
And no matter where you go
There you are
Some folks fall in love with guitar
Most of us don't get too far
Lotta people hang out in bars
Gives 'em somethin' to do
Some people love to smoke cigarettes
Live in a trailer drive a red Corvette
Give back half as much as they get

Could find theirselves in a mirror
CHORUS
Some folks drive a car just to speed
Others hang around all day smokin' weed
Take a break to do the dirty deed
But it prob'ly ain't gonna happen
Some break the law every time they take a pill
Others do anything just for a thrill
Hope I don't run into one of 'em who kills
But sometimes it ain't you day
CHORUS
No matter where you goooooo
There…you…aaarrrre!

Rousing applause. A few stood up from their seafood "mystery stew" (it was listed on the menu) or fried scallops. "Ah, you're too kind," said Riley. "Thanks so much."

He toyed with one of the strings, not because it was really out of tune but because he, like most musicians, was just a tad insecure about sound. He wound a knob slightly one way, then slightly the other, then pretty much put it back where it was.

"I got this problem," he said to the audience. "When I'm onstage, at first, I'm kind of nervous inside. People tell me I seem relaxed, but believe me, I'm not."

A smattering of chuckles.

"So I've written, like dozens of songs, and after I do the first one, for some reason, I can't remember a single one of the others."

He's kidding, right? Melissa thought. *It's all an act, all about being self-deprecating and unassuming and…human.*

"So I'm going to do a medley of old country songs, just to wind myself down a little. Coincidentally, I'll start out with a song called 'Wine Me Up.'"

Riley then played a verse and chorus of six or seven songs, starting with drinking songs ("Y'all drink, right?" he asked, hoisting a beer) and then segued to Hank Williams sad songs, a Hank Williams happy song, a George Jones tune, a Merle Haggard, a Johnny Cash.

The place went wild when he finished.

"Thanks so much," he said. "Most of those songs I learned because, number one, I love 'em, and number two, they're so damn easy."

Then, having raised the audience temperature with familiar standards, he kept them in thrall with a progression of his songs. He played for an hour, then took a break of twenty minutes or so, during which he and Melissa drank beer. Melissa noticed that each set began with one of his better songs, followed by several covers and closing with several more of his own songs.

During the second set, Riley played soft rock and pop. During the third set, with most of the diners having moved on in favor of drinkers, he turned to songs about drinking and getting stoned. For the fourth and final set, with only a few people still hanging around, Riley mainly took requests, two of which were for his songs and several of which were for songs he didn't know but tried to play anyway. He called it "chasing my voice with my fingers." Not bad, all things considered. He had to give Melissa the keys to the truck so that she could go back and fetch two XLs and a double. She sold ten CDs at fifteen bucks a pop, and eleven tee shirts for the same amount, and when he got a waitress to circulate a beat-up cowboy hat around the room, it came back with seventy-two dollars in ones and fives.

By the end of the night, it was all Riley and Melissa could do to scrape up their stuff and leave with the rough notion that nothing had been left behind. Riley chatted with the diehards who had stayed all night and autographed a few CDs and tee shirts. He stopped at a Circle K for cigarettes and rolling papers, paying with a wad of bills he had stuck in his pocket.

They crashed in each other's arms, fully clothed, and slept almost immediately.

♫

The first word Melissa heard the next morning was Riley saying "fuck" with some urgency.

She rolled over. "What?"

"Somebody's been in the room," he said.

Immediately, Melissa sprang up, alarmed.

"Thing is, they didn't take anything," said Riley. "They just rummaged through everything."

"Are you sure?"

"Yeah, I'm sure. I can tell. They found the weed. Tried to put it back the way it was. Didn't take nothin'."

"What do you think it means?"

Riley looked at the ceiling. "I reckon it means somebody really wants to know a lot about me. And one of the things he knows about me is exactly where I am."

"Shit," she said.

Riley sat down in the shabby chair next to the window for a while.

"Well," he said, "let's get going."

"We leaving?"

"No," he said, thinking. "We're staying here another night, maybe two."

"You really think we ought to hang around?"

"I think it'll be okay. I think it's just a matter of somebody in the goddamned government forcing me to do what they want me to do…and I'm not going to give them the satisfaction of having me change a single fucking thing."

CHAPTER ELEVEN
BLISSFULLY IGNORANT

Drizzling rain gently sprayed the windshield of the truck as Riley and Melissa headed up U.S. 1.

"Stop using your cell," Riley said simply.

"What?"

"Stop using your cell. I was just thinking. Whoever broke into the room probably knows who you are."

Melissa was silent, thinking. She'd had her purse with her at the seafood shack. Was there any identification in her bags? She had to think.

"I...don't see how they could tell who I am," she said finally. "I don't think there's anything in my bags that identify me."

"Well, better safe than sorry," he replied. "We don't know how, uh, sophisticated these people are. I don't think it was terrorists who went through our stuff. They woulda blew us up, not checked for weed. I mean, you can't be sure about anything, but I think it's the government. Or the Republicans. No telling what shit those fuckers can pull.

"Just keep your cell turned off. We'll figure out something. Maybe get some pay-as-you-go plan, some cell with a card with so many minutes. Then maybe we'll turn that in and get another one. We'll figure out something."

Listening to Outlaw Country, Riley lost himself for a few moments singing along with Jimmie Dale Gilmore, something about flying into Dallas on a DC-9 at night.

"When we get back to the room, we'll go online with my air card," he said at last. "I don't even know if the motel has wireless, but if it does, it's probably not encrypted, or whatever. Someone nearby can probably monitor, you know, the activity of anyone who uses it."

"What about the air card?"

"I don't know, for sure, if it's safe, but it's gotta be safer. I'll keep thinking about it."

♪

David Branham had his secretary put a call through to Banks McPherson at Homeland Security.

"David?"

"Yes, Banks, how are you? I wanted you to update me on the, uh, Riley Mansfield situation." Branham referred to a legal pad to retrieve Riley's name.

"We're on him," said McPherson. "The guy whose name you gave me? He's quite a character. In my mind, I've started thinking of him as the Christian Soldier."

"Jed's a true believer, all right," said Branham, smiling. "I don't suppose you've researched his background?"

"I admit, sir, I haven't had a chance. I just relied on your judgment."

"If you can believe it, he started out as a disk jockey."

"No."

"Reagan—not the president, the Administration—recruited Jed from Christian radio. He started out with the U.S. Information Agency, then from there he went CIA. He's been in all kind of shit abroad. Got shot in the shoulder somewhere in Africa. Jed comes from a long tradition of…your term, Christian soldiers. He reminds me of Stonewall Jackson, maybe even Nathan Bedford Forrest."

"Well," said McPherson, "Mr. Mansfield has come around. "We're in email contact with him. He wrote that he would come to a rally, shake hands with the President and sing a song or two."

"Have you told him that we wanted him to tour with the President?"

"We have, but we haven't heard back."

"Why can't you talk with him?"

"He isn't home and if he has his cell phone, it hasn't been on since shortly after the incident."

"Jed knows his location?"

"Yessir."

"Why don't you try to get through to him by phone in, what, a motel room?"

"We're pursuing that, sir," said McPherson, though, in fact, he hadn't thought of it. "I'll keep you apprised of the situation."

"Very good, Banks. Bye, now."

McPherson wondered vaguely why the National Security Adviser was so interested in all these details.

♫

Melissa, back at the room while Riley was out reviewing cell-phone options, was shocked. She had no idea how out of touch Riley was with what was swirling on the Internet. He had already morphed from hero to mystery man in the public eye. There were eyewitness accounts of his show at Timmy's Bar. By noon, blogs were being posted about a sighting in Flagler Beach. When she "Googled" his name, "about" 364,900 results showed up.

She signed on to Riley's email account and was reluctant to delete the hundreds of items. After considering it for a while, she only deleted the commercial offers.

Melissa wrote her mother a short note, then turned to the "official" emails Riley had been getting, with urgent instructions to call offices in the White House, the Republican National Committee, not to mention the Democratic National Committee, both parties' committees for the Senate and Congress, their home Congressman, both South Carolina senators and some person she'd never heard of who claimed he was running for Secretary of Agriculture somewhere.

She thought about deleting the ones from CNN, Fox News, MSNBC, did delete the ones from religious groups and wondered why both the Libertarians and the Daughters of the Confederacy wanted to champion Riley's cause.

Whatever it was.

Carefully she drafted a generic reply with Riley's basic guidelines. He'd only appear if he could sing at least a song. Music had to be involved. He would neither endorse nor appear in any commercial for any candidate of either major party. He would only reply to emails. Melissa thought about placing her own name at the bottom and listing herself as Riley's "representative," but then she decided he wouldn't like that for security reasons and realized she didn't like it either, which, in turn, left her a bit frightened.

She retrieved the film canister from the pocket of Riley's backpack and carefully rolled a joint. She went in the bathroom and smoked most of it. Then she found the Lysol and sprayed the bathroom. Placing a pack of cigarettes on the cheap wooden table, she went back to work. Her second was smoldering in the ashtray when Riley returned.

"Sup?" he asked.

"This is unbelievable, hon. You're more famous than the Pope."

"I write better songs than the Pope," he said, "but I bet you—and he—ain't gotta piss as bad as I do."

Riley returned from the bathroom smiling.

"Smells like you burned one."

"I sprayed it with Lysol," she said.

"Help it a little next time," he said. "Switch on the fan."

"I'm sorry."

"No reason. It's cool. I'll teach you all the tricks. You'll be an old pro in no time. You don't got, like, the rest of the joint, do ya?"

"It was real...thin. There's just a little left." She had the Aleve bottle in the pocket of her shorts, fetched it and handed it to him.

"Hey, we got to talk. Why come don't you blaze out here?"

"I threw caution to the winds yesterday," Riley replied. "That was before somebody broke in and looked around."

"Have you said anything to the lady at the front desk about it?"

"No use," said Riley. "Can't trust nobody. If they ain't in on it, maybe the police come, but they don't do hardly nothing but file a report. If they are in on it, they let somebody know we...know.

"Back in five."

Riley came out in a fresh pair of boxer shorts and began dressing for the gig.

"You good to go?"

"It's okay," she said. "I didn't get rained on. I'm fine."

"I need to take, like, a little bitty nap," he said. "Then we'll talk in the truck. It'll take thirty or forty minutes to get there. I want to know what's shaking. I'm just incapable of much attention right now. Thirty minutes, tops."

He slept for almost two hours.

♫

The rain had blown through by the time Riley headed up A1A, the sun starting to droop over the condos and golf courses arrayed across the road from the beach. Melissa tried to explain just how out of hand things were getting. "The Internet's ablaze," she said.

"It's because there was a terror threat," he said. "It can't get better if there's more of me to see. If I do the minimum, eventually it's got to die down. Everybody's a star for fifteen minutes. I just gotta wait mine out."

"On the news sites, there's all sorts of speculation," she replied. "For instance, why would somebody try to blow up such a little plane? Bunch of news stories are talking about al Qaeda opening up 'a whole new front' in the War on Terror."

"I wondered that myself," Riley said. "But what can you say? I don't know why. Maybe they're smart. Maybe they figured out that security would be more lax on commuter flights."

"But Nine Eleven killed thousands of people. If they're so interested in bringing us to down to our knees, why would they blow up a plane that would have, what, twenty people on it?"

"More like a dozen on the plane in question," Riley said. "What about the guy who tried to do it?"

"Wait a minute. I promised I was going to remember his name...Fatih...Ghannam...F-A-T-I-H...G-H-A-N-N-A-M."

Expecting Riley to be impressed, instead she saw him shocked.

"Whatsa matter?"

"Fuck," he said. Then he was quiet for a few seconds.

"An FBI agent told me the person they'd detained wasn't Arab. He said he was of Cuban descent, from South Florida."

Chills went down Melissa's spine, but she just said, "Had to be a mistake."

"That's an awful big mistake for one of them guys to make," Riley said.

After a few minutes of contemplation, Riley pulled the truck over near the ghost town that had once been Marineland.

"Could you fetch the weed?"

"Sure," she said, but stopped halfway from hoisting the backpack, now missing its laptop, from the bench seats. "Oh, shit."

"What?"

"I got it out and forgot to put it back," she said.

"Where is it?"

"It's…in the drawer next to the bed, where the Bible is."

"That's okay," he said. "I'll just drink a couple beers before I go onstage."

"Does it, really, like, make you better?" Melissa asked.

"No, but it loosens you up. I mean, you know the argument. You don't sound better drunk; you just think you do. But it's bullshit. When you get drunk enough or stoned enough that you lose touch with reality, that's not good, but when you just find that happy medium, when you've got that gentle little buzz, it's functional. You screw up more when you're nervous than when you're buzzed."

"But…you don't have to be drunk, right?"

"What is this, an intervention?" Riley laughed.

"No. Who am I to intervene? I was just curious."

"Yeah," Riley said. "It's a crutch."

CHAPTER TWELVE
UP A HILL AND DOWN

"Holy shit," said Riley, looking at the crowd gathered at the Oasis. He noted the telltale presence of the TV cars, trucks and SUVs, all decaled up with their action and eyewitness monikers and their chummy slogans. Your Friend Four. News You Can Count On. The radio stations were also represented, with their own boastful slogans, likely concocted because of some television-derived chips on their collective shoulders. The Mighty 96.9. Kick 103.7. Sexy 93. Riley and Melissa lugged their stuff in from a block away. The muffled sound of the Land Sharks jamming emanated from within.

"Fuck," he said.

"What?"

"This is just royally screwing everything up for Alan and Wes. I gotta do something. Stop a minute. Gimme a minute to think."

A wooden rail fence ran along the inside of the sidewalk. Riley leaned his guitar case against it and put the small box of CDs on the ground. Melissa was glad to drop the larger box of tee shirts. They both leaned against the fence.

"Okay," Riley said. "We'll go in and put this stuff somewhere. Alan's probably got us a seat saved near the bandstand at a table with friends. Either his wife Joanne and his two kids, maybe, or they're at home and some friends who are big fans are sitting there. He'll probably motion to me when he sees us walk in. The live-music area is upstairs.

"We know all these media people are around, probably outside." He looked to his right. "I'd be willing to bet both of them, the man with the perfect hair over there and the woman in her little bright pantsuit, are from TV. We'll both sneak in through the back, take the stuff up the stairs. Then you go back out the side door, down the outside stairs, and I'll go out the way we came in.

"Here's what we're gonna say. You introduce yourself as my

agent or representative or manager or whatever. I'm guessing I won't have to tell 'em who I am, so here's the deal. I'll be going on the stage in, probably, thirty minutes. They can shoot all they want of me onstage, talking between songs, singing, whatever. But if they want me to talk to them, they're going to have to shoot—and use, goddamnit—footage of the Land Sharks. They don't have to show much, just make reference to Riley Mansfield joining his longtime friends the Land Sharks in an appearance at the Oasis in St. Augustine Beach. We gotta get them some exposure; I don't care whether they run footage of me or not."

"What if they just say, 'yeah, yeah, yeah' and don't actually run any of it?"

"Well, that's a distinct possibility," said Riley, "but that's why we have to be as gracious and good-natured as we can, which ain't easy when you're talking about people used to everybody just falling all over themselves to be on TV. Be really gracious, and make some explanation about how it's difficult for me to get in the proper frame of mind to perform. We gotta seem so cooperative, even while we're not being as cooperative as they want—and believe me, give 'em an inch and they'll take a mile—that they'll do something nice for the local band. If they seem genuinely interested in the kind of music I play—if they act like they've heard of me, if they know any of my songs—give 'em a CD. If they're not that into it, offer 'em a tee shirt. The radio guys'll give away a tee shirt or a CD on the air, to the fifth caller or some such. Tell 'em I've got to go onstage shortly, but as soon as I finish a set, forty-five minutes or so, I'll go back outside and do interviews outside the door."

"I really got to get my act together on this, Riley," said Melissa. "Give me a minute."

"Take your time, beautiful," he said, flashing the boyish grin. "No pressure. You can't possibly screw up in my eyes. We'll just take the attitude that whatever we do, whatever we say, it's the right thing. We'll just eliminate all second-guessing from our minds. Power of positive thinking. When the going gets tough, the tough get going. If you won't be beat, you can't be beat.

"Sorry," he added, watching her laugh, "I lapsed into a recitation of slogans from locker-room walls."

"Okay," Melissa said. "Let's go."

The gig bag could be worn like a backpack. Riley and Melissa made their way inside. "Let me put this stuff away," said Riley, smiling as he encountered the TV "talent." "Be right back."

The Land Sharks were playing "Sweet Home Alabama." As predicted, Alan Isaac, effortlessly playing a solo on his Takamine electric-acoustic guitar, pointed at a nearby table with his eyes. Riley unzipped the gig back, retrieved his guitar and leaned it against the side of an amplifier. He placed the box of CDs under the table. Melissa did the same with her box, which was about three times as large but not as heavy. After brief greetings and introductions, they each excused themselves and went in separate directions.

Melissa worked the TV personalities while Riley concentrated on radio. He explained his conditions and chatted while, at the same time, monitoring what was going on inside. When he heard Wes Davidson, the lead singer, say they were going to do one more song, Riley politely excused himself. The band was still jamming—Alan cranking out some serious Stevie Ray Vaughn—when Melissa strode back in flashing a thumb's up.

Once she wedged her way in beside him, Riley asked—actually yelled above the din—if she had a notepad. Yes. She also provided a pen. He wrote a note and managed to get it passed up to the stage. It was a message to just give him a basic introduction, or none at all, and he'd take it from there. "Don't bother to mention the airplane thing. I'll take care of that."

So, while Alan and Wes, along with Chip Allison the bass player and Smoky Lee (whose real name, Riley knew for a fact, was Scheinblum) the drummer, unplugged, parked guitars and set things like drumsticks and sheets of tablature aside, Riley strapped on his guitar and mounted the stage.

"We're gonna alternate sets with our good buddy from South Carolina, Mr. Riley Mansfield," said Alan, simply.

The roar was embarrassingly loud, though it wasn't exactly maintained due to the fact that Riley had neither checked the sound nor tuned his guitar. The guitar needed only minor tweaks of the tuners, and the sound was pretty close to right. Besides, it would be better for Riley to perform with a sound slightly imperfect and not reset things for the band that would be coming back onstage after him. They relied much more on that sound. Riley, armed only with his guitar, relied more on the words of his songs and the sound of his voice. As long as his guitar didn't obliterate the sound of his voice, things would be okay.

"Anybody drinking tonight?"

The affirmative, overwhelmingly.

"Well, this song oughtta fit," he said, quickly diving into a cover of Charlie Robison's "Barlight," which the patrons didn't know but would pick up quickly. It was clear, though, that the crowd wanted to hear from the hero.

"Ladies and gentlemen," he said, "please bear with me a little. My world's gone crazy because, somehow, I got put in a place and time where just doing what anybody would do got me tagged as a hero. Believe it or not, my life would be a lot simpler right now if I was a coward.

"'Course, I reckon I'd be dead." Laughter. "Dead is simple, right?"

Nothing like gallows humor to rouse an audience.

"When this set is over, or after the night has run its course, I'll be glad to sit and chat and autograph these CDs and tee shirts I brought along," Riley said, followed by an introduction of Melissa.

He added, "I want to let you in on a little secret and ask for your help. You may have noticed that my appearance has raised the interest of the local media, and I want you to give all these media people a big round of applause. When they write about us, or talk about us on the radio and on TV, sometimes we may like it and sometimes we may not, but at least they're letting folks know what we're doing. What's that old saying? 'There's no such thing as bad publicity'? Well, the good Lord has given me kind of an extreme example...but I reckon I still believe it. We made a little deal standing outside the door while Alan and Wes and the rest of the Land Sharks were damn near burning this house down. In order for me to go on camera and talk to them, I made one condition, and they all agreed to shoot some footage of St. Augustine's own band, the Land Sharks, and run a little of it on the news tonight. I don't have any doubt but that these are honorable men and women, but if you turn on your TV to the news, and you see me, or hear me, but no footage of the Land Sharks, I want you to call your local station, or your local newspaper, or your local radio station, and raise holy hell!"

Old movie from the 1940s: What a swell guy.

"All right. These tee shirts of mine got this phrase written on 'em: 'No matter where you go, there you are,' and that ain't never been more true in my life than right this very minute."

As he sang "There You Are," the crowd clapped and yelled. At the end, he leaned over and said to the table in general and Melissa in particular, "I ain't even tore up," but he intentionally said it loud enough for everyone around to hear. Loud enough for one bearded fellow two tables back to yell, "Well, by God, I'll fix that," and send up a shot of Jagermeister while Riley was singing the Eagles' "Peaceful Easy Feeling."

After knocking back the shot, Riley said, "Funny you should send me one of those. This just happened to come up in a song I wrote recently. Just a happy-faced little ditty that goes like this here."

> *If the good Lord's willin' and the creek don't rise*
> *And my baby still loves me much to my surprise*
> *Life's too difficult to analyze*
> *When the lows ain't as low as the highs are high*
> *Good Lord's willin' and the creek don't rise*

I got up this morning it was pouring rain
Moving kinda slow due to lower-back pain
Probably a result of raisin' Cain
Man's got a reputation to maintain
Man's got a reputation to maintain
Can't make enough money to pay my bills
Factor in the cost of blood-pressure pills
Probably be better with a moonshine still
Either way you go it's all uphill
Either way you go it's all uphill
CHORUS
Wish I could buy me a brand-new car
The one I got's done been too far
Makes its way to a smoke-filled bar
Playin' for tips on this old guitar
Playin' for tips on this old guitar
Sometimes folks like to buy me shots
Most of the time I'd rather not
Some folks sneak outside and smoke pot
You can tell when you see 'em 'cause their eyes are
bloodshot
Tell when you see 'em 'cause their eyes are bloodshot
CHORUS
I don't know why I come this far
Just to sit here and play guitar
I just wanna sing my songs
Maybe one day you'll sing along
Maybe one day you'll sing along
CHORUS

Meanwhile, Melissa was scribbling away furiously on the notepad Riley had borrowed. She held back CDs and tee shirts for the media, making a note to herself on which size shirt she figured each could wear. She was preparing for a run on Riley Mansfield paraphernalia, and when he completed his set with an imitation-laden version of Hank Williams "Jambalaya," she got it.

Riley, too, had announced it when he was about to do his final song, and this alerted the TV cameras to get set up and ready. Riley slowly worked his way through the crowd like a politician, shaking hands and signing a few CDs.

Meanwhile, a bevy of journalists awaited him, secure in the knowledge that they would soon have tape recordings and video footage of Riley Mansfield they were just sure they could hawk to every media outlet from St. Augustine to Beijing.

Gotta knock this shit out so they'll leave!

Susie Quillen, from a Jacksonville station, asked Riley if he was "politically active."

"Well, I love my country," he said. "I vote. I've got political views, but I don't want to be political. I want to be like most Americans. We've got a secret ballot, and I don't much want to be, like I said, political. I just want to mind my own business, I guess. It's kind of ridiculous, when you get right down to it, for a musician, or a movie star, or an athlete, to presume to sway people on issues like, you know, the environment and health care and whatever else...foreign policy, you know. I've got opinions, but I'm not as informed as some other people are, and I don't mind admitting that."

"But why do you resist being honored by the president for an heroic act?"

"I'm going to, uh, I dunno, do something. I've agreed to that. I just don't want to be exploited by either side."

"But how can being honored by the President of the United States be exploitation?"

"I just want to make sure it isn't."

"Don't you think many good, hardworking Americans would rightfully object to someone, anyone, who would turn down a chance to meet the president?"

"I don't know." *Take a breath. Don't get snide. Be nice.* "I already said I would be willing, be glad, to be honored by President Harmon in a modest, appropriate way. It's going to happen. I'm just trying to work out the details."

"But…"

"Excuse me."

"Yes?"

"Is your station affiliated with Fox News?"

"What's that got to do with it?"

"Oh, nothing. I'm just not going to be browbeaten. That's enough." Riley walked to the next camera.

That's one CD and tee shirt I won't have to give away.

The other interviews were more pleasant, but Riley knew which one would be excerpted by Sean Hannity.

Back inside, he found Melissa, who was growing exasperated. He told her to take a break and signed tee shirts and CDs. Autographing tee shirts was harder than playing guitar, he thought, at least to master. *Thank God for Sharpies.*

All of a sudden, the sound next door subsided. *Jesus. It's already time to play again. Actually, come to think of it, that's cool.*

He passed Melissa on the way back to the stage.

"How'd it go?" she asked.

"Great," he said, "all except one."

"Cute little Susie," she said.

"How'd you know?"

"I could just tell."

"Well, it's a free country. You can't get bent out of shape if somebody doesn't see something the way you do. What's that Buffett song? 'Don't ever forget that you just might wind up being wrong.'"

"*Manana.*"

"I don't know what we'll do quite yet. Probably hit the road."

"No, not the word. The song '*Manana.*'"

"Oh, yeah. Right."

The Audacity of Dope

Riley began his second set with a new song:

> They told me that I had to go on furlough
> I said, man, you know, that don't seem so bad
> Ain't that when sailors go on shore leave
> Chase women, get arrested, shit like that?
> Turns out that ain't what it means to be on furlough
> They just make you go a while without a job
> They wouldn't even let me check my email
> By Friday I looked for a bank to rob
> Rich folks are the ones who need a furlough
> They're the ones who ran this ship aground
> Talking about the danger of class warfare
> While less and less money gets around
> My furlough coincided with tax time
> Where I typically have to write a check
> My bank account contained little money
> Less now since I got drunk and had a wreck
> I spent a night of furlough in a jail cell
> My mama couldn't even go my bail
> I sent her to my house on Friday
> Hopin' that a check was in the mail
> CHORUS
> I learned a few lessons on my furlough
> Turns out it was a sign of things to come
> Word got out that I had been arrested
> And I qualified for status as a bum
> They don't allow no bums to work at Walmart
> Though it's perfectly all right for us to shop
> Now I'm learning how to grow marijuana
> And learning how to buy off the cops
> CHORUS

"That little song is called 'Furlough Blues,' friends and neighbors, and I appreciate you listening to it."

Someone in the back yelled out, "Play 'The Gambler'!"

This actually worked, since Riley was fond of following up with a few covers after beginning a set with a song he wanted to showcase.

"All right, I don't think I can do the whole song, but, like everybody in here, I know a little of it," he said. "Tell you what I'll do. I'll do a medley of traditional country songs, and I'll kick it off with part of 'The Gambler.'"

He sang a verse and chorus of the Kenny Rogers tune, then moved on to "Heartaches by the Number," "Pick Me Up on Your Way Down," "Wine Me Up," "You Win Again," and "Is Anybody Goin' to San Antone."

The guy who'd requested "The Gambler" made his way through the throng and left a twenty-dollar tip and a shot of something that was really strong. Riley tossed the shot back. "God-damn!" he said. "What the hell is that? Absinthe?"

Laughter. "Actually, I have no idea what absinthe tastes like. I think it's green, though, isn't it?"

He sang several more of his own songs—"Gotta Be Somebody," "Inman Farms," "Tattooed Gal" and a set closer, "First I Took My Clothes Off (Then You Changed Your Mind)."

Riley greeted Alan Isaac as he picked up his tip jar.

"Hey, I'm sorry for this hullabaloo," he said. "The last thing I wanted to do is upstage you guys."

"Don't worry about a thing," Alan replied. "You're making us money, too. Shit. Let us follow you around."

"I'm not unaware of how ridiculous this is," Riley said. "Playing in a little half-empty coffeehouse is pretty much my speed. Y'all deserve this kind of attention. I should be playing during your breaks while half the crowd steps outside for a smoke."

While the Land Sharks made their way back onstage and got ready, Melissa informed Riley that the merchandise—his CD, *There You Are*, and the similarly-themed tee shirts—was all gone.

"Damn," he said. "Good problem to have."

She held up a wad of bills. "Nine hundred and twenty-four dollars," she said proudly. "What's in the tip jar?"

Riley had brought it with him from the stage. "Fuck," he said. "About a hundred from that set alone."

"How 'bout the first one?"

"Well, aren't you the pretty little capitalist? Don't know. Got a wad of bills in my pocket." He rolled his eyes. "We're rich! We're fuckin' rich!"

They laughed. And kissed.

The Land Sharks were just about ready. "Want to go have a smoke?" Riley asked.

"I'll join you in a few minutes," she said. "Let me tidy up a bit."

"I'll wait," he said.

"No, go ahead. I'll be out there in ten."

Riley made his way away from the bandstand, winding around the bar, getting slapped on the back and signing autographs. When he finally reached the wooden balcony that wrapped around the upstairs, he found a kid and his girlfriend, looking quite under-aged, smoking. Riley recognized Wes Davidson's son.

"Hey, don't worry," he said, noticing Dylan Davidson's look of mild fright. "It's usually safe when your old man's onstage, huh?"

Embarrassed, but smiling a bit conspiratorially, the kid said, "Yeah. Thanks for being cool."

The girlfriend had a certain Goth motif, the kind that suggested she would have been quite a bit more made up had she not been out to see her boyfriend's dad playing his antiquated music to his antiquated fans.

"Well, who am I to talk?" Riley pulled out a pack of smokes. "I'd be just like y'all if my mama was here, and I'm thirty-five fuckin' years old."

They laughed, conceding that, for a few fleeting moments, Riley Mansfield was cool for an old fart. When Melissa arrived, shortly after the young lovers disappeared back inside, they laughed about it.

"Hear no evil, see no evil, speak no evil," Riley said.

♫

By the end the crowd was thinner but composed almost completely of true believers, their devotion enhanced by drinking religiously. Riley played a short third set by popular demand. They had begun watching Riley with curiosity, decided they liked this guy, and the ones who stayed to the bitter end wanted to drink with him at the very least. They wanted to be his pals. Women wanted to take him home, judging from the way they stared in his eyes, wiggled their hips and snapped their fingers as he sang their songs. Riley wondered if Melissa was taking all this in and realized undoubtedly she was. *Ain't my fault.*

The Land Sharks had to stay until Riley finished—it was their sound equipment—so he cut it a bit short. He sang rowdy songs— "Stoned at the Crack of Dawn" and "Wake and Bake" from his own repertoire, then covers of "Family Tradition," "I Ain't All Bad" and "Panama Red"—but closed with an inspirational tune of his own, "Your Independence Day."

"Everybody be safe on the way home," he said. "Thanks for being so nice and hospitable and all. Pretty soon I'll be back down this way, once I stop being this big, walking, talking answer to the media's dreams. Sign up on Melissa's sheet for email updates, check out my website and keep those cards and letters coming."

While Melissa scratched figures on her notepad and got ready to leave—"Can we throw these boxes away since there isn't anything in them?"— Riley helped the Land Sharks pack their equipment. By the time he got back, the bar was empty and its employees itchy to lock the doors. Still there were a few who wanted to mingle.

"Ready?"

"Yeah," she said. "Everything's organized."

"You've already taken me farther than I've ever taken myself," Riley said.

As they walked down the street, hearing the crash of waves in the distance, Melissa said. "This is a little scary."

"Oh, yeah."

"I'm glad I'm not making this walk by myself," she said. "I've got beaucoups of cash on me."

"Shit."

"What?"

"Actually, security isn't a problem," he said, nodding to suggest she should look up the street.

Police cruisers were parked on both sides of Riley's Toyota truck. No lights were flashing, but Riley saw two officers sitting in the car in front and figured there would be two in the car behind.

"I think you picked a great time to forget the weed," he said quietly, smiling and waving politely as he walked past the first squad car.

They loaded the truck, which took practically no time. Riley opened the passenger door for Melissa, walked around the truck, got in, started the ignition and turned on the lights. That's when the police car's lights started flashing on both sides. Four officers hustled out.

"Well, it ain't drunk driving," said Riley. "Fuckers won't let me drive."

"Please get out of the car," the one who scurried around to Riley's window said. "Both of you."

Melissa walked around the truck, a little disoriented by the flashing lights.

"I think the term is 'spread 'em'," said Riley to her.

The policeman seemed crestfallen when he discovered that the wad in Riley's cargo shorts was cash. The one frisking Melissa said, "She's clean, too."

"What's the problem, Officer?"

"License and registration, please."

Riley fished out his wallet and handed over his driver's license. "The registration's in the glove compartment, so why don't you get one of your...friends to get it so I won't give you an excuse to shoot me?"

"Would you object to having your vehicle searched?"

Riley's eyes met Melissa's. "Of course not, Officer. I just don't understand why I'm under suspicion."

He didn't reply but let Riley and Missy stand over by the wooden fence while he and the three other officers searched the truck as if it had crossed the border from Mexico, which wasn't very likely, this being Florida.

"There's nothing, right?" Melissa asked.

"I'm pretty sure we're clean," whispered Riley. "I'm pretty sure we're really lucky."

"What if they gave you a Breathalyzer?"

"I'm pretty sure I'd flunk it. I don't think they're interested in alcohol. Guess it depends on how bad they want a piece of my ass."

"Is there anything on your record?"

"Not a thing. Clean as a whistle."

The process took half an hour. The main officer—according to the badge, his name was Nathan Nelson—went back to his squad car. They could hear him talking on his radio, but the doors were closed and little could be made of it.

Officer Nelson walked up holding a prescription bottle.

"What's this?"

"Uh, I'm pretty sure it's Tylenol," said Riley. "Maybe Extra Strength."

"There's a variety of...medications, Mr. Mansfield. I think these are Percocets."

"They are, Officer. They were prescribed for pain about two months ago when I had a fall and severely sprained my left ankle. They're in there because I got hurt again and put the pills in there, just in case I needed one. If you'd like to take a look at my black-and-blue back, I'll be glad to show you."

Riley put his hands up, turned slowly around and raised his shirt.

"Were you authorized to take this medication for that particular injury, Mr. Mansfield?"

"I haven't taken any of it, Officer. I merely brought it along as a precaution. Are you a doctor, or are you an officer of the law?"

"Could I talk with you privately for a moment?"

"Sure, Officer." Riley turned to Melissa. "Be right back."

Inside the police car, the officer turned to Riley.

"Look, I don't know why they're after your ass, but somebody way higher up certainly is," he said. "For what it's worth, I don't understand it, and it pisses me off a little, but we were instructed to go out and try to find a reason to bring you in. I'm going to catch hell for not being able to do it."

"I appreciate the information, Officer Nelson. And I appreciate you doing what's right."

"I didn't tell you nothing official now."

"No, no, of course not."

"Look, it's an honor to meet you. I enjoyed what few of your songs I saw you perform."

"Well, that's funny. I didn't notice you guys when I was singing."

"That's because we were there in street clothes," he said. "It was part of the first set."

"Well, thanks...for your help. I know you gotta do what you gotta do. I'd give you a CD but they're all gone. Give me an address...or, if you got a card..."

"I do," said Nelson, proffering one. "You and...Miss Franklin...take care, you hear, and be safe."

The ride back to Flagler Beach was mostly quiet.

"You know, when I was a kid," Riley said at last, "Daddy used to smoke a bunch of turkeys and hams on his barbecue pit. On Christmas morning, he'd take me and my brother and we'd go all around the county, delivering turkeys and hams to the preacher, the mayor, the police chief, the sheriff, the magistrate…the bootlegger."

"That's funny," said Melissa.

"I used to think it was the stupidest, most embarrassing thing on earth. As I've gotten older, I've come to understand my old man a little more, now that he's gone. He knew exactly what he was doing. It always helps to create a little goodwill with the people who count."

Silence.

"We were, like, sooooo busted," he said. Melissa laughed and laughed.

"And we are definitely getting the fuck out of Florida tomorrow," Riley concluded.

CHAPTER THIRTEEN
HOME FOR A LITTLE WHILE

Riley, up as usual before Melissa awakened, fired up the laptop and checked email. He donned gym shorts and a tee shirt and jogged a mile up and down the beach across the street. Riley was bathed, packed and dressed by the time Melissa rose. Eventually they drove fifteen miles or so to have lunch in a fine seafood shack, Hull's, across the bridge over the Halifax River in Ormond Beach.

Opening his polyethylene container on a picnic table out front, Riley said to Melissa, "You're gonna love this. I found this place one time when one of the locals recommended it. Everything I've ever had here is as good as any seafood I've ever had anywhere."

Melissa sampled her scallops. "Wow. Scrumptious.

"Where to next?"

"Home for a while, I reckon," said Riley. "I'm not sure whether it'll come together or not, but it looks like we might have a gig in Rockingham, North Carolina, on Friday night. Right now I'm thinking I'm going to put off Kentucky for a week.

"Are you still in? Are things getting too scary? If you want to have an extended visit home, see your mama, I can probably go that one alone."

"Why don't let's play it by ear," she said. "My first reaction is that spending a few days at home will be enough."

"Love to have you, but if you want the weekend free, I can swing back home."

"On the way to…Kentucky?"

"Yeah. It'll probably be just like this. Go home, pay some bills, wash some clothes. In Kentucky, we can crash there at a buddy's house as long as we want, if you don't mind sharing this huge, wraparound couch. I don't want to be around home for long, and Kentucky has always been sort of a refuge for me."

"Bet you never needed a 'refuge' as bad you need one now."

"No shit. Does your mother know you're, like, my manager?"

"Well," Melissa said, smiling," I think she suspects I'm your partner."

"You are. In every way."

The remark required a suitable silence. Mclissa sat across from Riley, smiling, for a few seconds before resuming the conversation.

"So what's the deal in, where is it, Rockingham?"

"Ever heard of it?"

"Isn't there a race track there?"

"Yeah," said Riley. "They used to run big NASCAR races there. Now, from what I hear, it's mainly a test track, but they have several races in lower series. One of them's next weekend. The gig is in the infield the night before the race."

"O…kay."

Riley laughed. "It's a long story. These guys, believe it or not, aren't musicians. They're racers. Some of them drive. They haven't made it big or anything. I met them by chance when they happened to see me play in Greensboro. Then they came when I played a minor-league baseball park in Kannapolis.

"What we were talking about?"

"Rockingham."

"Oh, yeah. So these guys tell me they're gonna bring me in for a party at the race track every time I see them. Turns out, there's about a week-old message in my email. Soon as I got the phone, I called this guy, Dell Howard, and he said the party was still on. It's the night before a Late Model race, whatever that is. I can just sell some tee shirts and CDs and solicit tips. Probably gonna be some serious drinking. Jugs of moonshine and shit. It usually helps sales and tips when people get fucked up, particularly when a guy's got a pretty girl to pass the hat around the crowd."

"So you want me to go?"

"If you don't, I'll have to find another pretty girl."

"Shitass."

Riley laughed. "I'm just kidding. I'd love you to go. But this has got to be turning into this weird, crazy world for you. I can understand if you want to get away from it for a little while."

"We'll be home tonight," she said, "and we've got all week."

"Nothing would make me happier. What say let's hit the road?"

Once on I-95, Melissa said she wanted to call her mother and tell her they'd be home tonight.

"Why don't you tell her we'll be home tomorrow?"

"I could do that," she said.

♫

"I just got here," said Sue Ellen Spenser, "and Riley Mansfield just left."

"Shit," said Garner Thomas, talking with her by phone from the offices of Sedgwick Sanford and Van Buren on K Street.

"He checked out of his ratty motel room this morning. I guess he could be headed back to South Carolina, but I don't know for sure. With this guy, there's no way of knowing. He's leading me on a merry fucking chase."

"Enough is enough," said Thomas. "It's obvious he's not going to play ball. Sit tight. Let me make a few calls. As soon as we figure out where he is, I'll book you a flight."

"You're going to keep me chasing this phantom? I mean, what's the use of this spy game? If you want to discredit him, isn't there plenty there just waiting to be leaked? I mean, he writes songs. There's got to be lyrics, things he's said…has he got a police record? Ever been busted for drugs or anything?"

"In regard to the law, he's clean. Homeland Security's got a man on him, too. We already tried to pick him up because we thought it was reasonably certain he had weed on him after he played music at this dive in St. Augustine last night."

"And?"

"The local police frisked him and a female friend. Searched his truck. Nothing. They weren't going to arrest him. They were just going to take him in. We had a guy at the station who was going to tell him the facts of life."

"Who's 'we,' Garner?"

"I'm not sure. The White House doesn't provide details. I don't know. FBI man. Homeland Security. Homeland Security furnished with an FBI badge. Or vice-versa. I don't know. Hell, I don't want to know."

"Again, Garner. What's the use of keeping me on this?"

"You're still wearing the kid gloves, Sue Ellen. We still need someone to make, uh, friendly contact."

"How about this woman he's traveling with?"

"We got her ID from the St. Augustine police. Her name is Melissa Franklin. She and Mansfield went to high school together. Ms. Franklin is a schoolteacher. I think it's reasonable to assume they're sleeping together; they shared the room in Flagler Beach. As best we can tell, she's acting as his manager, 'gofer,' tee-shirt salesman, whatever. Mansfield needed someone once his agent dropped him, so he must've convinced her to go along for the ride. School's out and she's free."

"She makes it difficult for me, Garner."

"If Mansfield's headed home, Ms. Franklin's probably headed home, too, and she's probably going to stay home. Just give me twelve hours to find him. Be ready to go to the airport. We may even fly a plane down to…Daytona Beach, I guess…pick you up and take you wherever we determine this Riley Mansfield is."

"This really stinks, Garner."

"Hang in there, babe. There's light at the end of the tunnel. Keep in touch. Bye." Thomas hung up hurriedly, not wanting to hear any more complaining. Sue Ellen cursed, glanced at the emails coming in on her Blackberry, placed it in the center console of her rental car and retreated to the Daytona Beach Hilton.

The Audacity of Dope

♫

Clark Powell Morgenthau LLC's Priscilla Hay was stuck in South Carolina, prowling the streets of Riley's hometown looking for a man who wasn't there. From her hotel room, in Spartanburg, she also made a call to George Grinnell, her boss, at the office.

"I'm lost," she said. "No one knows where he is, not even his family, or so they say. There's a broken-down pickup truck in the middle of a field behind Mansfield's house. A ten-year-old Toyota in the garage. I'm guessing whatever's missing from the two-car garage is what he's in."

"That would be a two-year-old Toyota Tacoma truck," said Grinnell, referring to his notes.

"What can you do to find him?"

"Not much other than what almost anybody could do," said Grinnell. "The truck's silver. You want the license number?"

"I don't see what I could do with it. I don't have a helicopter."

"The Republicans have a huge advantage. They've got the government. Hell, they've got the South Carolina government, the local government. There's no end to the strings they can pull, and there's not much anyone can do about it, legal or not."

"Oh, they've been known to pull a few strings."

"You've got to try to find him. Try to stake him out, but don't make contact, at least not overt. Go on the Internet. Check out his web site, look at MySpace, Facebook…look for clues of where he is and where he's headed."

"Hang on a minute," she said. "I'm calling up his Facebook page now. Ah. Here it is…He's in Florida. No mention, but there are some posts on his wall about performing at a bar, the Oasis, in St. Augustine Beach. Tagged photos from there, posted to his 'wall,' at what looks like a little dive in…Flagler Beach. No mention anywhere so far on whether he's staying down there a while. Mansfield doesn't post that much on Facebook; just links blogs, photos, videos from MySpace. I'm checking that out right now. Looks like his last post was…from right after the plane incident."

"How 'bout Twitter?"

"I checked that first, before I left," said Hay. "No Twitter."

"Ah, good for him," said Grinnell. "Keep in touch, and hang in there. Remember, it might be a long shot, but the stakes are so high, Priscilla. If we could get this guy, this guy who foiled a terrorist attack, to criticize the Administration, or even just stand up for us, it could make a difference. A big difference."

"I'll do my best," she said. After hanging up, she wondered how in the hell an honors graduate of the University of Texas, with a master's degree in journalism from the University of Missouri, had wound up trying to be a glorified private investigator in South Carolina.

♫

Federal Bureau of Investigation officers Henry Poston and Ike Spurgeon were headed up Interstate 26 between the South Carolina cities of Columbia and Spartanburg, en route to a bank-robbery investigation, when Poston's cell phone rang.

"Ike, would you answer that?" Poston was driving.

"Sure." He flipped open the phone Poston handed him. "Y'ello."

Glancing at his partner, Poston noticed a quizzical expression. Spurgeon put his hand over the phone.

"Guy from Homeland Security wants to talk to you, Hank."

"What? At the airport? TSA?"

"No. Actual Homeland Security. In D.C.," said Spurgeon, who had muted the phone. "Guy says his name is Banks McPherson."

"Jeez. That guy's a bigwig."

"I better pull off. Tell him I'll be right with him." At the Pomaria/Prosperity exit, somewhere below Newberry, Poston pulled the Ford Crown Victoria, government issue, off the exit and parked in the lot of a truck stop.

"He wants to talk about Riley Mansfield," Spurgeon whispered as he handed over the phone.

"Yessir, this is Poston."

"Mr. Poston, you and Agent Spurgeon conducted the interrogation of Riley Mansfield, right?"

"Yessir."

"Do you recall what you told Mansfield about the chief suspect?"

"The alleged bomber?"

"Yes," said McPherson. "Did you mention anything to Mansfield about him? His name. His nationality. Anything like that?"

"It should be in my report, sir."

"Well, the report is a little vague."

"I don't think so, sir. I'm reasonably certain that we withheld that information during the interrogation because we didn't want to provide any information that wasn't absolutely necessary. I can double-check my notes as soon as I get back to the office."

"Report back to me, Agent Poston, as soon as you know for sure."

"Yessir. Is that all?"

"What was your impression of Mansfield?"

"It's all there in the report, sir."

"I read the report," said McPherson. "Is there anything you can add?"

"Well, I'd say Mansfield is an easygoing, somewhat immature person, typical, I'd say, of musicians. He's highly intelligent but distrustful of authority."

"Do you think he's radical in any way?"

"No, sir, I think he just wants to put all this behind him and get on with his life. Based on the interview and our interactions with Mansfield, I don't think he's particularly political by nature."

"I see. Well, thank you for your insight, Poston. Get back to me and let me know what you find when you go over your notes."

"Yessir," he said. "It may be in the morning. Agent Spurgeon and I are on our way to a criminal investigation right now."

"Turn around and go back to your office. On my authority. I'll call your office right now so that arrangements can be made."

"Yessir," said Poston. "Is that all for now?"

"Yes," said McPherson. "Bye."

Looking troubled, Poston turned left out of the parking lot, crossed the bridge and headed back to Columbia.

"What's up?" asked Spurgeon.

"We're being sent back to the office to check our notes on Riley Mansfield. Homeland Security wants to know what we told Mansfield about the bomb suspect."

"As in…that the guy was a Cuban from South Florida, not an Arab from South Yemen?"

"I cut him a break," said Poston. "Something's really fishy about this whole thing, but I don't think Mansfield wants anything but his life back."

"You're treading on pretty thin ice, Hank."

"I know it. But something's not right. Why would a terrorist try to blow up a prop plane with thirteen passengers on it? Why would the alleged perp carry a driver's license identifying him as Philippe Tiant of Miami and be released to the press as Fatih Ghannam of Aden?"

"Out of our hands, man."

"You agree with me, right, that Mansfield's no terrorist?"

"No question. He did what was right. When something had to be done, he did it. He ought to be considered a hero."

"Well, I'm a little worried that something really…strange is going on here. I think maybe the cowboys in the Harmon Administration are up to something."

"You don't think they crashed a plane just for a political stunt?"

"Don't even go there, Ike. I'm not saying anything like that. I'm just really suspicious of this whole deal, and even if it's not something as despicable as that—I mean, shit, God forbid—there's some dirty dealing going on, and I think this Mansfield is in danger of becoming too hot for the Administration to handle.

"You and I both know they're not averse to stretching the rules."

"Uh, no," said Spurgeon. "They're not."

"First thing, they're shutting us out of the investigation completely after we were the first agents assigned to it. Then someone from Washington in Homeland Security is wanting us to go back through everything and see what information we divulged while interrogating Mansfield. And what this McPherson supposedly wants to know is whether Mansfield knows the guy isn't Arab. At the very least, we know the Administration is hiding the identity of the suspect, and also at the very least, that this has political implications."

"Wonder where Philippe Tiant is right now?" pondered Spurgeon aloud.

"Somebody's in Guantanamo," said Poston.

♫

"Riley," Melissa Franklin asked, "why do you think somebody wanted to blow up such an itsy, bitsy plane?"

They were driving through the coastal swamps of southern Georgia on Interstate 95, headed back home. They were both high, and it was quite a bit more evident in Melissa's case.

"I don't know," said Riley Mansfield. "I just don't fuckin' know."

"Why do you think the government arrested a man who was Cuban and turned him into a man who was Arab?"

"Don't know that either, babe."

"Why do you think...they wanna beat up the guy who kept the...fucking plane...from being blown up, and then they follow him around like he's a...bad guy...himself?"

"Well," said Riley, "I don't really want to know more than what I need to know. I want to get to the point where I don't fucking care. I want to do what it takes…to get things back to normal. I crave normalcy, though I don't like it as a word."

"What's wrong with normalcy?"

"It was invented by a shitty, dumbass president named Warren G. Harding, who was about the worst thing that came down the presidential pike before Richard Nixon and Sam Harmon."

"Where do you get that shit?"

"I am an absolute whiz at everything, my dear, that don't make money." Riley didn't get the chuckle he expected.

"Riley Mansfield," she said, "this is fuckin' America, goddamn it. You can't have shit like this in America. This is the land of the fucking free."

"Home of the fucking brave."

"Don't make a joke out of it, Riley."

"I make a joke out of everything. Ever listen to my songs?"

"But you're a hero, Riley. What do you get? They're trying to throw you in jail. They might be trying to kill you."

"Well, maybe you should take a little nap, Missy."

"Maybe I should," she said. "Maybe I fuckin' should. But it's pressure, Riley, there's so much fuckin' pressure. They might…fuckin' kill you."

"Sleep, honey. It's bad, but it ain't that bad. Nothing's that bad. We got each other. That's somethin'."

Fuck. I feel like I'm in a soap opera. A bad one.

"Okay, Riley Mansfield, world's most stubborn…independent man. I'll try to sleep."

"That's good, Melissa. That's good."

"But first I gotta use the bathroom."

♫

Darkness greeted Riley and Melissa as they finally reached the South Carolina Upstate. Melissa slept most of the way through Georgia and didn't stir until they were north of Columbia. She awakened thoughtful and sentimental. They stopped for coffee.

"Riley?"

"Yeah?"

"I think, maybe, you should drop me by my house. I better go ahead and check on Mama."

"That's cool."

"Things are just happening so fast," she said. "It's…a blur. I need some time to myself, just to think things over."

"Well, if you want to talk, call me. I mean, that's why we got the new cell phone. I don't know. I wonder if you can change the number every few days?"

"When is…you're going to, where is it, Rockingham?"

"Yeah. Friday morning, I think."

"What are you going to do between now and then?"

"I think I'm gonna keep myself pretty scarce, obviously. Maybe get some work done early in the morning and fairly late at night. I don't know. I'll have to think about it. I'll probably do some laundry tonight, maybe pay some bills, go online, check emails. I think, in the daytime, I might just go back on the farm with my guitar on my back, find a place to sit down and play some tunes, maybe write a couple."

"If I need to get away, I may join you, but right now, I need to think about things and get my head together."

"This shit is harsh," he said. "Just let me know what you're thinking, what you decide. This is all going to blow over eventually, one way or another. I can't blame you if you need a break from bizarro world."

Riley dropped Melissa off, helped her with her bags and said hello to her mother. Then he drove home, wondering a little about whether or not he still had a manager and a lot about whether or not he was losing yet another woman with whom he had fallen in love.

CHAPTER FOURTEEN
PIDDLIN' AROUND

Riley got up early on Monday morning and wrote an email to the White House. He used the address of the mid-level aide with whom he and Melissa had been corresponding. First he reviewed all the previous notes, reading Melissa's replies, which she had drafted in his name. Riley reasoned that having a lover—if, in fact, she was still his lover—as manager was not unlike a golfer having his wife as caddie. *Whoa. Don't even go there.*

> **Dear Mr. Ashton:**
> **I don't understand the problem.**
> **I've offered to make an appearance with the president, shake hands and sing a song. Any song the president wants. Or two. Or three. Whatever. I thought we had an agreement. I don't know the details, but that's only because I'm waiting for you people to make up your mind and give me a time and a place I'm supposed to be.**
> **So why am I continually being hassled? Why am I under surveillance? Why am I being accosted and harassed by law-enforcement officers?**
> **I don't understand the benefit of working with y'all. If I refused to do anything, at least there would be some justification, however perverse, for making my life difficult.**
> **Sincerely yours,**
> **Riley Mansfield**
> **"The truth is seldom more evident than when being vehemently denied."**

Riley remained uncomfortable about being at home. Home wasn't home anymore in any normal sense. Shortly after the sun rose, he placed his guitar in a bag and strapped it across his shoulders. He filled his cargo shorts with .12-gauge shells and carried his shotgun. He wasn't much of a hunter, but he had a shotgun, a Remington. It had been leaning against the wall of a closet for two years. He peppered an old, half-sunk rowboat grounded in the shallow end of the pond. He thought about trying to down a buzzard circling calmly a couple hundred feet above.

That wouldn't be nothing but meanness.

He walked to the back of the farm, once a fertile bottomland in his youth but now rapidly turning into a pine forest. He wanted the land opened up again, but it'd never happen. At some point, his father must have allowed a pulpwood company to plant back there. He wouldn't go to the expense of having all the middle-aged pine trees cut down and the stumps uprooted. It was a mistake that had already been made.

The spot he chose was a mile from any highway, and the only houses within a mile were his and his mother's. He found a stump, a remnant of five years or so earlier when Riley had actually cut wood for his own fireplace. Now what little was left of the wood was rotten, still stacked up next to the steps to the deck of his house.

He pulled out the guitar, tuned it, clipped a capo to the neck and started strumming away. Melissa was in his thoughts. He wondered how long it could last. How long would it be before the road, so invigorating at first, became hazardous and scary? She was probably, right this minute, getting back in her right mind. But he needed her and felt incapable of keeping her.

The incident with the police outside the Oasis might just have put Melissa over the edge. It had distressed him when she decided not to stay overnight, but that was because he longed for her body. Just thinking of her left him brimming with arousal. What scared him was the fear of losing touch with her soul. He needed to be more sensitive to her needs. He had been acting as if his crazy, dysfunctional life was normal because it was normal for him. For a time, Melissa had seemed capable of adapting seamlessly, but it was a façade born out of the excitement that, at first, had seemed so breathless. He rolled a joint and smoked half of it. Then he wrote a song:

Monte Dutton

Sittin' on the front porch in the rain
Wondering what became of me
And why I can't make things the way they used to be
I don't know why she don't love me
Don't know what she wants
Try my best to show my love
Even as I watch her slip away
I'm pretty sure she knows I love her
Just as sure she likes me a lot
But love and like are twice as bad
As fish and chicken in the same pot
If we can't make two lovers
Friends would still mean a lot
But when love gets in the air
It snuffs out all where love is not
Every time I even see her
All she says is that she's beat
Like she's the only hard worker
Who don't get too much sleep
I don't think she likes the pressure
Of knowing just the way I feel
It's drivin' me up the wall
Even as I watch her slip away
Here alone the blues consume me
Leave me wounded and depressed
It hurts to be humiliated
My life turned into a mess
What made me think she loved me?
Who was I to be so bold?
I don't even hold a grudge
It was merely insight to her soul
Even as I watch her slip away
Even as I watch her slip away

The Audacity of Dope

So…there.

It wasn't about her, but it was inspired by her. The story was incidental and a natural reaction to angst, which welled inside him, perhaps irrationally. He felt ill. It was getting hot, but the woods were shady. Time flew by. He just sat there alone, singing songs and trying to bring himself back.

One thing about being heartbroken: You'll get a damn good song out of it.

Riley wanted to call her, but more than that, he wanted her to call him. She needed her space. He needed to let this play out right. The United States government—most powerful nation on earth!—was trailing him and forcing him to do what it wanted. He'd been beaten with the butt of a shotgun similar to the one lying against the tree nearby. *Shit, it's like I'm some fucking sailor getting forty lashes.* He was going to have to stand up on a stage, God knew where, and sing a song of homage to a politician he reviled.

But the onus of the pressure was Melissa, with her sandy brown hair, her perfect complexion and green eyes, her perfect, not-too-small, not-too-large breasts. He put down the guitar. His fingertips tingled with the soft, irresistible feel of the curvature of Melissa's ass. Strings of a guitar proved insufficient. His tongue craved her bodily fluids as if they constituted the essence of his life.

Perhaps they did.

In the woods, Riley's thoughts turned to the memories of all the women, all the relationships, he had squandered over the years. He was struck by the seeming statistical inevitability of fucking this up, too. He felt completely powerless to do anything about it because he was completely confident that whatever he did would fail.

Smoking the rest of the joint helped a little.

♬

Hazel Franklin told her daughter she had decided to retire from school teaching. Melissa said she was thinking about it, too. She gave her mother a censored account of the Florida trip as the two of them drank coffee at the kitchen table. She didn't mention watching Riley being beaten by a fake cop, or hassled by real ones. She tried to explain his reluctance to take advantage of the cataclysmic, random event that had turned his life upside down. She said he wanted her to be his manager and travel with him. He needed her to manage the increasingly complex predicament.

Hazel lowered her head, peering at her only child over the top of her reading glasses.

"Do you love him?"

"Yes."

"Does he treat you well?"

"He's really sensitive, Mama. Even with all this…nonsense…bubbling all around him, he's still sensitive. He's stubborn and willful and…competitive…but Riley's sensitivity is never far away. He's a good person. Really. A very good person. But…he's never going to change. The way he lives his life, in his mind, is righteous."

"Well, honey, think about it. Make sure he loves you as much as you love him."

"He does."

"Just don't get carried away in the passion of the moment. You'll always be my baby, and I'll always be scared to death any time there's a tiny chance you might be hurt. Think this through, and make sure Riley's the kind of man you want to live with forever. I can't do this for you. I trust your judgment, and you've got to trust it, too."

"Thanks, Ma. I love you."

"I love you, too, honey."

Melissa curled up on the living-room couch for the rest of the morning, considering things while, at the same time, reading The Great Gatsby for what had to be the tenth time. As the narrative began its gentle descent into inevitable tragedy, Melissa wondered if Riley Mansfield's life would wind up being a different take on the same story. She had a sinking feeling, too.

The Audacity of Dope

♫

Sam Harmon strode across the White House lawn to board a helicopter that would take him to Air Force One. The President would be joining the First Lady, already ensconced with their college-age sons, at the family's vacation home on the Outer Banks of North Carolina. National Security Adviser David Branham walked Harmon to the helicopter.

"Where do we stand on this singer? What's his name again? Mansfield?"

"That's right, Mr. President: Riley Mansfield," Branham replied. "We're making the arrangements. Mike Ashton is handling the matter."

"What's the holdup?"

"No holdup. Mansfield is sort of...private. He sort of resents the intrusion on his privacy."

"He's an entertainer, right? Whoever heard of—what, he's a country singer?—a singer shying away from attention? Hell, doesn't he want to be a big star?"

"He is, mainly, a songwriter. His income is mainly derived from royalties. He performs extensively but seems to prefer the anonymity of small clubs. He's sort of made himself scarce ever since the incident occurred."

Harmon held up the takeoff, lingering with Branham at the foot of the steps. "What's he, a fuckin' Democrat?"

"He doesn't seem to be anything, Mr. President. He says he doesn't want to be...affiliated...with either party."

"He's a fuckin' Democrat. I was hoping we could get him to travel with the campaign, come out on stage, say a few words and, you know, perform a few songs. 'God Bless the U.S.A.,' shit like that."

"He's agreed to make an appearance, but, according to Mike, he just wants to do it one time. Says he wants to 'get it out of the way.'"

"Well, if we're just gonna get this guy once, it needs to be a pretty big production, don't you think?"

"Yessir."

"I mean, we need to get a big fuckin' bump from this hillbilly."

"Mr. President, we're making arrangements to have Mansfield perform a song—he wants to do 'This Land Is Your Land'—on the National Mall on the Fourth of July."

"'This Land Is Your Land,' huh? Yeah, he's definitely a fuckin' Democrat." The President seldom used the word *Democrat* without preceding it with the word *fucking*. "How, uh, inquisitive is he, David? Are we sure he doesn't know anything we don't want him to?"

"We've vetted him thoroughly, Mr. President," said Branham. "Michael has reviewed all the law-enforcement reports, watched all the footage of Mansfield…we've got an undercover operative following him around, and the RNC has someone following him around, posing as a fan."

"I tell you who we ought to put on his ass," said Harmon. "What's Sue Ellen Spenser doing these days?"

Branham smiled. "You're right on the money, Mr. President. She's at Sedgwick Sanford and Van Buren. She doesn't work for the committee. There's no formal link, no money changing hands."

"Can't hurt to get him laid," said the Leader of the Free World. "You know, I had a piece of that ass myself one time. Tell Sue Ellen I'd still like to see him sing 'God Bless the U.S.A.'"

"Will do, Mr. President. Have a nice weekend."

Harmon waved at the cameras trained on him and boarded the helicopter.

CHAPTER FIFTEEN
RILEY IN WONDERLAND

Cable news came back alive. Entertainment Tonight depicted "obscure hero" (occasionally "reclusive hero") Riley Mansfield. He showed up in the top ten of the Yahoo searches again. His email to the White House—Michael Ashton, maybe?—hadn't even been dignified by a reply, but Riley's agreement to perform on a national stage with President Sam Harmon had become a done deal in the media even though it remained vague in Riley's mind. There wasn't much in the way of details.

Riley's Tuesday morning was amusing. He sat in his trusty easy chair, guitar leaning against the couch, and listened while Don Imus called him "a lying weasel" on RFD-TV. A few days earlier, he had caught a glimpse of Fox News debating whether he was closer politically to Marx or Lenin, but now that heat had subsided. The tone was grudging praise. He saw a clip of Sean Hannity talking about it and thought he detected a bit of drool flowing from the edge of the conservative host's mouth. Fox now ran the same tape from outside the Oasis that CNN and MSNBC had been running. Previously it had been strictly the contentious exchange between Riley and Susie Quillen. He had a new fan in Joe Scarborough. Regis Philbin asked, "What is this guy? Nuts?"

Penthouse. Outhouse. Penthouse. Outhouse.

Nothing bothered him. On the other hand, nothing pleased him. Riley noted that he was at least buzzed and at times stoned in virtually every news clip. He wondered if it was as obvious to everyone else as it was to him. He was, after all, high when he watched most of it.

Yet it was all quiet on the home front. Apparently he'd made himself sufficiently elusive so that most everyone now relied on the canned, the manipulated, the hyped, the spun, the easy. The feeding frenzy was on autopilot.

Gee, there's a song no one would listen to or understand.

The phone rang. For some ungodly reason, Riley answered it.

"Hello."

"Riley Mansfield, please."

"Speaking."

"May I call you Riley?"

"Sure. 'Morning Joe' does and I never even met the guy."

Polite laughter. "My name is Adam Rhine. I work for *Rolling Stone*."

"Well, fuck. It's about time you guys called."

Silence.

"I'm kidding," Riley said.

"I'd like to do a story on you. Hang with you. Follow you around."

"See the seamy underbelly of the struggling musician, coping with sudden and unwanted fame?"

"Something like that,"

Riley sighed and thought a moment.

"Okay, first of all, yeah, I read *Rolling Stone*. I like it. I'm not too interested in baring my soul, but I'm not afraid of an honest…depiction. But I've got to, uh, make some modest, uh, requirements."

"Such as?"

"Well—how do I phrase this?—you can talk to me, you can observe me, write about the scene around me, whatever you want, but your story can't come out until after I've paid my debt to society."

"What does that mean?" asked Rhine.

"Uh, I've got to do something where I shake hands with the president and sing a song and—wait a minute, this has got to be off the record, agreed?"

"Agreed. I'm not writing a story now."

"So nothing we say right now is going to wind up in, like, 'Random Notes,' anything like that?"

"No. Between you and me."

"Umm-kay. Well, maybe we can work something out."

"That's cool. When can we hook up?"

"How 'bout I meet you next week in Kentucky? That ought to be earthy enough," Riley said.

"Then I'll just hang out with you right through the Fourth of July gig on the Mall?"

"You, uh, apparently know something I don't."

"Well, according to what I hear, you're playing a song in a celebration with the president at the National Mall on July fourth. Well, no, actually, it's on Saturday, so, strictly speaking, that's the fifth of July."

"That's fine," said Riley with a touch of weariness. "I told 'em I'd sing a song, shake the president's hand and then be done with it. I wrote an email saying I'd do something, within limits. They just haven't actually told me what it is."

"You're not making any campaign appearances?"

"Fuck, no," said Riley. "That's still off the record, right?"

"Right. Nothing you say to me on this phone call is for publication."

"Okay, so you can't print it if I say that President Harmon is a lying cocksucker. Hypothetically. I certainly don't have literal knowledge of this."

"You're a pretty funny dude."

"What say you meet me a week from Thursday? In Kentucky. You probably want to fly into Lexington. Maybe Knoxville."

"How do I get back in touch with you? You'll be on the road, right?"

"Likely. Being home's a real drag now. I kind of feel like I'm on the run."

"From being a hero?"

"Something like that."

Riley gave Rhine an email address and promised to check it regularly. He said he'd give the writer a phone number a couple days ahead of time, but even then, that number had better not get passed around.

"I give you my word," said Rhine.

As he turned his attention back to "Morning Joe," Riley thought about the song "Cover of the *Rolling Stone*" and figured out how to play it on his Pawless. He couldn't think of all the words, but maybe he should learn it. *Might be...topical.*

The news wasn't exciting. Nothing was exciting anymore. The numbness wasn't wholly a consequence of weed. *Nah. Couldn't be. Could it?*

It was Tuesday, and there wasn't any need on God's green earth to go to Rockingham any time before Friday morning. The phone rang again. *Fuck. Forgot.* Riley yanked the cord out of the back. Sight unseen of who it was.

It was almost nine. Riley felt the need to escape. Teams of dignitaries could be closing in on his messy, modest house at any moment. Or another alleged deputy like Barton Fleming. If somebody from *Rolling Stone* calls a man at 8:30 in the morning, anything can happen. *How 'bout a nice Hawaiian Punch?*

After a half-hearted shave and a disinterested shower, Riley headed to a nearby state park. No one was ever at state parks in the mornings, not even when the weather was beautiful. This day it was stormy. He played his guitar from a covered shelter on a rise overlooking the Enoree River. If there had been anyone there, they would have thought him pixilated. They would've been right. Then he just drove the back roads for a few hours, bought a hot dog and Diet Coke at a roadside stand and returned home.

Somehow he managed to kill another day.

It was almost dark when he snuck back in his house. Though he had the stereo on, listening to Slaid Cleaves, he barely picked up the sound of a phone ringing. His cell phone rang. *Yikes. Melissa. The only person, I think, who knows the number. Where the fuck is it?* It was attached to the belt on his jeans, which were hanging on his would-be exercise bike.

"Hello. Melissa?" She'd hung up. He called back. She asked how he was doing.

"Not bad for a troubled recluse."

"Mind if I come over?"

"Mind? I'll come pick you up. Where are you? Borneo?"

She laughed. "I'll drive over."

"Great. I hope you're feelin' me like I'm feelin' you. Charley Pride song. Sorry."

"It's okay," she said. "I like Charley Pride. I think."

"You do. He's a great American and a credit to his race."

She giggled again. "I'll be there in ten," she said.

Riley cleaned off the couch, using as much of the coffee table as possible to stack the magazines, books, harmonicas, guitar picks, change and peanuts. Under the cushion he found change and a pack of rolling papers. He put the cheap mandolin in his music room, hanging its stringy strap on a nail on the wall. He matched socks and folded towels, then put another load in the dryer. By the time he put his outside-in, green sweatpants back in the order God intended, Melissa was knocking on the door. That's because the doorbell had been broken for approximately five years.

Riley smiled brightly. "Kiss me," he said. "Show me your titties. Then tell me how I can pleasure you."

"Hold your horses, tiger," she said, blushing. "I just came by to talk."

"Shit. I'm no good at that," he said. "Come in and sit down. I can be decent if'n I gotta."

Melissa sat on the couch, crossed her legs and lit a cigarette. She motioned with the pack, offering Riley one.

"Thanks," he said. "I got some. I don't smoke much when I'm sober."

"You're sober?"

"Reasonably close. I probably could be...prevailed upon to...partake."

"Let's just talk," she said.

"How's your mama?"

"She's good."

"Whatcha been doin'?"

"Reading. Talking with Mom. Thinking."

Sinking feeling.

"Me, too," Riley said. "Only I gotta do my reading in undisclosed locations. Being caught with a book is a misdemeanor in these parts."

"You're funny."

"Yeah. It's the least of my vices. This is like a comedy monologue so far. Or one of those old Dockers commercials. I wish my whole life was a Dockers commercial. Beats being a hero. John Wayne was wrong, man. I wish I could star in 'The Truman Show.'"

"So, when we gonna talk about...us?" Melissa asked.

"I dunno. I'm...scared."

"You're scared but, at the same time, you're stubborn. Hell, you're brave. You can't fool me, you..."

"Stupid son of a bitch?"

"No," she said. "You're not both. I can't figure out if you're stupid or not, and I don't think you're a son of a bitch, but if I was rich and famous and important, I might change my mind."

"Poverty breeds character," said Riley, "and freedom's just another word for nothing left to lose."

"Janis Joplin."

"Kris Kristofferson. He wrote it. She just sang it. She sang it well."

"We could just go on like this forever, couldn't we?"

"We already did it for hundreds of miles. Want to make it thousands? Apparently we just got to make it for a few more weeks, and maybe, if I'm a good boy, we can get rid of some of the craziness between now and then.

"And besides, chitchat is a wonderful defense mechanism."

Melissa let that one pass. "What's new?"

"Well, according to the *Rolling Stone*, I'm playing a song or two on national TV on the National Mall, and I'm shakin' hands with the national president. It's gonna be on the fifth of July because, apparently, that's a Saturday. Bad guys ain't told me yet, but everybody but me apparently knows all about it."

"Wow."

"What? That I'm helping a good man like Sam Harmon get reelected?"

"No. You're talking to *Rolling Stone*."

"You think I'm funny? You're the one who's a fucking riot. Mind if I have a bong hit?"

"No," she said, tossing her hair. "Go right ahead."

"Be right back. I gotta use the bathroom anyway. Want some?"

"No. I'm good."

"Don't be alarmed if you hear a gurgling sound," he said. "Just for safety's sake, probably be best to blaze in the bathroom. My mood will lighten, no doubt, when I return."

"How could it?"

When Riley returned, staggering a tad, he picked up his guitar and starting singing funky. *Funkily?* He started experimenting vocally, which was his habit while inspirationally stoned. He sang lots of songs onstage in styles he devised while stewing in the easy chair, slightly baked.

When he was through, Riley said, "I got this friend who built this guitar. One time, I was at his shop, just picking up guitars he had there for repair, or maybe one he'd just finished, or one that was built by some Jewish guy in New York City in the nineteen thirties, and I sang this version of 'Jambalaya,' the Hank Williams song.

"That was the first song I ever learned on guitar, and I learned it because, when I first started out, I just knew two chords, G and C, and all 'Jambalaya' is, is G and C, back and forth. I sang that fuckin' song so many times that I got bored, so I started doing impersonations of old country singers. One verse Hank Williams. Next verse George Jones. Next verse Johnny Cash."

"Do it for me," she said.

Riley could tell she was really impressed when he rumbled down low for Cash, then soared up high for Marty Robbins. George Jones made her giggle.

"That's quite a crowd pleaser," she said.

"Yeah," Riley said, "I used to be so proud of being able to do that. So, I was out in Texas, and I sang it for my buddy the guitar maker. Name's Vince Pawless. And I got through, and he paused for a minute, and he looked me in the eye, and he said, 'That's good…but what does Riley Mansfield sound like?' And it floored me, man. It got under my skin, and I started trying to do every song I knew like nobody had ever done them."

"And it works best when you're stoned?"

"Well, not stoned, exactly. More like buzzed. Not stoned or baked. Buzzed or high. When you're stoned, you can't think. When you're buzzed, the creativity kicks in but the brain hasn't kicked out. It's a smooth combination."

"I think you just convinced me to have a bong hit," she said.

"That was my intention," he said. "I had the best of intentions."

Riley raised his left hand, palm outward and open, signaling he'd be right back. He walked to the bathroom and came back with the blue plastic bong, which was about a foot tall on a square wooden base.

"Fuck the bathroom. Here, let me prepare this for you, my dear." He tapped the ashes off.

"No, let me pack it," Melissa said.

"You don't trust me?" He laughed.

"Hell, no," she said. "What is it you just said? I need a buzz. Just a buzz."

She took the lighter and drew deeply. She held in the smoke for several seconds and exhaled smoothly.

"I'd say you're gonna get your buzz," he said. "Give it a couple minutes."

"What were we talking about?"

"Uh, buzzes."

Riley moved to the couch. Since he noticed a little smoke smoldering in the bowl, he finished off the weed Melissa had left. Then he put his arm around her shoulders.

"Rockingham," she said. "When are you going to Rockingham?"

"Friday," he said. "I wish we could leave right now."

"We?"

"I wish I could leave right now. Or, maybe, in the morning."

"What's it gonna be like?"

"Uh, I went there last year, and it was...okay. I really ended up just getting drunk and mainly singing songs around a campfire. But this year, supposedly, it's gonna be way better. They got a tent in case it rains. They got good sound, so I don't have to pack my amps. They're barbecuing a bunch of pork. Kegs. Chests of beer. Lots of these guys are gonna be stock car racers. Pretty sure it'll be relatively weed-free. I'm not gonna say there won't be a few people sneaking away, but the illegal substance of choice is likely to be homemade liquor, not homegrown weed."

"I've never drunk moonshine," Melissa said. "Will it kill you?"

"Not so far. No, it's cool if you don't get carried away. I'll probably stick with a beer and just take a swig of the hard stuff if it's, you know, handed to me on stage in some...rite of passage. In a party atmosphere, it's easy to get carried away. You just gotta watch yourself. I have to say, you know, I think different kinds of alcohol affect people in different ways, and a moonshine high reminds me a little bit of a weed high. I don't know why. It's just my impression. It's definitely not a show for first-time callers, though."

"That's an interesting play on words."

"I'm fucked up," he replied.

For a while, they watched Betty Hutton and Eddie Bracken in "Miracle of Morgan's Creek" on TCM. It was a screwball comedy, full of madcap antics.

"Go with me," he said at last. "I need you. I couldn't feel number if I was paralyzed from the waist down."

"You're high."

"That makes it better, not worse. I got this…overwhelming…sense of…nothing. I'm just drifting along, bong hit to bong hit, joint to joint. Nothing means anything. You're, like, the only antidote…to the rockin' pneumonia and the boogie-woogie flu.

"You know how Little Richard makes his voice go way up high?"

"What?"

"Little Richard. You know, when he sings 'Tutti Frutti'?"

"Bip, bop, baluba, buhlam-bam-boom?"

"That's good, but, no, that's not what I mean. In the chorus, when he launches his voice way up high, and he goes, 'Aaaah-aaaah-aaah'!"

"Oh, yeah."

"I can't do that," Riley said, "and it sucks."

Melissa's laugh was unusually raucous for her. When it died down, Riley said quietly, "Uh, we were talking about if, like, you'll stay with me. I mean, if you want to skip the Rock, that's cool, but I really do need your help."

"I'm there," she said. "Now let's fuck."

"Let's," Riley said.

CHAPTER SIXTEEN
RECKLESS ABANDON

"Why do you have an aversion to growing up?" asked Melissa shortly after Riley helped her pack at her mother's house on Friday morning. She had wanted to spend some time with her mother before they left for Rockingham.

"Well, that's quite a question," he said. "Hmm. I guess it's better to have your adulthood questioned than your manhood."

"Your manhood is not in question," she said.

There was no easy way to get to Rockingham, North Carolina. He charted a course of two-lane roads and small towns: Whitmire, Chester, Lancaster, Pageland, Chesterfield and Cheraw in South Carolina, then north on U.S. 1 to Rockingham, which was just a few miles past the border.

"I don't mean it as an insult," Melissa said. "What I mean is, you seem to just drift along, living by your wits. Do you ever think about settling down?"

"Oh, most of my friends were settled down ten years ago," he said. "They got wives and kids and lawns and cul-de-sacs. Funny thing is, when we get together—Fourth of July, Homecoming game at Piedmont, Christmas party—they go back to acting like we did when we were kids. I just never stopped."

Melissa digested the information. "Not to change the subject," she said finally, "but why are we in the car?"

Riley was noticing how half the businesses on the Chester bypass were shut down, including what once had been a mall, then some kind of "auto mall." Now signs were falling off the hinges and grass was growing through the pavement.

"Uh, I try to divide up the mileage," he said. "This Corolla'll get twice the mileage of the Tacoma, or, maybe, a third better, anyway. Betwcen the trunk and the backseat, there's plenty of room, and we don't have to tote any amps or sound equipment.

"Doesn't this reasoning sound grown up?"

"I'm just saying…"

"I know. You're right. I'm in suspended adolescence, and if I had any sense, I'd know I'm getting too old for this shit."

"You just don't like to do what people want you to."

"Yeah. I got that from my old man."

"You miss him?"

"Oh, I don't know," Riley said. "I think it's fair to say that most of the memories are fairly warm, now that he's dead. It was hard to be his son, though.

"My daddy, he was an only child, and he was spoiled rotten. Yet he just terrorized me. Nothing pleased him. When you're raised the way I was, there's only two ways to go, and both are kind of crazy. Either you'll be tough as shit, or you'll run away, drop out and wind up passed out on some big-city street corner."

"So, you're…playing it halfway?"

"I'm serious. I wasn't any good in football until I learned not to give a shit and just let it all hang out. That's the only way I could keep my fucking daddy out from under my skin. Do we, like, have to talk about this?"

"No," she said. "I'm just interested in how you got to be the way you are."

"Well, it's a pretty long story."

Riley turned up the radio. He sang along with Charlie Walker's "Pick Me Up on Your Way Down" on Willie's Place, the Sirius traditional country station.

"Only song I know with 'haughty' in it," he said, not to Melissa. It was just a general pronouncement. A fun fact.

He switched channels after hearing a song he didn't like. Riley was thinking, though, about the issues Melissa had raised and the futility of remaining silent. She'd hold it against him. Women always did.

"I kinda don't get it when people expect athletes to be, you know, wholesome, polite, humble. That's got nothing to do with sports," he said. "Football rewards you for being mean. Aggressive. Brutal. Ruthless. It's—what's that military term?—shock and awe. It's about kicking the shit out of those poor slobs on the other side of a chalk line. You gotta seize every opening, exploit every weakness.

"Eventually I just said 'fuck it.' To me, being reckless on the field was just natural to being reckless off it. Kick ass all day and raise hell all night. They just went together, and when I got kind of wild, it made me…good in football."

"But, about, growing up…"

"I'm getting to that," said Riley, "but I'm having a hard time putting it together. You know, articulating it. I'm kind of just thinking out loud and trying to make a convoluted explanation make sense.

"Okay, you know, it would make sense, when you play football, which is the ultimate team sport, that you'd be adept at being a team player in life. That's what they always tell you. Football is a microcosm of life. Shit. It's a microcosm of failure in life."

"Well, that's harsh."

"Do you know how many players from my high school team are dead? How many were in drunken car crashes? How many are wandering around town like zombies now, living on yesterday? It's, like, something you can't escape. It was great. It made you a man, in a way, and it made you think you were capable of anything, but in another sense, you just go off into the real world and you're totally unprepared…for all the wrong reasons."

"How so?"

"Well, in your mind, you think the best team is gonna win in life just like it does in football," he said, "and when you get out, here's what you see: The guys who are running the world? They're the same guys who couldn't make it through two-a-days. The world's run by ass-kissing weasels, and there's nothing for anybody else. When I first got out of college, I took a job for about six months selling athletic shoes. I traveled around a good bit, there was time to write songs and fool around with the guitar, and I worked hard. And it didn't do a bit of good. The guys who got the promotions, who moved up the ladder, were the ones who kissed every ass in the building. They didn't give a shit about cleats and running shoes and sneakers. They gave a shit about themselves and their future. Period. Fuckers would ask me what I thought, I'd tell them, and if the boss liked it, it was their idea. If he didn't, it was mine.

"Luckily, I sold my first song, I mean, got my first decent royalties, which led to more of my songs getting looked at, which led to me signing a contract to write songs for a living and maybe cut a CD or two myself. I got to Nashville, sat down and started cranking out songs, and it was like a factory, and all they wanted was songs that were catchy but, just as intentionally, stupid, and the people running the place were just like the ones in charge of sneakers. Same weasels. Only the names were changed to protect the guilty."

"Shit. Aren't you depressing?"

"You brought it up," Riley said.

"I think you're right, but I don't think it's much consolation when you're the only one."

"I make a living," Riley said, "and a living is all I want. I don't care about being rich. I don't care about being a star. I want to do what I want to do, and it just becomes a matter of making that into a living. I think I have, and I've gotten set in my ways."

Another quiet period followed, both imagining what the other was thinking.

Riley said, "I reckon you're thinking…where do I fit?"

"What?"

"In my life. Are you wondering where you fit?"

"I didn't say that."

"You're thinking it, though. I got this idea in my head that you and me might be different. We might can love each other because we got the same adventurous spirit. You ain't got as much experience as me, but you're learning in a hurry. I think you might find out you like it, once we can, like, go to the grocery store without getting beat over the head by every limp dick with a video camera. Once I can walk in my backyard without being whacked across the back by the butt of a shotgun."

"I'm just a little scared," she said.

"Well, you know what? Me, too. I'm a little scared, but tell the truth. Don't you get just a little exhilarated by this? Aren't you kind of getting to where you enjoy tap dancing out on the edge just a little?"

"I'd hardly call this a little."

Riley pulled off at a service station on the left, just past where Interstate 77 crossed.

"What are we stopping for?"

"How about getting me a Diet Dr. Pepper and a pack of nabs, and get whatever you want, and while you're in there, I'll roll a joint, and maybe, just maybe, we'll stop talking about all this serious shit."

She got out of the car, but before she was out of earshot, Riley said, "Oh, yeah. Chewing gum. Lots of chewing gum. Those Listermint strip things. Couple packs of smokes.

"Couple packs of rubbers." He smiled, and she gave him that "you!" look.

♫

North of Cheraw, just shy of the North Carolina border, Riley tapped Melissa lightly on the shoulder. She stirred and immediately her eyes caught the strobe-like blaze of lights. The lights of a patrol car.

"Shit," she said.

"Melissa. Be cool," Riley's voice was quiet and firm. "Everything's fine. Don't say a word. Don't look surprised. Don't look anything at all. Just trust me. Got it?"

"Yeah."

Riley rolled down the window.

A burly state trooper said, "Please exit the car, sir. You and your passenger."

Riley got out promptly. Melissa looked at herself in the flip-down mirror on the passenger side and tossed her head a little, then climbed out, obviously a little sleepy. A second cop frisked her.

The trooper glanced at Riley's driver's license.

"What's up, Officer? I wasn't speeding, was I?"

"Sir," he said with a formal air. "I'd like your permission to search the car."

"Sure, but…" One thousand one, one thousand two, one thousand three. "Wait a minute. I know what it is. Somebody must've called you, right? From, like, a convenience store?"

"Sir…"

"Hey," Riley said. "Here's what you want." He opened his hands, opening them outwards to the officer, reached with his right hand into the shirt pocket over his heart and retrieved a joint.

"Here."

Melissa, watching from across the roof, gasped.

"Smell it," Riley said. The trooper sniffed. "It's tobacco."

The trooper stared at Riley. Their eyes didn't meet because Riley still had sunglasses on. He motioned the other trooper back to the squad car.

"Drive safely, sir."

Riley pulled back onto the highway.

Before Melissa could even speak, Riley said, "I thought about this a couple days ago. It's hard, even for the White House, to get something like the Highway Patrol to do its dirty work. They can have them sent out to hassle somebody, but they can't share the details. Too many people would know, and even cops like to gossip. Local law enforcement is easy to corrupt but hard to keep quiet. Maybe somebody in that parking lot at the convenience store saw me rolling a joint and took down the license plate. Or maybe the Highway Patrol was out looking for my license number. Either way, it's pretty much the same.

"We're living life in a cell-phone world. I think probably someone put 'em on us. Whether that person made that call because he was, you know, a concerned citizen, or if it's somebody who's tailing us and just trying to cause mischief, I don't know. I haven't noticed anybody following us, but I probably ought to pay more attention. Odds are it was just some blue-haired lady who went apeshit."

"God almighty," said Melissa. "How do you figure that shit out?"

"I keep a pouch of tobacco in the console." He retrieved it. "See?"

American Spirit.

"I rolled two joints, one with weed and one with tobacco. Let me tell you where I learned this. One night I went to see a band because the lead singer wanted to write together. I waited in the green room while they were playing their encore. On the counter, they had this cigarette-rolling contraption and a big pouch of tobacco. Then, when the band rolled in from the stage, the first thing the bass player did was stash the tobacco. Then he pulled out a bag of weed, rolled a couple joints and they started passing 'em around. I figured it out. They just had the tobacco sitting out there on the table as a cover. Security always keeps people out of the dressing rooms, and the main reason is that, nine times out of ten, the band's gonna get high before and after they go onstage. Most places, it's sort of understood, and the cops don't hassle them, but you can't ever tell when some sheriff is interested in an easy publicity stunt. Security can't keep the cops out. Maybe it works. Maybe it doesn't. But it's worth a shot."

They checked into the Holiday Inn Express in Rockingham. All they did was leave their bags in the room. Riley went to the bathroom.

"All right with you if we head on out there?"

"Sure."

"Okay. I didn't know about it till I had already booked the room, but they're going to have several motorhomes out there around the site of the party, which is in the track's infield. It's gonna be a long night. If we get too drunk, we'll just crash out there at the track. Even if we do, we can drive back here at the crack of dawn and scrub up. We'll have to be at the track for breakfast, 'cause I'm playing again, but we can sneak out of there as soon as we get through with that."

"I've never seen a stock car race," Melissa said.

"It'll be fun, darling, and you just can't beat fun. I used to know a guy who said that all the time. He's dead now, but that's a story for another day."

"You're just fucking amazing," said Melissa. "I've never heard of anybody so good at thinking on his feet."

"Race-car drivers call it driving by the seat of your pants," Riley said as the track appeared ahead on the right. "Man learns a lot of lessons out there on the road.

"Besides, you ain't bad yourself. You're the one who thought to take pictures of me getting beat up in the backyard."

She blushed.

"I printed out those pictures," he said. "They're stored in the laptop, and the prints are in a manila folder in the backpack. I slid 'em in next to the laptop. Just know they're there…in case we need 'em at some point."

"You're so…unflappable."

"Yeah," he said. "I seldom flap."

CHAPTER SEVENTEEN
THE ROCK

After stopping by the ticket office, Riley drove through the fourth-turn tunnel into the Rockingham Speedway infield, which was still mostly empty at two in the afternoon except for a complex of two race-car haulers, a moderately large tent and four motorhomes. In other words, it wasn't hard to find Del Howard, Blake Agnew and a small band getting ready for a party. A keg had been tapped. Pork roasts were cooking in the pit, which had wheels on it and had been pulled as a trailer behind a Chevrolet truck.

Riley parked nearby, strapped his guitar on his back, hoisted his cooler and introduced Melissa to Del and Blake. Others had familiar faces, but Riley would need a while to reacquaint himself with their names.

While the pork barbecued—the plan was for it to be ready at dusk—barbecued chicken legs were stacked on platters for snacking. Riley ate three, made himself available to help with…anything, but all duties were fairly well assigned. Riley sat down and idly plunked away at his guitar, pausing for swigs of beer between tunes. Melissa wandered around, occasionally stopping by. Finally the stock cars stopped practicing and as the they coasted into the garage, Riley knew it was time to play.

"Will you introduce me to the crowd?" he asked Melissa.

"What?"

"I need somebody to introduce me, and you're the only person I know who won't make a big deal of the airplane and all that shit."

"Well, you gotta mention it."

"Yeah, but just don't say much about it."

"Okay. Got it," she said.

There wasn't a stage, just a mic stand. There weren't any wings for Riley to wait in, but he stood over on the right side, kind of in the shadows. Melissa walked up to the microphone.

"Ladies and gentlemen, my name is Melissa Franklin and I'm one of the lives that this man I'm introducing saved. I was on a plane flying from New York City to Greenville, South Carolina. There I was, getting ready to get home, sitting in 3C, and there was this big commotion behind me."

Fuckin' liar!

"I thought that man standing over there," she pointed him out, "was a raving lunatic. There was this great struggle, and I was of a mind to whack him one, if you know what I'm saying." The crowd was laughing now. "Then he threw this little tiny case—I reckon it had a guitar in it—right out the side door of that li'l plane, and, godamighty if it didn't blow up in the treetops! And that's when I realized Riley Mansfield was a genuine American hero. How 'bout a big hand for Riley Mansfield!"

Riley smiled and walked up. Melissa embraced him.

"You bitch," Riley whispered.

"You had it coming," she replied.

Riley walked up to the mic. "Aw, you're too kind," he said. "I, uh, didn't do anything that any…red-blooded…American wouldn't.

"I wrote this song when I went with a bunch of buddies to a stock car race. It was the first one they'd ever been to." He played the introductory chords. "They was musicians! Song's called 'Martinsville'! Reckon if I'd had any sense, I'd've named it 'Rockingham.'"

> *I went down to Martinsville*
> *Wish I had a Coupe de Ville*
> *But all I got is this old pickup truck*
> *I reckon that a man can dream*
> *Or that's my story any way*
> *I fell in with some long lost friends*
> *Some of them might be kin*
> *But all of 'em love to drink beer*

The Audacity of Dope

We saw races two days straight
Or that's my story anyway
Martinsville
A place frozen in place and time
Martinsville
It's north of Eden
A lover's leap east
Of Woolwine
When the roar of engines stopped
We built a fire, pissed off a cop
But he never even pulled his guns
I took a deep breath
And had me another beer
Pretty soon we drew a crowd
And it kinda got real loud
But everybody tried to get along
This guitar came in handy then
Or that's my story anyway
CHORUS
Jimmie Johnson won the race
Took the lead in the Chase
Tony Stewart acted like he was mad
Guy next to me had some moonshine
Or that's my story anyway
I had no business drivin' home
But it wudn't like I was alone
It ain't too hard to drive at a speed of five
I had some explaining to do
And yet this was my story anyway
CHORUS

Riley performed a couple more songs, then exhorted the fans to party in the third turn.

"When you get through socializing with all these fine and talented race-car drivers—by God, they're the real heroes!—stay and party with us all night long, ladies and gentlemen. If you don't watch out, I'll sell you a CD and tee shirt before you'n blink your eyes.

"Thanks for putting up with me, and enjoy the big race tomorrow."

Riley unplugged the guitar and walked over to Melissa. "I thought that went right well," he said. "In spite of your best efforts."

"Aw, just stick with me, kid, and I'll make you bigger than Elvis," she said. "I think I'll go find me a strappin' race-car driver."

She walked away without waiting for a rejoinder. Riley didn't have one, anyway.

Del Howard arrived on the scene. "I take it y'all are having your differences?"

"Not only is she pissed at me for some unknown reason," said Riley. "She is also shitfaced."

"If I was you, I'd get the same way. Be best if y'all'd play by the same rules."

Riley thought about how alcohol was such an inferior buzz.

♫

Riley was leaning on the Corolla, away from the crowd, when Melisssa walked over. She looked him in the eyes, smiling coyly.

"It was pretty funny, actually," said Riley. "Completing making up that story about being on the plane...sounds..."

"Like something you would do."

"A little."

"That's why I did it. I thought it was a dose of your own medicine."

The rain let up. Sun peeked out from the horizon. Darkness was about to fall.

"I'm guessing you need me to sell your shit," Melissa said.

"If you wanna. If you don't mind."

The Audacity of Dope

Riley played an hour-long set to a crowd of people balancing plates in one hand and beers in the other. Riley preferred standing up while he played, but stools had been placed on the stage, so, rather than looking for a place to put them, he just sat down. As a result, about thirty minutes in, the left cheek of his ass fell asleep. Lacking feel in the seat of his pants would've greatly hindered a stock car racer, but Riley was only mildly cognizant of it. He was a little uneasy at the beginning and botched the lyrics of his first song. It was doubtful anyone noticed. At the start, the tent was crowded but after the first couple songs, people started drifting back outside where the food was. After opening with "If the Good Lord's Willing (and the Creek Don't Rise)," Riley roared into a medley of old country songs. They were songs that were easy to play and fun to sing. Old standards—"Heartaches by the Number," "Wine Me Up," "Kiss an Angel Good Morning," "Big City" and "Folsom Prison Blues"—helped him relax. Sure enough, he was almost perfect for the rest of the set."

Blake, who joined him on the chorus and whatever else he could remember of another cover, "Margaritaville," said the crowd outside was listening, as if Riley would be insulted that people wanted to eat barbecue and grab another beer. He also brought a Mason jar of moonshine with him—it had a big peach floating in it—and insisted Riley take a slug.

Riley went back to his own songs, stringing five of them together to close the set.

"Thank you all so much," he said, noting with satisfaction that the subject of the blown-up guitar had never come up and anxiously awaiting the return of feeling to his ass. "I'll take a little break and be back up here onstage in a little while."

Riley sat down at a table with Melissa and autographed a few CDs and tee shirts. It only took a few minutes.

"We're not selling near as much stuff as Florida," Melissa said.

"I didn't expect to. This is just partying with friends, more or less. Next set, if you don't mind, could you take that crumble-up straw hat that's in the tee shirt box and pass it around? I'll open up with 'There You Are,' since that's what's on the front of the shirts, and I'll pump up the tee shirts during the guitar break."

"Why don't you put one on instead of the football jersey?"

"I think that might be a tad immodest," Riley said. "I don't feel right wearing my own tee shirt. Tell you what: I'll hold one up onstage at the end of 'There You Are'."

"That'll work. And I'll wear one."

"Cool," Riley said. "You eaten?"

"Yeah, I'm good."

"Well, I'm starving. It's kind of a curse when you're playing guitar. Every time I stop by the barbecue pit, the plate they just chopped up is either empty or what's left is globbed with grease."

It was completely dark now, closing in on nine o'clock. A small cluster of people gathered around Riley, who only made it close enough to the grill to grab half a pimiento-cheese sandwich from the folding table next to it. They all wanted to know about the plane incident and hear Riley regale them with tales of how he kicked the terrorist's ass. He politely corrected the exaggerations inherent in phrases like "I hear tell" and "they say."

"They say you whupped that Arab (ay-RAB) upside the head and then tossed the guitar out the window."

"Naw, I was actually too scared to do anything but shove the side door open and throw the guitar out it."

"I wish you'd th'own that goddamn terrorist out with it."

"Well, it was all I could do to get rid of my guitar," Riley said. "People thought I'd gone crazy and were tearing at my arms. I don't think I got it all the way out the door until I kicked at it while I was being drug back."

A chunky man with kind of a hungry look stood at the edge of the crowd. Riley noticed his penetrating blue eyes. As others drifted away after conversing for a while, the man, whose jet-black hair looked as if it had been dyed, moved closer, waiting for a chance at a private conversation.

The Audacity of Dope

Jesus. People with black hair should never dye it. Looks like Superman in the comics: black with glints of blue.

"Hi, there, Mr. Mansfield, sure enjoyed your music," the man said.

"Well, thanks. I try my best."

"You ever do any gospel numbers?"

"I wrote a gospel song when I was in Nashville a few years ago. Called 'Come on Down.' It's not exactly made for partying, but I'll do it for you next set if you'd like."

"That'd be just fine. Are you are a religious man, Mr. Mansfield?"

No, but I take it you are. This is what happens when you open up an orgy to the general public.

"Uh, I kind of attend the Tom T. Hall school," Riley said. "Me and Jesus got our own thing going. I say my prayers every night, and I believe in religion. I just don't much believe in organized religion."

"How's that?"

"Well, there's just something I've never enjoyed about churches," Riley said, feeling at the same time that moonshine course into his brain. "It sort of waters down the whole experience. There's something I don't like about a bunch of people sittin' in a building listening to a preacher tell 'em what to think."

"That's interesting."

"I think the teaching of the Gospels is kind of skewed," Riley said.

"How do you figure that?"

Why am I doing this? Because I can't help it. "When the preacher man's riding around in a Lincoln Town Car, he ain't likely to stress that stuff about Christ renouncing material values," Riley said. "And the Jesus I hear 'em talk about in church ain't the man I envision when I read the Bible."

"Well," the man said, "I reckon that's something to think about. Nice talking to you."

"Same here. I didn't catch your name."

"Name's Jed," the man said. "Good to know you."

By the end of the second set, Riley felt as if he were staggering around in a fishbowl. The harsh lighting, spotlights in the darkness, gave everything a stark look. He staggered into one of the race-car haulers and played Beer Pong a while, which wasn't really a good move since he wasn't really very good at it and had to drink quite a bit of beer in quite a short amount of time.

Aw, shit. You can't get that drunk on beer.

Midnight was closing in, and Riley's third set was boisterous. The good citizens had drifted into the night. Beautiful women were showing him their tits, right in front of the stage. Riley barely had enough sense to look over to the table, catch Melissa's gaze and dutifully roll his eyes.

A gorgeous redhead with big hair yelled, "Hey, Riley Manfield, you wanna fuck?"

"No, ma'am, I'm spoken for," he said. "Thanks for asking, though."

She leaned over grandiosely and pointed to her lips. If Riley had leaned over, she might have drug him off the stage with her tongue. But he didn't. He still had that much sense. He didn't have enough sense, though, to turn down requests. Several times he made attempts to play snippets of songs he'd never tried to play before. The set went on and on. Still sitting on the stool, this time it wasn't just Riley's ass that fell asleep. He lost feeling in his entire left leg. *Fuckin' football injuries.*

When the set was finally over—and he had sung everything from "Me and Julio Down by the School Yard" to "The Joker" to a short song he'd written about an agricultural festival in Georgia—Riley mistakenly thought he could walk off the stage despite the fact that his leg was asleep. When he stepped down from the stage, his left leg couldn't have folded any better if it had been aluminum foil. Thankfully, he just fell down on his ass and then rolled over on his side.

The Audacity of Dope

"I'm fine, I'm fine, I'm fine," Riley said as friends rushed to his aid. "My fuckin' leg's asleep, and like a goddamn idiot, I thought I could walk on it okay. I'm stupid as a mudhole."

All fretting about his well-being ended with the first fusillade of fireworks going off outside.

"Who do you think you are?" Melissa asked. "Fuckin' Ozzy Osbourne?"

For the next hour, Riley attempted to climb out of the fishbowl. He stopped drinking, drank water, breathed deeply. He wasn't sick. He was functioning. The fall hadn't been about being drunk, other than it being an indication of stupidity. Riley hadn't ever had his leg fall asleep onstage, but it had happened before when he sat awkwardly. Even drunk, he should've had enough sense to wait a minute or two before he put any weight on the leg. But…he hadn't.

"Probably be sore again in the morning," he told Melissa. "I'm 'bout to the point where it don't feel right not to be sore."

"Maybe I'll give you a massage," she said.

♫

The next morning Riley passed up a shave but took a hot shower. When he emerged from the steam, still drying himself, Melissa was still sleeping soundly. Riley put on a Dale Watson & His Lone Stars tee shirt and stepped into his jeans. Gently he sat on the edge of the bed and touched Melissa's shoulder.

She rubbed her eyes and squinted. "We leaving?"

"I gotta go to the track and play that breakfast. A bunch of people staying here are going to the race. I'll go down to the breakfast bar and hitch a ride to the track. All I'll need is my guitar. I'll leave the keys on the table, and you come get me later. You don't even have to stop by the office. Just leave the room key on the table. I'll pack my bag and put it in the truck before I go. All you'll have to do is put your stuff in the truck and drive out to the track. Make sure you keep that wrist band so you can get into the infield. As soon as I quit playing, they're going to be having

- 161 -

qualifying—that's when one car runs a lap by itself to set the starting lineup—and we can leave right then if you want."

Melissa yawned. "I kind of want to see the race. At least a little."

"That's cool, honey."

"Okay," she said and went back to sleep.

Riley and his guitar rode to the track in the backseat of an extended-cab Ford F250 that had "Jack Taft Racing, Goshen, Indiana, USA" printed on its sides. Riley presumed the man driving to be Jack Taft but wasn't sure. After riding through the tunnel, Riley offered his thanks and dismounted the behemoth. When he arrived at the party compound, no one was awake, so he sat on an ice cooler and softly sang "Green, Green Grass of Home." It was the bluegrass picker's idyll, commonly referred to as the "cold gray light of dawn."

The best-laid plans had called for music at eight. Now it appeared there wouldn't be anyone awake at eight. *Oh, well.*

Del Howard was among the first to rise. Blake Agnew was among the last. Breakfast was breathtakingly effective at diminishing hangovers. Ace Hawkins—saxophone in tow—arrived at about nine. He ad-libbed with Riley, using the sax, a mandolin and harmonicas at various times. Riley strummed away at simple songs and sang his ass (now fully awake) off, but Ace stole the show. They jammed right up until the first qualifier was roaring around the mile-long speedway.

Melissa arrived for the start of the race with minutes to spare. She and Riley climbed a ladder to the roof of one of the haulers in order to watch. Pop-up metal rails created a viewing platform.

As a field of thirty-six high-powered stock cars roared by them into the track's third turn for the first time, Melissa was transfixed. She started jumping up and down like a little girl at the Christmas Parade. On the seventh time by, a red car turned sideways right in front of the viewing platform. The screech of metal actually penetrated the engine roar as three more cars disappeared into the tire smoke and came careening out of it.

"I love this shit," Melissa said.

"What?"

"I fuckin' love this shit!"

"Oh," said Riley. "Right."

But about halfway through the race, with the field idling by and the yellow lights blinking for the fifth time, Melissa turned to Riley and said, "Okay, I'm good. We can leave now."

They got in the Corolla and buckled their seatbelts. Melissa counted money.

"Two hundred and seventeen dollars," she said. "That's how much we took in last night."

"Oh, well. It was damn sure something to do."

Del Howard knocked on the window. Riley rolled it down and Del handed him four twenties.

"That fair?"

"Sure," said Riley. "That's cool. I didn't come for the money, but it sure helps to make ends meet."

"You be careful," said Del, "and keep in touch."

"You don't get yourself killed neither, in no stock car, you hear?"

"I'll be careful as you," said Del, smiling as Riley and Melissa drove away.

CHAPTER EIGHTEEN
THE TECHNOLOGY CORRIDOR

After some rumination in the parking lot of a Food Lion, Riley and Melissa decided to make the three-hour drive back home, spend the night there, hopefully unbeknownst to all interested parties, and head up the road to Kentucky on Sunday. Riley decided to trade the Corolla for the Toyota truck, thus adding cargo space so could pack some equipment that might or might not be needed, a couple boxes of CDs and all the tee shirts he had left.

They got out of town a little after ten the next morning. Riley made a quick trip to the bank and the post office. They got biscuits and coffee at a Hardee's drive-through and headed up Interstate 26.

Melissa opened Riley's laptop and looked through emails as he drove.

"Now tell me one more time why we're going to Kentucky," she said.

"Well, we're gonna play some music with these friends of mine. Tonight we'll probably just move in and crash. I'd say, several nights this week, we'll just sit outside, under the stars, and play tunes, and people from town will come up, and we'll drink a little moonshine and drink some beer and smoke some weed.

"It'll be cool. Eric's house is up on top of a mountain. It'll be fairly empty in the daytime. He'll be off working, and there probably won't be anybody there but us and his dad. There's a pretty good chance nobody will know we're there, and even if they do, it'll be hard to find us. We can lay low, catch up on communications and email and shit, I can get some songwriting done, and hopefully it'll be just one big chance to relax and take a breath. Things might get a little...normal.

"Then, when the weekend comes, we'll go play with my friends at bars on Friday and Saturday night. They'll play, and I'll join them some, sing some harmony, and then I'll go on stage and play some of my songs with them. I might even play by myself when the band's on break. Then, a week from today, after time to think and communicate and make plans, we'll go somewhere else."

Melissa pondered this for a few moments.

"So it's kind of…a vacation?"

"More or less," said Riley. "They're my friends. I've got a lot of musician friends."

"No shit."

"They're people I can trust, and it's kind of rural. And a refuge. A safe harbor, I guess you could call it.

"That plus I need some weed," he said. "Badly. A good bit of it. It's plentiful up there."

"You'll be interested to know that, when you play at the America Celebrates America, you'll be joined by Claude Herndon, Lee Greenwood, major league pitcher Curt Schilling, comedian Dennis Miller, Lynyrd Skynyrd, the Beach Boys and others to be announced later."

"Hmm. What do you think the odds are we'll hear 'Sweet Home Alabama'?"

"Pretty strong," Melissa observed. "They want to know how many rooms you'll need for the band."

"I'm still recruiting the band, but let's see." Riley pondered the matter for a minute or so before concluding, "I think we need seven rooms."

"Check. I'll write back that we need seven rooms."

"Say we might need to fly a few people in. Inquire politely about expenses. It's not actually the Fourth of July, right? It's the Fifth, Saturday. We'll need to get there on, uh, the second. We can get together and rehearse. Mention that we'll need some place to do that, but I'm guessing they'll have everything set up and have some kind of schedule for sound checks and a dress rehearsal. On the third, maybe."

Melissa was typing right along with his instructions. "Okay, got it," she said. "Anything else?"

"When you mention expenses, phrase it so it doesn't close the door to being paid. Mention the need for transportation expenses and inquire as to how we are to be, uh, compensated."

"Umm, all right. That it?"

"Yeah, I think so. Send that mother.

"I got my printer in the truck bed," he said. "We can set it up in Eric's living room. He's got this three-part, wrap-around couch. I'm fairly sure that's where we'll be sleeping. We'll get all that straight when we get to Hyden."

"That's where we're going?"

"Yeah," Riley said. "It's this little coal-mining town. Ever heard of the Osborne Brothers?"

"No."

"They're a bluegrass duo. Or were. Bob and Sonny. One of them's dead now, I think. I saw them in concert once when I was a little kid. I was, like, eight, maybe. Opened for Charley Pride. My mother couldn't stand 'em."

"Do you know them? Are these guys in the band you know related or something."

"Nope," said Riley. "It's just a coincidence. Tom T. Hall wrote a great song called 'Trip to Hyden.' It's got some of my favorite words."

"So, did you, like, go there because you knew these songs, and look for musicians there?" asked Melissa, a bit discombobulated.

"No, nothing like that," Riley said. "I met Eric Hays and Wade McKeever and some gals from up there in a bar in Nashville. I admit, I thought it was kind of cosmic when I found out they were from Hyden, Kentucky, but we just hit it off, and next thing, we were writing songs together and, when I could get up there, we'd play together. Used to be we'd meet up in Nashville, where I had some gigs, but then Eric and Wade and them—the band is called the Grassy Knolls. Eric Hays and the Grassy Knolls."

"That's a cool name."

"Yeah," said Riley. "I like it."

Then Riley just zoned out, lost in thought. A couple times Melissa spoke and he didn't seem to hear her. The silence started with the rise of Interstate 40 into the Smoky Mountains past Asheville, North Carolina.

"You okay?" she asked.

Riley seemed to snap out of a trance. "Yeah, fine. Why?"

"You've been so quiet and glum since we got through talking about that email," Melissa said. "I feel like I'm sitting in a truck, riding hundreds of miles, with Stephen Wright driving."

"I'll get better. We'll stop in Knoxville and get some food. I'm just sort of contemplative 'cause I'm kind of meditating and thinking things through as I go along. Some of this shit you can plan, and some of it, you can't. Know what I mean?"

"Maybe," said Melissa.

"Hey, how much money we got? We should have a shitload of cash, right?"

"I got it in a zip-up sleeve in my travel bag," she said. "I'm sure there's, like, way over a thousand dollars, even after paying for the room in Rockingham."

"Yeah, and I still got the eighty dollars Del gave me. I put some songwriting money, couple checks, in the bank. I got a bunch of receipts in my wallet. Remind me to have you put them with the cash. Sometime this week, we'll work with the spreadsheets in my laptop. Gotta keep up for tax purposes."

"How much money do you make writing songs?"

"Enough to pay for most everything," Riley said. "There are royalties that get auto-deposited, and some that come in the mail. I've written enough songs that it's a pretty steady income. I've had, like, fifteen songs recorded by people that are…successful. None of them have been, like, chart-toppers or made into videos, but they've been recorded by fairly successful, critically acclaimed people, and several have been recorded by five or six different guys. People who have been nominated for Grammys. I think two of my songs have been on Grammy-nominated albums, one by, uh, this guy Brad Kent and another by the Cornhuskers, this roots-rock band in…"

"Nebraska?"

"Yeah. Nebraska. I think. I've never been there. Their shit's good, though."

"So you live on royalties from songs you've written?"

"Pretty much," said Riley. "I clear a little from playing in clubs, but songwriting pays the bills and keeps me on the road. I just try to make touring and recording pay for itself. I make, like, next to nothing on albums, but I've recorded, like, five. I've just been selling the latest one—it's about two years old—but I probably should get some of the others just to have available. Remind me to take care of that tomorrow."

Melissa added to the notes she was writing herself in a spiral notebook.

"And you have to sell 'em yourself?"

For the first time in the trip, Riley laughed a little.

"Nah," he said, "I just keep a few with me to fuck around with. They're in stores, usually the folk section or the Americana section or the alternative section. That's kind of weird because they're more country than anything else. But country isn't country anymore. Country is country for people who don't like country."

"I wouldn't be here," Melissa suddenly blurted, "if I hadn't watched you get cheap-shotted by a cop."

Riley glanced at Melissa, gauging her expression.

"Apparently a fake cop," he said, finally. "Pretty good message he sent, though. 'Don't fuck with Republicans, man.' They'll whup 'at ass. They don't like no back talk. They'll mess you up if you cross 'em.

"I'm their nigger. All white folks ought to know how that feels. I reckon I was overdue."

Riley thought for a few moments.

"I'm just sorting it out," he said. "I'm kind of in the rationalization stage. I'm about to do something detestable just so people will leave me alone. I'm trying to do the minimum that will get them to leave me alone and let me live my simple little pot-smoking, songwriting life. I don't want to be a hypocrite. It's hard. But I got to. And it's going to take some getting used to. I've kind of got a natural impression to do the stupid thing, which is usually, coincidentally, the honest thing. Some things, though, you can't be honest about. Sometimes you gotta play it smart.

"I fuckin' hate playing it smart."

They listened to music for a while. Not far from Newport, where civilization informally started again, Riley suddenly pulled the Tacoma into the breakdown lane.

"Something wrong?" Melissa asked.

"Nope. You see that sign?"

It read Tennessee Technology Corridor and was no more than ten yards in front of the parked truck. It was standing alone, surrounded by nothing but a mountainous landscape and manmade cliffs rising on each side of the highway. It struck him as funny.

"I'm taking a picture of that," he said. "Been meaning to for years. This time I saw it in time to stop."

"Why?"

"It's funny," he said. "It says Tennessee Technology Corridor and yet there's not a power line, not a house, not any sign of civilization in sight."

Melissa laughed. She got it.

Riley opened the bed cover, rummaged through a handbag and retrieved the digital camera. He took a photo of the sign, took a photo of Melissa with the sign and had Melissa take a photo of him with the sign.

"Already," he said, "the trip's first major accomplishment."

♫

On Interstate 26, earlier in the day, the pickup truck carrying Riley Mansfield and Melissa Franklin had been in the westbound lane at the same time a rental carrying Sue Ellen Spenser had been in the eastbound lane. By the time the pickup reached Asheville, North Carolina, Sue Ellen had sat in Mansfield's yard for an hour, driven around town aimlessly for a while and read a book while dining at a place called Fatz Café. Riley and Melissa were nearing the Kentucky border when Sue Ellen's cell rang.

"Hello, Garner."

"Abort the mission, Sue Ellen. Mansfield's all set. He's agreed to play ball, and all the details are being made. Come on back on the next plane."

"Can't wait," she said.

"I don't have the full details," said Garner Thomas, "but he's traveling up here a couple days early. Mike Ashton at the White House just copied me his email. I don't have any information about hotel or anything like that yet, but perhaps you can get together with him up here. I don't know. Everything seems to be fine, now."

"Why would I need to talk with him later?"

"Well, I don't think there's going to be any need. It's just that, from what I can gather, this Mansfield character's still kind of evasive. We might need someone to feel him out and make sure he's not trying to throw us a curveball of some sort. You might have to debrief him, but I doubt it. Somehow or another, he's apparently had the fear of God put in him, and I doubt he's got the balls to try to pull something. It sounds like he just wants to get it over with."

"All right," Sue Ellen said, sighing at the apparent waste of her time. "I'm headed back. Get me on the next plane out of Greenville-Spartanburg. I'll be at the airport in an hour."

♫

By the time the Republican Sue Ellen Spenser was headed back up I-26, the Democrat Priscilla Hay was checking into a Hampton Inn. She was unpacking and refolding her clothes when her cell rang. Her conversation, understandably, had a greater sense of urgency, and George Grinnell didn't know Mansfield had left town. He just knew that the reluctant hero had decided to be feted by President Sam Harmon on the National Mall.

Finding no signs of life at Mansfield's house, Priscilla saw the brick house across the pasture and surmised correctly that someone else in the family, most likely Riley's mother, lived there.

After knocking politely on the door for some time, it was opened to Priscilla by a middle-aged woman who seemed a bit impaired. She identified herself as Louise, Riley's sister.

"He's done gone," she said, grandiosely waving the hand that wasn't anchoring her to the screen door. "Kentucky, I think."

"Kentucky?"

"Yeah, I think he's in Kentucky. He's got music friends up there. I expect he's of a mind to kind of hide out till all this shit dies down. Know what I mean?"

Priscilla politely excused herself, a bit taken aback by this woman's not bothering to ask her name or a reason for being there. She made a call to George Grinnell to tell him she was pursuing Mansfield to Kentucky without bothering to tell her senior associate that she had no idea where in Kentucky he was.

What Priscilla found out back at the Hampton Inn, though, was that Riley Mansfield, like almost all musicians, had a MySpace page. There were numerous Kentuckians on the friends' list. At the top of Riley's "best friends" was the page of a band known as the Grassy Knolls. There were two members of that band whose individual members were also right at the top. Their names were Eric Hays and Wade McKeever. They lived in a town called Hyden, which was in southeastern Kentucky.

Priscilla booked herself a flight back to Washington the next morning, then made arrangements to fly on Friday to Lexington, Kentucky. The Grassy Knolls were playing that night in a bar called the Blue Moon Lounge in Richmond, Kentucky. According to her road atlas, Hyden and Richmond appeared to be at least an hour's drive apart. Priscilla reserved a room for herself in London, conveniently nestled alongside Interstate 75 and apparently equidistant to the two towns.

♫

The sun was setting when Riley pulled off the Hal Rogers Parkway and proceeded down a long grade into the hollow where the town of Hyden had settled like silt in a mountain stream. Signs paid homage to the Osborne Brothers, but the highway, the "pass," was named after Tim Couch, the underachieving pro-football quarterback.

CHAPTER NINETEEN
MAMA BLAZES

Riley and Melissa stopped at a BP convenience store entering town, where the cell phone had "no bars," so Riley called Eric Hays from a pay phone. He filled the gas tank and drove on through town. Most of the traffic consisted of coal trucks.

Riley took a right onto a gravel road a couple miles out of town, and from there they slowly made their way up, the road edging upward to the contours of a hill and passing occasional driveways.

"Eric's house is on top of this mountain," Riley said. "The privacy is unbelievable. You can sit out under the stars, and the only audience is God.

"I should prepare you a little, I guess. Eric lives with his dad, Ethan. Ethan's kind of reclusive. He's really quiet and maybe a little scary, if you don't know him. He's got kind of a haunted look, and, you know, I guess he's kind of a broken man. He takes medication, and Eric has to get up every day or so and fill up these little containers so that Ethan will take his medication at the right times."

Melissa had a wary look.

"Look, he's a really good man, a really tranquil man," Riley said. "Tomorrow, Eric'll have to go to work, and Ethan and I will probably be the only ones up for quite a while—as you have undoubtedly noticed, I rarely need much sleep—and we'll sit at the kitchen table and talk. He'll just sit there, smoke and drink coffee, and we'll talk quietly and he'll tell me little stories. It's cool, but he takes a little getting used to. It kind of makes you feel like you're going back in time, talking to a man who just stepped out of the Great Depression."

"Does he...blaze?"

Riley chuckled. "You're really getting pretty conscious of this, aren't you?"

"I just wondered," she said. "I mean, he's this Eric guy's father."

"I know what you're saying. That's exactly the way I felt the first time I came up here, but you'll find the people up in these hills amazingly tolerant. There's a lot of weed grown up here—it's kind of marijuana country—and it's a poor area. It also kind of reminds you of what you hear about back in the fifties, moonshiners and revenuers. They resent the feds coming in here with their choppers in the air, busting the pot growers.

"I guess this is Copperhead Road, when you get right down to it."

"But back to the original question…"

"There's kind of an informal understanding," Riley said. "When you go smoke a joint, you just go out on the porch. Or walk down overlooking the valley, where there are some chairs and benches. Ethan knows it's going on. Just as a general rule, if you know him, there ain't much he misses. But, I guess, since he's kind of, uh, different, the general rule of thumb is you don't want to…I guess, I don't know…tempt him or something.

"But you don't need to worry about talking about it or say 'hey, let's go burn one,' or nothing like that. You just don't blaze in the house, that's all."

"Gotcha," she said, and now Riley was getting up a head of steam, almost spinning the truck around and gunning it up a switchback that was almost too steep to manage without four-wheel drive.

"It's actually worse when it's dry, like now," he said above the spinning wheels and flying gravel. "When it's damp or rainy, the tires get more grip. I pity those folks in the house down behind us. We're throwing up a cloud of dust."

After another hard left turn at the top of the road, Riley pulled into the crowded front of Eric Hays' simple but fairly large house. Three cars, two pickups and a van were parked out front. Behind all the vehicles was a backhoe. An old riding mower was stopped in the yard, as if that were the place where it had broken down.

Riley grabbed his gig bag and slung it over his back. He unlocked the roll-back bed cover. Melissa grabbed her suitcase. Eric Hays and Wade McKeever emerged on the porch, offering help.

Ethan Hays, bearded and gaunt, sat at the kitchen table, expressionless. A couple of kids, probably in their late teens or early twenties, with their sweethearts, sat on the couch. The boy had a guitar on his knee. There were guitars everywhere: in a trophy case, on stands, one fashioned into a lamp, acoustics, electrics, electric acoustics, basses and a dobro. A mandolin hung from a column in the middle of the large room, which served as kitchen, living room and office all in one.

A jar of moonshine was on the kitchen table, almost full.

"This is Melissa," Riley said. "She's my new manager. I've known her all my life and I'm teaching her how to be my manager right now because my other one dropped me."

"Well, tell us about you being the big hero," Wade said.

"It'll come out gradual," said Riley. "Let's just play some music and let it come out when it wants to."

"We got some more friends might show up," Eric said.

Wade was on Eric's computer, working on the MySpace page.

"Melissa, I want you to get with Wade here," Riley said. "He's, like, a wizard on MySpace. He knows how to network. Their band's got more friends in their list than Springsteen."

"I don't reckon Springsteen actually fucks with MySpace," Wade said. "He's probably got two dozen pages set up in his honor."

"Come on," said Eric, "let's go out over the valley there and make us a bonfire."

Darkness was falling on the ridge as Riley and Eric stacked wood on a bed of cardboard and kindling.

"So, uh, what's with Melissa?" Eric asked.

"I grew up with her. She teaches school now at my old high school. If everything works out, though, I think she might give it up. I'm in a world of shit right now. If she can help me through this, she can probably help me through anything."

"What's the deal, man? What's up with this hero thing? Did you, like, keep some raghead from blowing up your plane?"

Riley sighed and told the story.

"Fuck," Eric said. "That's the goddamndest thing I ever heard."

"And here's the thing, Eric. Here's what I keep thinking about. If it hadn't been for the most unbelievable fucking accident in the history of the world, I'd be dead and they'd think it was me who had blown up the goddamned thing."

♫

Everyone save Ethan came out to the overlook, where the fire came to life to provide light and protection from the mosquitoes. They took turns playing songs—Riley, Eric, Wade and Chuckie, a kid, who had an affinity for John Prine—most of which they wrote but some of which they didn't. Riley followed up Chuck's "Illegal Smile" with another Prine song, "The Glory of True Love." Sips of moonshine followed a joint around the fire. Melissa took a decent sip.

"It's smooth," she said, turning hoarse for a second. "Strong, but smooth."

Riley smiled. "Ain't you glad you took a few shots in Rockingham?"

"Yep," said Melissa. "I'm learning a lot of shit from you. This is different, though. That moonshine in Rockingham had a peach floating in it."

"You see more of that in the Carolinas," Riley said. "It's kind of the moonshine version of brandy, sort of. Up here it's mainly white liquor."

The guitars were functional because they occupied everyone. They kept everyone occupied enough to avoid oblivion. They just "maintained."

Eric and Wade were first-class guitarists. Riley just knew

chords. He strummed; they picked. There was nothing, though, he loved better than sitting on that hill, around that campfire, hearing magical guitarists make his songs—his songs—sound heavenly.

Here's what heaven is, he thought. Eric had that Don Rich sound going. Wade was studying and experimenting and gradually adding in blues riffs.

At the end of "Tattooed Gal," Wade turned to Riley and said, "Son, I ain't never heard you sing this good."

"That's 'cause this is one of the few times you've ever heard me sing when I wasn't worried about the cops busting the motel-room door in at any second," Riley replied.

"It's not hard to cut it loose on this mountain," he concluded. "This may not be close to God, but it's a step in the right direction. It's just a closer walk with Thee, so to speak. It may be in a decidedly secular sense, but it's righteous nonetheless."

Then they sang a couple gospel songs—"Lord Help Me Jesus" was one—and passed another joint.

"Melissa," Riley said, "Why don't you sing us a song, darlin'?"

"I don't know…"

"Do you like to sing?"

"Kinda. I took piano lessons for several years when I was little."

"You still play?"

"A little."

"Gimme a song you know all the words to."

"You know that Sheryl Crow song? 'All I Wanna Do Is Have Some Fun'? Something like that?"

Riley chuckled. "I got no clue. Wade, you know that song?"

"I might can pick it out a little."

"Sound good with a slide, wouldn't it?"

"It might," said Wade, who rather amazingly approximated the opening licks.

Melissa did know all the words. She could sing, too. Like an angel.

"Would you kindly excuse my candor?" asked Riley afterwards.

"What?"

Riley lowered his voice and whispered conspiratorially, "I'm pretty sure I want to fuck you here in a little while."

Alas, it was not to be. By two in the morning, it was a miracle there were no casualties from the group staggering back to the house. Melissa and Riley settled for a tender kiss in the darkness and bedded down on opposite wings of the three-piece couch.

Riley went to sleep obsessed with the notion of getting a room.

♬

Naturally, Riley rose early and retrieved a trash bag from behind the passenger seat of his truck. In it were a checkbook and a mountain of magazines, checks and bills. Predictably, Ethan quietly joined him, turning on the coffee pot and sitting down at the opposite side of the kitchen table while Riley looked at the contents of envelopes and wrote checks.

"I hear tell you's some sort of hero," Ethan said quietly.

"Nah. People want to make me one. I just saved my own skin."

"Was you on some kind of airplane?"

"Yeah, there was this guy who wanted to blow up the plane. And just by pure luck, I came across the bomb. So I threw it out and it blew up. Everything else started blowing up then, too."

Ethan lit a cigarette.

"I remember back when me and my brother Chuck got interested in stock-car racing," he said. "Next thing I knowed, we'd done built ourself a car and was racing at a dirt track over there in Winchester. We didn't never win none. Chuck got flustered at hisself a'ter he wrecked it a couple times, and he said I ort to give it a whirl myself."

Riley just kept on paying bills, considering what determined the course of Ethan's wandering mind.

"One time, we 'uz setting there back behind the third turn— that's where you could work on the cars and all—and this little bird lit on the edge of the truck bed. And I looked at it, and it seemed like it looked right back at me." Ethan paused a while to take a drag off the cigarette and chase it with a sip of coffee. "Then, there, after a little while, it hopped a little and flapped its wings and landed right thahr on my shoulder. It stayed thahr for quite a while."

Riley walked away for a short time to fetch a little zip-up bag that held receipts, envelopes and postage stamps.

"You were talking about the bird sitting on your shoulder?"

"Yeah," Ethan said, searching his psyche. "Oh. Well, y'see, after that little bird come and gone, I reckon it left something that told me I didn't have no business trying to race that car. So, when I told Chuck that, he just loaded the car back up on the trailer and we went home and didn't never go back no more."

"Do you still got that car off somewhere?"

Ethan considered the question. "I don't rightly know," he said.

♫

Riley fetched his electric shaver, turned on the television—it had been on all night and Riley wondered how it had gotten switched off—and watched MSNBC. Seemingly, he had faded from the news again. Nineteen had been killed in a suicide bombing; Riley wasn't paying enough attention to discern whether it was in Iraq, Afghanistan or someplace else. The Dow was falling. Gas was rising. Not even Pat Buchanan had much nice to say about President Sam Harmon.

Eric paraded across the floor back and forth from the bedroom to bathroom, pulling on his jeans as he made the return trip. He had to go to work, and Riley timed him from the moment the bedroom door opened till the front door closed behind him. Twenty-seven minutes. *Not bad*, Riley thought.

He pulled out an old paperback he was reading—Dodsworth, by Sinclair Lewis—and chuckled at the deft satire being hurled at the meat-and-potatoes industrialists of the 1920s.

Melissa arose slowly, with several fits and starts, until finally she strolled over, smiling, and plopped down next to Riley, who put his arm around her. They snuggled.

"You feel ah'ight?"

"Yeah," she said. "I'm good. Still a little dreamy. You?"

"I hardly ever get a hangover. Never when weed's involved."

The room was still darkened. Ethan was still sitting silently at the kitchen table.

"Who's here?" Melissa asked.

"Just you and me and Ethan. Eric left a few minutes ago."

"Let me go to the little girls' room," she said.

It was an overcast and cool day, the air so damp that it seemed almost like a light drizzle. Riley took his guitar and held hands with Melissa as they walked slowly to the overlook. They sat down on the bench, which was fashioned out of a crosstie. He leaned the guitar next to him, lit a joint, took a hit and handed it to Melissa on the other side.

"I got a motel room for tonight," he said. "There's a Hampton Inn in London. Two, in fact. I took the cheaper."

"You called 'em?"

"Laptop," he said. "Remember? The Sprint card works just fine up here."

"Tonight?"

"Right up to Saturday. We'll have to help load the equipment then. After the gig Friday, Eric'll leave everything at the club. We'll drive back to the room; it's not as far as it is from Richmond to here. Saturday night it'll all have to be brought back here. They could probably use some space in my pickup. So we'll spend Saturday night here again."

"Isn't that, like, a lot of money?"

"Hilton points," Riley said. "I got a lot of Hilton points."

"We should live up here," said Melissa. "Everybody's really friendly. They're so…"

"Honest?"

"Yeah."

"They're the least hypocritical folks ever I been around."

"Riley?"

He held in a lung full of smoke. "Yeah?"

"You're starting to sound like them."

He coughed his guts out.

"They don't drug-test you when you teach school?" Riley asked.

"Haven't before," she said. "They're starting this year."

"Whoa."

"Explains a lot, doesn't it?" Melissa lit a cigarette. "I was looking for an escape."

Riley smiled. "Surely you didn't target little old me for a way out?"

"Well, I was looking," she said. "That night at Timmy's, I was going to talk to you about it and see if you could give me some advice. 'Course you beat me to the punch. Went out and had to be a hero."

"Uh, until recently, I had this girl on the road," he said. "One that meant a lot to me."

"And?"

"We had this real, uh, real bad breakup," he said. "It was right before I came up here the first time."

"Funny thing about getting your guts ripped out. You get a fuckin' great song out of it."

"Oh, yeah?"

"I played it at Rockingham. 'Slip Away.' Remember it? 'Sitting on the front porch in the rain…'"

"Yeah," Melissa said. "I really liked it. It's probably the song I love the most out of the ones I've heard you sing."

Riley pointed at Eric's house. "That's the front porch I was sitting on in the rain."

"I got a bong," said Melissa, from out of nowhere.

"Your mama know?"

"Mama blazes."

CHAPTER TWENTY
BIG WHEEL KEEPS ON TURNIN'

When Henry Poston and Ike Spurgeon arrived at the Federal Bureau of Investigation office in Columbia, South Carolina early Monday morning, the Deputy Director of Homeland Security was waiting for them, and they were ushered into a conference room.

"Agent Poston, Agent Spurgeon, we need to talk about a matter of grave concern," said Banks McPherson. "I've reviewed your report regarding the aviation incident at Greenville-Spartanburg Airport. According to the transcript of Riley Mansfield, there's some…confusion regarding the context of his remarks. Who wrote the report?"

"I did, sir," said Poston.

"Here's the section I have some questions about. Mansfield is quoted as saying, 'You think this was all an elaborate publicity stunt?' Then his next response is, and I quote, 'I'm assuming you arrested the Muslim-looking fucker who rammed that little bomb into my guitar.' Then Mr. Mansfield is quoted as saying, or asking, 'I mean, you do have him in custody?'"

"Yes, sir."

"By phone, you told me that no information was divulged to Mr. Mansfield about the profile of the suspect."

"Yes, sir, that's correct."

"Are you absolutely sure of that?"

"Yes, sir, it's policy except in certain instances where it might be useful in advancing an investigation."

McPherson turned to Ike. "Agent Spurgeon, you also participated in the interview in question?"

"That's correct, sir."

"And you are also absolutely sure that no information was provided Mansfield about the profile of the suspect."

"Yes, sir."

"Why was a complete transcript, including both questions and answers, not included in the report?"

"The gist of the questions was included," said Poston.

"Do you have the tape?"

"Uh, no, sir. We used a digital recorder, and it was erased after being transcribed for the report."

"Is this official policy?" asked McPherson.

"We save and download the interviews when it is deemed necessary, Mr. McPherson," said Poston. "In this instance, Mansfield wasn't seriously considered a suspect. My conclusion was that the perception that he saved the lives of the passengers on that plane was the correct one. We quickly concluded, after reviewing transcripts taken from the flight attendant, pilot and co-pilot, that Mansfield was involved only in stopping the prime suspect's attempt to destroy the plane."

"Why did you not question him more specifically?"

"Because," said Spurgeon, "we had already reviewed the transcript of a detailed interview of Mansfield by local law-enforcement officials. Our interview was merely supplemental."

McPherson shuffled papers and considered what the agents had said.

"You will provide me that transcript?"

"Yes, sir." They spoke at the same time.

"Very well," he said finally. "Thank you for your time."

"Is there any particular reason," Poston asked, "why you flew all the way down here to talk to us?"

"That's proprietary to the investigation, of which this office is no longer involved," said McPherson.

"This is just a whistlestop for me, gentlemen," he added. "I'm working on a report on the incident that was requested by the White House and Congress. I'm proceeding from here to several other locations today and tomorrow."

"Then that's all?"

"Yes. Thank you, both of you, for your cooperation."

♫

McPherson met Jed Langston in a Cuban restaurant near Miami International Airport. This was to be McPherson's first encounter with David Branham's fundamentalist hit man. He imagined John Brown, but the man who sauntered over to his table didn't look like a fanatic. Red hair, carefully combed. A round, freckled face. Only the bright-blue eyes betrayed Langston. The eyes were intense, which set them apart.

"Jed, I presume?" McPherson stood up to shake hands.

"Yessir, it's good to meet you, Mr. McPherson."

McPherson motioned for Langston to sit down.

"We are two blocks away from Tiant's Hardware," said McPherson. "Philippe Tiant doesn't actually have much to do with its operation."

"It's a front?"

"Yes, a front," said McPherson. "We run some undercover operations out of there. This has been in place since the CIA was involved in some operations in Central America back in the nineteen eighties."

"Iran-Contra."

"That's correct. Tiant usually comes into the store early each morning and leaves at about the time the doors open. The store maintains a retail presence. The front of it is stocked, and there's a modest amount of local business. There's no advertising, selection is limited and prices are a little on the high side. The building is designed in a way that suggests that the back of the building is empty and unrented. But that's where Tiant will be. He usually arrives no later than seven each morning. Park in the back and wait for him."

Langston ordered a Cuban sandwich and iced tea. McPherson ordered fried grouper accompanied with rice and plantains. And a Diet Coke, which came in a can accompanied by a glass of ice. Though the waitress was bilingual, no one else in the restaurant was speaking English, and there were only a few other patrons. McPherson reasoned that it was the kind of place where the great majority of business occurred after five in the afternoon.

"What instructions have you got for me?" asked Langston.

"Identify yourself as being with Homeland Security. Go inside with Tiant and discuss the incident at Greenville-Spartanburg with him. See what he has to say. Reassure him that his role in the incident has been completely hidden and that his safety is assured. Gauge his mood. Listen carefully. Don't betray any opinions. Just be a listening post."

"Do you anticipate a problem?"

"Well," said McPherson, "we are a bit distressed that he might be somewhat desperate and angry."

"And that is because?"

McPherson sighed. "It's hard to say this delicately. He is undoubtedly concerned about the incident…because…he had been led to believe that the bomb he was carrying was not actually capable of exploding. What was pitched to Mr. Tiant was that he was to be detained after the plane landed. Then we would switch him for another suspect, an Arab, and the incident would be a means of…elevating citizen awareness regarding the threat of terrorism."

"Thus helping President Harmon get re-elected."

"Correct."

"But someone in the White House decided that wouldn't be enough."

"Not the President," said McPherson.

"The Vice President?"

"Not the Vice President."

"Lee Cartwright."

"I met with the Chief of Staff last night," said McPherson.

Food arrived. Both men ate quietly, digesting the conversation, as well.

"And, after gauging Mr. Tiant's state of mind and evaluating the risk factors, what am I supposed to do regarding the conclusions made?"

"You are to take whatever action you deem necessary," said McPherson. "Cartwright and Branham have the utmost confidence in your judgment."

"Will I have some assistance?"

"Two other Homeland Security agents will accompany you. I believe you are familiar with Leeds McCormick."

"Yes, sir, we go back ten years to when we were both working abroad for the NSA and CIA, through the U.S. Information Agency, and he's been involved with me in the Riley Mansfield…case."

"The other agent is Kurt Hasselbeck. They will be present merely for assistance. You are to interview Tiant alone."

"And take whatever action I feel is appropriate."

"Correct."

"The Lord's will be done," said Langston.

"Amen," said McPherson, shocking himself when the word escaped his mouth.

♬

"Did I tell you this reporter with *Rolling Stone* was gonna be hanging out for a few days?" Riley asked.

"Riley, you have this unbelievable knack for springing surprises early in the morning," said Melissa. "Why would you grant an interview to *Rolling Stone*?"

"Oh, I don't know," he said. "Maybe because it's, like, the most important music magazine there is."

"But how about all this secrecy you've been surrounding yourself with, this hiding and avoiding the media, for the last three weeks?"

"I talked to the guy on the phone a few days ago. I told him we could hang out under the condition that nothing could be published until after the Fourth of July. Nothing online. Nothing at all until the deal in Washington is over with."

"And you trust this guy? You remember his name?"

"It's in my laptop…somewhere."

Melissa started laughing.

"What?"

"I was just thinking," she said. "What if we were supposed to meet this guy, and there was this knock on the door, and you opened the door…and it's that deputy? Barton Fleming."

"That's not funny," Riley said, but he started laughing, anyway.

"When's he getting here?"

"Barton Fleming?"

"*Rolling Stone.*"

"Sometime today."

"Oh, great."

"C'mon, Missy. He works for *Rolling Stone.* He's cool. We don't have to change nothing. He'll just be cramped up in that bench seat in the truck, that's all."

They laughed a little more.

"How do you know he's so cool?" Melissa asked.

"I read *Rolling Stone.*"

"And he's gonna follow us around and write about everything."

"Yeah."

"And you're not worried about that?"

"Nope," Riley said. "After the Fourth of July, I ain't worried about nothing."

♫

"So…what's your impression of Riley Mansfield?" asked Jed Langston, who was riding down LeJeune Road in the passenger seat. Kurt Hasselbeck drove the navy-blue Crown Vic. Langston turned around to hear Leeds McCormick's response.

"I think he'll do what the president wants him to do," said McCormick from the backseat. "The main thing I saw in his eyes was fear."

"I had a conversation with him at a wild party in the infield of a race track. Rockingham, North Carolina," said Langston. "He's a friendly enough fellow, but all you've got to do is listen to his music to tell he's a liberal. And a druggie.

"Okay, Kurt, take a right a block before that red light, drive a block and see if you can park on the street."

The back of Tiant's Hardware had a small blacktop parking lot, but it was obscured by a yellow frame house between it and a side street. Hasselbeck parked with a clear view of the road connecting the street to the lot.

"Either of you had any dealings with Tiant?" Langston asked.

Hasselbeck shook his head. "Heard the name," said McCormick.

"I met him once, I think," said Langston. "He's a little guy. Cuban refugee. Has relatives back in Havana. He got active in the Cuban community because he hates Castro. We put him in business partly because he's somewhat alone. Has few family ties. He's just a simple guy, really, who got energized by what happened to his family."

A burgundy Ford Contour pulled into the lot behind the store.

"I'll walk," Langston said. "Stay right here. I've got a text message I've saved in my 'drafts' folder. When I'm ready for you to drive up, I'll send the message."

Langston started to get out.

"Have any idea what you're gonna do, Jed?" McCormick asked.

"Nope," he replied, "but I've prayed about it."

♫

Melissa was almost dressed. Riley looked up from the laptop.

"Guy from *Rolling Stone* won't be here till tomorrow," he said. "Adam Rhine. R-H-I-N-E. Like Lenoir-Rhyne, the college. Only I think the college has a 'y,' not an 'i.' He's coming by sometime late in the morning, I think."

"So what are we doing today? Going back to Hyden?"

"Why don't we take a road trip?"

"I'm up for that," said Melissa.

"We'll drive down the parkway to Pikeville. I don't know what we'll come across, but it'll be scenic. I'll take the guitar, we'll stop and get some fried chicken and we'll have a picnic somewhere."

Melissa nodded to the laptop. "Everything okay out there in the Great Unknown?"

"Nothing that can't wait a day," Riley said. "Let's go somewhere and relax."

♫

"Hey, hey, Luis," said Langston. He called the short, chunky man Luis, not Phillipe, because the former pitcher Luis Tiant was the only other Tiant with whom Langston had been familiar. "Jed Langston. We worked together once…over near Tampa, I think."

"Jed, good to see you," said Tiant, sizing him up. "You know, El Tiante is a distant cousin of mine. Come in. Something to drink? Coke?"

"Diet, if you got it." Langston sat on a dusty gray couch. Everything seemed to be gray, right down to the canisters of arms lined up on shelves.

"Can I take your jacket? It will take a while for the air conditioning to kick in."

"Don't bother. It's just seven in the morning. I'm a bit cold-natured."

Tiant handed Langston a Diet Coke and sat down. "Now what can I do for you?" he asked.

"It's just follow-up, Philippe. Agency took me off surveillance for a few days and put me to work doing a report on the incident at Greenville-Spartanburg." Langston pulled out a digital recorder from the jacket pocket on his left side and flipped it on.

Tiant's expression darkened. "It was not supposed to blow up, Jed. It was not even supposed to be a bomb."

"It wouldn't have blown up, Philippe. The reason it went off is because the grove of peach trees where it exploded was thirty feet below the altitude of the runway."

"That's risky, no?"

"The device did exactly what it was programmed to do," said Langston. "Highly sophisticated and reliable piece of equipment."

Tiant sat quietly, considering what Langston had said. "No. I don't believe you. If it hadn't been for that man, it would've blown up on the plane."

"That's ridiculous, Philippe."

"Branham told me it was not a bomb. He said I would be detained after the plane landed."

Branham. The National Security Adviser. In the White House.

"They decided I was expendable," said Tiant, voice rising. "They decided the passengers on that little fucking plane were expendable. All so the President could get—what is it they call it?—a bump in the polls."

Langston had had enough. He shut off the recorder. He'd made up his mind, secure in his understanding of God's will. "Can we trust you to remain quiet, Philippe?"

For the first time, fright registered in the little man's dark eyes. "Yes," he said, "but goddamn it, Jed, I want out of this business. I won't tell a soul, but I want out."

"I think that's completely understandable, Philippe. I just wanted to be sure we could trust you not to talk to anyone. You've had an unfortunate experience—I only know what I've been told, and that is that the bomb wasn't going to explode if that plane had landed—and I'm not going to write what you said just now. I'm going to make sure you get a nice, clean break. Because we're friends, right?"

"That's right, Jed."

Langston put his left arm around Tiant, yanking on his left shoulder to pull him closer. They walked together to the back door in a veritable bear hug, Langston fawning affection. A tin trash can sat next to where a shelf ended, short of the end of the wall, next to the door. As they reached the trash can, Langston removed his hand from Tiant's shoulder and grabbed his head, wrenching it toward the trash can.

"What? Jed!"

Langston quickly shifted his grip to the side of Tiant's neck and pinned his side against the side of the trash can. He retrieved a small pistol from his right jacket pocket and fired it into Tiant's temple point blank. Blood splattered into the plastic liner. Langston was pleased that the sound of the bullet penetrating Tiant's skull was muffled a bit. He slowly let the trash can tumble to the ground, replacing the pistol in his pocket and lifting the dead man's leg so that he could slide his upper body into the can, which was now laying on its side. He retrieved Tiant's car keys.

Pulling the cell phone from its holster, Langston called up the drafts folder and sent the message. *Done. Drive around.* The blue Ford pulled up as Langston walked out to greet it.

Hasselbeck and McCormick climbed out. "Make it a suicide," said Langston, who returned to the car, climbed into the driver's seat and prayed. He grabbed a small briefcase from the floorboard on the passenger side and retrieved a religious text that contained "The Pilgrim's Psalm," a modern adaptation from Psalms and the Epistles of St. Paul:

> *I will put on the whole armour of light that I may be able to stand in the evil day.*
> *The shield of faith, the helmet of salvation, the breastplate of righteousness, the sword of the spirit.*
> *God girdeth me with strength of war and maketh my way perfect.*
> *Yea, I will smite mine enemies, they shall not be able to stand, but fall under my feet.*
> *Blest be the Lord my strength that teacheth my hands to war and my fingers to fight, my hope and my fortress, my castle and my deliverer, my defence in whom I trust.*
> *I will not be afraid of the terror by night, nor for the arrow that flieth by day, for thou, Lord, art my hope,*

Thou hast set my house of defence very high.
I will go forward valiant in fight, and put to flight the armies of evil.
He that overcometh shall inherit all things.

After Hasselbeck and McCormick had finished their work, Langston gave Hasselbeck the keys to Tiant's Ford and a business card with the location of a garage near Calder Race Course. He and McCormick drove to Homestead Air Force Base, where a government plane was waiting.

"Shame about Tiant," said McCormick.

"Yeah. Shame. He was expendable, though. That's why they put him on that plane in the first place. In the greater scheme of things, he was just one more problem we don't have anymore."

At the landing strip, Langston handed the car keys to McCormick.

"Leeds, be sure to take every precaution. You stay down here as long as it takes. Avoid any conflicts with local law enforcement. Homeland Security has the right to handle the investigation of incidents affecting the War on Terrorism. You don't have to explain. You just have to be firm. You and Kurt take control of this. Go to Tiant's house. Go through all his personal effects. Review his records. Make sure you take care of every contingency. If everything goes well, Tiant will just be a man who barely existed in the first place. If necessary, make him disappear. If you have to go the suicide route, do it, but we don't want this getting any attention."

They shook hands.

"Just remember, Leeds, this country cannot withstand a takeover by the godless Democrats," he said before boarding the plane.

CHAPTER TWENTY-ONE
THE BLUE...GRASS STATE

Riley Mansfield was taken aback when he greeted Adam Rhine at ten on Tuesday morning at his motel room door. The *Rolling Stone* writer's attire was a bit off the beaten path for London, Kentucky. He looked as if he had stepped out of the pages of *Esquire*, or, even, *Rolling Stone*.

Rhine wore a brown, silk-and-cotton, suit and pin-striped white dress shirt. The shoes were buckled loafers, and Riley was willing to bet the socks were of some bright hue.

"We gotta buy you some clothes, man," Riley said.

"What?"

"Too fashionable for Kentucky."

"What would you suggest?"

Riley smirked. "Overalls, maybe. Plaid flannel shirt. Work boots. Straw hat. No, seriously. You got some sneakers?"

"Jogging shoes."

"I believe I'd wear them as a general course. This is jeans-and-tee-shirt country. You look good, man, but fashion is a good five years behind here and most of it don't get here at all.

"Hey, come in." Riley was barefoot, wearing sweatpants and a "Keep Austin Weird" tee shirt. He sat on the bed and motioned for Rhine to pull up a chair.

"So, how do you want to handle this? You want to begin with a, what, formal interview?"

Melissa came out of the bathroom, wearing her shorts and his shirt, with a towel wrapped around her head.

"Meet Melissa," Riley said. "Melissa, this is Adam. Melissa is my invaluable associate." She laughed. "It's all I could come up with," Riley said, "on such short notice."

"I'll be back shortly," she said. "Gotta dry my hair."

"So, you want to start with an interview?"

"Sure," said Rhine. "We can talk. Mainly I just want to hang out with you, ask questions, make observations. In a day or two, we'll have a photographer come in, as soon as I can make some judgments on what kind of art would fit the story."

Riley nodded and opened the drawer next to the bed. "You blaze?" he asked. "Of course you do. You work for *Rolling Stone*."

"I'll have a hit or two."

Riley got up, cracked the door and placed the "Do Not Disturb" tag on the knob. "Like I said…it's Kentucky."

Riley lit the joint, took a hit and passed it to Rhine.

"I always wondered," he said, before inhaling, holding in the smoke and exhaling, "when you read all these articles, and the writer just openly 'fesses up to taking drugs with rock stars…Why don't the writers get hassled by the cops? I'd be worried they'd be tailing me around, trying to catch me."

Rhine thought a moment, exhaled his own stream of smoke, and replied, "I guess it's a matter of not living in places where anybody gives a fuck."

"Pretty good answer."

"I wasn't really sure what to expect," said Rhine. "You're seen as somewhat of an enigma."

"I don't know what that is. I just want to preserve my life as best I can. I didn't want to be a hero. I just did what I had to do. My main priority was just saving myself. I don't really think it was that heroic, and I certainly don't want to be seen as any kind of hero. I just want to write my songs, play my little gigs and make a living, like before."

"Surely you recognize the impossibility of that."

"I guess. I just don't want to do anything to encourage it. Maybe things won't ever get back to 'normal,' okay? But I can try to get back to as close to normal as possible."

"You're performing at the Fourth of July celebration in Washington."

"Yeah. I didn't want to, but I've kind of been pressured into it."

"How so?"

Melissa emerged again. Riley handed her the joint and asked her, "Where are the photos?"

She took a healthy hit, extinguished the roach on the surface of her tongue and retrieved a manila envelope from her suitcase.

"Melissa took these," Riley said, handing the envelope to Rhine.

Rhine glanced at each. "That's you getting beat up by the cop?"

"Uh, huh. He was an imposter. Came to deliver a message that I needed to play ball with the politicians. I've also had my truck searched outside a bar in Florida and been stopped on the highway in North Carolina and searched again."

"So you decided to play ball?"

"I told them I'd shake hands with Harmon and do a couple patriotic songs. It's the least I could get away with it. They wanted me to tour the country with the campaign and shit."

"I take it you're not much of a Republican."

"That's one way of putting it."

"Most of the songs you've had covered were by country artists," said Rhine. "Is that one reason why you've been reluctant to express yourself politically?"

"I express myself in my songs," Riley replied, "but, to answer your question, no, that has nothing to do with it. I've got no particular incentive to get along with the music industry. I've been able to make a decent living in spite of it. No one hassles me for my beliefs. I just write songs, they look at them, and if there's promise, I guess, or if they think there's promise, I end up making money. I'm not significant enough for politics to be an issue. At least not until I fucked up and didn't get myself blown up in an airplane."

"Look, you staying here?"

"Yeah," said Rhine. "Room two fourteen. I actually got in late last night."

"Let me shave and shower, get dressed. You go back to the room and put some jeans on if you got 'em…"

"I got 'em."

"Good. I'll call you in forty-five minutes or so, and we can ride around, get some lunch, maybe stop somewhere scenic and shoot the shit."

Rhine switched off his recorder. "Can I get a copy of these photos?" he asked.

"Sure. I'll send the files by email. Let me guess: arhine@rollingstone.com?"

"Actually, it's 'awrhine'."

"What's the 'W'?

"Warren."

"Cool. Honorable name, Warren. I'll see you in a bit."

After Rhine left, Melissa sat next to Riley on the bed. "Well," she asked, "what do you think?"

"He seems okay. I think I'll take my guitar and we can go somewhere like that state park overlooking the waterfalls. Want to go?"

"I'll just stay here. I've still got a lot of catching up to do answering emails, stuff like that."

"That's cool," he said. "Adam's probably got a rental car."

"I'm not going anywhere. Take the truck if you like."

"You know, I don't want to play the Hollywood Bowl, and I don't much care to be a big star," Riley said. "But, you know, it'd be kind of cool to be on the cover of the *Rolling Stone*."

"I hope you're right about that," Melissa said as Riley headed to the shower.

♫

Riley and Adam drove the back roads for ninety minutes or so, conducting more a conversation than interview.

"First things first," Riley said, and he gave Adam a fairly detailed account of the incident on the plane. "I don't know what you don't know. Just ask me whatever you want about it."

"Don't you think the whole thing is kind of strange?" Rhine asked.

"Oh, yeah, it was definitely bizarre, man."

"I mean, why would anyone try to blow up this little plane, about to land at this little airport?"

"Maybe they—the guy on the plane, al Qaeda, Taliban, whatever—just figured they could get away with it easier than some giant airliner. Maybe it was 'cause they were smart. Maybe they wanted to get this message across that nothing was safe."

"That's what the government is saying."

"Well, I guess it's a way to make something that doesn't make sense seem like it makes sense," Riley said and left it at that.

Then he asked, "Where is the dude, anyway?"

"Who?"

"The dude who tried to blow up the plane. What's his name?...Fatih Ghannam."

"He's being held at Guantanamo Bay," said Adam. "He's supposed to be tried by a military tribunal."

"Wonder if I'm supposed to testify."

"Don't know. No one's communicated with you about that?"

"Not a word," Riley said. "I haven't talked to the FBI since they interviewed me the night after it happened."

Riley took a right at a stop sign and drove down a long hill into the tiny town of Booneville. They stopped at a place called Dooley's Diner, on the public square.

"You hungry?" Riley asked. They sat in a booth, surrounded by a half-full dining room of middle-aged men in overalls, smoking, and heavy-set women in old-fashioned dresses.

"Not so much," said Adam, staring at the menu. "I ate the free breakfast in the lobby this morning."

"Get a bowl of vegetable soup," Riley said. "Crumble up some cornbread in it. Be a good way for a city boy to get in touch with life beyond the malls." Riley knew the waitress, whom he got up to hug.

"Darling, I'll have me some country-fried steak with okra, corn, rice and gravy," he said. "My friend here'll have a bowl of vegetable soup. Sweet tea to drink for both of us.

"You'll like it, Adam. We gotta get you comfortable with your surroundings."

"I'll have a grilled cheese, too," Adam said.

Over lunch, Riley told Adam about Melissa, how he had grown up with her, lost touch and been sort of randomly reacquainted in the aftermath of the airplane incident.

"I assume she's your girlfriend," Adam said.

"I've fallen in love with her," Riley replied. "But, honestly, she's got more common sense than any ten managers, agents and publicists. She picks things up in a hurry. I'm sure people always say this shit about people they're fucking, but, really, she's something special. You'll see that if you hang around long enough."

After they had finished eating, Riley paid the bill and said, "Now let's find us a place where a man can smoke dope safely."

He drove to Natural Bridge State Resort Park, where he and Adam shared a joint riding the chair lift. Then after few minutes' pause, they hiked—Riley had his guitar strapped on his back— through something called the Fat Man Squeeze, which left them sitting on benches peering at the aforementioned Natural Bridge above them.

"Isn't it amazing," asked Riley, panting, "the lengths of physical exertion a man will subject himself to just to find a safe place to blaze?"

"I'm glad we did this," said Adam. "I didn't get a chance to jog this morning. You work out?"

"Nah," said Riley. "You know what this old blues man told me one time?"

"No, what?"

"He said, 'You know how you stay in shape to play music? You play some fuckin' music.'"

So, still pleasantly buzzed, Riley pulled out the guitar and entertained a handful of tourists who had happened by as well as Adam. He played some old, familiar tunes—"Pick Me Up on Your Way Down," "Big City," "Mr. Bojangles"—while really waiting for kids and parents to move on. Only a couple in their twenties remained when Riley decided to play a song he'd written on a napkin while watching the Land Sharks play in Florida.

"This one I wrote," he said. "It's called 'I'm So Sensitive'."

I'm so sensitive
I'm contemplative
I'm ruminative
I'm argumentative
And I'm talkative
That's why I wrote this song
I heard somebody say that I was all washed up
Never mind in general she was all fucked up
It pissed me off but I didn't let on
But deep inside it scared me to the bone
It's a lonely life sayin' what you mean
Without mincing words and wasting gasoline
It's easy to tell if you're my friend or not
Real friends are really all I got
CHORUS
A man's gotta do what he thinks is right
He can't be afraid to fuss and fight
He can't control what anybody thinks
Don't sweat the opinion of a rinky dink
My daddy taught me wrong and a little right
One thing was don't be afraid to fight
But lots of what he knew he didn't let on
I had to learn that shit all on my own
CHORUS

Riley gave the couple a CD he pulled out of the gig bag, and they moved on after profusely thanking him. He handed Adam the guitar.

"You're a fucking music writer," he said. "You gotta play guitar."

"A little."

"Shit. I'd be willing to bet you can play circles around me."

♫

Priscilla Hay arrived in London on Thursday, the night before she surmised Riley would be playing in Richmond, to the north. She couldn't find the Blue Moon Lounge on MapQuest. She unpacked her bags, took an hour-long nap, caught up on email correspondence, ordered pizza and made plans to encounter Riley Mansfield the next night. She retired early.

Riley, Melissa and Adam returned from a day in which they had taken in an afternoon movie and had dinner at the nearby Ruby Tuesdays. Dinner had involved a fair amount of drinking, so Riley and Melissa parted ways with Adam upon their return.

Unbeknownst to either, Priscilla was asleep in Room 327 while Riley and Melissa were fucking in 329. The next morning Riley and Melissa drove to Hyden to spend the day leading up to that night's gig.

Priscilla put a good deal of thought into what might be appropriate attire. She imagined the Blue Moon an informal place. A honky-tonk. Once she had been in Nashville for a senatorial debate. Afterwards, she had gone with other campaign workers to the line of bars on Lower Broadway, where she had been a bit overdressed. She had come prepared this time, and donned a pair of designer jeans. The blouse she put on, though, left her with the nagging impression that it might be a bit too fashionable. Exiting near Eastern Kentucky University, Priscilla found a souvenir store near campus and bought a school tee shirt. She asked several apparent students how to get to the Blue Moon Lounge. None of them had ever heard of it.

She drove to a convenience store and changed into the tee shirt in the restroom. She then bought a pack of cigarettes, a lighter and some gum. This, she commiserated, had turned out to be an excellent opportunity to resume smoking. As she paid, Priscilla asked the weathered man behind the counter if he could provide directions to a place called the Blue Moon Lounge.

The man wore a beat-up cowboy hat. He handed Priscilla change and took a draw off a Camel smoldering in a glass ashtray that looked like the one in Priscilla's motel room. He looked her over, seemed to make a conclusion of some sort and chuckled.

"That's a place," he said, "I don't believe a young woman like you ought to be a-visiting."

Priscilla thought a moment. "There's a band playing there I want to see."

"Well, I tell you what, young lady, you'll be the best-looking woman walks in there tonight."

"Why, thanks," said Priscilla, flashing a thoroughly insincere beauty queen's smile.

"That might not necessarily be no good thing," said the cashier, but he told her how to get there anyway.

♫

By the time Riley, Adam and Melissa arrived at the rundown Richmond club—Adam drove his rented Impala—all the equipment had been set up. Two other band members were there, along with Eric and Wade. Riley greeted the bassist and drummer warmly, introducing Melissa as his manager to Sammy Quinn and Harley Harvey.

They had beers. Riley and Wade walked outside. The sun was still well above the rim of the hills. The world would have to start looking bleak before the patrons started drifting in.

"Little late, ain't you?"

"We didn't get to Hyden till y'all had already left," said Riley. "So then we had to hightail it over here and find the place. We'll go back down the interstate to London tonight."

Eric came ambling out to join Riley and Wade. They chatted, leaning against the back of Eric's van. The Blue Moon was in the middle of what appeared to be a working-class neighborhood. A small auto repair shop was up the street. Riley asked what Melissa was doing, and Riley said she was sitting at the bar, trying to get a wireless signal on a laptop.

"I better tell her to pack that thing up and hide it in the truck before much of a crowd shows up," Riley said.

"This is a little rougher place than that last one you went with us to," said Eric.

"They got anything to eat?" Riley asked.

"Peanuts, maybe," Wade said.

Adam showed up. Riley introduced him as a friend, neglecting to tell them he was writing a story for *Rolling Stone*.

"They's a Mexican joint about a quarter-mile that way," said Eric, pointing left and slightly downhill.

"When you go on?"

"Half hour."

"What say Adam, Melissa and me go get some food, and we'll come back with a shitload of burritos or tacos or something for your first break," Riley suggested.

"Sounds like a plan," said Eric.

♬

Riley Mansfield wasn't mentioned on the bill taped to the door of the Blue Moon Lounge, which Priscilla found odd since there was some celebrity attached to his name. *Maybe that's why it wasn't*, she thought. Maybe he was still trying to avoid attention. This seemed like a damn good place for it.

Once Eric Hays and the Grassy Knolls started playing, it was too loud for Priscilla to inquire as to the whereabouts of Mr. Mansfield. Priscilla surmised that the band's name wasn't politically inspired. They were more rock than country, but definitely country and blues influenced. Mostly they satisfied the appetite of an increasingly raucous crowd with covers of everyone from Lynyrd Skynyrd and the Rolling Stones to Merle Haggard and Johnny Cash. They sang, maybe, one original song during their first set. The quality of the musicianship was first-rate, though, and Hays could sing.

Priscilla felt surrounded by lunatics. Most of the audience, which was growing rapidly, looked as if they'd been working hard right up to the moment they began drinking hard. The men were younger than they looked. The women were mostly unattractive. They seemed supercharged, amped, out of their minds. Priscilla didn't realize people like this still existed. These were Depression scenes she was watching, sipping Coors Lights and feeling very uncomfortable. Several times lanky, gaunt men beckoned her to dance. She mouthed that she was "waiting for somebody" and "I can't" and tried to smile and be gracious because these men looked dangerous. She thought about spreading word, deceitfully, that she was a lesbian but concluded, surveying the crowd, that there was the possibility there would be business there, too.

So these are the Reagan Democrats, she thought, keeping a lookout for anyone who might be Riley Mansfield.

♫

"What do you love about me, Riley?" asked Melissa, a little drunkenly through a mouthful of crunching chips and salsa.

"I love your green eyes," he said. "They're beautiful. I love the way you never actually take issue with anything I say, but your expressions give you away and get the message across. I love the knack you have for revealing secrets at precisely the right time. You have an innate sense of drama."

"Know what I love about you?"

Riley raised his eyebrows and opened his palms.

"I like the fact that you're really smart and yet you really don't care much about money and fame."

"You may be first woman ever born who loves that."

"Like, I said. Like."

Riley couldn't help but laugh again. "Duly noted."

"Anything else you love about me?"

"You're gorgeous. You're smart. You're mischievous. You're rebellious, deep down," he said, staring at her. "Your titties are just right. Your nose is cute. I love your hair, partly out of jealousy because mine's getting a few flecks of gray."

"You're so sweet," she said.

"Let me pay the bill," said Adam, looking at his watch and feeling significantly out of place. "I think we need to be getting back."

♫

He's here, Priscilla thought. *That's got to be Riley. Good-looking girl with him. Must be his girlfriend.* There was a slight, black-haired guy. Slightly younger, perhaps. Strangely, he carried what looked like a large bag of tacos. *Must be for the band currently playing.* They were sitting at the side of the stage at a table someone had been saving for them. The woman looked a tad over-served.

In front of the stage was a massive fan, its blades enclosed in some black material, as if it came from under the hood of some massive truck. This was much larger, though. The besotted patrons treated the fan as if it were a religious artifact. They stood in front of, its wind in their faces, leaning back and raising their arms like Moses come down from the mountain.

Stupid things begat stupid things. In one little huddle on the dance floor, three men surrounded one plump little woman. For some reason, they collectively decided it would be wildly innovative to, between three of them, hoist the girl up so that she would be staring at the ceiling, lying flat in their arms, and all was well until the inevitable moment when they dropped the girl, and it looked as if the back of her head hit the floor, thankfully slowed somewhat by all those forearms and hands slowly sagging and giving way.

Eric closed up the set ("We're gonna take a little break 'cause, judged by what a big time y'all's having, we need to do some catchin' up.") and noticed, for the first time, Riley at stage right.

"What you think?" Eric asked.

"I sure love to watch those meth heads dance," he said.

"Wanna come on the next set and do a few tunes with us?"

"Sure."

"Wanna get high?"

"I'd love to, but I need to keep a watch on Melissa," said Riley. "I gotta make sure she don't get sick. I think she's gonna be all right, but she might need to take a nap in the truck."

"That's cool," said Eric, and Riley pondered the huge range of comments that his friend could answer with that phrase.

Priscilla worked her way across the dance floor but was still five yards away when Riley and the girl got up and retreated toward an adjoining room with pool tables. She got to the opening just as they walked through a swinging door to an open-air area where the air may have been open but not clean. She started out there, only to see the two go through another swinging door into the parking lot beyond.

Frustrated but realizing the impropriety of further pursuit, Priscilla did an about-face and walked back across the dance floor, which was much easier now that no one was dancing. She walked outside through the front door and lit a cigarette on the opposite side of the building from where Riley and Melissa had exited. It struck Priscilla as odd that no one else was outside until she realized that the crowd didn't need to step outside to smoke. Kentucky actually still had smoke-filled bars.

It was cool but not cool enough to be locked inside a truck. Fortunately, when Riley and Melissa had returned from Monterrey Mexican Cafe, the lot had been crowded and they had squeezed into a spot at the end, three rows back. Riley looked around and decided it was safe to leave Melissa asleep with the windows down.

"Honey, you take a nice little nap," said Riley. "Take these."

He handed her two Aleves and had her wash them down with what was left of a bottle of diet green tea that had been sitting for more than a day in the cup holder.

"Sleep a little while, and I'll come back and check on you as soon as I can," he said.

"I love you, Riley," she said and drifted off to sleep.

The Grassy Knolls roared back to life at about the time Riley returned to his table. After singing three more songs, Eric Hays spoke into the mic.

"Me and the boys have got a real good friend who's gonna come up and sing a few songs with us. He's a real good songwriter—a few of his songs have been recorded by some folks down in Nashville—and when we get done with this set, he's going to play you a few of his songs next time we take a break.

"Give a good ol' Kentucky welcome to…Riley Mansfield!"

The crowd clapped politely as Riley walked onstage, sans guitar. He'd done this before. He had to do songs that he and the band both knew. Eric hadn't mentioned the hero bit, and apparently, here in the hills, the patrons didn't recognize the name. He was just a singer. Eric and Riley stepped back from the mics.

"Whatcha wanna do?" asked Eric.

"Let's see. How many songs?"

"Four all right?

"Four's fine. How 'bout 'Folsom Prison Blues,' 'Mama Tried,' uh, 'Guitars, Cadillacs and Hillbilly Music' and…"

"'The Joker.' You can sing that. They'll love it."

"Ah'ight. So be it."

Wade plucked the intro of "Folsom Prison Blues," and off they went.

Priscilla, meanwhile, was still frustrated. How was she going to talk to this Riley Mansfield fellow, this hell-raising hero, if he was going to play during the next break? She devised a plan.

When Riley began singing "The Joker," Priscilla realized it was the perfect moment. She slid through the crowd and worked her way right in front of Riley at the front of the crowd. She began dancing as provocatively as she knew how. She and Riley locked gazes. She sang along.

Really like your peaches wanna shake your treeeees!

It made an impression. Before Riley left the stage, he and Eric stepped back from the mics again. Wade drifted over, grinning.

Eric said, "I reckon you noticed the looks that gal was giving you?"

"Yeah. She's good-lookin' too, ain't she?"

"Goddamn," said Wade. "We gonna do a slow song just to watch y'all dance."

"I don't think it'd be too smart. Girl that good-lookin's bound to have a man."

"She's been settin' by herself all night," said Eric, "waitin' on you."

The woman was still standing in front of the stage, still staring.

"Where's, uh, Melissa?" asked Wade.

"Sound asleep in the truck."

"I'd say you're damned if you do and damned if you don't," said Eric. "You might make a scene if you dance with her, and I'd say she'll definitely make a scene if you don't."

Riley sighed. "She is good-lookin'."

"Damned if she ain't," said Wade.

Riley had barely stepped off the stage when Priscilla Hay dragged him out on the dance floor.

The Grassy Knolls must have jammed fifteen minutes on some fine Stevie Ray Vaughan, courtesy of Wade McKeever's fine electric-guitar work. Riley sobered up pretty rapidly. Thankfully, the next song was a slow one, but even though it wasn't fast, it was loud, and Priscilla could make out what Riley said a lot better than Riley, who just nodded, smiled and pretended to understand. As best he could tell, she knew he was a hero. And she was mighty fun to rub up against.

When they finally parted, Priscilla said she wanted to talk to him later, and this time Riley just smiled and nodded even though he could understand her. The band was cranking up some Skynyrd when Riley walked back, looking down at the floor and pondering the situation. He was back at the side table when he looked up and saw Melissa sitting across from him again.

She looked pissed, very much awake, and they couldn't talk because of the loud music. Riley tried to shake his head and plead his case by expressions, but Melissa was a lot better at it. So they just sat there and Riley ordered a beer. Melissa didn't want one.

Finally the set ended. It was Riley's turn to go on alone.

"I didn't have a choice," Riley said, trying to keep a brief conversation private. "She drug me on the dance floor. There would've been a big stink if I hadn't danced with her. That's the honest truth, Melissa. Ask Eric and Wade. They saw it. I ain't talked to 'em 'cause they were playing. Get 'em to tell you what happened."

Riley had his gig bag under the table. He unzipped it and pulled out his Pawless guitar. Eric was nearby. With Melissa sulking, arms folded and back turned, Riley said to Eric, "She ain't near as drunk. She's mad, as you might expect. Go to bat for me, tell her the truth and if there's any way possible, try to get her high."

"That's cool," Eric said.

Riley took the stage mainly because there wasn't any reason not to. The crowd was too drunk to listen to lyrics, and not even they would dance to a guy on an acoustic guitar singing songs they'd never heard. If nothing else, Riley at least figured he could prevent the bar owner from cranking up rap or seventies disco. No just god could fail to look down with goodness and mercy upon a man who would prevent that abomination from happening.

Wisely taking the novelty angle, Riley sang "First I Took My Clothes Off (Then You Changed Your Mind," followed by one of his songs the Cornhuskers had cut, "Stoned at the Crack of Dawn." That was about as rabble-rousing as he could muster.

"I tell you what, before I get off this damn stage and put some real music back on it, let me do this little simple tune I wrote here over the last few days. It's called 'Gotta Be Somebody'."

The Audacity of Dope

I got some eggs ain't got no ham
Need some breakfast I'm a hungry man
Sure do hate to get up and around
Feels too rough to drive into town
Gotta be somebody
Gotta be somebody
Gotta be somebody
Lord it's gonna drag me down
Bossman says I gotta pee in a cup
Half the time I'm all fucked up
He don't give me no sympathy
All I wanna do is watch Court TV
They's an eighteen-wheeler rolling down the line
Man I hope she's right on time
Best as I can understand
That trucker's hauling contraband
CHORUS
My old lady says I don't pull my weight
Baby they's a whole lot on my plate
Rock 'n' roll you to the break of day
You know, honey baby, I don't play
It's hard for me to turn down a beer
Head don't work if it thinks too clear
I don't aim to hurt no one
All I wanna do is have some fun
CHORUS

That little two-chord song got 'em started. "You know," Riley said to the crowd, "a great Kentuckian, Tom T. Hall, said it could be that the Good Lord needs a little pickin' too. You ever thought about the word 'buzz'? I mean, you pick up the paper and there's this column that says 'the buzz around town.' You turn on the TV and it says 'the morning buzz.' People wanna 'cop a buzz.' I know I do. It's kind of a buzz word, y'know. I wrote this song called 'Inferior Buzz.' I'm gonna do the song, then I'm gonna give this stage to Eric Hays and the Grassy Knolls 'cause that's, like, where it rightly belongs."

> *The buzz is all over town*
> *Catch a buzz is what folks wanna do*
> *There's a whole lot of different ways to catch a buzz*
> *If you think they're all the same, it ain't true.*
> *I can shoot me a gun*
> *I can beat up my wife*
> *I can get liquored up*
> *Pull out a knife*
> *I can raise me an army*
> *Start up a war*
> *But inferior buzz ain't what I'm lookin' for*

Wade walked onstage and began playing lead. Harley Harvey jumped in on drums. The crowd started digging it. People were clogging and shit.

> *Y'know, they say money rules the world*
> *And I reckon that's prob'ly right*
> *But I'd never shut down a mine*
> *Without considering the poor workers' plight*
> *'Cause money is just another buzz*
> *As addictive as any pill*
> *It don't have to fuck up your life*
> *But if you make it fast enough it prob'ly will*
> *CHORUS*
> *Some get a buzz from poppin' pills*
> *Some get baked smokin' weed*
> *To some Jesus is a natural high*
> *Simple faith is what most people need*
> *As for me it varies day to day*
> *All depends on what I wanna risk*
> *Read a book write a song watch TV*
> *Say a prayer, smoke a joint, steal a kiss*

CHORUS

"Thank you, folks," said Riley. "Thanks for putting up with my sorry-ass, not-even-from-Kentucky self. Let me get out of the way, folks, and leave you listen to some honest-to-God music!"

The crowd roared.

Eric Hays jumped onstage. "Riley Mansfield, ladies and gentlemen!" he screamed.

Shit, thought Priscilla Hay, *this guy's pretty charismatic. The Reagan Democrats love him.* She sent several text messages to George Grinnell.

♪

It was after one when everything ended. Fatigue was no longer a factor. Riley was riding a wave of adrenaline. He'd pulled it off and had the crowd eating out of his hands. Being a hero hadn't even been an issue. They hadn't even known about it. They'd loved him anyway, and Riley was almost in a trance. Since the band would be back the next night, there were only a few guitars and electrical cords to be loaded in the van.

Melissa wasn't mad anymore, which seemed a good thing when Priscilla walked up to the truck as Riley and Melissa were getting in.

"Hello, Mr. Mansfield, I want to apologize if I was a little untoward when you were onstage. I didn't mean any harm, Miss…"

"Franklin. Melissa Franklin." She shook Priscilla's hand.

"You see—may I call you Riley?—I know what you did on that airplane. I know you don't want to make a big deal about it. I'm a Democrat, Riley, and I think you are, too, and I want to know why you're going to Washington so that the worst president this country's ever had can exploit you for his own means."

"So…you're not from around here."

"No," Priscilla said. "I'm not."

Riley took a deep breath. "Long story," he said. "I got no

choice. How can you turn down the President of the United States, no matter how much you disagree with him? How can you do that without looking unpatriotic?"

"How can you do that and be patriotic?" Priscilla fired back.

"Look, Miss…"

"I'm sorry. I'm Priscilla. Priscilla Hay."

"Priscilla. Like I was saying, I've made up my mind. I'm gonna do it. I don't want to talk about it."

Priscilla tried to reply. Riley waved his hand and somehow it silenced her for a moment.

"Anderson Cooper you ain't, and I ain't the president and this ain't a press conference," he said. He climbed into the truck, unlocked the passenger-side door for Melissa and shut the door on Priscilla Hay. He put the key into the ignition, cranked up the Tacoma, backed out and left Priscilla alone in the darkness.

"Fuck, fuck, fuck, fuck, fuck, fuck, fuck!" Priscilla exclaimed to no one in the darkness, Riley's red taillights now exiting the lot.

Melissa looked pleased, however, when Riley saw her expression flickering in the lights of the street.

CHAPTER TWENTY-TWO
WHEELS TURNING

Priscilla Hay drove straight home and went to bed. Riley and Melissa stopped off at a truck stop with the Grassy Knolls and a few girlfriends and relatives. Priscilla was sound asleep in Room 327 when Riley and Melissa finally arrived at Room 329.

"I'm still riding the adrenaline," said Riley. "Mind if I play my guitar for a while?"

"Don't you think you'll wake up somebody?" Melissa asked.

"Probably. I don't know. Maybe there's nobody in the rooms next door. I wish we were in Nashville. When I've met up with Eric and Wade there, always in their room, it's amazing how you can sing and pick all night and nobody seems to mind. Let's see what happens."

Riley retrieved a plastic baggy from the luggage and rolled a joint.

"You were good," Melissa said. "You got their attention. They loved you."

Riley lit the joint, took a hit and passed it to Melissa.

"That's not easy," he said. "It's best to sing your own songs in little coffeehouse settings 'cause that's what the people come for. They're attentive and pay attention to the lyrics. At a bar, everybody comes to drink and dance and pick up women. They don't want any heavy lifting. They want to drink and raise hell and sing along to songs they already know. It's kind of depressing, really."

"Yeah," said Melissa, "but you pulled it off. There were some awkward moments, but they heightened the drama, so to speak. First, it was kind of weird, but that's what drew their attention. Then you knocked 'em dead."

"I thought you were gonna knock me dead when I saw your face. You know, when you walked in on me with that Democrat woman? Were you still mad when she came out to the truck?"

"I was a little hurt." Melissa said, taking a hit. "Whenever something like that happens, when you leave some place for a while and you see the man you're with dancing with someone else, this whole suspiciousness just wraps you like a net or something. You're, like, 'fuckin' men.' You just feel like you can't trust them. With the slightest chance, they're just gonna jump the first pair of legs that open up for 'em."

"I guess she really did me a favor. Honestly, I really just danced with her because she was insistent and I didn't want to make a scene. No, I didn't want you to walk in right when you did, but I didn't do anything wrong and I wasn't pondering anything unfaithful."

Riley picked up the Pawless and played the Eagles' "Peaceful Easy Feeling."

"You know," Riley said, "when I was up there onstage, I wanted to show off my songs because I'm proud of them. But I love playing other people's songs, too, you know, songs that, for one reason or another, I just like. They're meaningful to me.

"When I was a little boy, I used to go with my daddy to horse and cattle auctions, and we'd listen to the Grand Ole Opry on the way home on the radio. That's where I learned to love traditional country music."

Riley proceeded to play a series of simple old songs: "Pop a Top," "I Know One," "Lost Highway," "Pick Me Up on Your Way Down," "Ring of Fire" and others. It was when he launched into a boisterous version of "Six Days on the Road" that the sound awakened Priscilla from her slumber in Room 327.

Priscilla's eyes opened wide and she swung her legs off the side of the bed.

"Shit!" She rubbed her eyes and tried to concentrate. *Wait a minute.* It couldn't be. That was Riley Mansfield's voice. She walked to the mirror and brushed her black hair. She still had the EKU tee shirt on. Priscilla stepped into her jeans and sat down again. She retrieved the cigarettes from her purse and lit one. She wiggled her feet into tennis shoes, finished the smoke, found her plastic room-entry card and walked outside.

Priscilla knocked on the door of Room 329. Inside, Riley put a roach out with his tongue and said, "Uh, oh." He swallowed it.

Riley thought a moment. "It would be better," he said, almost whispering, "if someone had been banging on the wall. Or if the phone had rung. When somebody knocks on your door, it might be the police. Then again, if it was the cops, they'd probably have knocked on the door a lot harder and started yelling, unless, of course, they were mindful of people trying to get some sleep, so they decided it would be better to just tap lightly on the door. I don't think there's a cop in Kentucky who would be that considerate. My mind is a ball of confusion."

The look on his face caused Melissa to giggle.

He said, "Don't worry, honey, just be cool," and grabbed a can of Lysol from his suitcase. He sprayed the room quickly, then squinted into the little viewing hole in the door. The Lysol didn't prevent smoke from billowing out the door when he opened it to find Priscilla Hay outside.

"Well," said Riley, "small world."

"I'm next door," said Priscilla. "May I come in?"

Riley frowned. "You blaze?" he asked, to which Priscilla replied, "Not recently, but I'm not against it."

"Well, come on in," Riley said, sighing.

"This is Melissa. What is your name again? Donna Democrat?"

"Actually, it's Priscilla Hay, and I don't, technically speaking, work for the Democratic Party. I work for a P.R. firm."

"Does it have a name?" Riley asked.

"Clark Powell Morgenthau LLC."

"Which one of 'em's your daddy?"

"None," said Priscilla. "If one of them was my daddy, he wouldn't have sent me off to South Carolina and Kentucky chasing down a country singer." She hadn't put her watch on. "Do you have the time?" she asked.

"Four o'clock," said Riley. "Three minutes till."

Priscilla did some quick math. "In a little more than two weeks, you're supposed to be on this big, grand stage telling everyone how wonderful President Sam Harmon is, even though we both know you don't believe it."

"How you know that?"

"Your song. It's on your MySpace page. It's called 'Misfits.' The words are in a blog. It expresses your contempt for the president and his policies. You've written several blogs on that subject."

Riley looked a bit incredulous. "I guess you've done your homework," he said. "But for what? What does it hurt for the guy who the media made into a hero to go up and shake hands with the president?"

"This isn't exactly the rose garden at eleven in the morning, Mr. Mansfield."

"Riley, ma'am. Please call me Riley."

"Riley, this is a nationally-televised patriotic celebration. You have been put on this show for one reason: to help this president draw attention away from his abysmal record and put his party's brand of propaganda into every home. If you played your cards right, Riley, you might just blossom into a full-fledged Lee Greenwood."

Riley laughed. "Them's fightin' words," he said. "Would you care to blaze?"

"Well, okay," Priscilla said, imagining that she was in some High Plains tepee and that Riley was a fierce chief signaling for the peace pipe to be fired up.

"Why the fuck would anyone care?" asked Riley, crumbling up little chunks of weed and scattering it in the folded paper. "Who could criticize me for singing a couple patriotic songs and shaking hands with the president?"

"He is up for reelection, and he is in big trouble, and if he can get the implied endorsement of an otherwise reclusive national hero, it would help him remind the American people that they should be scared as shit if anyone is their president other than Sam Harmon.

"You see, you've actually upped the ante, Riley. By hiding, you've lent a certain dramatic quality to your inevitable reemergence. You've become a priority item for the RNC."

"What's the RNC?"

"Republican National Committee."

"Oh. Guess that makes sense." Riley wet the joint he had just rolled with his tongue, lit it, took a hit and passed it to Melissa, who thus far had said nary a word.

"The RNC is desperate, and the president and the thugs around him are doing what they always do, which is try to scare the shit out of the American people, who otherwise would have enough sense to vote the sons of bitches out of office."

"Only men?"

"Huh?" Priscilla took a modest, but professional, hit.

"You said, uh, sons of bitches."

"Oh…okay, I get it…bitches, too.

"Riley, before we discuss this further, would you do me a favor?"

"Sure."

"Play 'Misfits' for me. I'd like to hear the tune."

"It's a stupid song. Just something I wrote when I was despondent and fucked up. My personal opinion is it's not very good."

"I read the lyrics," said Priscilla. "But the song wasn't posted on your MySpace page."

"Ah'ight'en," said Riley, and he proceeded to sing it.

"You're a fuckin' full-fledged, card-carrying lefty," said Priscilla. "You ought to be singing that song at Democratic town meetings and state conventions. Shit. Union halls."

"I don't want to be the Democrat Lee Greenwood," said Riley. "I don't want to be in a world where I can't sit on a motel room bed just like this one and blaze and play my songs. I want to have the freedom to live my life as I see fit."

"So you want to be the songwriting equivalent of Greta Garbo?"

"I don't follow you."

"I vant to be alone," said Priscilla, laughing.

Riley laughed. So did Melissa.

"Look, Priscilla," said Riley. "I...by the way, can I make a quick guess? You don't like to be called Prissy."

"I killed the last man."

"It's your sad fate to be forever plagued by affiliations with three-syllabled women," said Melissa, making her first contribution to the wee-hours summit.

"You're trying to change the subject," Priscilla said.

"So I am," said Riley, smiling. "Look, I got to. I got to. I got to. I hate myself for it but..."

"...ya got to," interrupted Priscilla. "My question would be, how come you got to?"

"Show her," said Melissa, producing a manila envelope.

Riley handed Priscilla the prints, which included a shot of his back taken a day after he'd been worked over by the fake deputy.

"Looks like a great, big, solid blue tattoo, huh?"

"Shit," said Priscilla. "They did this to you? I mean, Republicans?"

Riley told her of alleged Barton Fleming's visit.

"Those motherfuckers." It was stunning to hear Priscilla use such a word. She took a hit.

"Wasn't a real cop," said Riley. "Called the sheriff's department to give him credit for his caring staff. He'd already come to see me with a delegation of local Gestapo. I could tell, though, when I told him, he was shocked. He didn't know nothing."

"You'd never seen this beast before?"

"Certainly not in that particular state of beastliness," said Riley.

"No. Never. I'd like to see him hang, though, even though I'm against capital punishment. I'd like to see him hang, break his neck and survive. I'm no longer against maiming for life."

Riley grabbed a cigarette and motioned to Priscilla, "Want one?"

"Yeah, sure, why not?" Priscilla had left Washington, D.C., and the firm Clark Powell Morgenthau LLC far behind.

"Look, I can't blame you," she said. "Now I understand why you're doing it. But I feel like I know you a little. I know, Riley, you've thought about a way to turn the tables on them."

"Not seriously."

"But you've thought about it. You've imagined scenarios."

"Yeah," he said. "That's true enough."

"We can help you. I could pull some strings. I can figure something sneaky out that won't hurt you and will hurt the administration."

Riley finished the cigarette and thought.

"Okay," he said, at last. "What are your plans?"

"Well, I'm sort of thinking off the top of my head," Priscilla answered, "but I guess I should check out of here and get back to Washington. I could put some things together."

"Why don't you take my laptop with you?"

"What?"

"It's loaded down with emails with instructions and prepared remarks and all sorts of attempts to get me to tell them where I am, why I'm where I am and why don't I come to Washington right away 'cause they're extremely willing to come get me. Hell, if I'd do it, they'd put me on the road stumping for the president."

"Why don't you impersonate me?" Riley asked.

"What?"

"Online. Why don't you take my computer, pretend to be me and do with it what you will? I mean, I'm such an amateur at this bullshit. You're actually in politics. I can't really get out of appearing at this big hullabaloo, you know, but after I'm done with it, I've got a little something up my sleeve."

"Riley, what you are is a dirty trick. You've been forced to come to Washington to be a publicity stunt for the president and the Republican Party. What I'd like to do is turn the tables on the bastards."

"Me, too," Riley said. "That's why this dude with *Rolling Stone* is hanging out with me. After the big Fourth of July shindig—actually, I think it's the fifth of July—he's gonna write about me...and it."

"You got the balls?"

Riley laughed. "I'm surprised you phrased it that way. But, obviously. He's been riding around with me the past two days. He was at the Blue Moon. Short, slight guy. You had to notice him. He was more out of place than you. No turning back with this, though. I told him he could write whatever he wants, but nothing, not a peep, not a blog, not a 'Random Note,' can come out until after that deal in Washington.

"But, to answer your question, I got the balls. I've always had the balls. They're too big for my own good, and that's why I'm doing what I'm doing and why I'm right here in the middle of Kentucky in one way and in the middle of a shitstorm in another.

"See what you can do, Priscilla Hay. Try not to get me killed."

"Oh, shit, you're just paranoid," she said.

"Pretty much," Riley replied.

♫

Though he hadn't slept until six, Riley nonetheless rose before eleven. He'd stuffed a stack of magazines in his bag when they'd swung by home after Rockingham and was working his way through copies of *Rolling Stone*, *Esquire*, *Time* and *Sports Illustrated* when Melissa awakened.

"You know," he said. "Every one of these magazines except *SI* has tried to contact me for an interview. Plus *Details*, *GQ* and *Maxim*."

"No *Playboy*?"

"Not to my knowledge. I'm already down to a few graphs, though."

Riley leafed through a copy of *Time*.

"Listen to this. 'Riley Mansfield, the obscure songwriter credited with preventing an alleged terrorist from setting off a bomb on a May twenty-fourth commuter flight, has agreed to perform at a July fifth celebration scheduled for the National Mall.

"'Mansfield, thirty-five, granted several interviews shortly after the incident but has since avoided the media. He has reportedly spent only a few days at his South Carolina home. Videos of Mansfield performing at small clubs in North Carolina and Florida have been popping up on YouTube since the incident.

"'The former University of Piedmont quarterback reportedly agreed to the Washington appearance—where he will be honored by President Sam Harmon—only after considerable coaxing from Administration and Republican Party operatives.'"

Adam Rhine called at noon.

"Adam," said Riley. "You missed the boat last night, hotshot."

"Huh?"

"You went to bed. We had quite a jam session here in the room. Lasted almost all the way till dawn."

"Really? What happened?"

"Aw, nothin' much. It was just fun. That's all."

"Wanna get some lunch?"

"Sure," Riley said. "Melissa just got up. Give us to one or so. We'll come by your room."

He hung up. Melissa looked at him.

"Backing off on full disclosure, huh?"

"What?"

"You didn't tell Adam about Priscilla."

Riley laughed. "He didn't ask. I said I'd be honest. I didn't say I'd answer questions he didn't ask."

"I have to confess to amazement that you'd just hand over your laptop to Miss Hay," said Melissa.

Riley didn't know what to make of Melissa's formal reference to Priscilla but let it pass.

"We'll get another one," said Riley.

"Kind of expensive."

"That's what credit cards are for. I'm gonna give her my air card, but I'm going to tell her I don't think she should use it."

"Why not?"

"Well, I don't know, but I'm thinking maybe there's a way to track where we are by when that signal's transmitting. I don't have any way of knowing, but I'm just guessing the government's trying to monitor my whereabouts. Maybe not. Maybe I'm just paranoid, or I'm overestimating my importance, but I'm kind of concerned by how often people just seem to pop up."

"And you're giving your laptop to one of them?"

"Judgment call," he said. "It really doesn't take James Bond shit to figure out where I am. All you'd have to do is search MySpace and Facebook. Even though I haven't been posting anything, my friends have. You could look at my friends' list and check out stuff there to find out where I am and where I'm headed. I bet that's what Priscilla did."

A knock on the door. Riley got up and opened it.

"Funny you should arrive," he said to Priscilla. "We were just talking about you."

"I trust you spoke of me well."

"Oh, Melissa was just questioning the wisdom of handing my laptop over to you. Nothing to worry about. Just idle chatter."

Melissa gave him a look that would kill.

"Do you need to clean it out, take anything out of it?"

"I don't think there's anything in there that would surprise you," he said, handing Priscilla the canvas shoulder bag. "A few weed sites in the Favorites folder. I haven't been foraging through the dark underside of my soul or anything like that. I mean, I'd like you to respect my privacy, but there's not anything in particular I'm worried about, nothing that would shock or disgust you."

"It's comforting to know I'm not collaborating with a perv," said Priscilla.

"So what are your plans?"

"I'm flying back to Washington. Need to leave shortly for the Lexington airport."

"Here," Riley said. "I put together a list of user names and passwords for my email accounts. I've got three. They're in the Email Favorites folder. Two of 'em have the passwords saved already, so they'll just sign on without you having to type anything."

"Keep in touch via cell phone. You got the number, right?"

"Yeah. I'll give you mine. It's gonna change from time to time. I'll keep yours written down and probably memorize it, too. Now that I think about it, I can probably access the Internet here and there. If you should need to send an email, it might be a while, but I'll get it."

Melissa nodded, too, and scribbled notes.

"Well, I'd better get going," Priscilla said. "When I get back to Washington, I'll get right to work on this. I'll be in touch if I have any questions, but the first thing I'll do is look at all your email transmissions."

"Cool," said Riley. "You wanna cop a buzz for the road?"

"No, that's okay," said Priscilla. "I really don't need to get lost trying to find the Lexington airport."

"All right, then," said Riley. "Be safe."

CHAPTER TWENTY-THREE
SPENDING REPUBLICAN MONEY

Priscilla Hay called late Tuesday morning, finding Riley with his legs propped up in the motel room, pondering what to do and where to go next. Melissa was in the shower.

He knew it was her. "Priscilla, know all my deep, dark secrets yet?"

"Riley, there were lots of emails I get the feeling you didn't ever read."

"I tried to hit the high spots."

"Jesus, the money these people have is obscene," Priscilla said. "You could request the Mormon Tabernacle Choir back you up, and they wouldn't blink an eye."

"Yeah? Well, could I, like, assemble a band to back me at the big shindig, whatever it's called?"

"You can probably fly them in on Air Force One."

"Can you make some arrangements for me? Some travel arrangements?"

"Yes. I have this deep desire to spend Republican money."

"Could you line up expenses for a warm-up concert? A way to get equipment there, spend the afternoon rehearsing and give a show on Wednesday or Thursday night of next week?"

"Honestly, based on all these emails from the Republican National Committee…"

"RNC," Riley said.

"Very good. And stuff from Harmon's reelection campaign. Anyway, there's a process where I can enter an account number and spend all kinds of money. You were apparently reluctant enough, and they wanted you badly enough, that there are numerous offers that amount to giving you just about carte blanche to spend whatever money you want to spend."

"And you're me."

"I'm you."

"Are you a believable me?" Riley asked.

"Well, I went through all your sent emails and tried to pick up a feeling for your writing style."

"And why are you doing this again?"

"At the very least, I can spend the Republicans' money. But I'm working out some activities for you after you get off stage on the Fourth of July."

"Well, I'm sure you'll tell me all about it later. For right now, though, the rehearsal concert is going to be in a place called Ashland Coffee and Tea, in Ashland, Virginia. I've got a gig there. It's right near Randolph-Macon College. I think it's Wednesday week."

"Wednesday week?"

"A week from Wednesday. Southern term, I guess. It might be Thursday, but I'm almost positive it's Wednesday. Check my MySpace. It's supposed to be just me and my guitar—I've played this place a bunch of times—but I'll call and make it a band show. And I'll let the owners know it's going to be a preview of the show in Washington, which it really won't be 'cause all I'm doing there is a few songs, and I probably won't even do those songs in Ashland, but we can practice there all day and get the band working together.

"We'll need, let's see, one, two, three, four, better make it five hotel rooms somewhere on the north side of Richmond for next Tuesday and Wednesday nights. Then we'll head to D.C. on Thursday. Rehearsals for the show on Friday?"

"Yeah," said Priscilla, "full dress rehearsal at dusk."

"One more thing," he said. "You got some kind of expert opinions on whether my laptop can be traced?"

Priscilla started laughing. "That's the first thing I had on the agenda when I came in yesterday morning. Turns out, yes, they can and probably have been tracking you electronically. There's a way around it, though. I got some help from some of our black-ops dudes…"

"Democrats have black-ops dudes?"

"It's a figure of speech. Our way of sounding macho. We've got sneaky guys."

"What did the sneaky guys say?"

"They said there's a way that, here from the office, I can send everything from your laptop through phone lines to any destination, then have it emitted as a wireless signal from wherever I want. I don't know exactly how to do it, but I've got some assistance."

"Where am I now?"

"Pensacola, Florida, I think."

"Don't tell Melissa. I used to have a gal down there...Oh, here she is, coming out of the bathroom now. I may be in trouble, Priscilla."

Riley was speaking overloud, taunting Melissa, who was on to him.

"I'm sure she'll listen."

"Hey, one more thing." She could hear him telling Melissa, "It's Priscilla. We're in Pensacola. Right now. I'll explain in a minute.

"Can you, like, pay for me and Melissa to go to Oregon if we bring a mandolin player back with us?"

"Oh, I'll try," said Priscilla Hay. "I'll try."

"Listen. I'm depending on you for security, too. How much can you do on my behalf without telling anyone else about it?"

"A lot," she said. "My boss knows something's up my sleeve, but I've told him he's got to trust me and I can't tell anybody about it. He's kind of letting me run the thing. There may be a little plausible deniability involved."

"When I think of politicians, I don't think of a group of people very adept at keeping secrets."

"That's what I think when journalists come up," said Priscilla.

It took a moment for Riley to figure out that she was referring to Adam Rhine. "Adam's cool," he said. "You're cool, too. I'm just making sure we're straight."

"We're straight," Priscilla said. "I won't let anything out."

"Okay. Cool. I'll be back in touch soon. Bye."

Riley hung up. "Guess what?" he said to Melissa. "We're going to Oregon."

"To Oregon?"

"Ever been there?"

"Not within a thousand miles. What's in Oregon?"

"Neil. My buddy. He's getting married."

"Who?"

"Can't remember right now. He sent me an invitation, though. We got to know each other when he was a film student and did this documentary on Americana music. He and this other guy, Johnny. I lost touch with him, but Neil and I somehow kept in touch. They sent me a copy of the documentary. That was, oh, probably five or six years ago. Johnny might be either in the film industry or something like it. Last I heard, he was in L.A. Neil's still in Oregon, where he grew up, and he's getting married on Saturday. He sent me an invitation. And we're going!"

"Riley, I don't know," Melissa said. "I gotta see Mama."

"Hmm. Tell you what. Let's get packed. We'll drive home today. You can spend all day tomorrow with your mom. We've got to fly to Oregon Thursday, though."

"I may not go with you on this one, Riley."

Riley leaned back in the chair, sighed and thought for a couple minutes. Melissa sat on the bed, leaning forward and waiting for him to speak again.

"I've got an ulterior motive," he said. "My wheels were spinning when I was talking to Priscilla. One of Neil's best friends is a kick-ass mandolinist. I mean, he's famous. I'm almost sure he's going to be at the wedding. I want to go out there, jam with him, play at the wedding reception and persuade him to join me onstage in D.C."

"Your whole attitude about this has changed," Melissa said.

"Part of it's what Priscilla said. I'm spending Sam Harmon's money. Part of it is maybe, just maybe, I can play this thing right for once in my life. They think I'm selling my soul. They want my soul, but I don't necessarily have to do it or let them know that I'm not doing it. I can be like Eric Dickerson."

"Who's Eric Dickerson?"

"He was a great running back for SMU. They say he signed with SMU after Texas A&M gave him a car. He showed up at SMU driving a maroon Corvette. It may not be true, but it's kind of a cool story, anyway."

Riley opened the curtain a little and peered out into the Hampton Inn parking lot. "They cheated to get him, but he wound up cheating them," Riley said.

"You're high, aren't you?"

"A little," he said. "You were still asleep. I'm pretty much over it now."

She gave him a coy, disbelieving glance.

"Well," he said, "in any event, we're driving home. Start packing up as quickly as you can, and I'll go settle things at the office, then I'll come back and load the stuff on the truck. We'll talk about it on the way home—it's not like we ain't got six hours—and I'll book the flight tonight. We'll go Thursday and come back Monday, or I'll go Thursday and come back Monday. Hell, I understand if you don't want to go."

"What's to keep the government from tracing you?"

"Well, for one thing, they're going to think I'm in Pensacola, Florida, and for another, my full name is John Riley Mansfield, and even though I file income tax and everything else as Riley Mansfield, I have one credit card that lists me as John R. Mansfield, and that might just be enough to get us out there without being noticed."

♫

After hours, National Security Adviser David Branham changed into casual clothes and left the White House, his limousine taking him to Clyde's of Gallery Place, a fairly popular restaurant and watering hole near Chinatown. There Garner Thomas and Sue Ellen Spenser were waiting, and the topic of the meeting was one Riley Mansfield.

Clyde's was a popular place, but not particularly so on a Tuesday night, so the National Security Adviser was accompanied to a booth in a fairly remote corner of the second floor. Branham got a friendly assurance from the attractive young woman who seated him who knew who he was—that no one else would be seated nearby.

In truth, Thomas had already made these arrangements, and he and Miss Spenser were waiting in the booth when Branham arrived.

He slid into the booth alongside Sue Ellen. They exchanged brief pleasantries.

"Okay, the big celebration is ten days away," said Branham. "Where are we with this Riley Mansfield?"

"I'm happy to report, at last, that things are coming along nicely," said Thomas. "After weeks of only the most cautious and noncommittal forms of communication, Mr. Mansfield has been setting up the logistics of his performance. He's assembling a band to back him, he's getting together with them middle of next week in Virginia, and he'll be on hand for a full dress rehearsal on the night of Friday, July Fourth, on the Mall."

"What's he gonna play?" asked Branham.

Spenser spoke up. "He's going to open with the Merle Haggard song 'Fightin' Side of Me,' then sing 'This Land Is Your Land.'"

"Sue Ellen's been handling this," said Thomas. "She's been on the road, observing Mansfield in concert and heading up preparations from our end."

This caused Spenser pause, but she chose not to say what she was thinking.

I've never even spoken to Riley Mansfield.

"He's a songwriter, right?"

Thomas and Spenser said "that's right" in near unison.

"Well, why don't we let him sing one of his songs? That ought to warm him up a little. Get him to do some sweet, wholesome, little song about living out in the country or something."

"So, you think he should do three songs?" asked Spenser.

"Hell, why not? Let him be introduced by the emcee...who's that?"

"Bruce Willis."

"Oh, yeah, that's right. That'll be perfect. Get Willis to introduce Mansfield, he does a little feel-good song, then the President walks out gracefully, presents him with the Medal of Freedom, he sings a little Merle Haggard, little Woody Guthrie, and the crowd goes wild. The President comes back on stage and they wave to the crowd together. Then there's a long commercial break, the commentators on TV talk about this stirring scene of Americana, and who's next?"

"Claude Herndon," said Spenser.

"The Beach Boys," said Branham. "When are they on?"

"Early in the show. That's sort of the warm-up group."

"That's perfect. You order some wings?"

"No, sir," said Thomas.

"Let's get some wings. And a pitcher of beer. I let the limousine driver go. One of you two has to give me a ride home. Mrs. Branham is out of town," said the National Security Adviser. "Tripp and Juliet are with her at South Padre Island."

At which point Sue Ellen Spenser first entertained the possibility of spending the night with Branham. It wouldn't be sex for love. It wouldn't be sex for recreation. It would be sex for career advancement.

Thomas excused himself briefly to order the food and drink. A waiter accompanied him with the beer, and the Buffalo wings followed shortly.

For the next half hour, Branham poured the beer and passed the wings. He regaled the two political consultants with stories of tax cuts, arms programs and methods of redistricting that had effectively rendered most of Texas Democrat-proof. Though fairly unusual for Branham, he eventually turned his attention back to matters related to his job, national security. "Banks tells me Jed Langston doesn't trust Mansfield," he said, referring to a conversation earlier in the day with Deputy Director of Homeland Security Banks McPherson.

"Well," said Thomas, "he's no Claude Herndon, this Mansfield. I think it's fair to say he isn't a Republican, but really he isn't anything. His reluctance, we've discerned, is more a matter of privacy. He doesn't want to get involved with any politician."

"We've done our share of prodding," said Branham.

"I think we got our message across," said Thomas. "We've made it worth his time, let him know it would be unwise to pass up this opportunity, and after a period in which he was sullen and terse, I think he's come around. And I think Sue Ellen deserves a considerable share of the credit for that."

Sue Ellen flashed her best fake beam, learned from an earlier life as a cheerleader and beauty queen. She'd gone on a wild-goose chase, and somehow the goose had done what she wanted it to. She'd have to get acquainted with Riley Mansfield a few days earlier, just so she could act like she knew him without faking it. This "rehearsal concert" in Virginia…That would be the perfect place.

"There's one more item" said Branham. "We've got to rush through security clearances for the whole bunch of them. Has Mansfield himself been cleared?"

"Yes, sir," said Spenser.

"Well, we need to get the Socials of each of the band members, just run them through the system, and as long as there aren't any felony arrests, Homeland Security and the Secret Service can take care of it…expeditiously."

Branham stopped talking and smiled at Sue Ellen.

"Now, Miss Spenser, could I get you to give an old Texan a ride back to his humble home?"

"Why, yes, Mr. Branham, it would be an honor."

♫

Riley was armed with a notepad and shampoo bottle after making a final check of the room. He opened the Tacoma's tailgate and stuffed the shampoo into a bag.

"Can you drive?" he asked Melissa. "Just to Knoxville."

"Sure. No problem. It's not a stick."

"I just gotta get on the phone and make a bunch of arrangements. I've got to make sure everything's cool for the band."

"Have you talked to everybody?"

"Yeah, but this is evolving, and I just decided to get everybody together to play in Ashland next Wednesday night, so I gotta go back and make sure everybody can work things out."

For two hours, Riley made one phone call after another, consulting his notebook, leaving messages and trying in vain to procure social security numbers from musician friends who were probably in some mild form of impairment.

"Okay," he said at last as they reached the far side of Knoxville, headed for Interstate 40 through the Smokies. "Let's stop and eat. There's an Outback at the next exit."

"So, what's up with the band?" asked Melissa once they had been seated.

"It's a mess. Wade don't want to leave the state, something about some warrants being out, so I gotta work on that. So I called Alan down in Florida, and he's in, and Harvey's coming…"

"Harvey?"

"My friend in Greenville."

"Oh. So you're set," said Melissa.

"Well, getting there."

Riley looked across the table at Melissa, smiling.

"What?"

"I was just thinking, you're not exactly a schoolteacher anymore."

"You should know more schoolteachers," she said. "You'd be surprised."

♫

Melissa slept most of the way through the Smokies. When the truck emerged from the highest mountains, Riley's cell went off and there was a message from Eric Hays. Riley waited until he was past Asheville and safely on Interstate 26 before returning the call.

"I don't know how to say this," said Eric, "but Dad wants to go."

"To Washington? Ethan?"

"Uh, yeah. I can't explain it."

"When's the last time he left the county?"

"He's got a doctor he goes to in Hazard."

"I mean, I can't believe it."

"He says he's got to be there. Says there's some feeling deep in his soul. A bird probably told him."

Riley was speechless for a moment. "Riley? You still there?"

"Yeah, Eric, I'm here. I'm just thinking. I'll see what I can do. I like your old man, even if he is crazy. If he wants to go, I reckon he's got his reasons."

"He wouldn't hurt a fly," Eric said.

"I know it. Well, I'll call you back soon as I get something worked out. Bye."

Riley told Melissa, who by then had awakened. "I don't think I've ever heard anything in my life that surprised me that much," he said.

"You don't think he'd shoot the president, do you?"

"Nah," said Riley. "Not Ethan. Oh, shit."

"What?" asked Melissa.

"I forgot to fucking tell Adam we were leaving," he said. "Fuck."

Melissa started laughing. "Just call him," she said, exploding in mirth, "and tell him…"

"What?"

"…to meet you in…Oregon!"

CHAPTER TWENTY-FOUR
SECURITY LAPSES

Melissa spent the night at Riley's house. He rose first, as usual, and had coffee and breakfast ready when she emerged. They lingered in the living room, drank more coffee, smoked and watched *Imus in the Morning* on the RFD satellite channel.

"You're starting to enjoy this," she said.

"What? Imus?"

She merely smiled.

"I don't know about that," he said. "I feel like things are racing along, out of control, and I'm some kind of helpless passenger on a runaway train. I'm just letting it go, along for the ride."

"I think you're kind of learning how to play your cards," she said. "Pardon my mixing up the metaphor."

"Well, my life's going to change. I've accepted that. The trick is to have some control over the changes. There's no making the storm go away. Note the further mixing of the metaphor."

Melissa laughed softly.

"When Adam's story comes out, I'm going to end up biting a hand that's feeding me," Riley said. "But the alternative is to live a lie. I'm going to come across as petty and ungrateful to those who want to see it that way, but at some point, being a man means doing what you think is right. People ain't gonna like it. No getting around that. Well, I can't do nothing about that. To hell with them. I'm gonna do what's right and not worry about it."

"And you're going to do it vividly. Colorfully.

"Are you really going to Oregon?" she asked.

"Yep. I really am."

"Riley, I gotta see Mama. I can't just go running off again, what with the big shindig coming up."

"I totally understand. I was waiting to see what you said. I might even see if I can get Adam to spring for the flight. We could talk all the way out, and then the wedding ought to be a pretty evocative event for his story.

"I was pretty sure you weren't gonna go," he said. "If you had surprised me, I would've made arrangements. You're right. You need to see your mama. Mine's used to me 'gallivantin' out here, there and yonder'."

Melissa took a shower. Riley smoked a bowl. When Melissa emerged from the bathroom, he asked her, "What do you think the odds are of the three of us getting high?"

"Three of us?"

"Me, you and your mama," said Riley. "Be a good way for me to get to know her, don't you think?"

"She'd be mortified if she knew I told you that," said Melissa. "You can't ever let her know you know."

"We're so fuckin' weird."

"What's that supposed to mean?"

"Southerners," Riley said. "I mean, Southerners. We got this terrible habit of votin' dry and drinkin' wet."

He opened the shades and watched Melissa drive away, wondering if things would be the same when he returned from Oregon. He thought about a song for a few moments, but it wouldn't come together.

♫

Riley Mansfield was driving Adam Rhine crazy. The *Rolling Stone* writer was vaguely aware that something had been amiss. Something had happened that Riley and Melissa hadn't told him. He hadn't made an issue of it. His entreaties had been polite. But now, the two had roared out of Kentucky while he was still curled up in bed. Never mind that he had been curled up in bed until two in the afternoon.

Rhine had a bit of a secret. After a motorcycle accident two years earlier, he had developed a nasty addiction to Oxycontin. It wasn't hard to score when one was hanging around rock bands. As best Rhine could tell, though, this laidback folk singer was only inclined to use marijuana and booze, and not much booze at that. Adam's relative scarcity over the past few days had largely been because his body was screaming at him. He was out. His bones hurt. Now he was laid up in the London, Kentucky, Hampton Inn, and booze was the only relief. He had communicated with Riley only by email and text message, and now he was going to Oregon. He had some friends in Portland, if only he could…get there. If only he could figure out how to get himself together and from London, Kentucky to Atlanta, Georgia.

Riley was flying there on a commuter flight from Greenville-Spartanburg. They would meet at Jackson-Hartsfield for a flight to Portland. Adam didn't actually know where in Oregon it was that they were going, only that there was a wedding. He knew how he was going but not where exactly he was going. Musicians lived life spontaneously, but Riley Mansfield took it further.

Be resourceful, goddamnit! Drunkenly, he retrieved his laptop and turned it on. Adam didn't bother to pull out the power cord. What day was it? *Tuesday.* He'd already tried to straighten out once. The pain was unbearable. He couldn't possibly drive a rental car from Kentucky to Atlanta. What could he do?

Jesus. He could take a bus.

♫

"He's not there," said Banks McPherson by phone to Jed Langston, who was in Pensacola, Florida.

"Where is he?" Langston knew McPherson had been referring to Riley Mansfield.

"Probably at home. Our people aren't exactly sure how, but this Mansfield character has somehow managed to emit false signals, something about a DSL being routed into wireless transmission in another area. Either that, or he's shipped his laptop to Pensacola and gotten it to transmit by itself."

"Something's going on," said Langston. "He's got something

up his sleeve. He's playing with our heads. You want me to go straight to South Carolina?"

"No, take tomorrow off, Jed. We'll get you on an Air Force jet to the Northwest on Thursday morning."

"He's going to the Northwest?"

"Yep," said McPherson. "A ticket was issued in the name of John R. Mansfield yesterday. Greenville-Spartanburg to Atlanta to Portland. Mansfield's first name is John. Two tickets were purchased by Mansfield. One seat was for him. The other was for Adam W. Rhine."

"Do we know what they're going out there for? And who's Adam Rhine?"

"No idea. We're checking on Rhine. I'm sure we've got something, but I called you as soon as I got the name...Hang on."

McPherson came back on line. "Guy's a journalist," he said. "He works for *Rolling Stone*. His last story was on someone named Alicia Keys. You know who that is?"

"No clue."

"Me, neither."

"I don't like the sound of it, though."

"Well, this guy's a music writer. Mansfield's a musician. Guy's writing 'bout this musician who's this big hero. It's a story."

"*Rolling Stone* wouldn't be interested in making the President look good," said Langston.

"You're right about that. That's why we got to get you out there. We don't know what they're doing, where they're going. You'd better be at the airport when they get off a plane and tail them. Keep me apprised of the situation."

"Will do, Banks, I'll keep those lyin' weasels in sight."

"What are you doing on your day off?"

"I don't know, Banks. Thinking about seeing if I can find an abortionist to take a few potshots at."

"I'd appreciate if you wouldn't do that, Jed. Bye, now, and safe travels."

McPherson was never completely sure how to take it when Langston made his infrequent attempts at something akin to humor.

♩

Priscilla Hay called Riley on Wednesday morning.

"I didn't wake you, I hope," she said when he answered.

"No. I gotta bunch of shit to do. Wash clothes, pay bills, go to the trash dump."

"What are you doing now?"

"Watching *Imus in the Morning*."

"You're high?"

"Sure…Not bad, though. Just a buzz."

"I need to talk to you," she said.

"Go ahead," he said. "It's cool. Honest. You're, like, my mom, all of a sudden?"

"No. You're right."

"Well, go ahead. Give it to me straight, copper. I can take it."

Priscilla laughed, even though it was ridiculous. "What I'd like for you to do, after you play your songs, is leave the stage to the left, and you'll recognize someone there by what he's wearing. He'll escort you to the MSNBC satellite truck, and we're going to hook you up with David Shuster for a live interview. Can you handle that?"

"Yeah," he said. "Why not Keith Olbermann?"

"Your time slot in the Celebration of America—that's the official name, clever, huh?—is fifteen minutes before Shuster goes on the air. You can say whatever you want, but what we hope you'll say is that the appearance with President Harmon shouldn't be implied as any endorsement."

"All right. We can talk about that when I get to Washington, okay?"

"Yeah," she said. "That's fine."

"Okay, what else?"

"Fox News and CNN have also requested interviews after your performance. How do you want to handle that?"

"Tell them I'm granting no interviews."

"That might seem suspicious."

"What about me ain't? It might be suspicious if I hadn't been avoiding publicity for most of three weeks. What would seem suspicious is if we told them—or MSNBC told them—that I was talking only to them. I think you got to do two things, Priscilla. First, you got to lie through your teeth—it'll be me officially, of course, not you—because that's the only way you're going to keep them at bay, and second, you gotta make sure that MSNBC doesn't make a sound about me being on there until a few moments before I actually come on. I would suggest that very few people know what's going on."

"You've got pretty good judgment for a man who's stoned," she observed.

"I told you. I'm just a little high. Buzzed. Not baked."

"Well, I've got some bad news. I'm a little suspicious that they're on to us in regard to hiding your whereabouts. I got an email from a mid-level RNC operative that makes reference to you putting your band together. He made mention of your 'Oregon trip' and asked the name and social security of the musician you were bringing in from out there. Now, as far as I know, the only way they could know you're going to Oregon is either through intercepting these phone calls, which I don't actually think is likely, or by somehow stumbling upon your purchase of a plane ticket to Oregon. Are you flying into Portland?"

"Yeah. Adam Rhine is going with me. He's the guy from *Rolling Stone*."

"You don't think he could've tipped them off?"

"Don't think so, but I'll check on it when I see him tomorrow. Adam could've blabbed it to somebody who told somebody else, et cetera, but again, I don't believe it. What about your end?"

"What do you mean?"

"I mean, who knows, at whatever the name of that firm you work for, at MSNBC, at the Democratic Party, shit, I don't know? Who knows?"

"Nobody knows exactly what I'm doing," Priscilla said. "My boss, George Grinnell, knows I'm doing something, and he knows it has something to do with you, and he knows there's a pretty good chance that you're going to help us in some way, but I've told him that security is important and that I need his trust if we're going to pull this off. And he's cool with that. And I trust him as much as you apparently trust this *Rolling Stone* reporter."

"Well," said Riley. "I expect musicians and politicians probably run about neck and neck at keeping secrets. We might both be fools."

"Well, I'll hold up my end, and you take care of yours," said Priscilla.

"No choice, at this point," said Riley. "Bye, now. Keep in touch."

Riley put the phone down and leaned back in his easy chair. *God, why can't this be over?* He had to run errands and do a dozen other things he dreaded doing, and he had to get going because he was supposed to meet Melissa that night for wings and beer, or maybe Mexican food and beer. Something and beer. He needed to be all packed because his flight from Greenville-Spartanburg to Atlanta was a little after seven in the morning, he was pretty sure. He fumbled through his little, incomplete address book to confirm this. Seven fifty-five departure.

At the moment, though, Riley wasn't fit for anything but playing his guitar.

♫

Adam got himself together as best he could. He decided to leave the rental car in the Hampton Inn parking lot and wait until he reached Atlanta and call Avis to tell them to pick it up. He poured vodka into two Aquafina bottles, stuck them into the pockets of his windbreaker and called a taxi. The bus was to leave at 3:05 p.m. and arrive at the Atlanta airport at 1:20 Thursday morning. Along the way were stops in the Tennessee cities of Knoxville, Athens, Cleveland and Chattanooga, then a stop in Marietta, Georgia, then the main Atlanta station and a transfer to Jackson-Hartsfield. He'd have an hour stop in Knoxville right off the bat.

He'd just take the occasional swig of Absolut, just enough to keep the screaming of his bones and muscles at bay. Not enough to get sick. He needed to eat. Not enough to pass out. Enough to keep from whimpering, or crying, or howling like a dog in its death throes. He could do this.

He boarded the bus early, making sure he could get his two bags safely in the cargo area. As he watched others boarding, Adam couldn't help but be reminded of the bar in *Star Wars*. No one had tusks, but it was a tough looking crew. Tall, roughhewn, unshaven men in flannel shirts and blue jeans, presumably coal miners. Plainly dressed women, holding babies in their arms and leading older children with dirty faces and clothes. Adam stared at the vacant eyes and hungry looks, and it made him shiver.

Adam tried to bide the time by reading a Chuck Klosterman book, absentmindedly taking small swigs of vodka at intervals. He was close to nodding off in sleep when he picked up the slightest scent of cannabis in the air. A kid, maybe twenty, had just emerged from the tight bathroom, three rows behind him at the back of the bus.

A towheaded boy, maybe five, said, "Hey, Ma, somebody's smokin' pot!" Adam glanced at the child's mother, blushing and whispering for him to hush. The kid who'd been blazing had a cheap gig bag, undoubtedly holding a similarly cheap guitar, in the open storage shelf above his seat. Maybe he would change buses in Knoxville and head off to Nashville, there to have his dreams destroyed. Both arms were tattooed in snakelike patterns, and he wore a Tom Petty tee shirt with the arms gone and perhaps the grimiest jeans Adam had ever seen. These hadn't been bought with the knees worn out. Adam looked around and realized there were many grimy, dust-tinted blue jeans being worn by his fellow travelers.

In Knoxville, Adam followed the kid with the guitar off the bus, careful to watch his step as he wobbled slightly down the steps to the pavement. Predictably, the bus station was in the old part of town, fairly close to the University of Tennessee.

Once off the bus, Adam tried to score some pills from the kid with the gig bag. Kid just had the weed. They split a joint in an alley down the street. It didn't help much.

It was all Adam could do to stagger back up the sidewalk to the bus station. He drew a little interest from a cop on the beat, but the guy let him slide.

CHAPTER TWENTY-FIVE
FLYING BY THE SEAT OF THE PANTS

Riley Mansfield had been absentmindedly and passively reading *USA Today* when a rather astonishing incarnation of Adam Rhine appeared in front of him at the Jackson-Hartsfield gate.

Rhine was unshaven, sweaty and malodorous. He wore a beige blazer almost uniformly darkened by mucky stains. His shoes were muddy. By comparison, the rolling suitcase, obnoxiously designed to take up all the overhead space in the plane, looked almost new.

Riley had checked a bag but had with him the Little Martin he had purchased to replace the Baby Taylor that exploded in the treetops of Greer, South Carolina, near Greenville-Spartanburg Airport. His first return to the airport had been uneventful, Riley feeling neither traumatized nor sentimental.

Now, however, he was sitting across from Adam Rhine, who looked pathetic.

"Adam," said Riley, "I didn't know you were homeless."

"I don't know how I'm going to make it. I rode a bus through the night from Kentucky. I got to Atlanta at, I don't know, one or two in the morning. For most of the past eight hours, I've been in the middle of Atlanta, trying to sleep in a bus station."

"Which is scary," Riley said.

"Yes."

"Don't you think, like, some explanation is in order here? I mean, why in the fuck did you ride a bus? I mean, you do actually work for *Rolling Stone*, right?"

"We need to talk...privately," said Adam. "Let's go see if we can find a gate where there aren't people everywhere."

"That's pretty hard in this airport."

"Well, let's just do the best we can."

"Off the record?"

"Yeah."

"Remember when we first set the ground rules for this deal? No such thing as off the record."

"Fuck you. You're not writing a story about me."

"No, but I think a song is a distinct possibility."

Adam smiled, only slightly. "Just change the name, will you?"

"Sure," said Riley. "Adam's hard to rhyme."

Fifty yards away, they found a sparsely populated boarding gate, one with rows of chairs that were mostly vacant. Adam ran his fingers through his greasy hair. Riley waited patiently for him to begin. He knew it couldn't be easy.

"Back in oh-six, man, I got fucked up pretty bad in a motorcycle accident," said Rhine. "Guy ran a stop sign in a Volvo station wagon. He almost got it stopped but still hit my Ducati a glancing blow. I broke three ribs, my left arm and my right leg in two places."

"Shit."

"I was laid up in the hospital for a week, and when I got out, and went through all the rehab and shit, I got myself hooked on painkillers. Oxycontin, specifically."

"I don't know nothing about it, man, but I've heard that can be some evil shit to get off of."

Adam's eyes welled up. "My fucking bones throb, man. 'Cause, like, I don't have any."

"Bones?"

"Funny," Adam replied. "Normally, when I'm hanging out at music venues, you know, I know guys who can hook me up. But, for some reason, I thought there was an extra bottle in my bags when I flew to Kentucky from L.A. And, at first, I wasn't too concerned, but then what I thought was gonna take a couple of days wound up taking a lot longer, and I didn't notice I didn't have more of the Oxycontin until, well, I ran out. And, so, since Monday, I haven't had any. And, I don't know, man, by Tuesday, shit, I couldn't even function.

"All I could do was drink, man, and that's why I had to take a bus down here. I can't function well when I'm drunk, but, man, I can't function at all if I'm not."

"Well," said Riley, "I can't even relate. Pretty much all I've ever done is drink and smoke weed."

"Well, I wish right now I was you."

"You gotta get off it," said Riley. "Shit's gonna kill you. You gotta wean yourself off it. I got a good bit of weed stashed in my checked luggage. I'm sure there'll be some around in the wedding party."

"Man, I don't think weed's gonna cut it."

"It's gotta be better than vodka, man. You better eat something, though."

They found a Burger King. It wasn't easy, but Adam managed to down a small cheeseburger and some fries.

"We're sitting in first class," Adam said, peering at his ticket.

"Yeah. I'm fairly popular with the airline."

"Booze is on the house. God, I hope they're serving as soon as we board."

"You can drink doubles, man," said Riley. "We get on the plane, you take the window seat. It'll be easier if I'm on the aisle. I can shield you a little if you're in pain. And I won't drink. I'll just order booze and you can have mine."

"I think I'm gonna need it. The best thing for me to do on the flight out is pass out."

"Shit, man, it'd be a better story if it was me writing about you."

♫

"Vodka rocks," said Riley shortly after they boarded. Adam ordered the same and switched on his "voice-activated digital recorder."

It wasn't an interview. It was a wobbly conversation. Riley volunteered as much information as he could. Several times he had to calm Adam, grasping his forearm and whispering, as hypnotically as he could muster, soothing words and encouragement. Riley felt mildly as if he were in the movie *Midnight Cowboy.*

Riley was struck by the absurdity of this scene and this latest improbable twist in the tracks, careening along on this runaway train his life had become. But, after pausing long enough that Adam turned to stare, Riley forged ahead.

"Okay," he said, "fundamentally, at base, I'm a country singer, a country songwriter. I grew up on a farm, with an alcoholic daddy, and I've got a lot of memories of coming home late at night, from an auction sale or a horse show, him driving drunk and the two of us listening to the Grand Ole Opry on the radio. Most of the time, I could get along with my daddy better when he was drunk than sober. When he was sober, you couldn't talk to him, and when he was drunk, he might not make much sense, but you could talk to him.

"Anyway—what was I talking about? Oh, yeah, country music—I remember this time when I was in, like, the eighth grade, and some of my friends came up, we were in the library, and asked me what my favorite group was."

"What did you say?"

"AC/DC. I didn't know a single song. Or maybe Cheap Trick. Some group I was vaguely aware of being popular."

"Next time the nice stewardess—don't call her that, it's flight attendant nowadays—next time the nice flight attendant comes by, I think it's time we had another cocktail."

By the time Riley finished reminiscing more about his musical roots, he discovered that Adam Rhine had fallen fast asleep, still shuddering a little. Riley got a blanket from the overhead bin and placed it over him. He picked up the recorder and switched it off. He winked at the flight attendant and ordered another drink, this one actually for himself. He found a bag folded in the pouch of the seat in front of him. Riley flattened the sack and stuffed it behind his back so that he could provide assistance quickly if Adam suddenly sickened.

For about three hours, he later estimated, Riley slept. He awakened after he sensed, somehow, that the plane was starting to descend. Adam's face was a bit sweaty, but Riley managed to rouse him with relative ease.

"How you making it?" Riley asked.

"Aw, it's not too bad. I think I could use another drink. You?"

"I'm fine, man. I wouldn't mind a cigarette."

"I thought you didn't smoke except when you were high."

"That, too," said Riley.

♫

Jed Langston watched Riley Mansfield and Adam Rhine exit Delta Flight 1761 from the seating area of a nearby gate. Langston wasn't wearing the toupee he had worn when he encountered Mansfield at Rockingham, and he had shaved the mustache. He wore a black Springsteen tee shirt, new jeans, leather cowboy boots and a No Fear ball cap. He was a bit old for the attire, but that was his intent.

From behind sunglasses, Langston studied the two. Mansfield—lanky with longish, flowing, dark-brown hair, bright blue, penetrating eyes, plaid western shirt, jean jacket, New Balance sneakers—looked rested and affable as he chatted briefly with an airline representative, apparently asking directions to the baggage area. The *Rolling Stone* writer was quite the contrast. He was unshaven, sweaty, haggard-looking and, quite possibly, drunk. The writer had a backpack, undoubtedly containing his laptop, and pulled a small rolling bag. Mansfield had a small guitar strapped to his back. The writer trudged along, fatigued and wobbly. Langston gave them twenty yards, knowing he would have to dawdle in order not to overtake them.

"I need a drink," Adam said.

"That's cool," said Riley. "There's a bar…see…on the left. I'll go on ahead and pick up my suitcase. I'll just wait for you there. You'll be okay, right?"

"Yeah, I can make it. It's not that bad…as long as I can get this vodka buzz going again."

"Don't have but one," said Riley. "We'll smoke some weed in the rental car."

Langston watched as the writer peeled off in a bar and Riley kept going. What the…? He stopped for a moment in his tracks, considering. Then Langston walked into the small bar and found an open seat on a stool next to the writer.

"What'll you have?" the bartender asked.

"Just club soda, thanks. With lime." The bartender frowned a bit until Langston crammed a five into the jug on the bar.

Adam had ordered a double. Couldn't hurt. Perhaps he could have a second. He felt sort of accustomed to being drunk, not to mention feeling miserable. The Oxycontin had kept all this at bay, but it was scary how much Adam had found he needed it.

"How ya doing?" asked Langston.

"Umm, okay."

Rhine didn't even look up. Barely acknowledged it. This will perk him up, thought Langston.

Langston lowered his voice and leaned discreetly toward Rhine. "I, uh, don't suppose you're looking to score?" he asked.

Adam turned immediately and looked directly at Langston. "No, thanks," he said.

"I'm not a narc. I'm a friend. You look like you're in bad shape. I can get whatever you want."

"Thanks," Rhine said, "but…no thanks."

He did finish the drink and order another. Langston scribbled a phone number on a slip of paper. "Call me if you need me," he said. Then Langston motioned to the bartender, paid Adam's bill and walked away.

♫

It was dank and rainy as they exited the airport, courtesy of Avis.

"Where we headed? Nearby?" Adam asked.

"Nope," said Riley. "Headed to the coast. Little town called Gearhart. Best I can figure, it's a little over an hour's drive. Ninety minutes, maybe."

"Nice town?"

"Don't know. Never been there.

"My friend's name is Neil Wilson. He was a film student when he first contacted me. He sent me a wedding invitation. He's got this friend—I don't even know his name—but he plays in a band that's pretty popular out here. Neil's been telling me for, I dunno, years that we should get together. I got a weekend to spare before the big shindig in Washington, so I decided to come out here and recruit this guy to play in the band with me."

"For, like, two songs?"

"Three. The latest word is that I get to play one of my songs. I haven't decided which one yet. We're getting the band together next Wednesday in Virginia, and we'll have all day, at least afternoon, to rehearse, and then we'll do a show, all of us together, just a jam session, really, at this club called Ashland Tea and Coffee. It's one of my favorite places to play."

"And if he can't do it?"

"It'll still be cool. I already got another acoustic, an electric guitar, bass, drums, fiddle. This is just another excursion. It'll be cool to go to Neil's wedding. We'll drink, blaze, play music on the beach, make some friends. This is my one last chance, hopefully, to get away from everything."

"For God's sake, stop at a liquor store."

"In about ten miles, there's a state park," Riley said. "We'll stop there and blaze. It'll be fine, man. It'll be good."

"All right, I'll try," Adam said, "but stop at a goddamned liquor store anyway. You say blazing will do the same thing. I say I need a backup."

"Okay," said Riley. He patted Adam on the shoulder. "We'll get through this thing, man. You can do it. It's got to start getting better. Your body's gonna lay down the arms eventually."

"Fuck," said Rhine. "I hope so."

♫

Riley pulled out his new Little Martin, which he'd played for only a half hour or so.

"It's a good prop," he said. "If somebody comes along, I'll just start plunking away and it'll be cool."

Riley lit a joint, took a deep hit and passed it to Adam. "Smoke the shit out of it," he said. "It ain't gonna make you nauseated. It ought to just numb you up nicely."

"I know how to smoke weed," said Adam.

"I should hope so." Riley tuned the guitar.

They were both quite buzzed when Riley said quietly, "Shit."

"What?"

"Don't look around," he said. "There's some ranger or something in an SUV. He just pulled in and stopped, way down at the other end of the parking lot. Just be cool."

Riley popped a stick of gum and gave one to Adam. He retrieved a small bottle of clear, thick liquid from the zip-up pocket in his gig bag. He squirted some out and rubbed his hands with it.

"Wash your hands with this," Riley said, handing the plastic bottle to Adam. "It disappears and dries, and it'll get the smell of weed off your fingers. Sometimes the TSA confiscates it at the airports, but they never take but one, and I've always got another bottle stashed somewhere. Besides, they don't remove liquids from checked luggage."

"You're amazing, man."

"I also got a clean record," Riley said. "Gotta be cool to get away with shit. Man, is this beautiful, or what?"

Fog still hung over the trees, but somehow it only added mystery to the majesty.

"It's like being in Twin Peaks," Adam said.

"In more ways than one," said Riley. "Don't look now, but here come the cops."

Riley calmly picked up his guitar and began playing a song. A gospel song. The one he wrote. "Come On Down."

"Seeking help from the baby Jesus?" Adam asked.

"Fuck, I'll rededicate my life to Christ if that's what it takes," Riley said, between verse and chorus.

Riley kept strumming the guitar. "Be cool," he whispered. "Everything's cool. Smell's not an issue. The air already smells like pine. Sing along or something. Clap your hands softly. Tap your toes. Look natural."

A tall, rugged ranger opened the door of the SUV, coded in the same colors as his crisp uniform. Another remained inside.

Riley glanced over and waved. The ranger smiled.

Then the ranger stuffed a paper sack of doughnut wrappers and paper coffee cups into the waste basket next to the picnic table where Riley Mansfield was playing guitar and Adam Rhine was trying to be cool.

"Thanks for the tunes, fellows," the ranger said. Then he walked back to the SUV, climbed in and drove off.

CHAPTER TWENTY-SIX
TRIPPIN'

The coast looked kind of…Scottish. It was warmer, but the inn where Riley Mansfield and Adam Rhine were staying could have overlooked the Firth of Forth. No links-style golf course, of course, but Riley just imagined one because all he knew about the coast of Scotland came from watching the British Open on television.

It was mid-afternoon as Riley and Adam walked the beach. Riley had called Neil Wilson, who, despite the fact that he was getting married two days later, still had time to come pick up Riley and, presumably, Adam, for the raucous gatherings that would inevitably lead up to the ceremonies.

"Can we sit down?" asked Adam. "I need to rest, man."

"Yeah, sure. You gonna make it?"

"I'm fucked up. Major fucked up." Adam sat in the sand, which was all over the seat of his designer jeans. "I think I need to lie down."

Riley checked his watch. "We got a couple hours before Neil picks us up. You want to go back and crash?"

"If I can fucking make it. I don't know, man. I may not make it to the party."

As they walked back up the beach—Adam trudged, as if he were staggering home from war—a chunky man with red hair, maybe forty-five years old, walked past in the opposite direction, walking a large dog. Riley tipped his straw hat, thinking mildly that the man looked familiar somehow.

Adam recognized him right away. It was the man from the airport bar. The man who'd offered to sell him drugs. Why was he here? Could it be some unbelievable coincidence? *Couldn't be.* So how did he know where they were? Had he followed them from Portland? Why, he must have.

"Have you ever seen that guy back there?" Riley asked as they walked along a road carved into the sand, heading back up to the inn.

"What guy?"

"The guy with the dog," Riley said. "On the beach."

"Oh. No, I don't think so. I really wasn't paying attention."

Riley had noticed Adam had been paying attention. Riley, whose room was on the same floor but at the other end of a long hall, accompanied Adam to his room. Adam staggered in and sat on the side of the bed, sweating profusely. Riley watched as Adam's tee shirt—Death Cab for Cutie!—became dripping wet before his eyes.

"Man, we better get some air on," he said, finding a thermostat on the wall near the bedroom entrance and dialing it down.

"I do not think I can function," said Adam. "If I'm gonna ride this out, I might have to do it by myself."

"You wanna smoke a J? Prob'ly help you sleep."

"Nah, I got some booze. It's okay." Adam poured some vodka into a plastic cup next to the ice bucket. He took a shot.

"Let me have your key," Riley said. "You go ahead and crash. I'm gonna go out and get you some snacks. You gotta keep something on your stomach. I'll bring some nuts or pretzels, something, and some Cokes."

"Get some Red Bull, man. Maybe if I get some of that in me, I'll rally. Be up to hanging at the party."

"Do what you gotta do, man. Right now, you rest, and I'll be back in fifteen."

Riley took the rental car and found a country store on the main road, a couple miles north of the tiny seacoast town. Gearhart was kind of attached to Seaside, which was larger and more populated by visitors. Seaside was south. He didn't know what was north beyond the store, except, eventually, Astoria.

Riley returned to the room juggling six Diet Cokes, four Red Bulls and a bag of pretzels. Adam was sound asleep. Riley put the drinks in the fridge and filled the ice bucket at the machine down the hall. He left the keys on the desk, then went back to his own room, smoked half a joint, poured himself a Diet Coke and called Priscilla Hay.

Or let it ring a couple of times until he realized it was two hours later in the east, and Priscilla had left work and was probably out with some friends, or at some soiree at an embassy or something. She would see the number and call if anything important was up.

So he called Melissa. It was about eight in the east. She answered on the third ring.

"Well, hello," she said.

"Are you back in your right mind yet?"

She didn't know quite what to make of that remark. He could hear her say, "Mom, it's Riley." Then he knew she was walking out on the front porch. And he was pretty sure she was lighting a Marlboro Light. So, three thousand miles away, he reached for an ash tray and lit one, too.

"So, what's going on in Henry?"

"Uh, it's pretty normal."

"Quite a change, huh?"

She laughed a little. "Well, we haven't had to deal with any fake deputies looking for fake marijuana plants," she said.

"Well, that's good," he said. "It's still Shitstorm Central out here."

"Oh, no…"

"It'll be okay," he said. "Adam's in bad shape. Come to find out, he's hooked on drugs, and he can't get any, and he's kind of, like, in withdrawal."

"Oh, my God."

"I think maybe it's getting better. I'm helping him through it, best I can. I don't have any experience with shit like this. I've never taken anything that grabbed my guts and started screaming for me to get some goddamn more. I hope the worst is passed. He's asleep right now. I managed to get him out here without it looking too desperate."

"You never knew anybody else hooked on drugs?"

"Well, I guess, but it's something you don't actually know, I reckon, unless you're doing 'em, too. What I'm finding out is that I never knew anybody who was hooked on dope and ran out of it.

"But I'll manage. I think I got him convinced he's got to get off it, and the best way to get off it is to just grit his teeth and tough it out. He's desperate. He knows it's gonna kill him, I think, if he lets it."

"Well, call me if you need me."

"Oh, I need you, but I'm glad you're not out here right now. You've been through enough, for now."

"Well, I'm looking forward to next week," she said. "When are you getting back?"

"Sunday night late."

"When you going to Richmond?"

"Tuesday. Practice all day Wednesday, play a gig, go to D.C. on Thursday. I'll probably talk to Priscilla in the morning, see what she's got going."

"Anything scary?"

"As in?"

"Anybody following you? Anybody breaking into your room? Anybody searching your car?"

"Nah. None of that. I hope I got 'em off looking for me somewhere else. You know, you'd think they'd back off since I'm doing their goddamned show and all."

"They're just suspicious. They're control freaks. They get paid good money to make sure everything is just so."

"I guess," he said. "When's it going to end?"

"I'd say it'll end the minute you go off national television."

"There might be a few seconds of silence until *Rolling Stone* magazine comes out," he said.

"You think Adam's going to be able to write it?"

"Oh, I think he'd better. He's spent a shitload of *Rolling Stone*'s money. He's been writing long, ambitious stories for a couple years while he's been hooked on painkillers. With a little luck, he'll still be able to write once he gets off 'em."

"What's he like?"

"You mean, without any drugs?"

"Yeah."

"He can't function. He's been on a drunk since Tuesday, trying to keep enough vodka in him to keep from screaming and going nuts. By and large, he's succeeded, but it's painful to watch. He took a fuckin' bus from Kentucky to Atlanta 'cause he knew he couldn't drive."

"Damn," she said.

"You should've seen him in the airport. Dude was nasty, unshaven, barely able to act straight enough that the cops wouldn't hassle him. On the flight out, I kept on ordering drinks for both of us, then letting him drink 'em. It's taking a toll. I've been trying to get him to smoke weed instead, but I can't get him to completely buy into it. I'm about to go play music with Neil and his friends. I doubt Adam's gonna make it.

"I gotta go," Riley said. "Just wanted to fill you in on what's going on. Don't let it bother you. Enjoy the time with your mom. I'll be okay. Hopefully, I'll be nice and relaxed and ready to get the shitstorm over with in a little over a week. I wish you were here, but I'm glad you're not. That make sense?"

"Yeah," she said. "Be careful. I still love you."

"I love you, too," he said. "See you Monday, and I'll call whenever I got a minute."

Riley piddled around with his new guitar for fifteen minutes or so. Neil called to say he was on his way.

♫

Neil Wilson hadn't seen Riley in five years, when he and a college classmate had included Riley in their senior film project. They had accompanied Riley from place to place, watched him play his guitar and sing his songs, drunk moonshine with him, smoked weed, sat around and jammed, and, of course, interviewed him, though the interview had been sort of the least significant aspect of the experience. The topic of their documentary had been singer-songwriters who performed alone, trying to hold a crowd without the accompaniment of a band. They had explored the independence of loners like Riley and titled their work "The Loneliness of the Stage."

"So, you're not exactly in love with being a comic-book hero, huh?"

"It sucks, man," Riley said. "Sometimes I kind of wish the plane had blown up."

"Aw, man…"

"I'm just kidding. It's been interesting. I ought to be writing songs about it, but let's not talk about unimportant shit. Besides, it'll all trickle out in the next couple days if we just sit around, play guitar and catch up. When do I get to meet the lucky gal?"

"Tonight," said Neil. "It's all really informal. We're all just gonna party two nights, then get married and party some more. Sarah's gonna be there for all of it."

"No insistence on keeping the lovely bride hidden from public view?"

"As long as it's not, uh, public view in the sense of having a mug shot in the newspaper."

"Six o'clock news."

"Nah, we're trying to avoid that. We got good security," Neil said.

"So, where we going?"

"I'm just gonna run some errands and show you where my uncle's house is. I thought we'd just ride around and shoot the shit, then I'll take you back to the inn and you can drive over. Cool?"

"Works, man."

"So, it's gotta, like, be killing you to stand up onstage and sing a few happy tunes in front of Sam fuckin' Harmon," Neil said.

"Yeah, pretty much. I'm just trying to do the minimum, man,

then get on with life. It may never be the same, but it's got to get back to normal a little bit."

"This is kind of your ultimate test."

"Yeah?"

"Well, here's a thing that happened, and immediately, you got all kinds of changes, but also all kinds of opportunities. You can fuckin' exploit the shit out of this. But it's not you, is it?"

"Nah, man, I like my life the way it is. I don't want to play Vegas, man. I don't want to wear rhinestones. I don't want to perform on charity telethons."

"You know you're the only holdout?"

"Huh?"

"Me and Lane talked to five singer-songwriters, right? We really stressed you because you were the only guy we became buds with. All the others have left the simple troubadour's life behind. It's been four years since 'Loneliness' came out, and you're the only one still doing your thing. And thing is, man, you're the one who had sudden stardom dropped right in your lap. You don't fucking care."

"You might be the only one—well, one of the few—I know who doesn't at least think I've slightly lost my mind by not just getting swept away."

"Dude, you're a hero, not 'cause you kept some batshit fucker from blowing up a plane. You're a hero because you do what you fuckin' want to do."

"I'm fuckin' nuts is what I am. It's the weed."

"I got some," said Neil.

"I'm glad," said Riley.

♫

The house reminded Riley of the neat rowhouses that used to exist in the textile mill villages of Henry. Apparently a relative of Neil Wilson's lived in this neat, wood-framed house, and there was a garage in the back. Riley was impressed by the white picket fence that surrounded the little plot and by the burnt-black stain on the walls of the garage.

When Riley entered the garage, after asking directions at the front door from the nice lady who must be Neil's aunt, he immediately picked up the mild scent of cannabis. No one was rolling joints, though. A bong was being passed around. In fact, two. The one apparently owned by Neil was compact and made mostly of blue-tinted plastic. Another, more ornate and made of crockery, was presumably the property of Sarah Mahaffey, to whom he would soon be wed.

"Riley," Neil announced, "I want you to meet my friends. Hey, everybody, say hello to Riley Mansfield, folk musician and foiler—is that a word?—of terrorist attacks."

Introductions were exchanged as Riley unzipped his gig bag and retrieved his guitar.

"Want a hit?" Neil asked.

"Sure. Why the hell not?" Riley took the blue bong from Neil.

"Thanks," he said, coughing a little. "I needed that."

Riley leaned his little guitar against a stack of wooden boxes, all filled with paperbacks. Through the gaps in the wood Riley saw titles by George Orwell, Graham Greene, Dick Francis and Elmore Leonard. He sat in a wooden chair and listened a while. Sarah, whom he'd never met, studied him. He was older than anyone else, spaced neatly between this generation and their parents.

The mandolinist was named Cody Huard. Riley mainly listened, but sang a little harmony, to a couple Dylan songs. Cody's mandolin playing was, as Neil had promised, first rate.

"Play us one of your songs, Riley."

He looked around the little circle of musicians and singers, his eyes stopping for a moment to study Sarah. She seemed a little disapproving. She was about to marry his friend. He wanted to win her over.

"All right," he said, finally. "There's, uh, obviously, some of me in this song, but I actually wrote it about my ex-brother-in-law.

Monte Dutton

I'm not a great admirer of his, but I tried to get inside his head, kind of like the way Steve Earle does. I was…kind of into that for a while.

My woman ran off and left me
Ain't got enough money to raise my kids
My oldest boy goes to college
He makes a lot more sense than I ever did
I should've named him Abel 'cause his brother's Cain
They're a ray of sunshine and a sheet of rain
One might grow up to be president
If he can spring the other from the state pen
Gotta bucket of right
A bushel of wrong
That's why I sit here stoned at the crack of dawn
Sit here stoned at the crack of dawn
I got a Zip-Loc bag of weed
Comes in handy when I'm down on my luck
Get up early in the morning
Get a little bit high when the sun comes up
Shave and shower, wash away the smell
Go to work feelin' cool as hell

"I'm serious," said the mandolinist.

Know what I'm doin, don't get caught
I gotta heap of friends who work for the law
Couple of hits, the blues is gone
That's why I sit here stoned at the crack of dawn
Sit here stoned at the crack of dawn

Eyes danced with delight. Sarah laughed softly, her doubts evaporating.

Some folks prob'ly think I'm crazy
What the fuck I care about what they say?
They prob'ly think I need to grow up

The Audacity of Dope

Just another way to waste my life away
I never was into them asshole drugs
It's the groovy shit that I always dug
Ain't enough to say it ain't too bad
It's the coolest feeling that I ever had
Without a buzz I couldn't write this song
That's why I sit here stoned at the crack of dawn
Sit here stoned at the crack of dawn
That's why I sit here stoned at the crack of dawn

"That was quite germane to the subject matter," said Sarah, smiling.

The keg was full of something strong and local. Riley had pedestrian tastes as far as beer was concerned, but he drank with enthusiasm. How could the taste of beer seem, uh, *buttery*? *Oh, well.* It wasn't half bad.

"So, uh, what's the deal after the wedding? Where's the honeymoon?" Riley asked.

"No honeymoon, at least not for a while," said Neil.

"We have been co-habitating for quite some time," added Sarah.

"I bought weed instead," said Neil.

Two more bong hits and Riley was feeling no pain, which failed to set him apart from the rest of the group. He lit a cigarette. Expectation and smoke hung heavy in the air. They all knew who he was and what he had done. And they wanted to hear about it. All was silent momentarily. "Okay," he said. "I'm thinking y'all, like, want to know what the fuck happened."

Nods. He went through the spiel.

"So what's this shit about you playing music for President Asshole?" Neil was nothing if not direct.

"Just the minimum required," Riley said dreamily. "I'm no fan, I promise, in spite of my Southern accent. His goons tried to pressure me into, like, touring with the campaign. They did several things to get the message across. Finally I said, okay, what if I played a song or two in some kind of...non-partisan thing? Just general, across the board patriotism. I'll do that. Next thing you know, there's this big celebration on the National Mall. I just found out I get to play one of my songs—I wrote one called 'Your Independence Day'—and a Merle Haggard song and 'This Land Is Your Land.'

"It's weird," said Neil. "You're, like, in all the supermarket tabloids as some kind of recluse. Like you're the next J.D. Salinger."

"Or Howard Hughes," said Riley, holding up his hands. "See how long my fingernails are getting?"

"And yet, here you are, on a few days' notice, showing up for my wedding. Cool."

"I'm just trying to do what it takes to get everybody off my back."

"Why don't you want to be a star? You could be big, man." It was Cody, who played in a band that apparently wanted to be big.

"I'm doing okay. People record my songs. I get royalties. I travel around, pretending I'm some troubadour or something, and play little clubs, and that's what I like to do. What I don't like to do is be a hypocrite."

"So ditch the prez," said Sarah.

"I am. As soon as this is over, *Rolling Stone* is going to run an article. This guy has been following me around and interviewing me."

"So he's gonna write about all the shit you've been through?"

"He's gonna write what he wants to, but, yeah, he knows everything. I've given him access. He's been hanging out with me and Melissa, everywhere we go. He hasn't asked a question I haven't answered.

"That's the method to my madness." Riley looked around. "If your daddy's, like, a Republican Congressman, or, for that matter, a Republican alderman, I'd appreciate it if you wouldn't tell him this shit."

"What's an alderman?" asked Neil.

Riley laughed. "It's what they used to call the people on City Council back home."

"What do you think of the Democrats?" asked Sarah.

"I don't know," Riley said. "I haven't really been paying attention. The nomination's still up in the air, right? The former vice president, Murrah, right? Against a senator from Iowa. Baskin. I just figure anyone would be better than Harmon."

Neil's uncle—Larry something or other, last name wasn't Wilson—wandered through amiably, showing no sign of irritation at the sweet smell that hung in the air. He introduced himself to Riley, lingered to have a beer, then retired gracefully back to the house. When he left, Neil said, "Uncle Larry used to blaze. I kind of wish he still did. He's got it in his head that he's too old."

Between his stoner song and his liberal politics, Riley sensed he had passed Sarah's litmus test.

"Do you, like, do mushrooms?" asked Neil.

"I haven't," said Riley. "Blazing's pretty much all I've ever done in the...realm of the...extralegal."

"Well," said Neil, holding some tin foil he was unfolding, "if you, like, just ate a little, it would only mildly loosen up reality in a way that I think you would find aesthetically pleasing."

"I'm pretty high."

"That's what I'm saying, man. High enough."

He ate a little and chased it with a big swig of that butternut-tasting dark beer.

"Ah," said Riley with a bit of a burp. "Que sera, sera, whatever will be, will be."

Riley picked up the guitar and began singing simple words from country standards, heartbreaking, mournful words, and gradually, he thought to himself that he was singing these righteous words with a soulfulness that he had never achieved, which, in fact, quite possibly, no man had ever achieved.

The tinfoil was on a wooden barrel in the middle of the makeshift circle. Riley ate a little more.

The feeling was good. Real good. Sarah's face shone radiantly, but her friend, Lily, maybe, or Rose, some flower, reminded Riley of Glenn Close in *The Natural,* her face wondrously illuminated in the upper deck of Wrigley Field, and Riley thought about Roy Hobbs hitting that home run, and as he ran around the bases, something urgent came alive in Riley Mansfield's brain, and he blurted it out, as if he were sitting in the Wrigley bleachers, oh, seventy years ago or something.

"Wait a goddamn minute. The Cubs still got a bat, motherfucker!"

Riley wasn't just thinking it. He yelled it. Loudly. And a dozen people laughed uproariously, and all was good again. Riley wanted to fuck Lily Rose with all the power of his loins. She wanted him to. He could tell. Melissa Franklin had drifted far, far away, absent from his soul and equidistant in miles.

"Riley."

"Yeah…" Riley squinted his eyes and stared. "Neil."

"Are you, like, orgasming, man?"

Riley didn't know what to make of that remark. Finally he looked down. His right thigh was vibrating. It was the cell phone in his pocket.

Neil's face was somehow illuminated now. All else was darkness. Riley fetched the phone.

"Yeah."

"It's me," said the voice. "Adam. I think I'm all right now. Can you come get me?"

"Sure. Be right over."

He hung up.

"That was Adam. Adam Rhine. *Rolling Stone.* He wants to come over. I gotta go get him."

"Can you drive?" asked Neil.

"Yeah. Sure."

"I'll come with you."

"Oh, yeah."

The Audacity of Dope

Riley struggled with his bearings. The blackness dissipated. Now Sarah was there again. And Lily Rose. And all the couple's other friends. Sarah's brother—his name was apparently Eddie—drained a beer and handed it to Riley.

"I got a new song for y'all," said Riley. "I just wrote it."

"You just wrote it?"

"It's in my mind," Riley said. "Three verses."

"Shit," said Cody. "Let's hear it."

I went out to the Great Northwest
To see some friends of mine
We sat around and played guitar
Time after time.
When it was time to go
I wanted to stay there
Where they still have pretty girls
With flowers in their hair
Down by the sea side
Down by the sea side
Round a campfire gettin' high
In the sweet, by and by
By the sea side
By the sea side
My music ain't exactly
What's hit parade out there
But I like theirs
They like mine
We got no cross to bear
And every time I think
My accent must sound strange
It proves to be no problem
When we all feel no pain
CHORUS
When I make a list of places
Where perhaps I could thrive

Austin, Nashville, Fenway Park
Make me feel alive
But if I'm of a mind
To have a little fun
I know I can find it
On the coast of Oregon
CHORUS

"That's fuckin' amazing," said Cody, who had been staring at Riley's fingers on the strings and following him on mandolin. "You just wrote that?"

"Pretty much."

"You ever done shit like that before."

"Nope."

Neil said, "Well, I know you can drive a car. Let's go."

♫

"It's my rental car," said Riley, pausing in front of the black Impala from Avis. "But you know the area. Me drive, or you drive?"

"You drive," said Neil. "I'll keep you heading in the right direction."

They got in and Riley cranked the car. He pulled away slowly.

"So how is it?" Neil asked. "Are you seeing shit?"

"It's okay. Just sort of, uh, improbably bright. I don't even need the headlights, but I figure I better have 'em on anyway."

"Just keep in mind, man, that the weird shit, if there's weird shit, isn't real."

"So you're telling me that that car at the stop sign up ahead isn't really firing light beams that are zipping at us, then veering above and to the side?"

"Exactly. That's your brain being stimulated. The odds are overwhelming that it's just a normal Oldsmobile and that it's not inhabited by evil, flesh-eating aliens from the planet Mingo-12."

They drove past the car without incident. Riley resisted the inclination to look to see if there were evil, flesh-eating aliens.

"I shouldn't have done that," said Neil.

"What?"

"Said what I said about aliens. You shouldn't introduce the possibility of horrific images. It's your state of mind that stimulates the hallucinations. If you're feeling cool, you'll see cool things."

"I'm okay," said Riley. "It's mainly amusing, not scary."

"Good, man. You're hangin' in."

"Yeah."

They turned left onto the main road.

"What are we doing?" asked Riley.

"What do you mean?"

"I forgot why we're driving."

After five seconds or so, Neil replied, "Me, too."

Riley pulled off the road into a convenience store. Inexplicably, cowboys were roping calves, in a synchronized pattern, in a meadow next to a river on the other side of the highway. He got out of the car and lit a cigarette while he watched.

"What are you watching?" Neil asked.

"Cowboys."

"Oh."

"What are you watching?"

"Angels fucking," he said.

"Are they flying?"

"What?"

"Are they flying? Are they fucking up in the air, flapping their wings and shit, or are they down on the ground?"

"They're up in the air," Neil said. "Slowly they're ascending into heaven, and they're having this unbelievable, acrobatic sex. There are hundreds of angels, as far as the eye can see, illuminated by the moonlight."

"Oh."

They walked into the convenience store, which was called Jack's.

"I got it, man," Neil said. "We're going to your motel room. And we're picking up your friend. The guy who works for *Rolling Stone*."

"Yeah. Yeah. Hang onto that thought."

The girl behind the counter looked exactly like Marilyn Monroe, and when she turned around to face them, her dress whirled around, even though there was likely no steaming grate in the tile floor.

"Can I help you?" she asked.

"Sure," Riley said. "I'll have the usual."

"The usual?"

"Yeah. You know. Pack of cigarettes. Chewing gum. Rolling papers. And a lighter. A man can't have too many lighters."

"What kind?" she asked. Riley gave her a blank stare.

"Cigarettes. What kind of cigarettes?"

"Oh," Riley said. "Doesn't matter."

♫

Somehow, on this particular night, a full moon brought greatly enhanced powers of illumination, and it was extraordinarily light for nine o'clock. On the other hand, the hall in the motel was astonishingly dark, its lamps, posted at every door, providing no more guidance than a row of candles.

Riley knocked at Adam's door, and after a few seconds, Adam opened it.

"Adam, I'd like you to meet my friend Neil."

"Pleased to meet you, I'm sure," said Adam, and they shook hands.

Adam looked normal. He wasn't sweaty. His hair was combed. He was dressed neatly. He was completely shaved for the first time since Riley had met him. Or so it seemed. They walked down the hall and stopped in Riley's room, where, over about a fifteen-minute period, they passed around two joints.

They drove back to the party. Things gradually began to seem normal again. The party continued until well past four. Riley took Lily Rose back to the room when they left. Adam possibly had a woman with him, too, but Riley's memory was sketchy when he awakened a little after ten. As he gazed down upon the delicate, lovely face of Lily Rose, waves of shame fell upon him, mainly because he had been untrue to Melissa but also because he still wasn't entirely sure what Lily Rose's real name was and it was really going to be difficult and awkward not to make that apparent when she rose.

Fortunately, Riley found an Oregon driver's license in the pockets of her jeans that revealed her name to be Alana.

CHAPTER TWENTY-SEVEN
BAD DAY FOR A STRAY DOG

It felt to Riley Mansfield as if he were completely irrelevant as far as his own life was concerned. He was an unwitting participant, which was strange because he had always taken pride in being in control of where he was going. Now his comfortable little niche, his personal little compromise between success and privacy, was gone forever. Why couldn't his life always be the way he had chosen? Why did God have to give him just two choices? Hero or Dead. Choosing the option other than dead didn't seem sinful or selfish. Why must he be punished? Why must he endure the consequences of fame when he never sought them?

Quite possibly, it was because God didn't have a thing to do with it.

The inn was really made up of small apartments. Riley left the bedroom, where Alana seemed nowhere near awakening, and sat in the living room. He didn't turn the TV on but tried to read one of the books he always kept stashed in his bag. There were so many developments to consider, so much to get right in his mind. He pondered the incident that had led to this nightmarish dissolution of his life. Everything had moved too swiftly for Riley to absorb. He had just bounced along, responding to each development without ever pausing long enough to consider any greater truths.

The planned crash had been an inside job. More and more, that was all Riley could conclude. An embattled president needed something to give him a bump in the polls. Sam Harmon was a failed president. His foreign war was failing. The economy was tanking. The stern, responsible businessman portrayed in 2004 had morphed into the jovial buffoon implausibly seeking reelection. A white-hot, down-to-the-wire battle for the Democratic Party's nomination had stolen what little thunder Harmon might have had.

The only mild defense of his bungled presidency was creating some sense that the people weren't safe with anyone else. What better way to scare the shit out of the electorate than to take a plane down? Not a big one. A little one. A couple dozen random citizens were expendable, and they'd be dying for a good cause: Sam Harmon's reelection.

Riley remembered the haunted look in the eyes of the bomber, Fatih Ghannam. Riley wished he could talk to the guy and see if he was really some demented instrument of an outlandish Muslim God. The guy didn't really look so fanatical. When caught, he had been scared, not defiant. Could it have been that the bomb wasn't supposed to have gone off? The fact that it did, in the treetops a few hundred yards shy of the Greenville-Spartanburg runway, had been witnessed by Ghannam.

Was that why he had looked frightened? Perhaps he had stuffed the bomb into Riley's guitar because it was Riley who would've taken the fall. Maybe Fatih Ghannam—if that was who he really was—had expected Riley Mansfield to have been led off the plane in handcuffs. But someone had thrown Ghannam a curve. Ghannam had been the ultimate patsy because he had been hired as a suicide bomber who didn't know it.

Or perhaps Riley was crazy. He thought about turning on the cell phone but didn't want to face a call from Melissa Franklin or the latest debriefing from Priscilla Hay. Instead, he decided to roll a joint.

Riley sifted through the cobwebs of the previous night. Adam, whom he had left in a horrid state, had inexplicably gotten himself together, or so it seemed. Riley didn't really remember much, but since his mind contained no images of Adam retching, sweating profusely and being generally hysterical, he figured that Adam had been quite normal, which in itself seemed miraculous in view of the events of the previous evening.

While brushing his teeth, Riley heard Alana's light tap.

"Just a minute."

"I gotta go."

"Okay. Okay."

Riley opened the door. Alana didn't have to go too badly. She told him he tasted good.

♪

It was slightly after noon by the time Riley returned to the inn. Alana had wanted to roll around in the sheets all afternoon—the wedding was at six, with a reception following—but Riley had insisted, against all manner of resistance, that he had to get some things done.

When he finally turned on his phone, Riley was delighted to see only a text message from Melissa. He crafted a warm reply, which was a lot easier than actually talking to her.

Riley sat in the parking lot for perhaps fifteen minutes. He thought it wise to check in on Adam Rhine. He got out, leaned against the door and smoked a cigarette. The cigarette retrieved a buzz. He crushed it out and walked up the stairs.

Adam opened the door fairly promptly. "Hey," he said. "What's up?"

"Ah, just trying to get my shit together," said Riley, walking in. Adam sat at the flimsy little table in the kitchenette. Riley sat down across from him. Adam was already shaved, washed and dressed.

"Want to have an interview session?" Adam picked up a leather bag and pawed in the pocket for a digital recorder and notepad. He sat the bag, which was designed to accommodate his laptop, on the table between them.

"Sure. Whatever." Riley stared at Adam. "Hey, man, what's up with you?"

"I'm okay."

"I mean, like, you seem to have made a miraculous recovery."

Adam looked at his hands, intertwined on the table. "I guess," he said. "I guess I got it out of my system. It was rough, man, but I started feeling better after you left. I figured it'd be cool for my story to go see you interact with your friends. That's why I called."

"Did you come home when I did?"

"Yeah. You don't remember? You took the brunette chick back to the room. I was in the back seat."

"Well, I kinda remember," Riley said, smiling. Adam still hadn't turned on the recorder. "To tell you the truth, what I mainly feel now is guilty. Melissa and I aren't engaged or anything. There's no, you know, formal obligation, but what I did wasn't cool."

Riley watched Adam, and when Adam looked down, Riley cut glances at the leather bag. On the underside, leaning toward him, was a row of zippers. The bottom two were open. The top was closed. He noticed a slight bulge, one that might be the size of a pill bottle.

"I'm cool," said Adam. "Strictly off the record."

Riley was wearing a plaid, short-sleeved western shirt, tails out, and jeans that had been worn approximately four days since washing. He popped a pearl snap and pulled out a pack of Marlboro Lights.

"Cigarette?"

"Nah," said Adam.

Adam turned on the recorder.

"Are you high now?" Adam asked.

"Of course. Just a little. I could stand another."

"I'm cool."

"We'll have to go back down to my room. I need to get myself...presentable, anyway."

Adam got up. Riley crushed out the cigarette. He waited for Adam to turn his back and quickly unzipped the leather bag. He pulled out a bottle of pills—*Tylenol! Shit!*—and stuffed them in his jean pocket as he rose.

♬

No more than a quarter mile away, Jed Langston sat on a bench, overlooking the beach. He cupped his hands against the wind as he placed a call to Banks McPherson in the Office of Homeland Security.

Jed identified himself to a secretary, and Banks promptly accepted the call.

"Yeah, Jed, what's up? You find Mansfield?"

"His hotel is in sight. I picked him up at the airport and tailed him to Gearhart. It's a little hamlet on the coast west of Portland. I walked past him and the reporter on the beach yesterday."

"What's he like? The reporter? From *Rolling Stone*, right?"

"Relax. I've got everything under control," Jed replied. "Story's never going to be written."

McPherson suspected there was information here he didn't want to know.

"Be careful, Jed. Let's not let things get out of hand."

"I'm working for America, Banks, but my every act is also in the name of my Lord Jesus Christ."

"Praise Jesus," said McPherson, not feeling particularly spiritual. "Let me know if you need any assistance."

"I'm way ahead of you. I might need a couple agents to help me tomorrow morning."

"I'll get someone in touch with you within two hours."

♫

"How you mean to handle this?" Riley asked, rolling a second joint.

"What?"

"I mean, when you write this story, how you gonna handle your side of it?"

"The story's about you, man."

"But don't you think you plunging into drug withdrawal is sort of a vital part of the story line?"

"No, I don't think so," said Adam. "I'm not the story. I'm the narrator."

"Pretty fucked up narrator, don't you think?"

"Man, why you getting on me? I'm over it. I'm off it. You helped me. I appreciate it. End of story."

"At the very least, man, you should write a novel."

"Maybe I will. So, what's up for the rest of the day?"

"The, uh, wedding's out on this lawn, overlooking the Pacific. Then there's a reception—I'm supposed to play a few tunes, along with some others—and it's at some church that's within walking distance."

"Well, tell you what. You gotta shave and shower and get ready. I'll go back to the room for a half hour or so, then we can go grab some food. On me." Adam stood up and started to leave.

"Need these?" Riley pulled the Tylenol bottle from his pants.

"Give me those, man."

"Relax, Adam. I'm not gonna keep 'em away from you...or flush 'em down the commode. I just wondered where you got 'em. Sit down. You don't need the drugs now. Your face isn't sweatin' or nothin'."

"It's Tylenol, man. I just got a raging hangover."

"Yeah, right." Riley opened the bottle and emptied the contents in his palm. "They're little orange pills, like St. Joseph's Children's Aspirin. Only they got little 'OCs' on 'em. What you bet that stands for Oxycontin or oxycodine or something?

"Where'd you get 'em?"

Adam wasn't making eye contact. "I found a guy."

"What guy? Where?"

"I don't know his name. I met him in the airport while you were waiting for the luggage. At the bar. He just gave me a phone number."

"Was it the guy we met on the beach yesterday?"

"What guy?"

"You know damn well what guy. The guy we passed, and I asked you about him. Guy with the dog."

Adam looked up. "Yeah. That's the guy."

"I've seen him before," said Riley. "Several times. I talked to him once, in the infield of Rockingham Speedway. North Carolina. He's tailing me...obviously. I think he works for the government. I think the government can't be too happy about me talking to *Rolling Stone* when I'm supposed to be safely in Sam Harmon's pocket."

"What are you saying?"

"I'm saying this guy could be dangerous."

"You're high, man."

"Yeah. I'm probably just paranoid, right?"

"Yeah. It's a free country, man. Not even this government would pull shit like...what?"

"Well, let's take a look," Riley said. He poured the pills on the coffee table. "Look. Several of them are different. They're kind of pink instead of light orange. And they don't have any letters on them."

"I don't know, man, maybe a few of them are generic. Or he just threw in some fake pills."

"Placebos, huh? That would be nice, but I don't think there's any particular reason. There are, like, a couple dozen pills. Look, four of them are different. Let's find out what they are."

Riley took the pink pills—the ones that were slightly different—and placed them in a tiny zip-lock plastic bag that had contained weed. He handed the Tylenol bottle to Adam. "Go easy," he said, "and if I was you, I'd wait a few minutes before I popped another one. Come with me. I'll shave and shower later."

Riley stopped at a little market in town and bought a pound of hamburger, failing to bother Adam with an explanation. He drove through Seaside, the larger resort town just to the south, and curled east into the hills and forests.

"Where we going?" Adam asked.

"I'm looking for a trash dump," Riley said. "Or maybe just a stray dog."

"A fucking stray dog?"

"Well, it's like this. I think those odd pills might be poison. I think this guy in the airport, this guy with a dog, might be wanting to get rid of you. I think the government of the Land of the Free and the Home of the Brave might be interested in making sure no *Rolling Stone*, liberal, dope-smoking, godless, rock-and-roll article is written about me. Particularly not with an election coming up."

"You're fuckin' crazy, man."

"I might be, but it can't hurt to test the theory. My first thought was go find a cow, out on the edge of some ranch, just grazing. But it would be a terrible thing to risk killing a cow or a horse. It's a terrible thing to kill a dog, but it's less terrible to risk killing some stray that's probably gonna get run over anyway."

"This is unbelievably weird," Adam said.

"And if you write about it in *Rolling Stone* and imply in any way that it's me gulping Oxycontins, I'm not going to sue you. I'm gonna beat the shit out of you and wait for you to sue me.

"Whoa. Look. There's a dog." Riley skidded to a halt, which at first caused the poor canine, a rather unhealthy incarnation of a collie, to run away, only it couldn't run very well, its buttocks having been permanently bowed by an apparent and unfortunate confrontation with an automobile.

Riley took the hamburger and kneaded the pink pills into it, taking care not to put any two closely together. Then he rounded the pound of burger into a fairly smooth concoction that might have made a meatloaf with onions, peppers and bread crumbs instead of pharmaceuticals of an unknown origin. He wiped his hands with napkins still inside a Wendy's bag (*late last night?*) and got out of the car. The collie could be seen peering over the hill. Riley placed the plastic bag from the meat market in a sandy, rain-washed ditch, returned to the car, lit a joint and waited.

"Be relatively still," Riley said, passing the joint to Adam.

It didn't take long. The dog shed any wariness of the black car parked five yards away from the meat. Her route back down the hill was indirect and suspicious, but she was just too damn hungry. When she reached the tantalizing pile of tender, processed meat, she tore into it with more energy than it had appeared she had.

Then, suddenly, the hapless creature lurched. Her eyes seemed to pop out. And she fell in a heap, gloriously and instantly extinguished.

"Fuck," Adam said.

"Ain't no autopsy conducted for a dead dog," Riley said.

"How could they get away with that? Murder. How could someone, even the government, kill me? For no good reason?"

"I reckon they figure a big magazine story on some left-leaning folk singer is reason enough," Riley said. "And I expect they got the means. Still wondering why I'm walking up on a stage and singin' 'This Land Is Your Land' for god-fearing Sam Harmon?"

"Not a bit," said Adam.

"Now you're bound to write a good story about me," Riley said, "since I saved your life and shit. Meanwhile, the dog has severely compromised my opposition to capital punishment."

♫

The wedding was beautiful, though it drizzled for a while. The lingering moisture produced a rainbow over the blue-green Pacific. Afterwards the party, forty or so, walked right down the middle of the streets of Gearhart, making their jubilant way to the reception at a community center, or maybe a union hall. It might've been a church, Christian Science, maybe, but Riley wasn't sure, not even after he was inside.

He drank beer joyously. He and other musicians—everyone Neil Wilson and Sarah Mahaffey knew seemed to be musicians—performed. Riley sang John Prine's "The Glory of True Love" and his own song, mysteriously hatched and still remembered from the night before, "Down by the Sea Side." It was a simple song, and Cody Huard picked it up immediately. Between the second and third verses, everyone jammed for five minutes or so.

Having arrived blissfully stoned, Riley was now growing quite drunk from more of the dark, strong beer. Adam, though looking a bit peaked, even joined in to sing a few songs.

"You're not drugging, are you?" Riley asked him between songs.

"Scared to," he replied. "It's not that bad. Yet, anyway."

"You got the balls to throw it away?"

"Not quite yet," Adam said. "I'm gonna hold off if I can."

"You're kind of like a pitcher."

"Huh?"

"You need to face the minimum." *Hmm, that'd make a song.*

It was all Riley could do to remember one of the main reasons for the trip. He had to recruit Cody Huard, whom he didn't really even know. Cody didn't seem gregarious. What he seemed was brilliant. Riley didn't really know why he needed him to play with him in D.C. He just knew he wanted it.

After the music finally subsided, and the feast portion of the festivities commenced, Riley asked Huard if he could talk with him outside.

"Has Neil said anything to you about playing with my band on national TV?"

"Yeah, he mentioned something about it." Cody's voice was emotionless, monotone.

"Are you, like, free this week?"

"We don't have another show, I don't think, till a couple weeks."

"Are you working anywhere, like, on the side?"

"Kind of."

"Can you get off this week? I can pay your expenses and make it worth your while."

"I guess, man."

"Can you fly back east with me and Adam? Like, tomorrow?"

"Well, I could. That's awful soon."

"We just need to do it right," Riley said. "The show's on Friday. Rehearsals are on Thursday. I'm sure it's going to be quite uptight, but it's on the National Mall with a huge crowd, and I've assembled a band of guys I know can get together on short notice.

We're gonna get together in Virginia and practice all day Wednesday, then play a local show at a little venue on Wednesday night.

"You'll get introduced on national TV. I'll make sure there are close-ups on camera, with, you know, subtitles and shit telling who you are. The president's gonna be there and shit."

"I don't care about the president being there and shit."

"Well, will you go with me? You gotta trust me. I don't have the details now, but I know, thanks to the politicians, that money's really no object, or else I wouldn't have charged this whole trip just to get this mandolinist I heard about to take part."

"You came out here just for this? I mean, so you could stand here and ask me to play mandolin for one, no, two shows, with your band, which…"

"Has never played before. That's not completely right. I came out here to see Neil and Sarah get married. But Neil told me one of his best friends was a kick-ass mandolinist, and I knew if he said it, it must be true. I wanted to get away from all the shit swirling around me, and now, I want you to play music with me. I don't even have a band, normally. But if I got to do this, I might as well have a cool time doing it."

Cody thought about it a few moments.

"Okay," he said finally. "I guess I can jam with you, man. When will I be back?"

"Sixth of July, I reckon," Riley said.

"Okay, man. Cool."

"You're from here, man. Do you think people would get too bent out of shape if I smoked a joint down there by the creek?"

"Nah, man," Cody said. "Not out here. Just don't, you know, flaunt it. I think there might be a few dudes, like, wandering around already."

CHAPTER TWENTY-EIGHT
BARING SOULS

At the Portland airport, Riley boarded a USAirways flight—the way back was through Phoenix, not Atlanta—with Adam Rhine and Cody Huard. Riley took a window seat near the front of the plane, eighth row, with Adam on the aisle, an empty seat between them. No first class, this time. Cody was somewhere in the back of the plane, his seat having been recently booked by Riley's on-line alter ego, Priscilla Hay.

Adam looked a little sickly but nothing like on the way out.

"You okay?" Riley asked.

"Not too bad," Adam said. "I'm weaning myself. I was taking, oh, four or five a day before Kentucky. I might take one sometime, maybe the layover in Phoenix. I'm all right."

"Try not to, man."

They sat mostly silent for a while.

"Being honest is lonely, man," Riley said.

After ruminating for a couple minutes, Riley said, "I learned a lot in college, but the number-one lesson was learning how to just please myself. I learned that one of the consequences of living in a free country is that you really can't control what people think. They can like you 'cause you're a jock or dislike you 'cause you're a jock, or because you're Christian or Muslim, black or white, I don't know, fat or skinny, blue eyes or brown. So, if you can eliminate the...mud in the water, the murkiness, of people's expectations, and just do what you think is right, it really eliminates a lot of unnecessary stress.

"So I got to where I didn't want to be a star. Didn't want to be famous. I just wanted to make a living doing my thing, which is writing songs. Other people can sing my songs on the radio, man. It's making me money."

"Do you make money playing live?"

Riley laughed. "Yeah, I clear a little, but it's because I take advantage of the generosity of friends. I sleep on couches. Women take me home, or, at least, they did until I met Melissa. She sort of came along with the rest of the hurricane."

Riley and Adam exchanged glances.

"I've still got some getting used to it in front of me," Riley conceded.

"How much do you make, though, traveling around and playing clubs?"

"I keep a ledger and try to live within my means. If I buy a new guitar, like the Little Martin I bought to replace the one that…blew up, it comes out of profits from playing live. But, for the most part, what it all comes down to, driving around and playing music on the road is…"

"What?"

"Weed money," Riley said.

♫

Sparing no expense, Jed Langston had assembled the same team that had accompanied him when he murdered Philippe Tiant. Kurt Hasselbeck and Leeds McCormick were experts at tying loose ends. They were professionals. Langston was just ruthless. The three arrived at the Gearhart Inn, flashed government badges and requested the room number of Adam Rhine.

"Mr. Rhine checked out early this morning," said the desk clerk.

"I see," said Langston, who expected him dead. "Thank you for your cooperation."

Back in the car, McCormick said, "What now?"

"Nothing," said Langston. "I've wasted your time. Let's get out of here."

"Where to?"

"Well, I reckon you two can head back to Atlanta. Me, I'm heading to Washington."

"You sure there's nothing left to do?" asked McCormick.

"Not unless you want to go rogue and kill a folksinger," said Langston. "I promise you one thing, though. The next time I try to kill somebody, I'm gonna watch him fall."

♫

The layover at Sky Harbor Airport in Phoenix was more than two hours. Riley and Adam were off the plane first and waited for Cody. Riley had his backpack and miniature guitar. He towered over both his companions at six-foot-three.

"How you feeling?" he asked Adam.

"I've been better. Not too bad, though."

"Do you think a few shots of booze would replace taking one of them pills?"

"Worth a try. I don't think it would make sense to drink and take one of them. That's kind of...unpredictable."

"So, if we have a couple drinks, you think you can stay off the Oxycontin?"

"Yeah."

Riley looked at Cody. "Long story," he said. "I'll fill you in."

Cody nodded. He wasn't the most talkative fellow in the world, but not much bothered him.

"Let's drink," Riley said. "It's an inferior buzz, but it's just too fucking difficult to get high in an airport."

Adam and Cody sat on either side of Riley at the airport bar.

"Man, I don't know a damn thing about you except that you can play the shit out of that mandolin," Riley said to Cody. "Tell me something about yourself, man."

"I come from kind of a religious family," he said. "My dad was in a gospel group, and I learned how to play mandolin so that I could be with him. I was just, like, twelve when I started playing it, and as I got better, we became more and more bluegrass/gospel."

"So how'd you get away from that?"

"Uh, my dad and I drifted apart. There were some ways that,

you know, he disappointed me. I'll leave it at that. But I started listening to some other music, you know, old stuff by The Band, and I really got into Nitty Gritty Dirt Band when I was little."

"How about you and Neil? How'd you get to be friends?"

"It was in college, man. We lived on the same hall as freshmen."

"You're paying attention, like, to what's being written about me, aren't you?" Riley asked Adam.

"There's not really that much."

"No. I mean in those supermarket tabloids. *Weekly World News*. *National Enquirer*. The shit publications."

"Oh, yeah, you're still getting the small color photo on the cover, generally one that makes you look either crazy or ridiculous."

"I never talked to anybody from any of them," said Riley. "Not a word. What are they saying?"

"Oh, you're reclusive. Defensive. Secretive. You might be gay."

Riley laughed. "Being gay might've been a lot less trouble. I'm afraid I've been destructively straight all my life."

"You want to read it?" Adam pulled one of the cheap tabloids from his backpack.

"Nah, that's not what I need. I mean, do they talk to real people? I can't imagine any of my friends saying shit about me."

"That's not the game, my friend," said Adam. "Those rags aren't about balance, man. They just talk to your enemies."

"I don't have many enemies," said Riley. "Come to think of it, I don't have many friends, but the ones I got, they're good ones."

"Got any ex-girlfriends?"

"Well, there's that," said Riley.

♫

Langston was on a layover of his own, in Cincinnati, when he called McPherson.

"What's up, Jed?"

"I think Mansfield's headed back east to get ready for the performance on the mall. The reporter's still with him, I think."

"Do you think that's something to worry about?"

"Yes, this guy Mansfield is going to try to disrupt things. I know he is."

"All the arrangements have been made, Jed. We know the three songs he's going to sing. One of them he wrote. It's called 'Your Independence Day.' Uplifting. Everything's going to be fine."

"He's not one of us, Banks."

"He's going to play ball. One of the reasons is the pressure you've been able to put on this Mansfield character. You've done what I asked. You should take pride in a job well done."

"I'm the guy who's been following him. He's sneaky and mischievous. He's tried to get inside my head."

"Nonsense. He knows that he's made a solemn agreement, and he's going to keep his end of the bargain. You've helped him realize what he's up against. You don't think he's a fool, do you?"

"He's not a fool," said Langston. "But he's a punk. He's got no respect for authority, or the Lord, either, for that matter."

"Everything's going to be fine, Jed. We've done a lot of work on our end, too."

"Well, I'm coming to Washington, Banks. I'm going to be there to make sure."

McPherson sighed. "Come see me when you get here."

♫

Riley and Adam slept until the plane crossed the Mississippi River at dusk. Riley stared quietly at all the doodles and curves in the mighty river's path, marveling at the rounded, cut-out lakes that had been separated by silt from the coursing current.

"I was just thinking," Riley said. "You know, there are areas where the government really is like a childish monster.

"You know, I was thinking about weed being illegal. I really don't think it's a matter of it being bad. I think, if you just point out, say, that it's not nearly as bad as alcohol, most people don't even dispute it with much enthusiasm. It's personal, man. It's not the right and wrong about the law; it's having the temerity to disobey the law. It's kind of the ultimate 'my way or the highway,' which is something I kind of got used to playing football. The simple issue of marijuana being a really trifling thing to spend billions of dollars to eradicate is completely irrelevant. The reason it continues, on and on, never effective, just, uh, bothersome and annoying, is just a childish example of, you know, 'it's the law, goddamn it, and whether you like it or not isn't important.' It's all 'how dare you?' and 'you will behave as we say you will.' Half the cops know it's stupid. I split a joint with a cop outside the back door in Baltimore one time.

"It's more like a stern lecture by a parent to his kid. 'Don't dispute my word.' My old man used to say that to me all the time. ''Cause I said so.' 'It's not your job to question, mister. It's your job to do as I say.' Well, man, that might have some traction if you're some little, fucked-up kid, but it's not the relationship there ought to be between a citizen and his government. That ought to carry some mutual respect. We as a country ought to be above that shit."

"It looks like Murrah is going to be the Democratic nominee," said Adam. "You think beating Sam Harmon's gonna get weed legalized?"

"Of course not," said Riley. "Democrats can't just cut through that shit. They've got to deal with the same attitude. But it'll be a step in the right direction. You know what I told Eric?"

"Eric in Kentucky?"

"Yeah, Eric asked me about politics. He's not, you know, that political, but he's probably Republican. Most of them up in the hills are. I told him if the Democrats got elected, there'd be a lot more chance of getting the feds to back off with all the choppers in the air. Man, weed's a business up there. Folks grow it 'cause there ain't no other way to make decent money and it beats the hell out of the mines. It's just like *Thunder Road*, man. You ever seen the old movie with Robert Mitchum? It's about moonshiners in the forties or fifties or sometime. It's so much like that now with pot."

Adam Rhine was probably no more than five-foot-six, slighter even than Cody Huard, who, while short, could liberally be described as chunky. Adam's black hair seemed dry and stringy. He looked sickly, and Riley wondered if he had always looked that way and how much it was derived from an addiction to Oxycontin.

"Here's what I can't figure," Adam said. "Why are you doing this?"

"Somebody's got to tell my story somewhere approaching right."

The plane began its final descent.

CHAPTER TWENTY-NINE
PLANS, PLANS, EVERYWHERE PLANS

The first phone call of the day was from Melissa Franklin. Priscilla Hay was probably waiting until business hours.

"Hey," Riley said, having already recognized the number. "How you making it?"

"Fine. Miss me?"

"With all my being. I had a hard time remembering lyrics because I was thinking of you every minute."

"Well, that's nice," she said.

"What?"

"Oh, nothing."

Oh, shit. She knows. She knows. She knows.

"I'm just high," he said. "Gotta get my shit together. Today's gonna be a bitch. This is my day of tying loose ends."

Riley was vaguely aware of Adam Rhine stirring in the guest bedroom, which opened into both the kitchen and the living room. It wasn't much of a bed that was in there, barely enough room to crawl in amid the guitars, speakers, recording equipment and desk. He half expected to hear Adam curse from stubbing his toe on a guitar stand or something. Cody Huard, who had slept on the couch, was out jogging, or walking, or something. He had been headed out the door, already hooked into music via ear buds and iPod, when Riley had staggered into the kitchen to gulp down his daily vitamins.

"Did you get in late?"

"Yeah, it was after midnight by the time we drove from Charlotte."

"Who's with you?"

"Adam's just getting up now. Also, this mandolinist, the one I think I told you about. I met him at Neil's wedding, and he flew back with us. I just got through looking him up—his name's Cody

Huard—online. The group he's in got nominated for a Grammy, man. I had no idea."

"When can I see you?"

"You can come over now if you want, but what say I try to take care of some of these details—I know Priscilla is going to call any minute—and then meet you for lunch? You can come back and help me with everything, if you want. I can use your help, but I understand if you got things to do."

They agreed to meet at the Holiday Inn out on the interstate. It would have less locals, and they could speak more frankly without recognizable diners situated around them.

Adam straggled in, shoved a blanket to one side and said, "What's going on?"

"Fuck," said Riley. "Melissa's on to me. I could tell it on the phone. Women are amazing."

"Are you high?"

"A little."

"Well, you're probably just a little paranoid. Besides, it doesn't matter."

"Huh?"

"Women are always suspicious, but they're also in denial. They don't want to know what they suspect. The only way a man can truly fuck up is to spill his guts."

"You're right," Riley said. "You're absolutely right. Thanks. So, you got the craving from pain-killing?"

"I'm going without today, man. I'm not even going to drink. I'm just going to rely on my friend and interview subject to keep me stoned all fucking day."

"That's the spirit," said Riley, gesturing to the coffee table, "I'm not sure I can hang, but there's a bag and a bong. It might not be a bad idea to go out on the deck. We've had some untidy visitors around here lately."

"Strictly for medicinal purposes," said Adam. "Literally." They laughed, and Riley began strumming his guitar.

♫

Sue Ellen Spenser was, yet again, closing in on the little town of Henry. Although she had yet to lay eyes on Riley Mansfield, she felt as if she knew him. Her first priority was to make sure everything went perfectly, to the letter, at the National Mall on Saturday the fifth of July. Her second goal was to fuck Mansfield. Oft times, in her experience, the goals could be intertwined.

"So best we know, David darling, this Mansfield is at home, right?" She had the National Security Agency's David Branham on her cell phone.

"Yes. He's either at his house or close by. He flew home with two others. One's a reporter. The other is a musician. We don't know if they're staying at his house or elsewhere. Neither is registered in any of the nearby hotels."

"They're probably sleeping on the fucking floor," said Sue Ellen. "Shit."

"It's probably not that big a deal, Sue Ellen."

"Oh, I'll make do. Play it by ear."

"Fly by the seat of your pants," said Branham. "You're good at that. Keep me in the loop."

♫

Cody Huard returned. Riley fetched a towel so that he could dry off before joining Adam on the couch.

"Bong hit?" Adam asked.

"Let me cool down," said Cody. "Not healthy to blaze while you're still cooling down from a jog."

"Hey, Adam, you're not gonna believe who it was on the phone just now."

"President?"

"No, smartass. It was the fucking sheriff."

"No shit?"

"No shit, man. He asked me if I needed help with security. Said he's gonna post a deputy to make sure no one bothers me while I'm preparing for the big show in D.C."

"What if it's, like, a guy who wants to sell you some weed?" Cody asked.

"You're, like, on a natural high, aren't you?" Riley asked, chuckling.

"Yeah. It bears some similarity."

The doorbell rang. Riley opened the door to find Sue Ellen Spenser standing there, dressed to the nines and tastefully fragrant.

"Hi," she said. "I'm Sue Ellen Spenser, and I represent the Republican Party and President Sam Harmon."

"I'm guessing it won't do any good to say I gave at the office," Riley said. "Come in."

Sue Ellen entered to find marijuana smoke wafting in the air, one short guy sweating in green jogging shorts and a yellow soccer jersey, and another short guy sitting next to him on the couch, pondering the weed he had stuffed into the bowl of a blue plastic bong but not yet smoked.

"Sorry about the mess," said Riley. "What can I say? We're musicians."

Riley pulled up a chair from the kitchen table, and Sue Ellen sat down. The only other option was the love seat, which had at least two dozen books, a backpack and an electric guitar lying across it. Adam and Cody sat on the couch atop a rumpled blanket and sheets. It was almost ten.

"It's okay," she said, smiling. "I would expect nothing less from the great Riley Mansfield."

"That's a bit much," he said.

"Oh, I know all about you, Riley. May I call you Riley? I've become a big fan. Your songs are brilliant. And I like this business about you being the private artist instead of the public personality. I'm sympathetic about all these intrusions into your public life."

"Did you, uh, come across that song of mine, 'Misfits'?"

"Oh, yes. It's not my favorite, but I know you're not, dare I say, fond of the president. Hell, I've got some misgivings, too. But you're not endorsing him. Oh, God, no, we all know just how much you want to keep your political opinions, uh, obscured but uncompromised. This is about America, Riley. You're not endorsing anybody. You're just going up on a stage and paying tribute to the country."

And if it helps President Harmon get re-elected…"

"Well, that's just an incidental consequence. In politics, we call what you're doing 'plausible deniability.' You're covered."

"Well, Sue Ellen— may I call you Sue Ellen?—that's all really irrelevant at this point, isn't it? I'm going to do what I'm going to do. I've taken some liberties to put together a band that will, with a little practice the day after tomorrow, just rock the crowd. And, maybe, just maybe, I can get out of all of this with my life somewhat intact, and everybody will be happy."

Adam wanted to puke, and not because he needed an Oxycontin. Cody just took it all in, the fatigue of running cultivating an expression devoid of suggestion. Riley thought to himself that Cody could've passed for retarded.

"It's really nice to meet you, Sue Ellen, but I've got a really busy day, full of making arrangements and getting the musicians all up to Richmond…"

"Could I have some of that?" Sue Ellen asked, pointing at the bong.

Riley motioned in the affirmative.

"We Republicans have all too few opportunities to, uh, indulge," she said, packing a bowl. "Oh, and I can share. I've got some coke."

"Uh, I hate to disappoint you, Sue Ellen, but I don't, uh, do coke," Riley said. "I don't even drink all that much. I just blaze. That's all."

Sue Ellen was sort of flabbergasted that she was sitting with a group of musicians—she hadn't yet put it together that Adam was the reporter, and she didn't know he worked for *Rolling Stone*— who apparently didn't like drugs as much as she did.

"Oh, well," she said. "To each his own."

"See, I've actually quite a bunch of stuff to do," Riley said.

"Well, that's what I'm here to help you with," said Sue Ellen, letting a burst of smoke escape.

"I know, and I appreciate it. But there's lots of, you know, music shit, and I got to call everybody and make sure everything's good to go about all of us getting together in Ashland, Virginia, on Wednesday morning."

"Ashland Coffee and Tea. Or is it Tea and Coffee?"

"I'm really not sure, but, the thing is, I've been away from my girlfriend for several days, and I also need to spend some time with her, and I'm supposed to meet her for lunch, and we're supposed to, uh, spend some time together this afternoon and, like, tonight."

Sue Ellen's disappointment was palpable. Before she could manage a spluttering reply, Adam Rhine spoke: "Let me help with this, Riley. Sue Ellen, my name is Ron McKernan. Riley and I go way back. Maybe we can make some arrangements. I'll take notes and make sure Riley's straight on everything."

It was all Riley could do to suppress a laugh. He knew Ron McKernan had been a founding member of the Grateful Dead, and he was pretty sure McKernan had died sometime in the seventies. He was hopeful, and pretty confident, that Sue Ellen Spenser wouldn't know this. What Riley wasn't sure about was whether or not Adam Rhine wanted to spend time with Sue Ellen for her cocaine or his story.

"Time out," Riley said. "Sue Ellen, let me apologize but Cody and me, and Ron, need to discuss this a bit in private. Be right back."

They walked through the guest bedroom into the garage. Riley closed the door behind him and pushed the button that prompted the garage door to rise. They walked out into the sunshine. Riley opened the door of a utility building and pulled out two flimsy chairs and a plastic bucket, which Cody sat on after turning it upside down.

"Oh, man," said Cody. "You're gonna get a song out of this one."

"No shit," said Riley.

"You don't, like, have a joint, do you?"

"Nah. It's all inside."

"I got one," said Adam.

"Good," said Cody.

"We got unbelievable security," said Riley. "Look down the lane, man. There's a sheriff's deputy handling security."

"Killer," said Cody.

"Okay," said Riley. "Adam…I mean, uh, Ron…"

"My first name is really Ronald," said Adam. "My mother calls me Ron. I won't fuck it up."

"You name's Adam Warren Rhine," Riley said.

"Well, I still won't fuck it up."

"All right, man, you think you got your shit together, huh? All I can give you for advice is lie like a motherfucker."

"So, what's up with me, man?" Cody asked, taking a hit. "I don't need to be with you and your old lady, man, and I don't need to be hanging out while Adam bangs this Republican broad."

"You know how to ride a horse?" Riley asked.

"Yeah."

"I can hook you up."

Inside, Sue Ellen Spenser snorted coke.

♫

"I'll have a Reuben, and a Diet Coke," said Riley to the nice waitress at the Holiday Inn. Melissa ordered a salad with baked chicken. And sweet tea.

"I just got off the phone with Priscilla," he said, once the orders had been taken and beverages delivered. "She's totally been impersonating me, making all the arrangements, booking rooms and…"

"What's she get out of it?"

"She's just helping...and, you know, using her contacts and knowledge of Washington to make everything work out."

"No, I mean, why's she interested in helping?"

"Well, you know, she's a Democrat, and her job right now is to, uh, minimize the success of Harmon's re-election campaign. After we get off stage, I'm going to go on several TV shows and say that my appearance was just to, you know, honor America on the Fourth of July and that I only agreed to do it with the understanding that it isn't any kind of implied endorsement. I may say that I oppose what Harmon has done, but I'm not really inclined to be active in either party. I guess I'll talk about the airplane thing, say what happened one more time, and, hopefully, be done with it."

Riley looked directly into Melissa's green eyes. "She's no replacement for you, honey. We're gonna do everything together, as long as you'll have me. I'm so glad you're going with me to Virginia and D.C. Your head's on straighter than anyone I know."

Melissa modestly looked down at the table, muttering "that's nice" in little more than a whisper.

"How was Oregon?" she asked.

"It was great. I love the people out there. I was kind of in the middle, you know, a little older than Neil and Sarah and their friends, and a little younger than their parents. They're, like, twenty-five, I'm thirty-five, and their parents are fifty."

"So, did that feel awkward?"

Riley smiled. "No. I probably acted like I was younger than anyone there. That's probably my level of maturity."

"Oh, bullshit," Melissa said, causing Riley to look around to see if people were watching. She saw his expression and burst out laughing.

"You've got more sense than anybody I know," she said. "You just smoke a little too much pot."

"And the problem...is?"

They were laughing when the food arrived.

"So, are you and Priscilla, you know, pretty close?"

"Melissa, don't tell me you're actually jealous of a woman whose only contact with me, I mean, other than with you and me, has been by phone and email."

"A little," she said.

"Priscilla likes me," Riley said. "That's a fact. But she's got a great career. She's doing what she wants, and it's so…antithetical…to everything about me. This whole deal is probably so totally different from anything she's ever done—she's told me that—that it's kind of different, kind of exciting. After next week, the only time we ever hear from Priscilla is probably going to be when we get a Christmas card."

"I know."

"You shouldn't feel any heat from Priscilla," Riley said, matter-of-factly. "The woman you should worry about is back at the house right now."

Melissa's eyes widened.

"Relax," he said. "The Republicans sent their own woman to see me this morning. She comes barging in, I'm in sweat pants and a tee shirt, unshaven and looking like hell. Adam's stoned out of his mind, the bong sitting on the coffee table, smokin' a little, and Cody—Cody's the guy who came back with us from Oregon—is sweaty 'cause he just came back from jogging around the farm."

"My God."

"What does she do? Marches right in, pulls up a chair and asks me if I want to do some cocaine."

"And you…"

"Don't do cocaine. Never have. Never will. I told her that. And I bailed as quick as I could take a shower, after me and Adam and Cody kind of discussed the situation outside for a few minutes."

"What's this…bitch's name?"

"Sue Ellen…something. Spenser, maybe."

"And she's at your house right now?"

"If I was a betting man, I'd say Adam's getting laid right now."

"How's he?"

"Better. Much better. Obviously," he said, smiling. "It's a long story, one I'll tell you when we're on the road tomorrow, but he's turned it around. He's actually done me some really fine favors lately, the latest example being kind of stepping up to entertain Miss Republican while I get the hell out."

"Well, he *is* getting laid," said Melissa.

"There's that."

"This is just a crazy world."

"Yeah. Totally. It's just about over, though. Things may never get back to normal, but it's gonna get better."

"So you're…reasonably happy, reasonably balanced?"

"I'm just bumping along," Riley said. "I'm just standing there, taking one big chance, one more crazy fuckin' something, after another. There's no goal beyond just getting from Point A to Point B and then seeing where Point C is. There's a part of me that seems human and a part of me that seems, I don't know, like a robot."

"Do you really think this is ever going to end?"

"I don't know. I don't seem to have any choice. You know how people say, 'Watch what you ask for. You might just get it.' I didn't ask for this. But, shit, that's just the way it is."

"You seen your mom?"

"Went by on the way here. I sat in the driveway for fifteen minutes, talking to Priscilla on the phone, then I went inside. As usual, she was reading a book in her room. We just talked. I picked up my mail. I told her it would all be over soon, and things would be back to normal, and she looked over the top of her reading glasses and said things are never normal in this family, and she's right. In an insane world, sane people feel awkward and out of place."

"Normal's boring?"

"Yeah," Riley said. "Kind of.

"On the down side, I've got kind of, I don't know, kind of a foreboding."

"What do you mean?"

"I mean, I've been so lucky. It seems like I've dodged so many bullets. I'm tired of being followed. I'm tired of weird shit happening left and right. I'm worried that my luck is going to run out. I just want to see things through and get it all over with."

Melissa grasped Riley's hand and squeezed it.

"Things'll be all right, baby. Things'll be all right."

"How's the salad?"

"Fine. The Reuben?"

"Good. I like a Reuben if I haven't had one in a while." Riley picked up the check. "Want to follow me back to the house?"

"I think maybe it'd be best if I let you, uh, take care of things with this Sue Ellen."

"Having you around might help."

"I trust you," she said. "I just don't think I can do this scene."

"I don't blame you," Riley said. "I'll call you later."

Riley stared at Melissa for a few seconds. Finally, he started laughing.

"What?" she asked.

"Aw, nothing. I was just thinking to myself that weed is kind of a Democrat drug, and cocaine is kind of inherently Republican. And everything else…almost springs from that, in a way."

♫

Rather than return to the house, Riley took to the interstate, where the cell signal was decent. The phone rang before the truck was down the exit ramp.

"Oh, I forgot to tell you." Naturally, it was Priscilla. "We've got a problem with one of the band members."

"Yeah, who?"

"Ethan Hays."

"That's Eric's dad."

"He's got a felony conviction."

"When? What?"

"He got busted in nineteen seventy-nine for growing marijuana. Served six months in federal prison."

"Well, they say marijuana can ruin your life," said Riley, "and the government makes sure of it."

"That aside…"

"Look, Priscilla, I don't even know why Ethan Hays wants to be there. When Eric told me, I was…flabbergasted. But his son is my friend, and he is my friend. He's gonna be there with us, and if they turn him away, there's going to be a scene."

"And probably an arrest."

"Look ,this was thirty years ago. Shit. Maybe Harmon can pardon him."

"I don't think so."

"Well, they'll just have to pardon him at the security gate, or whatever it is. Look, I know you've got things to do, and I know it's ridiculous for someone like you to have to deal with things like this. You want me to handle it?"

"No."

"Well, if need be, once we get up there, I'll get involved, go to bat for Ethan, whatever."

"What instrument does he play?"

"Harp," Riley said, lying. "You know, harmonica."

"All right," Priscilla said. "I'll keep working on it. You know, being Riley Mansfield isn't all it's cracked up to be."

"You're a lot better at it than me, all things considered," Riley said.

"You are very adept at straining the system."

"Well," he replied, "the system is very adept at straining me."

"I know," she said. "I'll do what I can. Bye."

♫

Riley found Adam Rhine half-asleep on the couch.

"Well, you look like you've been rode hard and put up wet," Riley said.

"Shit. You have no idea. I think I know why Republicans are against legalizing weed. They have no interest in it. They don't want anything that'll settle 'em down. They want something that'll blow their brains wide open."

"There's a part of me that hates I missed it."

"That woman doesn't fuck for love," Adam observed. "She fucks to enslave."

"D'you do some coke?"

"I had to, man. First she gave me a blow job. Then she demanded that I eat her pussy."

"Okay. Fellatio. Cunnilingus. That's good."

"It's not funny, man. When it actually came time to fuck, I didn't think I could get it up. That's why I took a snort. Just a little one."

"It do the trick?"

"Yeah, I made it through." Adam looked sheepish for a moment, then laughed a little.

"I appreciate you, uh, taking the heat, man. There's worse ways to do a favor for a friend. So, you play organ like the real Ron McKernan did?"

"That's good, man. You picked up on that. She actually knew I was a reporter, man."

"Ooh."

"But she didn't know I worked for *Rolling Stone*. I told her I work for *Reason*. That's a Libertarian magazine. I've got a friend I went to college with who works there. I told her you were actually a Libertarian."

"I don't suppose your friend was actually named Ron McKernan?"

"Uh, no. But I thought the bullshit was believable. I think it's kind of…plausible that you would hold Libertarian views."

"Specifically, I'm guessing you were referring to the fact that many Libertarians advocate the legalization of drugs."

"Well, that, too, but I was thinking about how Libertarians

believe in individualism and self-reliance, and that kind of lines up with you."

"Yeah, the difference is that I recognize that there are very few people actually like me. Thank God."

"That's smart, though," Riley added. "I'm fairly amazed at your ability to, uh, act extemporaneously. We make a pretty good team, actually. It sounds like Sue Ellen's got a little Libertarian in her."

"Not really," Adam said. "She's a typical Republican bitch. She thinks, because she's from money and has all the social graces, that she's able to do things like snort coke and she can handle it. She doesn't want the riffraff taking drugs. She wants to send them all to prison so she and her friends can have it all for themselves. She's really a repugnant individual."

"Who fucks like a rabbit."

"Well, yeah."

"Seen Cody?"

"Uh, the last I saw of him," Adam said, "he was sitting on the deck, with that huge quarter horse tied up, and I suspect he was getting high…I think he went off riding again later."

"Well," said Riley, "it's probably really unlikely that ol' Sunglow is going to run away with him. So, where's Wonder Woman now?"

"She said to tell you she was at the Holiday Inn."

"Think I should call, maybe take her to dinner?"

"I'm pretty sure she'd pick up the tab."

"I could take Melissa along, just to quell Sue Ellen's, uh, appetite. But that would take a lot of advance briefing. It sounds like I've just got to portray myself as a far-right-wing Libertarian, and maybe her little spy mission will be complete, and she can go back to Washington feeling the mission is accomplished."

"I think she's fucked the president before," Adam said.

♫

"The reason I won't endorse the president is that I don't agree with him," Riley said to Sue Ellen, sitting across from him in a booth at Fatz Café, another eatery adjacent to the interstate. "He's not a true conservative."

"Oh, you're just going to throw away your vote and let the damn liberal Democrats take over," she said.

Melissa was eating alone, across an aisle, about three booths away. Riley could see her over Sue Ellen's left shoulder.

"I didn't say that," Riley said. "I just said I don't want to endorse him. I agree that Harmon is better than Stuart Murrah."

"Lord knows, Jimmy Carter is better than Stuart Murrah."

"I won't say, 'I'm for Sam Harmon.' I'll shake hands with him, smile for the cameras, do the three songs and go on my way."

"You need to go on TV afterwards. Fox News. O'Reilly. He's a nice guy. It'll be easy. He won't ask any questions you don't want to answer."

"No. I won't go on a news show. When I get through, I just want to go home and fade away."

Sue Ellen started to speak.

"No, wait. How about this? How about if I give an interview on the edge of the stage, soon as I get through with the songs?"

"I really must insist that you should go on 'O'Reilly.'"

"Ain't happening," Riley said. "As it turns out, I ain't hungry, neither."

He got up and walked out. Melissa followed at a safe distance.

Sue Ellen settled for an appetizer and left. She drove back to her room, snorted a line and placed a call to David Branham's cell.

"Hang on a minute. Let me step outside."

Branham whispered to his wife, "Be right back, this is a call I gotta take," and walked out onto the patio of his McLean, Virginia, home.

"Everything's just fine, darling," Sue Ellen said. "We've got nothing to worry about with Mansfield. It's not what we thought. He's not to the left of the president, sugar, he's to the right. He's a fucking Libertarian."

"I understand there's a reporter following him around."

"I've spent some time with him. Ron something or other. He's writing a story about Mansfield's right-wing beliefs. He told me Mansfield's probably going to vote for the president but that he just doesn't want to get involved in politics. He's just a typical, reclusive Libertarian. It all makes sense, now that you think about it. One of his songs, I thought, was liberal. Actually, when you look at the words, it reflects a good bit of Libertarian belief."

"Good work, Sue Ellen," said Branham. "That's very good news indeed. The president will be very gratified."

♫

Riley and Melissa reclined next to each other on lounge furniture, staring at the stars from the back deck of Riley's house. Cody and Adam had gone to bed after a couple hours of music in the living room.

"I think I played it pretty well," said Riley. "And Adam played it even better. They'll probably catch on, but this'll have 'em questioning their own information for a while. Maybe they'll leave us be till we get to D.C."

"She's a beautiful woman."

"Sue Ellen? Yeah. She's hot. You know what Adam said? He said she fucks to enslave. You gotta be a writer to come up with that. I hope he uses it in his story, though it may be hard, given the circumstances, to work it in."

"Yeah, and you picked a fight with her."

"I had to figure out a way to get away before she tried to sink her teeth in me," he said.

"That's fairly brilliant," Melissa said.

"No, it wasn't. You were nearby. That's probably what was brilliant."

"And you're still getting laid tonight," Melissa said.

CHAPTER THIRTY
UP AND AT 'EM

Naturally, Riley was up first on Tuesday morning. Cody got up at seven and left on his jog a few moments later. Melissa drifted out of the bedroom a little after eight, yawned, smiled and emitted a barely recognizable version of "good morning," then disappeared into the bathroom.

With Cody gone, Riley picked up the remote and the television came to life. He tuned to RFD-TV to watch "Imus in the Morning."

When Melissa emerged from the bathroom, Riley got up from a stack of bills to kiss her as she breezed by and sat on the couch.

"Oh, shit," Riley said.

"Is that oh-shit-good or oh-shit-bad?"

"It's good. Real good."

"What?"

"Alan Jackson's gonna record one of my songs."

"Which one?"

"Uh, 'Your Independence Day.' I wonder if he knows I'm gonna sing it on national TV."

"Is that a problem?"

"Shit, no. Can't do nothing but help. I'm just trying to figure out if he's recording it because it's a good song or because he knows it's going to get exposure on television."

"Does it matter?"

"Well, no. Oh, maybe a little. I'd rather people record my songs because they're good, not because I worry the shit out of them. I could probably make a lot more money if I weren't too proud to beg."

"But you're gonna make a lot of money out of this?"

"Oh, yeah," Riley said. "It'll be big. We should probably do something to celebrate.

"How about if we get high?"

"I'm good," she said. "Big day, you know. When we gonna pull out?"

"Oh, ten, eleven, noon. My clothes are packed. I gotta load the truck with speakers and mixing board for the Ashland gig. It's, maybe, seven hours to Richmond, and we got rooms in the Homewood Suites near the airport. We just need to get in there at a decent hour, have dinner, get a good night's sleep, and then we'll spend all day Wednesday at Ashland Coffee and Tea, rehearsing, and then we'll do our show Wednesday night. It's gonna be great. I haven't played with a band in a while."

"Is everything good to go with everybody getting to Richmond?" she asked.

"Everything's cool," said Riley. "I know what you're thinking. In some ways, yes, I'm pretty slipshod. But the music, that's important. I kind of overdid it on purpose. Sometimes you got to ask for twice what you want just so's you wind up getting what you need. So, like, I requested everyone I wanted, knowing something would come up with one or two.

"My guys from Greenville are coming. Chad's gonna play drums. Harvey's gonna play bass guitar. I wish he could play stand-up bass, but that won't work because, if he plays bass guitar, that means Eric can pick up the bass and free up Harvey to play some fiddle. I'm not really worried about the show in Ashland. We'll be a little rough, but the quality of the instrumentals will be unbelievable, and a little improvisation—hell, a lot of improvisation—will work well in a live audience of music fans.

"For the big crowd in Washington, we'll have to be tight and precise. We probably need more work on three simple songs for D.C. than we do to play three hours at Ashland Coffee and Tea."

"How's everybody getting there?" Melissa asked.

"Let's see. Eric, Wade and Ethan are driving over the mountains from Hyden. God knows how you get there. I'm guessing they're probably going east to Pikeville, and I don't know, up into West Virginia and over, I reckon. Chad and Harvey are flying. We gotta take the equipment, so that's why we're driving. Same with Alan. He and Dan are flying up from Jacksonville or Orlando, I forget which. We're supposed to all be in Richmond by dark. Hotel's right next to the airport. We'll all go out to dinner. We'll try to get a good night's sleep, then we'll go find a Shoney's breakfast buffet in the morning, we'll go to Ashland, maybe, at ten, we'll set up and practice all day, then we'll do the gig and, God knows, it probably starts going downhill from there."

"You dread that thing on the Mall, don't you?"

"Fuck, yeah," Riley said. "In a way, maybe it'll put everything behind me, and in a way, it'll stir things back up for a while. I'll be glad to get it over with. Maybe some good'll come out of it."

"Still got the foreboding?" she asked.

"Yeah. I don't know if it's really, you know, some portent of doom. It's just that fucking numbness, that drifting-along feeling. There's been some scary shit, and I think, maybe, I've got…combat fatigue. It's just, you know how, when you have a close call? Say, something flew through your windshield…I mean, that never happened to me…but some fucking boulder goes through the passenger side of your car, and luckily nobody was sitting there. And you go, 'well, shit.' Well, things like that, along those lines, been happening left and right, and I'm just wondering, well, when's it gonna happen where I just make the wrong move. I just…fuck up."

"Relax, sugar. We've weathered the storm. Now it's just a matter of fulfilling commitments. Just do what you said you'd do."

"I'm the easiest guy in the world to set up," said Riley. "But I do love commitments."

♫

The West Wing office of National Security Adviser David Branham was the scene of an afternoon meeting attended by Banks

McPherson, Jed Langston, Michael Ashton and Sue Ellen Spenser, who arrived a few minutes late after landing at Reagan National.

"Sue Ellen, I'm glad you're here," said Branham. "I'm hoping this meeting will be relatively brief and that we're well prepared for the celebration. It's just four days away. Michael has been in charge of coordinating all the entertainment. Michael?"

"Thank you, David. Everything is progressing smoothly. Claude Herndon and his band are due to arrive on Thursday night. Dennis Miller will be here for a Friday rehearsal, too. All the arrangements have been made. The Beach Boys are going to open the show, then Lee Greenwood. Riley Mansfield has assembled a band for his segment of the show, which will come after Mr. Miller's comedy routine and before the president's brief address. Then Mr. Herndon will close the show."

"When will Mansfield be here?"

"He's arriving, uh, late morning on Thursday, and he's requested time at the site for rehearsal that afternoon," said Ashton. "That leaves the bulk of the rehearsal time on Friday for Claude Herndon. We'll have a run-through, a dress rehearsal, if you will, on Friday afternoon, beginning at around four, I think. The director and all the TV production people will be on hand for that."

"Very good," said Branham. "Banks, I understand you have some concerns about Mansfield."

"We've had a tail on him practically from the moment the airline incident occurred," said McPherson. "Jed here has headed up this effort. He considers Mansfield a security risk, but I'll let him tell you of his evaluation of the situation."

"Security risk? This Mansfield's a national hero," said Branham.

"Mr., uh, National Security Adviser..."

"Jed, for God's sake call me David. We're all friends here."

"David, Mansfield may be a hero, but he's no patriot. His political views are liberal. He's written songs that romanticize drugs and alcohol and sex."

"Aren't they humorous songs, Jed?" Branham asked.

"Well, you could say that."

"I believe, if I'm not mistaken, that Claude Herndon has had some hit songs that have drug references…"

"That's different, David. Claude Herndon has endorsed the president. He's playing the convention. We know he's on our side. I don't think Mansfield is. I know this is late, but I think we should pull the plug on Mansfield's appearance."

"Hasn't he agreed to play three songs we approve?"

"Yes, sir," said Ashton. "The three songs are 'Fighting Side of Me,' a Merle Haggard song, I believe, then a song Mr. Mansfield wrote, 'Your Independence Day,' and then close with 'This Land Is Your Land.' It's all pretty much set in stone."

"Why should we not trust Mansfield, Jed?"

"Because he's sneaky, and evasive, and a liar, and I've got a very strong suspicion that he's going to do something to interfere with the president's message."

"Well, we can't just pull the plug on part of the show with four days to go, and what, two days until rehearsals?"

"David, what if Mansfield has suspicions about what happened on that plane incident?" It was McPherson.

"Do we have any evidence of that?" Branham turned to Langston. "Do you have any evidence of that? Any wiretap? Anything he said to you? Anything from a phone call or an email?"

"No, sir. I still think there's reason for concern."

"On what basis?"

"On the basis, sir, that he happens to have been the anonymous target of that whole mission. That plane was supposed to go down, and he, the musician, whose guitar the bomb got randomly stuck inside, was supposed to take the fall."

Those were words Branham didn't like to hear. He didn't like them being said within the confines of the West Wing. He thought the words better left unsaid, but he held his tongue.

"We don't just cancel it," said Langston. "We have him arrested. Bust him and his friends for marijuana possession. Easiest thing in the world. I guarantee he'll have it on him, or in his room, or in his truck."

"Is this not a threat that has already been tried?" asked Branham. "Banks, didn't you tell me there was something, some ploy, where we were going to threaten Mansfield with arrest as a mean of making sure he cooperated?"

"You mean, was there a setup?"

"Yes. A setup."

"It didn't work," Langston blurted. "He dodged it. Several times. This guy's smart."

"Sue Ellen, what do you think?" asked Branham.

"With respect to Mr. McPherson and Mr. Langston, I don't think we have anything to worry about. I've spent some time with Mr. Mansfield, and he doesn't have anything like that in him. He's not even for Murrah. He's to the right of the president, not the left."

"And what about the dopehead reporter?" Langston asked.

"I spent some time with him, too," said Sue Ellen. "If anything, the story he writes is going to reveal Mansfield to be an eccentric. His political views are Libertarian. He doesn't support the president's foreign policy, but he told me Riley's going to vote for the president. He just doesn't want to endorse him publicly."

"That's ridiculous," said Langston.

"How much have you talked to Mansfield?" asked Branham.

"It wasn't my job to become his friend," said Langston. "It was my job to observe and gather information."

"And I'm going to ask you again: Do you have the slightest bit of evidence that Riley Mansfield, this obscure folksinger, has it in him to somehow booby-trap the celebration on the National Mall? What? Is he going to set off a bomb of his own?"

"No," said Langston. "He's not going to blow anything up. He's going to depart from the script, though. You bet he is."

"Have we not made it clear to him that doing that would be his own ruination?"

The question hung in the air.

"Jed, your job has been surveillance, and I appreciate all you've done. But Sue Ellen's job has been to find out what makes this character tick. She's befriended him and those around him. She's…infiltrated the group."

"I know him," Spenser said, fully aware of how much she was overstating her experience. "He just wants to get this behind him. He called it his 'duty' to me. He wants no part of politics. He just wants to get this done and go back to writing songs and smoking dope and whatever else it is he does."

"All right," said Branham, "I appreciate your input, Jed, and Banks, but I see no reason for concern. This call has to be made, and at this point, making any other call would be, in my estimation, absurd. The process has brought us to this point, and the process is working. We wanted to identify the president with a hero. Regardless of what else there is in Riley Mansfield, there's no question he's a hero. There's also no question that we have been very good to him and spent a lot of money to make this presentation work. We've paid him well. We've allowed him to assemble a band of his choosing. We've done everything he's asked, and Michael could give you some details to the effect that some of it hasn't been easy.

"I think he's in our corner now, and I don't think there's anything to be concerned about. It's a lot harder to discredit a hero than it is to celebrate him. That's my call, and I'm making it, and I've got some other matters to attend to, so let's adjourn this meeting."

On the way out, McPherson said to Langston, "We made our case, Jed. Let it go. Everything's going to be fine. We'll keep our fingers crossed."

"He took the woman's opinion over mine, that's the bottom line, and it's just stupid," Jed said. "I bet he's sleeping with her."

♫

Riley took a seat at one end of a large table, with Melissa at his right. Everyone else sort of sat down in line, Adam on the far side of Melissa, followed by Cody, Chad Dunham, Harvey Kitchens at the far end, and then Dan Bond, Alan Isaac, Wade McKeever, Eric Hays and Ethan, Eric's dad. They gathered for the first time at the TGI Fridays, which adjoined the Homewood Suites near the Richmond airport.

Ethan looked like a ghost. His complexion was gray, his stringy hair mostly black and his beard unkempt. Riley struggled to figure out who Ethan looked like. At first, he thought of photographs from the Great Depression, but at last, he realized that Ethan Hays bore a resemblance to Confederate General Stonewall Jackson. Since Ethan wore a gray shirt, even looking at him seemed to be in black and white.

After pitchers of beer were ordered, Riley attempted to strike up a conversation with Ethan, who was ill at ease and withdrawn.

"I'm surprised you wanted to come, Ethan," Riley said.

"I'm right surprised, too."

Ethan offered nothing else, and Riley couldn't think of a reply. He bided his time, making sure everyone knew who everyone else was. "Don't anybody get worried," Riley said. "It'll be cool. Everybody's just gotta act like we know what we're doing. Tomorrow we'll just jam all day, and then we'll get up in front of the crowd tomorrow night and do the best shit we played around with during the day. No need to be, you know, overly organized."

Everyone ordered food, all except Ethan Hays drank beer, and they gradually got to know each other. Riley combed the nearby booths and tables and didn't find anyone familiar or suspicious.

"Where's Priscilla?" Melissa asked.

"She'll be at the show tomorrow night. She's worried about security, thinks some of the Republicans might recognize her if she was part of the group."

"What about the little Republican bitch?"

"I expect we'll see her when we get to Washington," Riley said. "Or she might be here already. Adam might have her stashed in his room."

"Actually, no," Adam said, "I think eventually she's going to be really angry with me."

CHAPTER THIRTY-ONE
STIRRING THE POT

At seven on Wednesday morning, Riley Mansfield regretted forgetting to switch his cell phone off. He had stirred a bit but was far from up when Priscilla Hay called.

"Hey, sorry to call so early," she said. "I'm in the lobby."

"Uh, why?"

"Because I don't think Republicans get up this early," she said. "Can I come up?"

"Well, Melissa's still sound asleep. How 'bout if I put some clothes on and meet you? Can we, like, drive somewhere? I'm not in a state where I want to show myself in public."

"Sure," she said. "A bit musky, are we?"

"A bit. Give me…ten minutes."

Melissa Franklin looked the part of an angel, her light-brown hair tousled, adorned with a print nightie, mostly red, that barely concealed her breasts. Riley awakened her gently.

"What? Hey."

"I gotta go meet Priscilla. Want to come?"

"No," she said. "She'll be all right. I don't think she's in any danger."

Riley smiled. "I know," he said. "She just has some shit to tell me, I guess. I just wanted you to know where I was. I should be back in an hour or so." As the cobwebs dispersed, Melissa laughed.

"Yeah. I got you," she said, rubbing her eyes. "You're meeting Priscilla to talk about arrangements. Well, I'll make some arrangements in a half hour or so. Tell her I said hi."

"I'm sure you'll see her tonight," he said, and kissed her gently before he slid into his blue jeans, fetched a fresh tee shirt from his bag, pulled on his cowboy boots and walked out the door.

As Riley expected, Priscilla looked quite a bit more prepared to meet the day. Riley saw her, head buried in the morning *Times-*

Dispatch, before she noticed him coming. Riley sized her up. *Very pretty but sort of ashamed of it.* Priscilla's black hair was long and straight, parted in the middle. She'd have looked as if she walked right out of "The Addams Family" if not for the fact that she was so damned pretty.

She stood up as he approached. *Probably caught the smell*, Riley thought. They embraced, and he kissed her on the cheek. He had a guitar strapped around his back.

"I'm sorry I'm not more presentable," he said.

"The lack of presentability is part of your charm."

"Is that a word? Presentability? Maybe I should learn it."

"Nah," she said. "It'd do you no good."

They walked outside. Priscilla drove a white Prius. "This your personal car?" he asked getting in.

"Yeah. I love it."

"Believe it or not, I've never been in a Prius," Riley said. "Let's go and just sit around somewhere."

"Where you got in mind?"

"I just thought of it," he said. "That's why I brought the little guitar. Let's go to Cold Harbor. It's a Civil War battleground nearby. I've been there several times."

"Is it a place that's fairly safe for a musician who wants to smoke a joint?"

"Well, that's not altogether the reason, but it is awfully early. I wanted to play a new song for you."

"Well, show me how to get there."

They arrived at about eight. The visitors center didn't open until nine, so at least from appearances, the grounds were deserted.

"Let's walk across this field," Riley said. "I think there's a bench or something over at the other end, and it's in the shade. I mean, we can walk the battlefield, if you want. I've done it a couple times, but I just thought, well, it'd be a place that afforded some privacy."

"That's okay. Let's just walk over there then."

They ambled past the visitors center and essentially followed the prescribed route in reverse.

"You know, my boss, George Grinnell, caught his teen-aged son with some pot a couple weeks ago," Priscilla said.

"How old's the kid?"

"Sixteen, I think."

"That's probably a little too young," Riley said. "I was pretty goody-goody until I was almost out of high school. I've thought about that, at times. I think most of my friends who wound up, you know, being on drugs, or alcoholics, you know, having a problem with it, they all started when we were in junior high school. I was mainly just lucky, I guess, but I think it's harder to, uh, manage it when you're young because your body can't handle it."

"I take it you consider yourself as being able to manage it."

Riley turned to Priscilla and winced slightly. "I probably blaze too much," he conceded. "I'm not pretending to be objective—nobody is—but I'd like to think I've kept it from being a destructive force. I hope your boss didn't come down too hard on his kid. When you're under-age, beer and weed seem kind of equally illegal, and a kid doesn't need an ID to buy pot."

"Oh, it was just one of those family emergencies that come along. George told me about it at lunch last week. George Junior's a pretty good kid, actually."

"George Junior, huh? Lotta pressure. How much the kid have on him?"

"A joint."

"He's probably just blazed a couple times with his friends. He's probably pretty ashamed at being busted by his old man. He'll probably stay away from it now. For a while, anyways."

"He plays guitar."

"Well, that may be a problem, then," Riley said. "I'd offer to give the kid some pointers, but I'm guessing his dad knows enough about me to think that probably wouldn't be such a good idea. I'm not much of a role model."

"I don't think you can make that claim anymore," Priscilla said. "It doesn't matter whether you like it or not."

"The problem isn't the model. It's the role."

The sat finally on a bench at the edge of the woods.

"The coast looks astonishingly clear," Riley said, fetching a joint from the plain blue tee shirt, which conveniently had a pocket. He lit it, took a second hit and offered it to Priscilla.

"No, thanks," she said. "I've never smoked early in the morning."

"Hell, I've written songs about it," Riley said. "Two of them, actually. So, what's new?"

"Here's the way it's basically going to work," Priscilla said. "As soon as you get through..."

"I've got to talk for a minute live on Fox News," he said.

"What?"

"They wanted me to go in studio," he said. "I turned them down. I got them to agree to a brief interview—like, thirty seconds—at the edge of the stage, right after I'm through."

"Shit."

"Don't get all huffy, Priscilla. It's going to be as inoffensive and, uh, apolitical..."

"Who's it with?"

"O'Reilly."

"Oh, great."

"Look, if he asks me a smart-ass question, I'll fire back. It's supposed to be about music and patriotism in general. That's all."

"Bill O'Reilly loves it when people fire back," Priscilla said. "If they try to turn you into a propagandist, just say 'I'd rather not talk about it. Let's talk about America in general, not politics.'"

"That's a good tip," Riley said. He offered the joint again. "You sure you don't want just one little hit?"

"No, that's fine."

"Well, I'm gonna save it then," he said, crushing it out on a roughhewn wooden rail.

"Remember, I can't be there," said Priscilla, "but I'll be on the grounds. There's gonna be a satellite truck, parked just to the left of the tent complex, where the dressing rooms for entertainers are. There'll be security to hustle you out of there as soon as you get offstage. All you've got to do is duck into the tent, and then maybe duck right back out and walk fairly quickly to the back of the satellite truck. They'll be waiting for you."

"And then?"

"MSNBC isn't televising the show live. Fox News basically has an exclusive, but that's because the other networks, MSNBC and CNN, didn't really want to be a part of it. They're gonna cut away from regularly scheduled programming, and I've arranged for you to go on live remote with Chris Matthews."

"Nope," Riley said. "No Chris Matthews."

"Why the hell not?"

"He yells too much. I like him all right, but I hate situations where the guy who wins is the guy who interrupts the most. Yells the loudest."

"Well, who do you want?"

"We talked about David Shuster earlier. That's okay, but I'd really like Keith Olbermann."

"Impossible. He's taking the weekend off. In upstate New York or somewhere."

"Well, Rachel Maddow, then. I'd settle for David Gregory."

In spite of her disagreeable look, Priscilla said, "I'll see what I can do."

"How much does Matthews know?"

"Nothing, yet. I haven't told anyone. I was worried about word getting around that something big was going to happen. But George—George Grinnell—is going to be with whoever we get—Maddow, Gregory—and an hour before you get off stage, George is going to make some of the photos you gave me available."

"The ones of me being beaten by the fake deputy?"

"Yes."

"Oh, goddamn," Riley said. "This is really gonna be a clusterfuck."

"This shouldn't be a surprise, Riley. I've communicated with you at every point along the way. You knew this was going to be tough."

"Yeah, I know," he said. "You want a cigarette?"

"No, thanks."

"Aw, c'mon. You do."

"Okay, okay."

"Let me play this new song for you," said Riley, unzipping the gig bag.

"That's not the guitar you're playing onstage, is it?"

"Nah. It's my songwriting guitar. I bought it for thirty dollars in a truck stop. Planned on giving it to one of my sisters' kids. Got home, and I liked this flimsy thing better than another one I gave my nephew. It's good to thumb-strum. I like to play chords with my thumb when I'm writing songs."

"It's not, like, pertinent to this situation, is it?"

"No," said Riley, "it's just a song. I want you to hear it. And I'm high."

She smiled and said, "Go ahead, then."

Life's about knockin' people down
Then pickin' 'em up off the ground
You don't want to hang around
Or you just might get burned
Guy says hey, let me know
I can take you where you wanna go
Drift along where the river flows
And you just might get drowned
There's just got to be a way to find a balance
Between what you want and what you really need
And a man can only get so far on talent
And he can't make a living just on greed

(Unless he works for Enron or one of them Wall Street
investment firms)
A woman chased me like a pup
Kissed my ass like a suction cup
All she did was soften up
My fragile point of view
She left me in a pouring rain
Might as well have been a hurricane
Couldn't've caused me no more pain
If she'd shot me in the street
CHORUS
(Some have tried: Kinky Friedman, Orson Welles,
maybe … Ron Paul on the right, or Dennis Kucinich on
the left)
Friends say they wanna have fun
But they're lookin' out for number one
If your life hits a rut
They're sorry as they can be
If you ever asked 'em for a loan
They'd say, hey, man, you're on your own
You're just a dog lookin' for a bone
And I'm tired of hangin' out
CHORUS
(They all get theirs in the end: Ken Lay, Jack Abramoff,
maybe even…Michael Vick)

Priscilla laughed. "Congressman Kucinich will be very happy to hear that you consider him a dreamer," she said. "No, seriously. I think he will."

"So you like it?"

"Love it. Yet another in a long series of Riley Mansfield populist anthems. It's a little disjointed, though. Don't you think?"

"Yeah, I know," Riley said. "This one wasn't written to be a hit, just a coffeehouse crowd-pleaser. I understand what I'm talking about. Fuck it."

They took their time walking back across the field. The first tourists of the morning were outside the visitors center, waiting for it to open at nine, which was about ten minutes away.

"How'd you pull the satellite truck?" Riley asked.

"That was all George's doing. He's, uh, very well connected."

"But he's pretty much known worldwide as a Democrat, right?"

"He's got friends on both sides of the aisle," Priscilla said. "And believe it or not, there are actually Republicans who cannot stand President Sam Harmon."

"They want him to lose?"

"Some think they can't reclaim their own party unless they take a beating in November. In some ways, being out of power has its advantages. If Harmon isn't reelected, the Republicans go back to impeding everything the Democrats try to do, and they're a hell of a lot better at saying no than coming up with solutions of their own."

Priscilla dropped off Riley at the Homewood Suites and said she'd see him in Ashland that night.

"Come early if you can," Riley said as he waved goodbye. "The good shit's probably going to be in the rehearsal."

As Priscilla started to back out, Riley banged on the window glass. She stopped and lowered the passenger-side window. "I need some money," he said. "For the guys, I mean, I haven't been real specific about how much they're getting paid, but I definitely told them they would get paid."

"How much?"

"Just get what you can," Riley said, "preferably in cash. I'll divvy it up best I can."

"Like everything else," Priscilla said, sighing, "I'll see what I can do."

"Everybody'll be in a much merrier mood if I can give 'em some money sometime today," he said.

For the next fifteen minutes, Riley loaded a few essentials in the truck, then went back to the room to shave and shower.

Afterwards, everyone gathered in the lobby, and Melissa provided directions to the Shoney's on Staples Mill Road in Henrico for a breakfast suitable to get everyone through a long day of rehearsals and a night of live music.

♫

Ike Spurgeon was on the way to the Columbia, South Carolina, FBI office, when partner Henry Poston called.

"Henry, what's up?"

"We've been called into the home office, Ike."

"When?"

"We've got to fly up there in the morning. Flight's at eight thirty-five. Be there till Sunday."

"Do you have the slightest idea what this is about?"

"Apparently, it's got something to do with the Greenville-Spartanburg incident and the attempted bombing."

"Saturday's the fifth," Spurgeon said. "Riley Mansfield is playing on national television. That's got to have something to do with it."

"I honestly don't know for sure—I just got the news—but apparently they're calling in everyone who has had any dealings with the case. I mean, who knows? Maybe they're worried about Mansfield. Maybe they're worried about protecting him. Apparently, we're going to be there, or that's my guess."

"Something ain't right."

"That's been the story with that case, all along," said Poston. "We'll talk more when you get here."

♫

By the time breakfast had been eaten, the venue had been located, all the equipment had been set up and the sound checked, it was about eleven. The band was thrown together, but everyone but Cody Huard had played together many times over the years. Fortunately, Cody proved to be the most skilled, adaptable and spontaneous musician in the bunch. Riley's songs were simple, none requiring more than five chords and many no more than three. The process wasn't really that difficult. Riley would say a few words about each song, strum an introductory chord pattern, perform the song, and, in no more than three or four takes, everyone would have it down. After the second or third verse, Riley would back away from the microphone, tilt his guitar toward one of his fellow musicians—Cody on mandolin; Eric, Wade and Alan on guitars; Harvey on bass or fiddle; Chad on drums—and run through a series of solos. Then Riley would step back up to the mic, having been playing chords all along, and sing the final verse, or the final two. Sometimes songs with four verses would include two solo segments.

"Ain't no work to this," said Wade, who occasionally stepped outside for a smoke after completing his turn. "This is just fuckin' fun."

When Priscilla Hay appeared, Riley decided it was time to take a break. Eggs, bacon and grits were still heavy on everyone's stomach, so there wasn't much need for food. Dan, who had been scouting around, led them to a nearby facility known as Carter Park, which was spacious and, owing to the early-afternoon heat, almost deserted. They gathered at picnic tables in the shade of the woods that covered most of the landscape.

Priscilla handed Riley an envelope containing eight thousand dollars in twenty-dollar bills.

"Jesus," Riley said. "Who says the government can't act quickly?"

"Actually," Priscilla said, "it comes from the Republican National Committee. It was deposited in your bank account at nine thirty-three, which was slightly over an hour after you requested it."

"How'd you—they—get into my bank account?"

"You gave me your ATM card and account information," Priscilla said. "Remember?"

"When was that?"

"Right before you went to Oregon, silly. It was part of letting me be you."

"Oh. Well...cool."

Riley took the wad of cash and returned to the large picnic table where a joint was being merrily passed around. Riley counted out a thousand bucks in twenties—one, two, three, four, one; one, two, three, four, two; one, two, three, four, three—and gave each musician his share. There were only seven musicians, though. Riley took his share and realized he had a thousand to spare. He gave Eric two hundred dollars for his father, no longer acquainted with the use of money, and gave the same amount to Dan and Melissa. He kept six hundred dollars in reserve. *Shit. Could be a need for bribery at some point.*

"There'll be more," Riley said. "I don't know how much more, but we'll get it before we take the stage on Saturday."

Ashland Coffee and Tea was only a short distance away, but Riley wanted to make sure he wasn't going to need to try to bribe any cops in the next few minutes. Riley being Riley, he saw no peril in driving himself, but he made sure Dan drove the van Eric had driven from Kentucky.

On the way back, Riley said to Melissa, "You know, I feel like something I heard a comedian say on TV the other night. I think it was Craig Ferguson. He said he went to a rock concert on his first trip to America and, afterwards, he went down on his knee and said, 'I shall dedicate my life to drugs and rock and roll!' And then he said, 'What could possibly go wrong?'"

Melissa's laughter was a bit nervous.

"Everything's gonna be fine," Riley said.

"What happened to the foreboding?"

"It left with that swig of moonshine," Riley said.

Back at Ashland Coffee and Tea, rehearsals turned to songs by his fellow band members. Since Riley wasn't much needed—there were, after all, three other guitarists, all infinitely more proficient than he—he and Melissa hobnobbed with Barney and Helen Stegner, the proprietors. They were fine, selfless people, dedicated to live music. They assured him the place would be packed, and Riley told them he didn't want a dime, that he had made arrangements for the performance to be underwritten, somewhat unbeknownst, by the Republican National Committee.

"Should I read a certain irony into that?" Helen Stegner asked.

"Oh, yeah," Riley said. "I might be sleeping with the enemy, but the enemy's got to pay."

The Stegners obviously hit it off with Melissa, so after a polite period, Riley left the three of them gossiping at the coffee-and-food counter. He walked back into the main floor, joining Ethan Hays, who sat like a stone statue at one of the tables, smoking in spite of several signs placed to inform him he couldn't do that.

"How you making it?"

"I'm having trouble with the shakes," Ethan said. "I ain't rightly used to straying far from the house."

"Be good for you."

"I didn't want to come, to tell you the truth. I just felt, down in my bones, I had to."

Riley knew Ethan was prone to falling off his ladder when his medication wasn't regulated properly.

"Aw, everything's gonna be fine. You think you can handle all this? They's gonna be a real big crowd when we play that gig in Washington on Saturday."

"Be a waste for most of 'em," Ethan said. "I been a-listening, and y'all boys got somethin' the likes of which I ain't ne'er seen. I don't b'lieve city folks can appreciate it like they oughtta."

"If you don't think you can handle it, you can stay back at the hotel and watch it on TV," Riley said. "We can get somebody to keep you company. It's likely to be hotter'n hell."

"I don't want to go," said Ethan, "but I don't think they's no other choice."

Riley had no reply.

"I've just got this feeling, all about me, and I been hearing voices. And they's been some strange things occurrin'…and I think every goddamned thing I've been a-doin' in my whole mis'ble life been leading up to this one thing, and it's got something to do with that concert on Sat'dy, and I know in my bones I'm s'posed to be thar."

A part of Riley wanted to believe that Ethan Hays was as crazy as a steer shocked one too many times by a prod, and a part of him felt chilled to the bone by Ethan's words. He had always seen a touch of the mystic in Ethan, which is why he hadn't objected when Eric had told him Dad wanted to come. But Ethan was acting as if he was going to Washington, D.C. to die, and the thought didn't do much to quell the foreboding that still flickered, disavowals notwithstanding, in the recesses of his mind.

Riley walked to the back of the stage, rummaged around in Eric's bag, and took himself another swallow of moonshine. Then, when the current jam ran its course, he strapped on his Pawless and went back to work.

A couple hours before the gig, the band rode off in Eric's van, allegedly in search of pizza. Riley, Melissa and Adam remained. The Stegners provided sandwiches.

"You got any questions?" Riley asked Adam.

"Yeah. How do you feel about the end being near? Are you more relaxed? Or are you feeling the pressure?"

"I got some shit I take for the pressure," Riley said, laughing a little, but then he leaned back in the chair, took his left hand and ran it across his face, then ran it through the part in his dark-brown hair.

"I don't know," he said. "The main emotion, I think, is weariness. I don't need rest; I need relief. But it's not relief and it's not pressure. I don't know if it's emotion or lack of it. I've just been bumping along ever since the goddamned plane landed. It doesn't matter whether I'm high or sober, whether I'm driving down the highway or playing a song. I feel kind of anesthetized or something.

"What about you, by the way?"

"I'm good and getting better," Adam said. "I still got a little, oh, yearning in my bones, for want of a better term, but I think I'm almost there. Life's reasonably cool."

"When the gates open, we'll sneak out for a couple minutes. When I was a kid, my daddy used to pick me up at the show— that's what we called going to a movie, going to the show—and I could always tell when he was drinking because he'd be licking his lips when I got in the truck. He'd have a Fresca between his legs and a pint of Jack under the seat, and he'd look at me and know what I was thinking. 'Oh, just a little something to knock the chill off, Riley boy,' he'd say."

"Before the show, we just need a little something to knock the chill off."

"It's ninety degrees," Melissa said.

"But it's air-conditioned in here," Riley replied.

The three of them ate somewhat quietly, exchanging simple pleasantries. Riley picked at his club sandwich, leaving half of it uneaten. At about six, Priscilla bustled in. After going over some fairly mundane details, she retrieved a note from her purse and handed it to Riley.

"Who's Henry Poston?" she asked.

"Let's see. Name seems vaguely familiar. Oh, yeah. That's one of the FBI agents who interrogated me after the plane thing. Slim white guy. Horn-rimmed glasses. His partner is black. Big guy built like a linebacker."

"Well, I got an email," she said. "Or you got an email; I just read it. It was from a personal address, Yahoo or something. The note said you needed to give him a call. That's the number."

"Okay. That's kind of strange, don't you think? FBI agent sends me an email from his personal address. Maybe that's good. Wants to tell me something off the record. Maybe. I'll call him first thing in the morning, before we go to Washington. How we going to Washington, by the way?"

"We could've done this any way you wanted, but I thought, all things considered, it'd be best for all of you to drive up to the hotel."

"Which is?"

"It's all in packets I left for you and everyone else at the front desk of the Homewood," Priscilla said. "You're all at an Embassy Suites. Tenth Street Northwest, I think."

"Umm. Hilton Points. Wonder if I can get 'em even though I didn't pay for the room. Can't hurt to try."

"How do we get to the venue?" Melissa asked. "The National Mall?"

"Transportation will be provided. A bus will take you directly back and forth from the hotel to the Mall. All the rehearsals are going to be on the stage where the concert is. You've got two to five tomorrow afternoon. Your rooms will be ready. You just need to get settled in by noon."

"What's it, an hour's drive?" Riley asked.

"From your hotel, a good hour and a half, I'd say. Probably be best to leave around nine, so you'd hit D.C. traffic at about ten-thirty."

"Check," he said. "For all my vices and weaknesses, I'm remarkably punctual."

"Be careful," Priscilla said. "You need to act the good Libertarian, principled and humble."

Melissa laughed. A chunk of chicken flew past Riley's left ear.

♪

At seven, the doors opened. Ashland Coffee and Tea was packed within twenty minutes. The band had straggled back in. Riley and Adam had blazed after finding some open space near the railroad tracks. Lanky Riley nearly fell after tripping on the tracks.

"I probably need to wear my cowboy boots a little more often when I'm not on the stage," he said to Adam.

"It's remarkable how long it's taking to walk about fifty yards."

"Shit," said Riley, "look at that."

"What?"

"Sue Ellen Spenser, getting out of that black Audi. She's got some guy with her in a coat and tie."

"Good little Republicans," said Adam. "Checking in on their investment."

"Think you can play the little Libertarian blogger a little more?"

"I don't know, man," Adam said. "Don't you think she probably checked up on me or something?"

"Well, we could find out."

"How would I handle that?"

"Don't 'fess up to a thing," Riley said. "Make 'em tell you what they know. If they know you work for *Rolling Stone*, say you were hired there because Libertarians believe in legalizing drugs and the magazine wanted to give some attention, you know, to that point of view."

"That would help explain why I'm stoned as shit, too," Adam said.

"Yeah. Exactly."

♫

"Surprise, surprise," said Sue Ellen Spenser.

Priscilla Hay, sort of idly perusing the crowd filing in, was standing face-to-face with Sue Ellen and the president's National Security Adviser, David Branham.

"Look who's here. David, this is Priscilla Hay. Do you two know each other? Priscilla works at Clark Powell Morgenthau."

"I don't believe I've had the pleasure," said Branham. "Good to see you, Miss Hay."

"What brings you here, Priscilla?" Sue Ellen asked.

"Oh, just checking out the competition," she said, smiling politely. "I thought I'd review the act to see how much we're gonna get hammered by the president's grand extravaganza. I was in town already, saw this was going on in the *Times-Dispatch* and, really, I just came over out of curiosity."

"Small world," Sue Ellen said.

At this point, one might have expected an invitation from Sue Ellen and David for Priscilla to join them. It didn't happen. Priscilla broke the awkward silence.

"I'm here with a friend. An old school buddy."

"Well, David and I are here to check out this Riley Mansfield, too. I hear he's very clever. Enjoy yourself."

"Thanks," said Priscilla. "Glad to have met you, Mr. Branham."

Priscilla loitered until Spenser and Branham entered Ashland Coffee and Tea. Then she fairly fled to the back entrance near Riley's truck, her Prius and Eric's van. After entering, she quickly found Melissa.

"Psst," she yelled. "Come over here."

"What?" Melissa asked after joining her, out of view from the seating area.

"Sue Ellen Spenser's here. She's with the president's National Security Adviser."

"Wow. That's a really important position, right?"

"Well, yeah. Here's what I've got to know: Does she know you? Have you ever met?"

Melissa took a breath and touched her light-brown hair. "I've seen her. I don't think she's ever seen me."

"What do you mean?"

"Riley met her for dinner. I was in the restaurant within sight. It was back in Henry. I'm almost positive she didn't notice me."

"You sure?"

Melissa sighed again. "Yes. I'm sure."

"Good. I told Sue Ellen I was here with a friend. We can sit together during the show."

"We better go see Riley."

They found Riley and Adam in what passed for a dressing room. The rest of the band probably didn't even know it existed.

Riley flashed a brief look of annoyance when they fairly bustled in. "I'm kind of trying to get my head straight," he said.

"This is important, honey," Melissa said. "Sue Ellen Spenser's here, and she's got one of President Harmon's top guys…"

"National Security Adviser," said Priscilla.

"David Branham?" asked Adam. "David Branham's…here?"

"Yes," said Priscilla. "With Sue Ellen."

"So what? It doesn't change anything," Riley said. "I'll just do my show. I wasn't planning on doing 'Misfits' anyway. We're not playing anything that…I don't know…subversive.

"Do you think I need to acknowledge this guy Branham's presence? Should I introduce him, or him and Sue Ellen, from the stage?"

Priscilla thought a moment. "No," she said, finally. "I don't think so. Branham's married. Saying he's there with Sue Ellen might make him uncomfortable. It probably wouldn't be wise even to introduce him. It would cause people to stare at his table and wonder who the woman is."

Riley smiled. "And you are concerned that one of Harmon's top advisers might be uncomfortable?"

"Sometimes you've got to lose a few battles in order to win the war," Priscilla replied.

♫

"We're so proud to have back at Ashland Coffee and Tea one of our favorite songwriters," said Barney Stegner from his stage. "Things have really changed lately in our friend Riley Mansfield's life. He singlehandedly thwarted a terrorist's attempt to blow up an airliner in Greenville, South Carolina, which is near his home. On Saturday, he will perform on national television at a celebration hosted by President Sam Harmon on the National Mall in Washington. Through all of this, Riley has remained true to his songwriting roots, and when he called Helen and me, and said he needed a place to perform with the band he has assembled, we were so honored. Without further ado, please welcome to our stage...Riley Mansfield!"

Riley ambled out, having put on a long-sleeved flannel shirt, left unbuttoned, over his tee shirt.

"This is a Steve Earle song," he said when the applause settled. "I'll do mainly my own, but I'm kind of superstitious about doing a cover first. It's called 'Home to Houston.'"

Eric Hays took Harvey Kitchens' bass for the opening song, freeing Harvey to intro with a "zip-zip" fiddle lick. The song was about a trucker in Iran, so naturally, being an Earle song, it had a bit of an anti-war tone, but it was subtle and acceptable to conservatives. As Priscilla listened, she marveled at what a tactful choice it was. She glanced across the room at Branham and Spenser. They appeared to be enjoying themselves.

"I was in, uh, New England, when our country was attacked by terrorists on Nine Eleven," Riley said. "Uh, this isn't a patriotic song."

The crowd oohed a bit.

"It just occurred to me when I had this incident in a general store. It's called 'I Got Cash Money...and I'm Workin' Steady.'"

Eric had handed the bass back to Harvey and carried the load on electric guitar in Riley's second song.

> *I got cash money*
> *And I'm workin' steady*
> *Used to go to church*
> *My mama's name is Betty*
> *I pay my bills*
> *Work my job*
> *Always at the ready*
> *'Cause I got cash money*
> *And I'm workin' steady*
> *I drove through this town*
> *Thought I'd stop and have a bite to eat*
> *The lady at the counter looked at me*

Like I wasn't wearin' nothing on my feet
She told me that the deli had closed five minutes before
And would I please shut it when I walked back out the
door
I got the impression she didn't want to see my ass no
more
And I could not just sit there
And let it slide
(So I stopped at the door, turned around and said)
CHORUS

Eric's first lead had sort of a Don Rich sound to it, then Alan
jumped in with the slide and Wade brought the house down with
blues riffs.

(I'm taking you back quite a few years now…)
Sometimes I was too young when I wanted to buy beer
I already had a taste for it
Didn't' want to wait another year
So I smoked some weed and got my nerve up
To flash that fake ID
The asshole at the counter said, hey boy, what's in this
for me?
He made me realize that he was his own charity
And I could not just sit there
And let it slide
(So I looked that sonuvabitch right in the eye and I told
him)
CHORUS TWICE
I got cash money
And I'm workin' steeaady!

"I really like this," said Branham, clapping furiously. "I'm glad
you convinced me to come. We should use some of his music in
the campaign. I mean, he might have to be…selective."

"As I said, Mansfield shies away from politics."

"No, but I mean, maybe we could play some audio. Warm up the crowd at rallies, that type of thing."

"I think that could be arranged," said Sue Ellen, beaming.

Onstage, Riley and the band breezed through "There You Are," which was recognized by many in the crowd.

Wade McKeever motioned him over.

"Yeah?"

"Let's do 'Stoned at the Crack of Dawn.'"

Riley looked dubious but sleepy-eyed.

"Fuck it," Wade said.

"Ah'ight. Hell, yes." Riley turned to the band. "'Stoned at the Crack of Dawn,' it is."

He walked back to the mic. "Sad to say, but this song was written about my ex-brother-in-law."

Halfway through the second verse, Branham turned to Sue Ellen and said, "Do you think he's stoned?"

"What?"

Branham spoke up. "I said, do you think he's stoned? You know…on something?"

"Maybe a little pot," she said. "After all, David, he is a Libertarian."

"I guess you're right. You don't think he'd actually smoke marijuana before he goes on Saturday?"

Sue Ellen winced. "I tell you what, David. I bet you he doesn't smoke as much marijuana as Claude Herndon. Everything's fine. Security is in place."

Meanwhile, Barney Stegner responded to an urgent message from Helen concerning some disturbance at the gate.

Jed Langston had arrived late, having no idea at all that the concert might be sold out. Even though he flashed his Homeland Security badge, Helen steadfastly denied him entry.

"I'm sorry," she said. "There are regulations. We can't legally allow any more people inside. We already admitted several officials to provide security for an aide to the president."

"Who?"

"David…"

"Branham?"

"I think that's right."

"Well, you don't understand, ma'am. I'm here to provide security for the entertainers. We've been tracking terrorist movements, and I'm here to provide security for Riley Mansfield."

"You think there might be a terrorist attack…here?"

"No, ma'am, not at all. I'm just going to keep my eyes open and monitor the crowd. Nothing's going to happen, but in my business, you can't be too careful."

Barney arrived, and Helen briefly explained the situation.

"You won't get in trouble with the fire marshals," Langston said. "I can assure that. Besides, I'm here alone. I'll watch from the wings. Or at the back of the crowd."

"Okay," Barney said. "Come on in."

Onstage, Riley introduced another song. "On this next song," he said, "we're going to highlight the mandolin work of a friend I just met last week. How about a nice round of applause for the great Cody Huard."

Cody wowed the crowd with his intro to Riley's "I'm Responsible":

I'm responsible
For my mother
Responsible
For all the others
Responsible
For my sisters
Responsible
For all their children
I got so much responsibility
Who in the hell take care of me?
Grandma left it all to me

The house, the farm, the pecan trees
None of them bring money in
Very much to my chagrin
Well, I don't mind keepin' up my mother
Never hear from my brother
Never get no appreciation
Mainly just repudiation
CHORUS

During the instrumental break, Harvey put away the bass and spontaneously added some fiddle licks to Cody's mandolin.

I can barely afford to pay the taxes
I'm a man who seldom relaxes
Don't hear nothing till it's bad
Ain't no use in a-getting' mad
Kids won't even wash the dishes
Ain't a one of them's ambitious
I don't know who's to blame
For all them young'uns playin' video games
CHORUS
I got so much responsibility
Who in the hell take care of meeeee!

Riley and the band bathed in applause. It was the perfect band with the perfect crowd. Riley's eyes watered, partly because he was sentimental and partly because he was buzzed, and he and the band ripped with remarkable cohesion through "Go Big Red," "Martinsville" and the new song, "Find a Balance." Then Riley closed his first set with a medley of covers, introducing the band members one by one as each performed solos during the transitions from each song to another.

The crowd, populated in no small measure with students from nearby Randolph-Macon College, was in a state of collective ecstasy.

"Thank you so much," said Riley. "You're too kind. Right now

I'm going to take a break, mainly because I'm not good enough on guitar to hang in with these guys, but we want to showcase the band because, well, really, it's not my band, they're my buddies, and these guys all got great songs of their own. I'm gonna walk off for a little while so I won't be standing around lookin' stupid."

"Aw, what the hell," Riley said to himself as he locked the dressing-room door behind him. He smoked a roach as quickly as possible, then retrieved a handy can of Febreze from his bag and sprayed the room thoroughly. He gargled with some Scope at the simple sink, washed his hands conscientiously and left to join Melissa.

"Look at that," said David Branham from across the room. "Isn't that Priscilla Hay, the woman you introduced me to, sitting with Mansfield at his table?"

Sue Ellen almost panicked but regained her composure quickly.

"Mansfield's single," she said. "That table is right in the corner, nearest the dressing room. He's probably just trying to get laid."

"That's quite a coincidence," Branham observed.

"Oh, I'm sure Priscilla's sizing him up. It's a done deal, though. She's probably just trying to pick up some details. Whether he's going to endorse the president, what songs he's going to sing, stuff like that. Personally, I hope he tells her everything," Sue Ellen said.

Standing in the back, next to the windows, pressed up against others admitted for standing room, Jed Langston also observed Riley Mansfield with interest. Jed knew Melissa was his girlfriend, of course, and the other woman seemed vaguely familiar. He couldn't place her, though, and figured she was just a friend of Melissa Franklin's who had come to see Mansfield perform.

♫

It was closing in on eleven when Riley and his friends slowed the tempo to close the show.

"Thank you so much, folks," Riley said. "I don't think I've ever had a better time playing music."

The Audacity of Dope

Enthusiastic applause rose and fell. They all left the stage, and then, naturally, they all returned for the encore.

"This number is about hard times in small towns," Riley said, strapping the guitar back across his shoulders.

> *I don't know where I am and I don't know where I'm*
> *goin'*
> *I reckon it's best not to say*
> *What factories are left here are mainly hiring Mexicans*
> *I reckon that they'll work without much pay*
> *I sell a little weed and I barely keep my bills paid*
> *Probably smoke too much of it away*
> *And my life's not that hot*
> *And I'm past the point of caring*
> *About all the things*
> *I ain't got*
> *(What I ain't got)*
> *My friends all moved away and they live in big cities*
> *Where they fight all that traffic every day*
> *While I sit here and rot in this godforsaken town*
> *That gets older and sadder every day*
> *I fell into this ditch and before I could climb out*
> *I realized I was bound to stay*
> *CHORUS*
> *I don't give a damn and I don't care what happens*
> *What happens is gonna happen either way*
> *I'm a ship without a rudder, adrift with no sails*
> *But the water's still choppy on the bay*
> *I flounder around, either drown or run aground*
> *It's really gonna suck either way*
> *CHORUS*
> *(What I ain't got ...)*

"Thank you so much," said Riley above the applause, "and how about a big round of applause for the band: Cody Huard on mandolin…Eric Hays, Wade McKeever and Alan Isaac on guitars…Chad Dunham on drums…and my old friend and partner in crime…Harvey Kitchens on bass and fiddle!

"Have a great Fourth of July, everybody! Let freedom ring!"

They all left the stage, and when Riley walked into the dressing room, they all followed.

Riley said, "Fuck, that was unbelievable, wasn't it?"

"We kicked ass," said Wade, and everyone else nodded.

♫

"Sue, this is just extraordinary," said David Branham, still at the table, though Sue Ellen had suggested they skip the encore. "It's a shame this guy…how old is he?"

"Thirty-five."

"It's a shame he won't just join the campaign. Does he know we could make him a millionaire?"

"Oh, he knows," said Sue Ellen. "Says he's only interested in success on his own terms."

"A shame that a man so talented can be such a fool," the National Security Adviser concluded. "He might get the president re-elected on Saturday alone. And, by extension, you might get the president re-elected based on your taking charge of making everything work just so."

Sue Ellen blushed, or tried to.

"I want to meet him. We'll get a room afterwards."

"You're…"

"Madelyn thinks I'm with the president at Camp David," Branham said. "I'll call her in the morning and tell her I got called away to Richmond to take care of a security issue that cropped up."

Meanwhile, Jed Langston had left early. He knew this Sue Ellen Spenser had foiled him yet again. He had to concede that bringing along David Branham had been a master stroke. There was no way he and Banks McPherson were going to convince

Branham that putting Riley Mansfield on a national stage was a bad idea. He had attended the concert hoping he could find something, anything, that would turn the tables on Mansfield. But Branham had seen—and obviously enjoyed—the same show he was hoping to use as a last-ditch argument to put an end to Mansfield.

Langston said a prayer as he sat in his government-issue sedan.

"Holy Father, give me the strength and provide me the opportunity to glorify Thy presence. Help me preserve the glory of the United States of America, a country founded in Thy name and dedicated to Thy honor. Help me, oh Father, to eliminate the wickedness on this earth because I know it is Thy will that the godless Democrats be prevented from taking over this poor, naïve country, and give me the strength and opportunity to prevent this imposter, this Riley Mansfield, from undermining the greatness of this nation and despoiling the glory of the Kingdom of Heaven.

"In Thy name I pray, amen."

♬

"Oh, shit, the souvenirs," said Melissa. "We gotta sell some tee shirts, honey. And CDs. You gotta sign some autographs."

Suddenly, Riley's mood changed.

"Why don't you let Priscilla give you a ride back to the hotel? I think Sue Ellen and Harmon's bigwig adviser, David, uh, whatever, are still out there."

"She doesn't know me."

"She knows Priscilla," Riley said. "And there's another guy who was in the crowd. The guy who tried to poison Adam. He was here. And he knows you. And he probably knows Priscilla."

"That guy's out there?" said Adam. "I didn't see him."

"Oh, he was out there. I think he left before the encore. I couldn't find him in the crowd when we went back out."

"He's right," Priscilla said. "We better get out of here."

"Dan, you can sell tee shirts, right?"

"Yeah, yeah, no problem."

"Guys, just take your time. Load the shit. I'll go out and sign autographs. Probably be some folks out back wanting all y'all's autographs.

"Adam, you better go, too."

"No shit, man."

Branham and Spenser were in line between a couple of likely stoners from Randolph-Macon and a middle-aged couple from someplace called Chester. Branham bought two CDs but passed on the tee shirts, the most popular being the ones promoting Riley's song "Wake and Bake."

Oh, my God. We never even did that song.

"I haven't enjoyed anything so much in a very, very long time," said the smooth National Security Adviser, looking terribly out of place in gray suit and red-and-blue-striped tie. "The President wanted me to express his gratitude for participating in this celebration of America."

"Well, uh, thanks, uh, Mr., uh, National Security Adviser."

"Please call me David. May I call you Riley?"

"Well, like, of course."

"When this is all over, Riley—it may be when the reelection campaign is over—but I want you to come to my house for a cookout. It can be just you and your guitar. It'll be a grand time."

"Thank you, uh, David. It'll be a...pleasure. I'll be back in touch, or I'm sure, you, uh, being in the government and all, that your, uh, people can figure out how to get in touch with me. Yeah, I'm pretty sure of that."

He laughed. Branham laughed. Sue Ellen laughed.

"I'll see you Saturday, if not before," Branham said, and they left.

CHAPTER THIRTY-TWO
GOOD TO GO

Riley Mansfield was still basking in the glow of the Ashland Coffee and Tea show on Thursday morning as he and Melissa Franklin drove up Interstate 95, headed for the District of Columbia.

"This is the first time I've really thought, deep down, that everything is going to work out," he said.

"Forgive me for saying this, but that's scary."

"Yeah, I guess you're right." Riley thought for a few moments. "Oh, yeah. I gotta make a call."

"Who?"

"This guy Henry Poston. He's the FBI agent who, uh, interrogated me after the bomb blew up in the peach trees near Greenville-Spartanburg. Priscilla gave me a message and phone number yesterday."

Riley fished a slip of paper out of his pocket, handed it to Melissa and pulled out his cell phone. "Give me the number," he said.

"Okay...eight oh three, five five five, oh seven five four."

"Got it."

Poston answered on the third ring.

"Agent Poston? This is Riley Mansfield."

"Gimme just a minute."

Riley waited, figuring correctly that Poston wanted some privacy.

"Where are you?" Poston asked.

"Driving between Richmond and D.C. We got a caravan: a truck, a van and a car. You in Columbia?"

"No," said Poston. "Special Agent Spurgeon and I were called in to headquarters. You remember Agent Spurgeon?"

"Sure. Your partner. Black guy."

"We'll be at the…extravaganza…what's it called?…on Saturday."

"Good. I don't know what it's called, either. 'Tribute to America.' 'America's Birthday Celebration.' Something like that. So what's up? They got y'all assigned to the 'keep Riley in line' patrol?"

"We, Agent Spurgeon and I, have actually cut you several breaks, and we've played a little fast and loose with Bureau regulations to do it, too," said Poston.

"I appreciate that, I reckon," said Riley. "I'm well aware that I can be a bit too much of a smart-ass, at times, but it's easy to get paranoid when the government's been following you around and forcing you to do what they want done. So, why are you here?"

"They called in everyone with any relation to the terrorist investigation. Agent Spurgeon and I are going to be in the security force at the show mainly, apparently, because we know…about you.

"We need to talk, Riley. I can't be completely sure this connection is secure."

"Boy, I know that feeling."

"Granted," Poston said. "Look. What's your schedule?"

"We, uh, gotta do rehearsals all this afternoon. Tomorrow I don't think it's that, you know, busy. There's a dress rehearsal late in the afternoon, where there's everything, I guess, except a crowd. I don't really know, exactly, what's going to be asked of us before that. We're supposed to get all our rehearsals done today."

"We've got a bunch of meetings, too. What about before the concert? I mean, several hours before it starts."

"That'll work," Riley said. "I'll come early, if need be. The show starts at two, I think."

"We need to talk somewhat privately. When do you think the crowd will start filing in?"

"I'm guessing…I think I saw that gates open at noon. Hang on.

"Melissa," Riley said, "I gotta little bag behind the seat. There's a zipper compartment on the front. There's some paperwork about the show there. See if you can see when the gates open on Saturday.

"Agent Poston, I'll be there whenever you need me. Is there something here I need to be worried about?"

"Well, I don't know, and I'm not at liberty to say…"

"If you don't know, why are you not at liberty to say?"

Silence.

"Yeah," said Melissa. "Noon. Gates open at noon."

"Noon, Agent Poston. So, what if you meet me somewhere around the stage at ten-thirty or eleven?"

"Fine."

"I'll save this number," Riley said. "You text me, or I'll text you, and we'll get together. I'll tell you whatever you want to know."

"All right, let's get off this line for now," Poston said. "Call me if you need me between now and then."

"Thanks. Give Agent Spurgeon my regards."

"You'll be seeing him," said Poston. "Bye."

♪

Working out the songs was effortless and beautiful. For the opening song, Merle Haggard's "The Fighting Side of Me," Eric and Alan concocted an intro, similar to the original, that began with Hays' picking and ended with Alan's slide riff. Wade took over during the first break, and then after the latter verse and chorus, Cody performed a mandolin solo that led, in turn, to singing the chorus a second time. Then came Riley's song, "Your Independence Day," in which Eric switched to bass and Harvey picked up the fiddle. His lovely fiddle riffs ran in and out of the melody throughout the song, and it was breathtakingly beautiful. Alan, who had played a Stratocaster on "Fighting Side," switched to an acoustic slide for Riley's song. Then the ease and familiarity of "This Land Is Your Land" just turned into a patriotic jubilee.

Riley thought he knew the song but hadn't realized it had five verses. Riley had to use a Teleprompter, which he had never done before, but the frequent breaks—beginning with the chorus, then verse, then chorus, et cetera—gave everyone in the band a chance to solo. In the first take, Chad and Harvey even opened with a combo bass-drums solo, but Riley decided that made for an awkward first break, so Eric opened with a country lead, followed by Wade playing the blues, the bass-drum run, Alan on slide, Harvey on fiddle and, finally, Cody on mandolin.

After about three hours, the band was good to go, but everything had to be coordinated by the TV director, who insisted on precision and wanted each song to comply with a predetermined time limit. Wade, in particular, got angry, shot the director the finger and stomped offstage.

After what began as a heated exchange, Riley got the little, beret-wearing director, whose name was Ian Costello even though he seemed the least Irish of anyone Riley had ever met, to settle down.

"Why don't we do it this way? Instead of starting with a number—minutes and seconds—let's start with the song. Time it the way we do it first, we'll do it that way on Saturday, and you adjust the schedule to that," Riley suggested.

Exasperated, the director offered token resistance but eventually came around to Riley's point of view. The initial schedule called for "Fighting Side of Me" and "Your Independence Day," followed by a two-minute commercial break, and then "This Land Is Your Land." Riley said he preferred to do the first song, then go to the break and come back for the final two songs.

"The reason the one song closes is that, after it's completed, that's when you greet President Harmon."

"But look at it the other way," Riley said. "The shortest song is 'Fighting Side.' Why not have the president come on after that? It's patriotic. It's right-wing. It's perfect. I know President Harmon is scheduled to speak for a few minutes. Why have him greeting me detract from that? Instead, I greet him before the break, then, after the break, we come back and do our last two songs, and then the camera cuts to the president and all the attention's on him. He doesn't have me standing nearby, looking stupid."

"Mr. Mansfield, this has already been carefully worked out. This is too late."

"Too late? This is the first time we've even rehearsed! What if, maybe, someone had talked to me about it before, like, now? I guarantee, I fucking guarantee, that when Claude Herndon comes up here tomorrow, he's gonna already know what he's doing and it's gonna be pretty much what his people said it was gonna be. What you're basically saying is his guys are pros and my guys aren't."

Riley realized, of course, that he was, quite possibly wrong. Priscilla Hay, acting in his stead, had probably just rubber-stamped the details.

"All right, all right," said Costello. "Let me think this over. I'm going back to the trailer…"

Ooh. He has a trailer. Where's my trailer? Bet Claude Herndon has a trailer. Never mind. Claude Herndon has a bus.

Everyone muddled about onstage, waiting for the director to return.

"Here's what's gonna happen," Riley said. "He knows I'm right, but he can't just collapse and let the inmates run the asylum. He's got to go back, turn it into his idea, make a couple calls, make the same exact argument I just did. And if they don't like it, it's my idea, and he'll say, 'I know it. He's just a whiny-assed prima donna,' and if they do like it, it's his fucking idea. Watch what happens."

Costello came back and said he was willing to go with the "alternate schedule." Everyone smirked. The band played the three tunes, which the director timed, including Riley's words of introduction, which had been scripted. Then they ran through it again, within five seconds of the original run-through.

As Riley was fond of saying, they were good to go.

♫

On Thursday night, Riley, Melissa and Adam Rhine attended a Washington Nationals game. Cody Huard, Alan Isaac and Dan Bond went to the movies, with Cody watching *Wall-E* and the Floridians enjoying *Get Smart*. Chad Dunham, Harvey Kitchens and Wade McKeever hit the Georgetown bars. Eric took a walk around the National Mall with his daddy until, realizing that Ethan wasn't up to much of a hike, caught taxis to the Lincoln and Jefferson memorials.

As the Nats got drilled by the Florida Marlins, Riley spent more time than he would have liked swapping text messages with Priscilla Hay. Riley basically spent three innings occupied.

"Shit," he said finally, flipping the phone off at last. "What did I miss? How'd the Nationals score?"

"Home run by Ryan Zimmerman," Adam said.

"I didn't even notice. You're not gonna believe what happened."

"What?" asked Melissa.

"Well, the higher-ups—I don't know, Republicans, White House, Harmon himself, for all I know—watched a videotape of our run-through, and now they say we gotta chop off the last two verses of 'This Land Is Your Land.'"

"What the fuck for?" asked Adam.

"The last two verses are the reason I wanted to do the song. They're just about hard times for the common man. That's patriotic, too, goddamn it. It's not about fucking Republicans and Democrats. It's about America."

Riley recited the lines: "'As I was walking, I saw a sign there; And that sign said no trespassing; But on the other side, it didn't say nothing; Now that side was made for you and me.'

"And the best one's the last: 'In the square of the city, in the shadow of the steeple; Near the relief office, I see my people; And some are grumbling, and some are wondering; If this land's still made for you and me.'"

"God knows, we wouldn't want anyone to suggest that everyone isn't well off," Melissa said.

"So what now?"

"Priscilla said they're going to replace the time by having me run through the band, jamming with me introducing everybody. That leaves three verses. I think what we'll do is, we'll eliminate the three instrumental runs wrapped around between the first two verses—remember, it begins with the chorus—and then we'll string them all together before the third verse, which is now the final verse. It's probably going to mean we shorten all the solos."

"How's that going to work on time?" Adam asked, as Nick Johnson struck out.

"It'll work," Riley said. "Problem is, we don't have any more time to rehearse, just the, you know, dry run. Dress rehearsal, I guess you'd say."

"Well," Riley continued, "we'll talk. And then I'll wear a watch, I reckon."

♫

Jed Langston called Banks McPherson to ask about Mansfield's activities.

"Everything's fine, Jed," said McPherson. "Relax. He and his girlfriend are at a baseball game. The rest of the band is out on the town. They're all being transported by supervised limousines. They're all protected. No one's going to get in any trouble. I'm told the rehearsals went great. Maybe a few minor revisions, but I'm hearing rave reviews about this band."

"Ah," said Jed, "you've been talking to Branham."

"How'd you know that?"

"He was there, with that Sue Ellen Spenser woman, on Wednesday night in Virginia. I was, too."

"And did anything go wrong?"

Pause. "Well, no."

"You gotta get off this, Jed. I know you don't like Mansfield, but we need him to set the tone for November. After this celebration, the Democratic Convention's coming up, and that's going to affect the polls. If we can boost our numbers going in, it'll keep us ahead no matter how good a job the Democrats do, and since Murrah's just barely going to win the nomination, I'd be willing to bet the Democrats have a little problem putting together a united front. There's going to be divisiveness at the convention. Murrah's too much a centrist for the lefties."

"Murrah's a socialist."

"Yeah, well, if Murrah's a socialist, then Baskin's a communist."

"I hear you," said Langston. "What's the traffic with Mansfield? What's he been saying on his cell phone? Any interesting text messages? Emails?"

"Emails are clean. They've always been clean. We gave up on the other surveillance."

"Why?"

"We haven't ever been able to track him thoroughly. Either he hasn't had one, or he's been changing from one to another. What does it matter? He's not off somewhere in the country. He's right here in town. We got five people within fifteen yards of him at Nationals Park right now."

"I want to work the crowd on Saturday."

"Why work the crowd? Why don't you hang around backstage? Does Mansfield know who you are?"

"Probably," said Langston. "I'll give him this: He's pretty smart. Too smart."

"Well," said McPherson. "Having you around'll probably keep him in line. Imagine you've given him a little reason to be scared of you."

"He ain't scared of me. He ain't scared of nothing, the punk. I don't want him to know I'm watching him. I want to be in the crowd, five or ten rows back..."

"Five rows back, you'd be twenty yards away, Jed. There's

going to be a mass of people in front of the stage, waving and cheering. We're rehearsing that, too. We've got five busloads of College Republicans coming in, waving placards and dancing—tastefully, mind you—in front of the stage. They're gonna be there for the rehearsal tomorrow night, too."

"Then I want to be in there amongst 'em, Banks. Just for security purposes. I want to be right there to make sure everything's going perfect."

"Well, everything's going to go perfect, regardless, but I'll make arrangements," said McPherson.

The Deputy Director of Homeland Security thought for several moments and decided to hedge his bets. McPherson made arrangements to place one of his agents, Langston, in front of the stage. He also added an additional observer to be placed on the roof of the National Gallery of Art. That agent would be charged with surveillance of Jed Langston. Photographs would be circulated to National Park Service Rangers who would, like Langston, be working the crowd in front of the stage.

McPherson's first priority was to make sure no one—not Riley Mansfield and not Jed Langston—fucked up the President's reelection campaign.

♬

Dennis Miller was ingratiating. Lee Greenwood was slimy. Claude Herndon was self-assured and arrogant. Riley and his band mates mingled with them all, not to mention the somewhat star-struck members of several military bands and an array of GOP politicos. Only the VIPs were getting a personal viewing of the run-through.

The rehearsal was in the late afternoon, earlier than originally scheduled. Nice and cool, though, thanks to a breeze and mainly overcast skies. The politicos were there for the photo ops. The musicians were there for the final rehearsal. A public show would follow an hour after the dress rehearsal, at nine. The Beach Boys would perform. This had been added as a compromise when the

Beach Boys apparently felt slighted at having Claude Herndon—the country redneck, in their view—as the headliner. The Beach Boys didn't mingle. Apparently, they were in a bus, in a tent, in a snit somewhere.

"Where are all the Democrats?" one congressman crowed.

"They're out yonder," yelled Herndon, "huggin' trees!"

Riley had to weather several posed photos, both group and individual, with his home state's Congressional delegation—less Democrats, of course—and take part in a press conference, which was a snap. The questions seemed to lack spontaneity, but more were interested now in Claude Herndon, not Riley Mansfield the Hero. Riley took some comfort in the notion that very soon he would truly be old news.

"Hey, man!" Riley turned around. It was Herndon, who didn't introduce himself because he didn't need to.

"You're Riley Mansfield."

"Yeah."

"Call me Claude."

"Hey, Claude."

"You're fucked up, ain't you? Stoned."

"A little," Riley said.

"Me, too. Let's go slip back to my bus, if you wanna. I got some good shit, man."

"Thanks, but I'm good."

"You wrote that song that George Strait's cutting, didn't you?"

"Yeah. You heard about that?"

"Shit, yeah, that's a good song, man. 'Your Independence Day,' right?"

Riley nodded.

"I wish the cocksuckers who work for me had found it. I just wanted to tell you, man, you do know the opportunity you've got, right?"

"Uh, I think so. I mean, I'm playing music with my friends on national television."

"Aw, shit, that ain't the half of it," said Herndon. "Ol' George ain't releasing that song till the fall, man. You get to sing it on that stage tomorrow, and the whole fuckin' country's watching. You could get the hit on that song for yourself, man. You get that thing released, and next thing you know, you'll be filthy rich from your own version and George's both."

Riley didn't know how to respond.

"I can help you, man. You can release it through my label. They tell me that band of yours is kick-ass. Why don't you and your buddies head straight from here to Nashville? Cut it while it's fresh and y'all are still together. I can pull strings for you, man, and I'll do you right."

"I don't know what to say. Thanks."

"Let's get together tomorrow," Herndon said. "Hang around after you get through playing. Let's meet up on the bus tomorrow night. We'll get a little buzz and talk some business."

Riley shook hands. "All right," he said. "Count on it. I'll get together with you after the show."

Walking away, Riley seethed.

What a two-timing shit that guy is. He's interested in me for one reason: to fuck George Strait. That's the Strait who's recorded two Riley Mansfield songs before. Claude Herndon ain't done shit for me, and, in the end, he ain't gonna do shit for me this time, either.

Adam Rhine walked up. "What'd Herndon say to you?"

"He wants to make me a big star, just like him," Riley said. "When that fucker dies, they'll line up down the street just to piss on his grave."

CHAPTER THIRTY-THREE
REPUBLAROO

Even at ten in the morning, four hours before the beginning of the great patriotic extravaganza, activity bustled behind the stage. For once, the story of Riley Mansfield wasn't just personally assigned to a solitary journalist. He had been a good boy during all the press conferences and side interviews with glib TV guys and gals. In a perverse sort of way, Riley had kind of enjoyed all the bullshit. He was getting so accustomed to being a Libertarian that he thought it might be time to buy a gun.

Little late, ain't it?

Riley rang his apparent Federal Bureau of Investigation friend, Henry Poston. "Look," he said, "people are everywhere back here. I think it's pretty much deserted out in front of the stage. Why don't you meet me there in, what, thirty minutes?"

"Ike and I are just pulling up," said Poston. "I can be there in ten."

"Okay, cool. Is Agent Spurgeon joining you?"

"I don't see why not."

"Oh, I'm probably just paranoid," Riley said. "I promise, I've got every reason to be. Why don't we slip into the orchestra pit? We can sit in the chairs and not be as visible."

"That's probably a good idea. I'll be there shortly."

Riley exited the tent and squinted as he rolled his head, staring at the panorama of the sky. It was getting hot, but it was going to be a beautiful day. Riley worked his way through a maze of gates and found there wasn't any way to get from the VIP area to the actual audience without hopping a fence, which, even hours before the show, might draw some security attention. Riley retraced his steps, walked out on the actual stage, and ventured down a half-dozen stairs into the orchestra pit. It was quite well-appointed. The chairs, though they unfolded, were cushioned and comfortable.

Riley was impressed at how much craftsmanship had gone into an edifice that would undoubtedly be completely dismantled by dawn on Sunday.

Vaguely recognizing the man entering the pit as Henry Poston, Riley stood up and shook hands.

"Why no Agent Spurgeon?"

"He may join us in a moment. Ike decided to walk the grounds, check out the security setup and see if he could find something interesting. He's dressed informally because he's going to be in the crowd. I'll be backstage."

"Okay, look," Riley said. "I'm going to tell you some things that you may not believe. You may think me kind of suspicious and conspiratorial. You can think what you like. You gonna tape-record this?"

"Sure."

"Well, I realize I have no business saying this, but I'd appreciate it if you'd just lose this shit if everything goes fine. If something goes wrong, you've got some information that you wouldn't have had otherwise. Deal?"

"We'll see."

"Look, Agent Poston…"

"Call me Henry. May I call you Riley?"

"Sure. You know, this is the second time you asked me that. There's something I gotta ask you? What happened to the guy on the plane? That day, you told me he was Cuban, from South Florida. Then I read where his name was Fatih Ghannam."

Poston said nothing but looked a bit anxious.

"Where is he?" Riley asked.

"Who?"

"They guy who tried to blow up the fucking plane."

"He is interred at Guantanamo."

"What about the guy you told me about? Was that some bullshit thing you said to try to rattle me? Or was there really a Cuban guy from Florida who ran a hardware store?"

"You allegedly smoke quite a bit of marijuana," said Poston. "I find it rather impressive that your memory is so sharp."

Riley looked at Poston and laughed. "So what the fuck happened to the Cuban guy, Henry?"

"His name was Philippe Tiant."

"Was?"

"He was murdered, week before last, in an apparent break-in at his business."

Chills went down Riley's spine. He shuddered and made a sound that was a greatly understated version of a horse slobbering. Riley had grown up around horses slobbering.

"Does anyone, besides me and your partner, know that you told me the bomber was Latino?" he asked, and even the FBI agent entertained the mild notion that Riley's blue eyes were laser beams.

"I hid that."

"No shit?"

"No one but Ike and me knows. The tape was erased. The report omitted it."

Riley looked away from Poston. He gazed over the shining white walls, festooned with red and white bunting, to the tops of trees and the roofs of distant buildings. Already there were marksmen on roofs. Riley thought of the Civil War term: sharpshooters.

"Look, let me just tell you a few details of the past few weeks. Turns out, you may understand why I'm a bit paranoid, after all, but you don't know the half of it. Let me just tick off a few things. Just a day or two after the plane landed, a group of local bigwigs, led by the sheriff, came to try to pressure me into, well, doing this. I told them, politely, to get fucked. Then a bogus deputy stopped by my house—had the squad car, uniform, whole deal—got me to go with him back behind the house, and proceeded to beat the shit out of me. He didn't punch me or nothing. He knocked me to my knees with the butt of a shotgun, then hit me again and knocked me from my knees to being flat on the ground. Then he grabbed a handful of my hair, yanked my ass back up off the ground and told me I'd fucking play ball with the president or it'd be my ass.

"That's why I'm here."

"What name did he give?"

"Wait a minute. Let me finish. Barton Fleming's what he told me, but let me finish. I kind of just took off, Henry. I wanted to get 'em off my back. I got rid of my cell phone and stopped writing emails. Then I'd get different cell phones and buy those little minute cards. But I wouldn't use 'em much. I got somebody else to pretend they were me and tend to all the details. In Florida, my motel room was searched. Cops tried to bust me after a gig. I've been playing music for fifteen years, and that's never happened. On the way to Rockingham, North Carolina, I got stopped on the highway and hassled again. Both cases, they were looking for drugs. Both cases, they didn't find any."

"Was that because you didn't have any?"

"No," Riley said. "It was because I was lucky and a little smart.

"But here's the worst one of all. I've had this reporter traveling with me. In Oregon someone—someone I'm pretty sure works for the government, or the Republicans, somebody—tried to kill him. And I know what the guy looks like."

"What'd he do?" Poston asked.

"I didn't know this going in, okay? But Adam, the writer, was hooked on painkillers. I was trying to help him wean himself off of 'em. It's all…fucked up. Anyway, while I was elsewhere, this guy introduces himself to Adam, leaves him a number. They hook up, and this guy sells Adam some Oxycontin. I went to a wedding out there, by the way. Adam shows up at the bachelor party, and he's okay all of a sudden, and I get suspicious so I confront him about it the next day, and I find the drugs. In the bottle, there were several tablets that were a slightly different color. They were poison."

"How'd you know?"

"Well," said Riley, "I killed a stray dog with 'em."

Poston had to chuckle.

"I put it in some hamburger. Adam and I watched the poor, miserable wretch die. I think it, uh, greatly speeded up Adam's rehabilitation process." Riley pulled out a pack of Marlboro Lights and offered one to Poston, who declined. "So, look," Riley said, lighting up. "When the band and me played a gig Wednesday night north of Richmond, the guy was in the audience. I'm guessing he's probably going to be somewhere today. If I can pick him out sometime, somewhere, I'd really appreciate it if you could keep an eye on him.

"I mean, if he works for the government, that means he could get in here with a gun, right?"

"You don't have a name?" Poston asked.

"No. I'll just to have to look for him. I'll get Adam to help. There's probably nothing to worry about...for once...but I'll let you know."

"What does he look like?"

"Red hair. Kind of pink complexion. Just a little stocky. But it's also true that I've seen him when he was disguised, different color hair. Aren't there supposed to be a bunch of kids in front of the stage? I think they're trying to advance this 'Republicans are hip' image. This guy's middle-aged, probably around fifty. He'll stick out in the crowd."

"I'll be backstage. Ike's going to be in the crowd in front of the stage. If this guy's anywhere close, he'll keep an eye on him. Let me know."

The FBI agent left. Riley finished the cigarette.

When Riley returned to the tent, where he had his own "tent room," the whole area around and behind the stage was even more cluttered, mainly because there were young men and women dressed in formal military uniforms. The show would begin with band music. Riley quickly picked out Army, Navy, Marines, Air Force and noticed there were others.

Coast Guard, maybe? Yeah. What about Merchant Marine?

Harvey, Chad and Wade were rumored to be in Claude Herndon's bus, undoubtedly getting high. Eric, who had been hassled somewhat gaining Ethan's admittance, was grumpy, probably because he felt he had to look out for his old man and was really wishing he was in Herndon's bus. Alan and Dan were out "mingling" and probably boozing it up a bit with the dignitaries. Melissa hadn't arrived yet. Riley had a cooler of his very own, stocked with Bud Light. Adam showed up after a while.

"Grab a beer," Riley said. "Don't cost nothin'."

Instead, Adam lit a cigarette.

"You're the reverse of me, man," Riley said.

"What do you mean?"

"I usually just smoke when I got a buzz. You only smoke when you don't."

Adam smiled. "How do you know, man? How do you know I haven't been partying with Claude Herndon?"

"Because I know you. Because I expect you hate that motherfucker as much as I do."

"His music's actually okay, man, some of it. He just turns me off, personally."

"What gets me, right now, is, you know, Herndon told me he'd record me, and he'd bring all the guys into the studio. Cut a CD."

"No shit?"

"Yesterday. It's all bullshit. He found out George Strait was recording 'Your Independence Day' and he figured if he could hustle me into the studio and get the single out, right after this performance, he could make some money and fuck up Strait at the same time. It's pretty damn clever in a diabolical way."

"You gonna do it?"

"Shit, no. I told him I probably would. Right now he's buttering up Harvey and Wade. Chad'll probably just take it in, but Wade and Harvey, man, they're gonna be all over me wanting to record at Claude Herndon's big studio in Nashville. I just need to nod my head—'great, man, that's cool'—for now. It'll take care of itself.

Once this day is over and I go on TV, and the whole story comes out, I'm pretty sure the offer from Claude Herndon is going to be rescinded."

♫

A half hour before the show was scheduled to begin, Riley ambled out on the stage, sat on it, his feet hanging over the edge. He noticed some people gawking and pointing him out. He was separated from them by the orchestra pit, though. The first military band was setting up. A few regarded Riley with suspicious looks, but he was out of the way and no one hassled him. Perhaps, he thought, they figured he was slightly stoned. He wasn't. He'd had several beers, three, maybe. He wanted to go onstage, still hours away, with a bit of a buzz. Some kind of buzz. Beer would have to do.

Maintain. Just need to maintain.

The lawn in front of the stage remained mostly unpopulated. Fox News wanted the wholesome young Republicans to be swaying and clapping to good, old, patriotic country music. They'd probably all file in to see Lee Greenwood, then they'd laugh uproariously to the act of Dennis Miller. And then they were just going to dig Riley Mansfield when he sang "The Fighting Side of Me."

Thing is, Riley really liked the song, and the more he thought about it, the more he thought it could cut both ways. Written in response to the radicalism of the sixties and seventies, it still played as an anthem against radicalism, and the radicalism of the new century was of the right, not the left.

Riley looked past the first set of restrictive barricades and saw, basically, his hometown filing in. They all looked like they were from Henry, and their placards bore the same slapdash style that might have been painted for the high-school football stadium by fans wanting to make "High School Friday Night" on the local network affiliates. But instead of "Go Big Red!" or "Snuff the

Cyclones!" they had messages like "Defend the Constitution!" or "Send Illegals Home!"

Then Riley saw him. The guy. He was wearing khakis and a light-blue, buttoned-down, short-sleeved shirt. And a cap. Riley squinted his eyes: Atlanta Braves, maybe. The guy was wearing sunglasses, naturally. He had a black windbreaker over his left shoulder, anchoring it with his fingers. He had emerged from the shade trees on the left and was walking slowly toward the stage. Riley was wearing shades, too, so he stared at the man while his head pointed to the right of him. Riley wondered if the guy was staring at him, too. Or if he'd even noticed he was sitting there. Riley abruptly pushed himself off the edge of the stage, into the opera pit. He almost fell on landing.

Shit. Bigger drop than I thought. Must be eight feet. Fuck.

Riley righted a chair he had displaced when he staggered into it. He sat down on it and rang Henry Poston.

One ring. "Excuse me," he could hear Poston say. "Yeah. What's up, Riley?"

"I see him. There's no crowd. Let me show him to you."

"In front of the stage?"

"Yeah. I mean, that's where he is. I'm in the orchestra pit. I just, uh, dropped down here. I saw the guy when I was sitting on the stage."

"Ike's nearby. I'll send him to you momentarily."

"Okay, hurry. Dude's just dawdling around right now, but I don't want to let him get away."

In less than three minutes, Ike Spurgeon bustled in.

"Hey," Riley said. "Good to see you again. Please sit down.

"Okay. The guy's wearing khaki pants, a ball cap, sunglasses, a light-blue button-down, and he's got a black windbreaker he's carrying. Just get up and walk over next to the stairs and look to the left, about thirty yards away from the stage. Red face. You'll see him."

Spurgeon calmly followed Riley's directions. He scanned the

lawn. He saw Jed Langston, though he didn't know that was his name...yet. Spurgeon studied for a while, taking in all the features, estimating his height and weight, trying to pick up some distinctive mannerisms. Then Spurgeon walked back and sat down.

"Can I call you Ike?"

"Sure. Riley."

"You play ball, man?"

"Yeah. University of Houston."

"Wow. We played Houston in a bowl game when I was at Piedmont."

"I played in that game, too. Defensive end."

"Oh, hell. I remember you now. You're the guy who cleaned my clock on the next-to-last play of the game."

"Yeah," Spurgeon said. "Small world, huh?"

"Yeah," said Riley. "How 'bout protecting me this time?"

♫

Melissa had arrived by the time Riley returned to the tent. Knowing nothing of the day's events, she was rather ebullient, and Riley let her be. Adam was still there but walked outside after chitchatting with the two of them for a couple minutes. Adam didn't know shit, either.

Damned if I ain't cut a side deal with the FBI.

"There's really not any way we can, like, get high," Melissa observed.

Riley smiled. "It's not physically addictive," he said.

"What?"

"Marijuana. It's not physically addictive, which can't be said for that beer in that cooler or the cigarettes in your purse. You can do without, man."

"But what if you don't want to do without?"

"Well," said Riley, "it is quite psychologically addictive. I would really like to get high. You know, little buzz, nothing scandalous."

"Me, too."

"Come with me," Riley said. They walked outside and then over to the paved area where Claude Herndon's bus was parked. Then they sat in the shade nearby.

"Be cool," he said. "Let's just wait and watch a while."

Herndon emerged from the bus, surrounded by cronies and probably at least one bodyguard, that being a crony who took steroids.

"They're going to shoot a segment for TV," Riley said. "I think at the Vietnam War Memorial. That's what Claude's about: honoring the men who died to keep us free. I think that bus is the only place on these grounds where marijuana is, right this minute, totally legal. I bet some of them Republican insiders been toking up with Claude this very morning. If Sue Ellen's been in there, there's been some serious coke-snorting, too, or that's what Adam says.

"I think it's time for us to mosey on over, right this minute."

They walked over, knocked on the door, it was opened and they walked up the three steps that took them inside.

"Quite palatial," Melissa said under her breath. Now, with the crowd having left to accompany the superstar, only a few band members and a stray roadie were inside.

"Hey, guys. Riley Mansfield."

"Your shit's good, man, I'm serious," said a burly musician with shaggy hair and a ZZ Top tee shirt.

"I was, uh, wondering if me and Melissa here—Melissa Franklin, she's my agent—could smoke a little weed in here."

"Yeah, man, sure. That's why we're in here. We got our own bus, man, but Claude keeps his good shit in here."

"That's okay, man. I brought my own."

"Aw, man, feel free. It's some really good shit. From Hawaii, I think."

"I don't know, man, I probably can't handle it. This Kentucky stuff I got is probably 'bout my speed."

"Well, use the bong anyway, man. Good to meet you. I watched your set last night, man. That band you put together is really tight. Good guys, too. We had a couple of 'em come by for a visit earlier."

"Yeah," Riley said, laughing. "I expect they been wandering around aimlessly ever since."

Riley and Melissa slid into a booth, with the bong between them.

When Riley and Melissa emerged from Claude Herndon's party bus, it was jarring to be walking stoned, in the heat of the day, with John Philip Sousa blaring.

The two of them had little interest in going anywhere. They sat in the grass, under a tree, and smoked cigarettes. They watched quietly as Claude Herndon and his entourage returned. Then someone noticed them, and with Herndon back inside the bus, the crowd of Republicans—congressmen and women, a senator, musicians, one well-known fisherman, a quarterback and two placekickers, some guy who Riley recognized from infomercials, a guy whose name Riley couldn't remember but knew was hot shit in the National Rifle Association—descended on poor, stoned Riley Mansfield. Sue Ellen Spenser was among them. And so, wonder of wonders, was Shawna, the flight attendant from the plane. Riley helped Melissa up and fairly dragged her toward the black woman he'd thought he'd probably never see again. This did not please Sue Ellen Spenser, whom Riley walked right past.

"So good to see you again, Shawna," Riley said. "I want you to meet Melissa. She's my gal. Melissa, Shawna was the stewardess—I mean, flight attendant—on the plane."

"You mean, *the* plane?"

"Yeah, that's the one. Shawna, I didn't know you were gonna be here. This is quite a surprise."

"Yeah. The pilot and co-pilot are here, too. We're going to be introduced."

Sue Ellen appeared. "Riley, who are your friends?"

Introductions were exchanged. It occurred to Riley that Sue Ellen had undoubtedly noticed Priscilla Hay sitting with Melissa at the Ashland show.

Okay, okay. Sue Ellen didn't know who Melissa was until Ashland. Right? I think, uh, that's been established. Okay. Priscilla and Melissa were sitting together. And I went and joined them. Shit. Sue Ellen...she saw it all right. But she probably thought I was just looking to pick up some trim. Being a man and all.

The women were gossiping. Exchanging pleasantries. It all scrambled in Riley's head. He stood there, wearing a goofy grin. Finally, he abruptly grabbed Melissa's ass.

"Hey!"

Riley put his arms around her and delivered one long, lascivious kiss. *Come on. Go along.*

First Melissa tensed, but then, she relented. Relaxed.

"Come on, baby," he said. "Let's me and you go back to the tent."

"Well, that was strange," said Shawna after a moment.

"Oh, don't mind them," said Sue Ellen. "They're just high."

As they walked away, hurriedly, Riley said to Melissa, "That was just to cover you."

"What?"

"You and me and Priscilla were together at the table in Ashland. Sue Ellen was there with that presidential aide. Now she just thinks you're some broad I picked up at Coffee and Tea."

"Oh. I was kind of looking forward to fucking."

Man. Adam wishes he was here to see this.

Twenty minutes later, Adam Rhine did reappear. He appeared to be a bit drunk.

"Other guys around?" Riley asked.

"Yeah. I'm pretty sure everybody's in the area. Alan and Dan are just outside, in the main tent area. I think Cody, uh, Wade, Chad and...Harvey are somewhere between here and Herndon's bus."

"Knowing him, he's probably trying to get 'em too fucked up to play," Riley said. *I am one to talk.*

"How about Eric and Ethan?"

"They're in front of the stage, watching the bands play."

"Hey, man, I just wanted to tell you. The guy who sold you the pills is here."

"Man. That sucks."

"Don't worry about it. It's gonna be fine. I got the feds on him."

"I thought he was the feds."

"Yeah, but let's just say I've befriended a couple of FBI agents. They're the ones who first interrogated me after the plane landed."

"So, like, that was in South Carolina. What's the reason they're here?"

"I don't know, completely. They just got flown up here. I guess they, I don't know, wanted all the people who...knew about the case? I just know they offered to help."

"And you...trust them?"

"Yeah. What? Do you think they're, like, double agents?"

"Could be."

"Well, I...don't think so. You gotta trust somebody, man. This whole deal, man, I've been getting along by my wits, my judgment. I always have believed in my ability to read people. Yeah. I trust them, all right. I told 'em all about the shit that's been pulled on me from the time the plane landed. I saw the guy, and I got in touch with one of the agents, and the other one met me, and I pointed the dude out. And they're gonna watch him. 'Cause he's, like, fucking evil."

Adam pulled out a notepad. "What are their names?"

Riley thought. "I can't tell you, man."

"Yes, you can."

"No. I can't. You write their names and they get fired. They're fucking helping me. I can't rat on them."

Riley turned up the air, closed the door and, emboldened, proceeded to roll a joint and get high again with Melissa and Adam.

"Spray some of that air freshener around," he said to Adam afterwards. "Melissa, wanna go watch the show?"

"Lee Greenwood?"

"Sure," Riley said. "God bless the USA. I really want to watch the crowd more than anything else. Let's go see the Republicans party."

Greenwood performed onstage alone, accompanied by the orchestra that actually populated the pit now. A huge video screen displayed images of flags, soldiers, baseball players, farmers, the Grand Canyon, power plants, hunters, NASCAR, cheerleaders and, occasionally, extremely wholesome and well-dressed black people.

Riley and Melissa stood at the edge of the stage.

"I wonder if they'll show the same amber waves of grain when I'm singing," Riley said.

"No."

"Why? You think they're so...high-tech and, you know, organized...what's the word I need?...that they won't duplicate anything?

"No," said Melissa. "I don't think they'll show amber waves of grain 'cause that's the wrong song, stupid. Amber waves are in 'America the Beautiful.' You are singing 'This Land Is Your Land.'"

Riley broke up. "Oh, yeah." He sang a few lines.

"It's not the redwood island," Melissa said. "New York island. Redwood forest."

"I'll be fine," Riley said. "I've done this...hundreds of times. Besides, there's a Teleprompter. I can still read. The music'll just flow. I'll get the words right. I won't even have to look."

Melissa rolled her eyes.

Riley motioned, across the stage, for Cody to come join them. He finally caught his eye. In a few moments, all four stood together as Greenwood sang some other patriotic song he wrote that no one had ever heard of.

"Look," Riley said.

"What?" asked Cody. "Lee Greenwood?"

"No. Look at all the little Republicans, wearing their polo shirts and cargo shorts and fucking Yankee caps. Drinking their beer...no, they're probably not even drinking beer. God forbid that a Sam Adams—that's the only domestic beer they drink—show up on national TV. They probably had to leave the beer on the bus. They get to cheer a shift, and then they go back to their bus, drink some, maybe snort a few lines, and another bus empties between sets, and a completely new crop of Republicans arrives during the break to cheer for Dennis Miller. That's the 'laugh like hell' squadron. Then, maybe, the first squadron comes back—or maybe there's an entirely new squadron, there may be four or five—to cheer on that noted super-patriot, Riley fucking Mansfield."

Riley smiled. "That's me."

When Greenwood left the stage, an entirely new group of young Republicans replaced the first. And it didn't seem much different to Riley than it would have had he had some of those good old Oregon mushrooms.

CHAPTER THIRTY-FOUR
THE FIGHTING SIDE OF RILEY

Riley Mansfield's home-state senator introduced not Riley, but the President of the United States, Sam Harmon, who entered left as Jim DeMint exited right.

"Fellow Americans, it is with great humility and even greater honor that I introduce our next guest," said Harmon. "Riley Mansfield is an established songwriter whose compositions have been recorded by some of country music's greatest stars.

"But Riley is much more than a talented artist; he is a true American hero. On June first of this year, Riley was a passenger on a USAirways flight from New York City to Greenville, South Carolina. An enemy of America attempted to destroy that airplane. Riley subdued the...suspect, wrested a bomb from his hands, kicked open the door of the plane, only a few seconds before landing, and dispensed with the bomb, which exploded in the treetops below."

He can't even get the story right. Subdue the suspect?

"Riley is a humble man who sought no credit for his act. He told me he merely did what any man would do."

Told you? I've never even met you.

"He has no interest in capitalizing on his fame, but we were able to get him to agree to take part in this wondrous celebration of America's birthday. Please join me in welcoming...Riley Mansfield!"

Riley strode onstage to join the band. He shook hands with the president, who patted him on the shoulder, then turned to the crowd and put his arms around him. Thousands of flashbulbs went off, which was absurd since no flashbulbs were needed in the bright sunlight that still flooded the Mall at five o'clock.

"Thank you, Mr. President. Happy birthday, America. No celebration is complete without a little Merle Haggard."

Riley turned to the band and nodded to Eric Hays, who dove into the intro of "The Fighting Side of Me."

Duh-duh-DUH-duh-duh-duh, duh-duh-DUH-duh-duh-duh, duh-duh-DUH-duh-duh-duh-duh-duh-DUH-duh, duh-WOW-wow-wow, duh-WOW-wow-wow...

While Riley sang that he heard people talking bad about the way they had to live here in this country, he couldn't actually see any of them. The song was a rabble-rouser, but there wasn't any rabble. All the blonde, blue-eyed Republicans in front of the stage roared on cue. Even amidst this weirdness, Riley wanted to stir them beyond the emotional level required for canned applause. It was an audience.

At the instrumental break, Riley backed away from the mic. As his three guitarists took their turns, each in a different style, their names and hometowns were all displayed in television close-ups. The camera steered clear of the gaunt, bearded man clapping his hands and stomping his feet at the edge of the stage. Garner Thomas, senior partner at Sedgwick Sanford & Van Buren (Sue Ellen Spenser's alleged employer), likened the man to one of those old black and white photos of the Depression, and the sight of Ethan Hays made him uncomfortable.

To Jed Langston, standing still amid the tumult of the all the enthusiastic Republicans, Ethan was a vision of John the Baptist. He inspired prayer in Langston.

At song's end, Riley's attention drifted off in the distance, where all the good people—Henry, his hometown, cubed—cheered with placards bouncing and something approximating Rebel yells booming above the applause.

"This is a song I wrote," he said. "We're going to highlight my friend Harvey Kitchens' sweet fiddle on 'Your Independence Day.'"

You've had hard times
Most self-imposed
You've taken long trips

The Audacity of Dope

Down rocky roads
But for every hill you've tumbled down
It's been worth it all
Having you around
When the sun comes up on that bright morn
In the quiet that follows every storm
When the demons have all died away
We'll celebrate your independence day
You've thrown all caution
To the wind
There are few rules
You haven't bent
You've turned your life into a game of chance
On the tightrope of life
You love to dance
CHORUS

As Harvey subtly ran the bow up and down his fiddle strings, Cody stepped up to deliver an equally nostalgic mandolin solo. Riley turned to his band mates briefly, but he couldn't help but stare in wonder at the crowd. Now the boisterousness had subsided. They were swaying side to side and clapping in unison. Riley wondered if it was the words or the instrumentals that moved them. It wasn't a patriotic song. It had, in fact, been written about drug addiction. It could have been written about Adam Rhine, but Riley had written it a few months before he ever met the *Rolling Stone* writer. Riley had suggested it to Priscilla Hay after landing in Portland. She had shipped the lyrics to the "planning committee," whatever that was. They probably approved it for the same reason Riley had suggested it: The title seemed patriotic even if the song, strictly speaking, wasn't.

You can't live
On bread alone
When you're nothing

But skin and bones
You've got to get your nourishment
They'll throw you out
If you can't pay the rent
CHORUS
We'll celebrate your independence day
We'll celebrate your independence day

Television went to break with Riley humbly smiling in the sunlight. Cameras panned back, casting first the singer, then the band, then the crowd, basking in the backdrop of the Capitol Building.

"I think we got a couple of base hits," Riley said to the band. "When we come back, let's drive in the winning run."

Well, that was fucking stupid.

Even Jed Langston was moved. He relaxed. This was going to be fine. Ten yards away, Ike Spurgeon noticed the apparent change in the mood of his suspect. He relaxed, too. The Administration, by the way, had been very happy to have him in the crowd. Because he was a Negro. At the behest of his superiors, he now wore a "Keeping America Secure 2008" tee shirt over his buttoned-down dress shirt. He was, after all, they informed him, undercover.

Sue Ellen Spenser barged out on the stage and told Riley the president wanted to see him.

"I'm about to do the last song."

"Riley, honey, you've got more than four minutes before the commercial break ends," she said. "They're going back to the studio first before they cue you again. You can't very well refuse a personal audience with the President."

Patience. Patience. All my trials, Lord, will soon be over...

"Okay," he said. "Fine."

Sue Ellen led him down a row of stairs at the back of the stage. There awaited Sam Harmon.

"You're a fine singer, Mr. Mansfield," said Harmon. "Thanks so much for coming."

"Thank you, Mr. President."

"May I call you Riley?"

"Of course." Riley knew he couldn't call the president Sam.

"I really wish you'd endorse my reelection campaign," he said, smiling. "We've got a lot in common, you and me. We're both from the Carolinas. We both know we've got to get America working again. We've got to restore this country's goodness, its values. We can't let this opportunity get away."

How naïve does this fucker think I am?

"Mr. President, don't you think this is, pretty much, an implied endorsement?"

"It's not enough," said Harmon, "and look at your career. Join hands with me and we'll both benefit. You help me get reelected, and I'll make you a millionaire. Look at the man who preceded you onstage. Lee Greenwood. Ronald Reagan made him an American icon. I can do the same for you."

It was, in fact, difficult to stand face to face with the President of the United States, and say no.

Even though I'm high.

"All right," Riley said. "All right, Mr. President. If you'll still have me after I get back up there and botch the next song, I'll help you out."

"Son, I've been listening to you," Harmon said. "You couldn't fuck this next song up if you tried."

Sue Ellen was laughing uproariously, wrapping her arms around the president's shoulders and telling him what a wit he was as Riley headed back up the stairs, retrieved his guitar and waited for the cue to resume.

Riley thought the booming voice—*must be some guy with a mic in the wings somewhere*—sounded like God Himself.

"And, now once again, ladies and gentleman, a genuine American hero, Riley Mansfield!"

Riley wished Priscilla Hay was around. For the first time, he read from the Teleprompter. The first words he was supposed to say were "God bless America." Instead, he said, "I love America. And Woody Guthrie, who wrote this song, loved America, too."

Through his ear set, Michael Ashton, the presidential aide who was nominally in charge of the show, heard Ian Costello say, "Oh, Christ, he's departing from the script."

"Still right on time, though," said another voice.

Ashton excused himself from the group surrounding Harmon.

"Everything's fine," he said. "Ian, don't worry about it. This is Ashton. Everything's fine. Mansfield couldn't be doing better. Relax. The President is very pleased."

Whoever heard of opening "This Land Is Your Land" with a mandolin solo? Cody Huard nailed it.

Riley sang passionately, filling every syllable with emotion and breaking his voice with a touch of a yodel on "Gulf Stream waaaaah-ters.

"This land was made for you and me!" Then Riley introduced his band.

"From Portland, Oregon, I'd never heard of him till a week ago and, come to find out, he was nominated for a Grammy last year...Cody Huard!"

Cody strummed the melody to riotous applause.

"My longtime friend, from West Pelzer, South Carolina, once punted for the University of the Piedmont...for almost two weeks...on the bass and fiddle...Harvey Kitchens."

Harvey grinned as he plunked out a bass solo. A few television viewers may have suspected, from watching his lips, that he said "You fucker!" to Riley, who leaned back and laughed before returning to the mic.

"Another old friend who showed me I could sing twice as good with him playing drums behind me. From Whitmire, South Carolina, where the Indians bring in their beaver pelts to trade for lightning water, on the drums...Chad Dunham!"

This is it, man. It'll never be better than right now. Just at this moment, right now, all the shit was worth it. Not a minute ago. Not tomorrow. I'll sell my soul when this is over. At the moment, though, quite frankly, I am free.

Riley's eyes met Adam Rhine's. As Chad tapped away at his drums, Riley smirked. And Adam thought, *What's he thinking?*

"This guy taught me—well, he didn't actually teach me—he showed me that I was never going to be good enough to play lead guitar…because he plays lead guitar. From Palm Coast, Florida, he can slide a man right to the Pearly Gates…Alan Isaac!"

Alan's slide gave "This Land Is Your Land" an eerie majesty. Riley thought of Jimi Hendrix doing the national anthem at Woodstock.

"Here's a good Republican from the hills of southeastern Kentucky. Playing that good ol' country lead guitar, a man who knows how to look out for his buddy when he's feelin' low. From Hyden, Kentucky…Eric Hays!"

Eric had been applauded for his guitar work on "Fightin' Side," and now he launched into a rock 'n' roll riff Carl Perkins would have cheered.

"In Kentucky, they can play the blues, too, man. Ain't got no worries. Also from Hyden, Kentucky…Wade McKeever!"

Woody Guthrie would've loved his song performed this way, Riley thought. He looked at Melissa and shook his head a little, smiling. Then he took his hands off the guitar and opened both palms upward. *Like Allstate. The Good Hands People.*

"Oh, my God," said Melissa.

"What?" It was Adam.

"He's gonna do something."

Riley walked back up to the mic, smiling broadly. He knew where he was. He had picked him out in the crowd. Riley stared straight at Jed Langston and walked to the left of the mic as Wade completed his solo. The words to the third verse were on the Teleprompter. Riley pointed at Langston. Though Langston couldn't actually hear him, for Riley just spoke, he didn't yell, but what he said was, "This one's for you."

Adam touched Melissa's shoulder, and when she turned, he said, "He's got a new verse."

"You know this?"

"No. Not at all. I just thought of it. I bet he's got a new verse."

Sure enough, Riley did. They weren't up to Guthrie's standards. He had just scribbled them as a lark, sitting on a patio overlooking the ocean in Oregon.

I faced temptation
And they betrayed me
With the voice of angels
They tried to slay me
But in my mind
The words were righteous
This land was made for you and me

Then Riley sang the chorus. Twice. In retrospect, it took too long.

Jed Langston's mouth dropped open. So did Ike Spurgeon's. So did Sam Harmon's. Mansfield stared at Jed. Leering, Jed thought. The verse was a double entendre. The crowd thought Riley was singing about terrorists. He was singing about his own government. Unfortunately, his own government knew it even if others didn't.

Then Riley turned, and his eyes met each of the band members, one after the other.

He'll have to shoot me in the back.

Barry Kowalski, a marine sergeant from Elmhurst, Illinois, had been assigned to monitor the pudgy man in the black windbreaker and ball cap. It was a shift change for the young Republicans, and the crowd in front of the stage was thinning, though not as quickly as before because some of the youthful conservatives seemed to be agitated all of a sudden.

Langston pulled a revolver from a holster beneath the windbreaker, but he held it low and the jacket shielded the view from the left. At first Spurgeon didn't notice. Langston took a step toward the stage but was briefly distracted.

From the wings, as if by magic, Ethan Hays staggered out, vacating the space previously occupied by Mansfield. In fact, Ethan was between Riley and Langston, in the line of fire.

He pointed at the heavens, words unintelligible. Fox News hastily went to break. But then, Ethan just kept on charging…and plummeted into the orchestra.

Ike Spurgeon heard the suspect yell.

"For God and country!"

Spurgeon started walking toward Langston. A young man bumped him. Ike threw him out of the way.

"Who do you think you are, nigger!" The words didn't register.

Now Jed pointed the revolver at Riley, who was walking away and toward the steps at the back of the stage where he had recently met President Harmon.

Sergeant Kowalski blinked at the possibility that the man in the ball cap might be about to shoot the president, who actually wasn't even onstage. He had the man in the crosshairs, via high-powered scope, from a hundred and fifty yards away. Kill. Shot.

Spurgeon smashed into the suspect. A shot rang out. *No, two.* The other band members hit the deck. Riley was already near the stairs and ran down them. Sue Ellen, sitting on the left side of the stage, reacted more slowly. Her first reaction was to stand up, not lie down. The stray bullet from Langston's .38 dented the metal in the back of Sue Ellen's folding chair and ricocheted into the ass of United States Senator Jim DeMint.

Barry Kowalski's intended kill shot wasn't. It ripped through FBI agent Ike Spurgeon's flesh just to the left of his neck. The wound was serious, though, because Kowalski's rifle was high-powered.

At the back of the stage, for perhaps five seconds, almost nothing moved. The crowd milling there drifted a few steps toward the stage. Collectively it searched for the President. Sam Harmon was sipping bourbon in front of the hospitality tent, chatting with Claude Herndon, when the shots rang out. He was fine. Riley looked for familiar faces. He saw Henry Poston, but Poston was running toward the front of the stage. Then people came from everywhere. Secret Service agents shoved Harmon into a limousine, which abruptly drove away in a hastily assembled motorcade.

Someone had him by the shoulders. "Riley, come with me!"

"Who are you?"

"George Grinnell. We're going to that satellite truck right over there."

But they weren't. Law enforcement was everywhere, as if by magic. Policemen. FBI. Secret Service. God knew what else. Everyone who had been onstage was accompanied—herded, really—into the entertainers' tent. The police "secured" the tent and built a perimeter outside. No one in. No one out.

"What happened?" Grinnell asked.

"I think maybe this guy tried to shoot me," Riley said.

"You okay?"

"Oh, yeah. Fine. Numb. Strangely calm."

"I gotta figure out a way to get you out of here."

"Is everything cool now?"

"There haven't been any more shots."

Riley looked around. Eric Hays was brawling with cops.

"My goddamn daddy's out there, you sonuvabitch!"

Riley dove into the scrum. "It's okay! It's okay!"

"Daddy fuckin' got shot by the bullet intended for you!"

"I don't think so," Riley said. "I'll make sure, man. It's gonna be okay. Just give it a minute, ah'ight? We don't want 'em to fuckin' taze you, man." Slowly, still tense, Eric got up, looking as if he might re-erupt at any moment. Riley pulled out his cell and rang Henry Poston's cell. It took six rings but Poston answered it.

"What?"

"Is anybody hurt?"

"Ike's hurt. I'm about to go to the hospital. He's gonna make it, but he's lost a lot of blood."

"How about the man onstage?"

"Senator DeMint got hit by a ricochet, apparently. He's got a minor wound."

"Nobody else?"

"Apparently not. The guy who charged out onstage fell into the orchestra pit. He's just got, like, broken bones. He's already on the way to the hospital."

"I know Ike's your partner," said Riley, "but he's gonna be all right?"

"Yeah, yeah. Once they get some blood in him, he's gonna be all right, I'm pretty sure."

"I need one more favor, Henry."

"Shit. What?"

"Don't get in the ambulance. I need you to spring me from this tent."

"What?"

"They got us sealed off in this tent. I've got to get out."

"Why?"

"Because…it's like the plane thing. Everything's gonna blow up again. People gonna be knocking down my doors again. This'll end up being my fault. I didn't get killed, man. I'm not gonna be a hero anymore. But if you don't help me get out of this goddamned tent and into a TV truck about twenty yards away, I'm gonna end up being the world's biggest bad guy."

"No."

"You're the only guy who can help me, Henry. You helped me already, 'cause you know how much I been fucked with. It's gonna happen again. It's not wrong, man. It's right. You gotta bust me out of here."

Poston hung up on Riley, but then he told Ike he couldn't go with him, got out of the ambulance and walked briskly toward the entertainers' tent, flashing his badge at checkpoint after checkpoint.

"I need one of the musicians in there," he said.

"Sir, we're under orders," said a burly policeman. "No one gets in. No one gets out."

"Well, I'm under orders, too, sir," holding up his badge once again. The officer seemed unimpressed.

Henry pulled out his cell phone and started punching numbers. "Perhaps you'd like to talk with the President of the United States?"

He handed the phone to the policeman, who stared at it, started to hold it up to his ear, then stopped.

"Go ahead," he said.

Poston quickly found Riley. "You know where you need to go?"

"Yes, sir."

"I have to go with him," said Grinnell.

"No, can't pull it." Turning back to Riley, Poston said, "All right, when we walk outside, as soon as you get through, walk, don't run, to wherever it is you're going. Right now, running might get you shot." He grabbed Riley by the shoulder and got him through security. Then he pushed him and said, "My work is done here."

"Thanks again," said Riley over his shoulder as he walked away.

♬

David Branham sat across from the President in the limousine.

"Well, David, what the fuck happened?" Harmon asked.

"Mansfield's last verse…"

"What? I wasn't listening."

"He apparently sang a verse that wasn't part of the song."

"And…?"

"Jed Langston tried to shoot him."

Harmon leaned back and sighed.

"What happened to Jed?"

"He's in custody, Mr. President."

"Oh, mother of God." The President of the United States buried his head in his hands.

♬

Riley tried to open the door of the satellite truck. He banged on the door. Priscilla Hay opened it.

"I was wondering where you were," Riley said.

"Can you handle this? Do you need some time to get yourself together?"

Riley took a deep breath. "No. Let's get it over with. Who am I talking to? Rachel Maddow?"

"As you requested."

"She can ask whatever she wants," he said. "I'm still numb. Calm. Sober, even."

Priscilla smiled. "Let's go, then."

Hurriedly, someone else led Riley to an office chair behind a steel-gray tabletop. An MSNBC logo was in the background. A tiny microphone was attached to his shirt. The monitor showed sirens flaring from squad cars in an aerial shot from a helicopter. "The crawl" streamed across the bottom of the screen.

BREAKING NEWS: SHOTS RING OUT AT WASHINGTON PATRIOTIC CELEBRATION. PRESIDENT HARMON PRESENT BUT UNHURT. TWO WOUNDED. PRESIDENTIAL PRESS SECURITY SAYS PRESIDENT WASN'T ONSTAGE WHEN SHOTS ERUPTED. UNIDENTIFIED MAN HELD IN CUSTODY.

Maddow, looking a bit unsure of herself, appeared onscreen. "We have breaking news," she said. "Riley Mansfield, who had been honored for preventing a terrorist attack on a private airliner earlier this year, is a musician who had been invited to perform at the celebration that took place today on the National Mall. Mr. Mansfield had just completed a song when, as I understand, shots rang out in front of the stage. We have Mr. Mansfield with us, live from the scene.

"Mr. Mansfield, can you tell us what happened?"

"I had just finished singing my last song, 'This Land Is Your Land,' when I turned to leave the stage. But before I could, I heard two shots."

"Were they from the same gun?"

"No, they were different. I think one came from far away. I

think it may have been from someone who saw the guy pull out his gun, but I don't know that for sure."

"You had your back turned?"

"Yes, but I'm almost sure I know who it was that tried to shoot me."

Maddow had what appeared to be a pencil in her hand. She twirled it between her fingers.

"Why do you think you know who it was?"

"I had stared at him when I finished the song, and I sort of sensed that he...well...that he hated me."

"Did you know this man?"

"I don't know his name," Riley said, "but he was familiar because, I believe, he's been following me ever since the plane almost...got blown up. I'm pretty sure he works for the federal government, and that following me around and making my life miserable was...his assignment."

"Why do you think this man, whom you say works in the government..."

"I think the government. He may work for, you know, the Republican Party or something."

"And why do you think he had been following you?"

"Uh, I didn't want to be a part of this. I didn't want to be used as a political tool. I'm against President Harmon's reelection, but really, I'm not that political, and I just didn't want to be exploited."

"And, so, there was some kind of campaign of intimidation...is that what I'm gathering?"

"I was beaten by a man impersonating a local deputy at my house a few days after I returned home. After the bomb thing on the plane. My, uh, manager, Melissa Franklin, was in the house at the time and took some photographs from the back window."

A progression of photos, showing Riley being beaten by a law enforcement officer. Then there were shots of Riley's black and blue back.

"And this was the man who shot at you?"

"No. The only time I've ever seen this man, who gave his name as Barton Fleming, was at my house...when I...got beat up."

"And you reported this to the authorities."

"Well, at first I did, but the sheriff..."

"This is in Henry, South Carolina?"

"Yes. The local sheriff didn't have a deputy by the name of Barton Fleming. When he told me that, I just, I don't know, said never mind. I realized then that it wasn't any good to alert the authorities, because it was the authorities who were out to get me. That's when I agreed to appear with President Harmon, but on the condition that I wasn't going to endorse him or anything. Just shake hands, and perform three songs, and, you know, that was it."

"But what is the connection with the, uh, would-be assassin?"

"I thought something might happen. Uh, let's just say that, along the way, I found some...people in law enforcement whom I...thought I could trust. So I told them about this man and, this morning, when I saw him in front of the stage, before the show started, I identified him for one of those...people. I gave another all the information I could, uh, about him."

"You don't know the name of the man?"

"No. I think...the authorities...might've. I mean, by the time the concert started, or sometime soon after."

"Can you cite an example of anything this man had done specifically to you?"

"Not specifically to me, but a week ago, uh, last week, he tried to kill someone who was traveling with me. A reporter who was writing a profile on me. He tried to poison him. There's no need to go too much in detail—I guess this is all going to be under investigation—but what happened is, I'm pretty sure, verifiable."

"So, let me get this straight, Mr. Mansfield..."

"Wish you'd call me Riley. I'm just Riley."

"Okay," she smiled. "Riley. You're saying that this incident was not a threat to the president but...instead...something in which the Harmon Administration was involved."

"I can't tell you, Rachel—I assume I can call you Rachel, too—if the president was involved, but there's no question that this whole deal—following me, trying to threaten me with arrest, beat me up, kill the guy who was writing a story about me—was by the government. I don't know where in the government the people work. I don't know where they're assigned. To some extent, the Republican Party, or Harmon's campaign, is involved, and I'm guessing there's some connection between those people…and the government, like, Homeland Security, CIA, FBI…I don't know the details, and I don't mean, I'm sorry, to throw out some names of agencies when I don't, uh, specifically, know which ones were involved. But, if you can believe me, there's no doubt that there was some effort, some serious, dangerous effort, to intimidate me into doing what the…Harmon Administration…wanted me to do."

"Thank you…Riley. We appreciate your agreeing to come on in such frightening circumstances."

"You're very welcome, Rachel."

♫

Almost instantly, Riley Mansfield's words spread via video clips to all the newspapers and web sites, the networks and all the cable channels. Fox News coverage was heavily edited, and several commentators, Bill O'Reilly and Sean Hannity among them, immediately questioned his motives. It was futile, though. They couldn't pull it off, and as the hours passed, more and more details came out. Photographs of Jed Langston. His employment at Homeland Security. Details of his background and his association with Banks McPherson.

FBI special agent Ike Spurgeon's condition was listed as stable. He was said to be resting comfortably. This time Riley wasn't the hero. It was Spurgeon, who once pummeled Riley the same way he had Langston. This time the result was a bullet wound, not an interception with nineteen seconds remaining in the Independence Bowl.

It was midnight when a full-blown motorcade finally returned Riley Mansfield to the Embassy Suites Hotel. FBI agents helped him wade through the lobby, where, once again, cameras, lights and photographers were waiting for him. The agents took him all the way to his room, where, at last, Melissa Franklin was waiting.

"I didn't even know what I was writing about," he told her as they prepared for bed.

She kissed him. Delicately. "What?"

"The last song I wrote, the one I performed for the first time in Ashland. 'Find a Balance.' 'Life's about knockin' people down…then picking 'em up off the ground.'"

"I remember," said Melissa. "'You don't want to hang around…or you just might get burned.'"

"It's a good story for a month," Riley said, "but not for a life."

CHAPTER THIRTY-FIVE
TWO MONTHS LATER

Riley Mansfield sat on a stump at the edge of the fish pond below his house. Idly he worked an earthworm around his hook and cast a line into a shallow area beneath a stand of cedar trees. He had gone out and bought a cheap rod and reel earlier in the day. Once he had wandered off a couple of times a week just to fish and listen to baseball games on the radio, but it had been so long that he'd forgotten whatever happened to his fishing implements. Perhaps they had been stolen out of the garage and he'd never noticed. It was vexing.

Dusk was falling. The late-summer heat was gradually subsiding. In the quiet, he heard gentle rustling in the long grass between the house and the pond. Melissa Franklin arrived, carrying a small cooler and a Tupperware container of ham-and-egg-salad sandwiches. Keeping an eye on the float, Riley walked closer to the water and sat on the small earthen ledge above the hard sand ringing the water. He patted the space next to him and Melissa sat down. He put his left arm around her, keeping the fishing rod in his right.

"What's going on in the music business?" he asked.

"We might have a bus."

"Oh, wow, probably be good to get a band to ride in it."

"Got a name yet?"

"I was thinking. How does Riley Mansfield and the Left Turns sound?"

"I like it."

"So when we gonna tour?"

"Last two weeks of October. Then you go out alone the last two weeks of November."

"Alone?"

"No. I'll go. It's coming together pretty well. For now, we'll play music two weeks a month, every other month with the band.

Then we can hang out at home and you can write songs. Then, in the winter, we can record the album."

"Take the band to Nashville? Or sessions guys?"

"Up to you."

"I'll talk with the guys. They're all over the place, and they all got their own deadlines and commitments. I think everyone agrees that two weeks, every other month, is doable. I think the timing's just right. All the shit's dying down a little. People still know who I am. I think touring two weeks a month will draw decent crowds, and by then they'll mainly be music fans, not gawkers and nutcases and celebrity hounds. I'm tired of being breaking news."

He opened the Tupperware. "Woman's touch," he said.

"Huh?"

"You cut the sandwiches in squares. Nobody's done that for me since my mama when I was twelve."

"You don't like it?"

"No. I love it. It's...cute."

Melissa pulled two cans of Diet Dr. Pepper from the cooler.

"I'm starting to feel, oh, happy again," he said.

"Are you high?"

"That, too, but just a little. Things are getting better all the time. Still got people wanting to talk to me all the time, but at least now I can be a recluse without getting beat up.

"How 'bout you?"

"It's all good."

"You high?"

"A little," she said, laughing.

"Talk to your mama?"

"She's fine. Says she's a little lonely with me living over here."

"Well, shit, tell her she can move in with us...if she brings some weed."

"Asshole." They both laughed, though.

Riley had returned home the previous night from two days testifying before Congress.

"You know," he said, "I really didn't mind it that much."

"It was funny what you said when that senator asked you about Sue Ellen," Melissa said.

"That was the only one who was kind of hard on me. He was from Utah, I think. Actually asked, point blank, if I had—how did he put it?—'had relations with Ms. Spenser.'"

"And you, with the world's most shit-eating grin on your face, said..."

"I did not have sexual relations with that woman."

"Even senators were laughing," Melissa said.

"Did I tell you I found out who Barton Fleming was?"

"No..."

"Apparently his name is Leeds McCormick," Riley said. "I don't know much, really, but I hear he's going on trial. He and another guy are, you know, some kind of co-conspirators or something with Jed Langston. I don't think they arrested him for beating the shit out of me, but somehow it got out that he was the guy."

"Well, I sure hope he burns in hell."

"I'm satisfied he'll just go to prison. The first thing I thought of was that, if my name was Leeds McCormick, I might claim to be Barton Fleming.

"But...you know what the biggest thing was? What the highlight of my big C-SPAN gig was?"

"What?" Melissa didn't feel the need to point out that Riley's testimony had aired on half the channels on cable.

"I got to do something I've always wanted to do. After a lifetime of watching lawyer shows on TV... you know how the prosecutor always browbeats the witness? Guy starts to answer and he screams, 'Yes or no! Yes or no, Mr., uh, Schultz!'"

Melissa laughed uproariously.

"So that senator pulls that shit—'Yes or no, Mr. Mansfield!'—and I just turned to the other senator and said, 'Mr. Chairman, when I took that oath, I said I'd tell the whole truth, and there's no possible way I can tell the whole truth with yes or no.'

"And he backed his ass right off, didn't he?"

"It was quite a contrast to that night outside Timmy's Bar, way back when it was all just starting," said Melissa. "It seems like a long time ago."

"I reckon I'm getting media-savvy."

Riley sighed. "Sitting down here is probably a pretty good place to be. Right now, I'm gonna go back to the way I felt then. I'm not talking to anybody but the local newspaper and the local radio station.

"Or Adam. If he calls."

"Have you talked to him?" Melissa asked.

"Yeah," Riley said. "It's funny how that deal worked."

The float dunked. Riley dropped a half-eaten sandwich square and yanked the pole. He quickly pulled in a puny round bream. "Shit," he said. Then he slowly worked the hook out of the side of poor gasping fish's mouth, reached over and dropped it in the edge of the muddy water. It seemed paralyzed for a split second, then jerked and swam away.

"Nothing but little runts," Riley said. "I don't know whether there's too many of them or whether the kids from the projects have fished all the decent ones out. I'm a soft touch for a black kid with a bamboo pole.

"What was I talking about?"

"Adam."

"Oh, yeah, Adam. We talked about how I ended up having him in a bind, but one that worked out for the both of us."

"What do you mean?"

"Well, Adam didn't feel inclined to go into the sordid details about his own little side story, so, it kind of made it difficult for him to publish whatever sordid details he might have included about me. It wound up being kind of a puff piece, but one he's probably gonna win the Pulitzer Prize for."

Rolling Stone's cover had depicted Riley's lanky frame lounging on the steps of the Capitol, leaning backwards with the

Pawless guitar around his neck, fingers pressing a "G" chord. The headline had read:

THE FOLK SINGER WHO TOPPLED SAM HARMON

The President of the United States had resigned three weeks before the Republican National Convention. The Vice President, Edward Morrow, had been passed over, and a former governor of Arkansas had been nominated hurriedly to represent the GOP. The Democratic nominee, Stuart Murrah, was twenty points ahead in the polls.

"How about Priscilla? You heard from her?"

"Oh, yeah," Riley said. "She called about a half hour ago. She wants me to play at the Inauguration if, you know, Murrah wins."

"You gonna do it?"

"I told her I'd do it for nothing, but I had to get to do what Willie Nelson did at the White House."

"Which is?"

"When Carter was president, Willie went up on the roof of the White House and smoked a joint."

"What'd she say?"

"She didn't turn me down. I asked her if there was any chance she could be appointed head of the DEA. She said she didn't think so."

"So," Melissa said, "it's nearly three months later and you're still a hero."

"We're heroes." He laughed. "You know that Dan Aykroyd line in 'Blues Brothers'? 'No, ma'am, we're musicians.'"

"I'm not a musician," Melissa said.

"Sure you are. You can sing like an angel. Especially when you got a buzz on. I think you should be a backup singer and sing harmony with me. You can be just like Emmylou Harris on those old Gram Parsons albums."

"You're joking, right?"

"No." Riley smiled mischievously.

"Who's gonna sell your CDs and tee shirts?"

"I wouldn't want you to sing with me except on special occasions."

"I don't think I could do that onstage."

"Then sing with me in the studio."

"You've lost your mind," she said. "Give me some of what you're smoking."

"No time," Riley said. "Let's go back up to the house, brush our teeth, wash our hands and go over to Mama's house. We can see if anybody's gotten arrested lately."

Author's Note

Writing about NASCAR, I fly a lot. The events of September 11, 2001 made me keenly aware of airport security, and what I resolved in 2001 was that I would never let my life be altered by the threat of terrorism.

Two conclusions came to me from observing security guidelines in airports and sports venues: 1. A guy who looked like me could blow up anything he wants, and 2. most security isn't geared as much to prevent terrorism as it is to comply with insurance regulations.

Having never had fiction published before, I thought it important to come up with a story that was timely. Combining two significant issues, terrorism and marijuana reform, is what made me determine that The Audacity of Dope was a compelling and marketable concept.

My first idea was to write a story about terrorists attempting to create mayhem at a sporting event. Writing True to the Roots allowed me to gain insight into the lives of musicians. I scrapped the original idea and started to think about what would gradually become The Audacity of Dope.

Here's how Riley Mansfield evolved. I put a character in a setting similar, at least geographically, to my own. I had to create a plausible character in that setting who was capable of doing what the protagonist in my story did. Quite obviously, Mansfield couldn't be based on me or even be very much like me. I made up someone younger, bolder, more attractive, rebellious and self-reliant than I. Then I tried to get the character straight in my mind and think the way he would.

The most noteworthy thing Riley Mansfield and I have in common is that I wrote his songs.

I've wanted to write a novel since I was in high school. When I couldn't find a publisher for an attempt I made more than 20 years ago, I sort of came up with a plan. A newspaper beat covering NASCAR gave me a chance to write books about NASCAR. Those books created the opportunity to write a book about something else: music. I hoped the next step would be a novel. I feel fortunate to have been right.

Author's Acknowledgements

My father has been dead for 18 years, but if he were alive, I'm satisfied he would refer to this as "one of them Dutton deals." If I could, I'd tell him that his dysfunctional raising of me was not entirely detrimental.

My mother, Betty Dutton, always tried her best to counterbalance the cataclysmic reality of being Jimmy Dutton's wife. In that, she was never quite successful, but being the spouse of a force of nature wasn't easy. I expect her saving grace is being the daughter of Hudson Davis, the most serene man I ever knew. My mother has been there, done that.

Writing The Audacity of Dope required encouragement and support. At a particularly perilous moment, Nate Ryan wrote me that what I was doing was "admirable," which had never occurred to me and probably won't occur to others. At a time in which my spirits were sagging, Nate's words came in handy.

It helped to have a person who has done it believe that I could do it. Peter Farris filled that role ably and with considerable sarcasm.

I'm thankful to Donna Font for allowing me to persuade her I could pull this off and her husband, Joe, for designing a cover as gutsy as the content inside it.

There are, of course, many others, but I wouldn't want to tag them with guilt by association.

Also by Monte Dutton

Pride of Clinton: Clinton High School Football, 1920-1985

At Speed: Up Close & Personal with the People, Places & Fans of NASCAR

Taking Stock: Life in NASCAR's Fast Lane

Rebel with a Cause: A Season with NASCAR's Tony Stewart

Jeff Gordon: The Racer

Postcards from Pit Road

Haul A** and Turn Left

True to the Roots: Americana Music Revealed

Monte Dutton lives in Clinton, South Carolina. In high school, he played football for a state championship team, then attended Furman University, Greenville, S.C., graduating in 1980, B.A., cum laude, political science/history.

He has written regularly about NASCAR since 1993, and has written for the Gaston Gazette (Gastonia, NC) since 1996. He was named Writer of the Year by the Eastern Motorsports Press Association (Frank Blunk Award) in 2003 and Writer of the Year by the National Motorsports Press Association (George Cunningham Award) in 2008. His NASCAR writing has been syndicated by King Feature Syndicate in the form of a weekly page, "NASCAR This Week."

The Audacity of Dope is his first novel, and he is hard at work on his second.

Made in the USA
Lexington, KY
02 November 2011